For Elizabeth –
Thank you for reading!
Enjoy the mystery & the
journey.

THE REDEMPTION
OF
RED FIRE WOMAN

Kathleen Rude

This is a work of fiction. Names, characters, places and incidents
either are the product of the author's imagination or are
used fictitiously. Any resemblance to actual persons,
living or dead, events or locales is entirely coincidental, except for
Karl and Mona Maser at the Ute Lodge. They are the real deal.

Cover Design: Dianne Hanau-Strain

The Redemption of Red Fire Woman

ISBN-10: 0615920969
ISBN-13: 978-0615920962

Green
Quill
Press

www.greenquillpress.com

This novel is dedicated to Clifford Duncan.
Thank you for your teachings, friendship
and blessing of this story.

Griffin the Wonder Dog, the best companion on and off the hiking trails.
I miss you.

GRATITUDE

I want to thank and celebrate all who helped me bring this story to life and into print.

Anna Mae Grimm, dear friend, for our writing weekends where I birthed the first chapters and for your years of brainstorming, encouragement, friendship and love.

John Mullin, for believing in me, and for your loving incentives, including giving up sugar, to help me finish what often felt like an impossible task.

Dianne Hanau-Strain, for your steadfast support and insightful fellow-writer feedback, for creating my book cover and designing the interior.

My other writing circle friends—Blair Hull, Bernice Selden and Carol Tessler—who kept me on task and made me a better writer.

My sister, Elizabeth Rude, whose extensive edits, creative ideas and loving support have been invaluable.

The folks who read and critiqued this manuscript and who shared expertise: Clifford Duncan, Tamyala Grabil, Regas Halandras, Bruce and Wanda Jewell, Mary-Lou Rude Leidheiser, Joanna Macy, Karl Maser, Mark LeFevre, Marissa LeFevre, Miles Posen, Chuck Skelton, Nan Streicker, and members of the Tussie Mussie Hussies Book Club—Pam Buffington, Carol Fix, Sherilyn Galeener, Cydney Johnson, Mona Maser, Betsy Nisse and Karin Ruffatto.

Michael Schwaba, for introducing me to the beautiful state of Colorado and Tom Yocom, for sharing the location of the secret box canyon that inspired this novel.

My teachers and guides in indigenous spirituality and environmental conservation who influenced this novel: Clifford Duncan, Jim Goss, Jeff Ham, Bill Kight, Chuck Skelton and Jim Stutzman.

CHAPTER ONE

THE LATE AFTERNOON SUN beat in through the truck window as Duncan Hawk drove down the gravel road, kicking up a trail of dust behind his red Ford pickup truck. He had the air conditioning turned off, preferring to feel the early summer desert heat of western Colorado. The sandy-gray and aspen-green foothills of the Milk Creek Valley, with its beautiful sagebrush starkness, stirred feelings of sadness and joyful homecoming. He traveled the thirteen miles from Meeker with a thirst he would not slake until he had finished his work. Having had no food or water that day, he felt empty, like the cloudless blue sky. Focusing his mind and his emotions on the task at hand, he trusted that he'd know what to do when the sun went down.

He looked out across the valley of prairie grasses and the winding waterway that afforded only glimpses of the creek through bushes lining the banks. No barns, homes, cattle or trucks met his gaze. It appeared as though Duncan Hawk was alone in this place, but he knew differently.

On top of the next rise, he saw what he was looking for. He parked his pickup on the side of the road, rolled up the windows and locked the doors. Having recently turned 70 years of age, Duncan hated to acknowledge the back pain that long drives on dirt roads now inflicted. He stretched to relieve the tension before putting on his cowboy hat with red-shafted flicker feathers tucked into the beaded headband. He wore his salt-and-pepper hair in a long ponytail. His eyes twinkled when he smiled, but the seriousness of his mission today hardened his gentle brown face. He shuffled slightly as he walked the short path to a fenced-off piece of ground where he stopped in front of two mismatched monuments—the old one was made of white marble; the modern sandstone cairn stood twice as tall. He had come to this place many times before and knew its significance. The cairns commemorated a battle where his grandfather had been wounded, a conflict that led to removal at gunpoint of the Ute people from their homes.

Duncan regretted that today few of his people felt any connection to their native Colorado mountains. The desolate Utah reservation was all they had known. But he had felt the calling of his ancestral homeland, even as a young boy. With that calling came responsibilities he didn't always understand, but throughout his life, he had faithfully heeded them. He had been summoned to be in this place tonight, to watch the sun set behind the mountains. For what reason, he did not yet know.

Walking past the cairns, he headed down the hill to sit on the ground close to the creek and to watch the sun's rays reflecting on the water. Never lifting his eyes, he saw the dusk settle on the valley through the flowing mirror before him. Quietly he sat, as the world seemed to glide past him, then away from him, as an inner world of spirit and vision slowly washed around him.

In the twilight they came, ghostly figures of Ute people streaming past, heads bent, despair etched in their faces. Men on horseback, women with babies, young boys and girls dragging travois piled with belongings. No one looked at him as they struggled on.

I must go with them, he thought, but his body would not move. He remained rooted to the ground as a short, muscular man with ebony skin and long white hair stepped through the crowd and stood before him. He had red eyes like the setting sun and was wearing only a breechcloth made of buckskin. The Ancient One smiled at Duncan and signaled for him to rise. Together they walked away from the creek, but Duncan was reluctant to leave these people behind. "I should be with them," he said. The Ancient One said nothing.

Suddenly Duncan gasped as icy water gripped his legs; he felt the slippery smoothness of rocks beneath his feet. They stood in a mountain stream, surrounded by red and tan cliffs towering above them. As they walked out of the stream and onto the bank, Duncan noticed a large vertical crack in the stone of the canyon wall, three times as tall as he was, and a small clearing directly in front of what appeared to be an opening to a cave. Cautiously, he stepped closer but froze when he caught sight of a huge grizzly bear sitting among the trees. The bear looked at him without any sign of aggression. Duncan watched as a Ute man appeared next to the bear. He wore his hair in two long braids, an eagle feather tied in each one, was bare-chested except for a large bear claw that hung from a simple beaded necklace. His breechcloth and leggings told Duncan he belonged to a time long ago.

The Ute nodded at him. Duncan returned the greeting and pulled out his tobacco pouch to offer a prayer in honor of the ancestors standing before him. But when he looked back up, the man and the bear had vanished. He quickly turned around but saw only the Ancient One, his face as still as stone. Looking back at the slit in the rock, he noticed a small stream of water flowing from the opening. The clear rivulet quickly darkened to murky brown, then bright red, as water turned to blood. Duncan approached the cave and peered in, seeing nothing but darkness. Then a piercing wail reverberated inside the cave. He startled backwards, his heart pumping.

A figure stepped into the light, a woman dressed in a dirty, torn buckskin dress. She walked with obvious discomfort, her right side hunched and twisted. She pressed her left hand, tightly fisted, across her chest. Her face was obscured by a wild tangle of matted red hair. Young or old, Duncan could not tell. She lifted her head to reveal a disfigured face wracked with pain. Her right side showed no blemish. But the other bore evidence of an old brutality that left her with broken bones and a ragged scar. She stared at Duncan with one penetrating green eye; the other stared blindly, a ghostly white.

She spoke in a voice both pleading and commanding. "I could not protect you. I could not save her. Because I could not stop *him*." Her left hand began to twitch, then she pounded the fist against her heart. "But now the ancestors cry out for healing! I must make amends. You must help me stop him before he brings ruin to the land!" Her voice quivered with rage.

Duncan did not understand her message and yet he knew he could not refuse her. She was the one his grandmother had told him about many years ago. Looking down, he fumbled with his tobacco pouch, but his offering came too late. The red-haired woman was gone.

Duncan faced The Ancient One. "The Ancestors are calling you to help heal these wounds of long ago," the spirit spoke. "But the path will not be clear."

"I do not know the meaning of her words," Duncan said, "but I feel the power of them as an ache in my heart. How will I know what to do?"

Silence answered. The last thing Duncan saw before darkness enveloped him was The Ancient One smiling.

Duncan did not know how long he'd been sitting by the creek, but his throat had grown raw with thirst. His body ached as he stood. Respectfully sprinkling tobacco on the water, he offered thanks to the creek for his vision and walked slowly back to the truck. The woman's tortured voice still echoed in his head. While he did not know how to honor her request, he did know her name. Red Fire Woman.

CHAPTER TWO

"WHY DOESN'T COFFEE ever taste as good as it smells?" asked Sarah as she put down the tray holding steaming cups of cappuccino and herbal tea. "Even the beans smell better somehow." Sarah's rapid-fire comments emphasized her nervousness. Unable to meet her sister's eyes, she stirred her coffee a bit too intently.

"Can't wait 'til I can have coffee again," Ruth said, reluctantly claiming the herbal tea. She was five months pregnant. "Sarah, what happened back there?"

"You're the psychotherapist, you tell me."

Ruth wrapped her hand lovingly around Sarah's and smiled at her older sister. "Come on. What's going on with you?"

"Just a bit of flight anxiety maybe. The airport was so crowded, people rushing and pushing, the stale air, I felt nauseated," Sarah said, pushing a strand of straight blonde hair behind her ear. "I freaked and needed to get out of there. I just couldn't get on that plane."

"How are you now?"

"Better, thanks. Although I must say, the decor in this coffee house isn't exactly soothing, is it?" Sarah remarked, looking at the oil paintings on the cracked plaster walls.

"Oh, I don't know," Ruth replied with an impish grin and pointing to her right. "I could see putting that one in the baby's room. I've been looking everywhere for a scene of two red feet cut off above the ankles, standing in a field of brilliant green grass. I consider myself pretty hip, but I sure don't understand modern art!"

"I'm with you, Sister O' Mine," Sarah said, licking hot foam from her upper lip.

Even though Sarah and Ruth differed in temperament and lifestyle, the casual observer immediately identified them as sisters. They shared the same bold laugh that made no apologies for filling a room. Their eyes twinkled the same way too, though Sarah had Grandma's hazel green coloring while Ruth's blue eyes took after their mother's. Loving sisters with no other siblings, they also had become each other's best friend.

"I hope this Colorado project won't take longer than three months," Sarah said. "I want to be here when my niece or nephew is born!"

"I want you to be here too, believe me," Ruth agreed, as she removed a black satchel from her purse. "So you'd best get your butt out there so you can finish up and get back in time for the Big Show!"

Sarah appreciated her sister's attempt at levity, eager for any diversion from her apprehension. Sipping her coffee, she watched her sister unzip the satchel on the table. A quick prick of a finger drew blood as red as those painted feet, the blood dropped onto a thin strip that she fed into a small computer that analyzed blood sugar levels on the spot. "I think this baby is going to be late," Ruth said as she pulled out a small vial and a syringe. "I sense a stubborn streak in this little one; she's in no hurry to go anywhere." Ruth lifted her blouse ever so slightly, exposing an inch of skin too familiar with the routine. A quick jab of a needle, a steady push on the plunger, and back into the black bag. No one around them noticed. They never did, which continually surprised Sarah. Probably because Ruth never made a big deal out of it.

At least three times a day every day, Ruth injected herself with insulin. Except for some miracle, she would need it for the rest of her life. Waking up every day to a needle had molded her somehow, given her an inner strength even she was not really aware of. Sarah saw it though, and loved her sister all the more for it.

In fact, she wished she had some of that inner fortitude right now. How was she going to get on that plane? She had told her client in Colorado, who also happened to be a friend of her father, that she would be arriving this week. She did not want to make a bad first impression or disappoint her father with such unprofessional behavior.

As a painter and muralist, Sarah knew a big job like this one came along once in a lifetime, if ever. But why did it have to be in Colorado?

Once she left the state seven years ago and moved to Chicago, she never wanted to go back. The ticket to Denver felt like a twenty-pound weight in her purse that grew heavier with each passing minute.

As the sisters ran out of chitchat, the teenage busboy with baggy pants and thick matted hair picked up their tray. Ruth shifted her gaze from the menagerie of colored chaos on the walls and looked straight at her sister. "I'm concerned about you. You aren't afraid to fly, but you are afraid of something. Going back is harder than you thought, isn't it?"

"Geez, you get right to the heart of the matter, don't you?" Sarah said. Ruth possessed an uncanny ability to see into her sister's heart, a gift Sarah did not always welcome, especially now.

"Look, I know you may not want to talk about this, but you've got to deal with it sometime," Ruth gently chided, tossing her thick auburn curls for emphasis. "You've got to get on that airplane eventually."

"I know. I just feel so silly. I couldn't step onto that walkway."

"Have you stopped to consider what going back to Colorado really means to you?" Ruth asked, cradling her mug close to her lips. "It's been a long time since your accident, but this will be your first time back. I don't think you've ever really given yourself time to process all that. You're always on the go."

"Look, I left Blue in the past long ago. He's not some ghost. I've moved on," she asserted. "I made a new life for myself, a good life. I don't even think about him any more. Don't be so melodramatic, Ruth. I just got a little queasy. I've gotten so little sleep in the last few days, getting ready for this trip. Colorado's just another state, it holds no ties for me anymore."

"I know that's what you want to believe," Ruth said, "and I really do hope it's true. Either way, I'm here for you no matter what."

Before leaving the café, Sarah gave her sister a long hug. "I'm sure I'll be able to walk on to that plane tomorrow. I don't want to let the past have a hold on me. I need to be stronger than that."

CHAPTER THREE

THE CLAY-RED CLIFFS of the Rocky Mountains had never become just scenery to Patrick. Having spent most of his thirty-five years in Colorado, he continued to marvel at them, especially when the first rays of sunshine reinvigorated their rich color after a rainstorm. He loved to drive through the mountains early in the morning, before the rest of the world took to the roads. He'd soak in the beauty as it unfolded at sunrise, eyes ever sharp for the faintest movement of wildlife. His trained biologist's eye gave him an advantage over most folks. When he saw black flecks in the distance, he recognized what they were: bighorn sheep, mule deer, golden eagle, coyote. He knew by their shape, their movement, their location on the mountain or in the air. Rarely would any of his friends spot an animal before he did.

Patrick was returning to Black Elk Valley, the project site where he'd been working for the past year. He put his cup of coffee in the cup holder, ran his fingers quickly through his unruly dark brown hair and reached for his sunglasses on the dash of his Blazer. He still wasn't used to wearing the uniform. The tan shirt with its official emblem looked respectable, but the pants were the most awful shade of brown. He was convinced that the person who designed the U.S. Fish and Wildlife Service uniform must have been colorblind or had a sick sense of humor. As soon as he got out in the field, away from the office, he would stuff the pants in the bottom of his duffel bag and pull out his blue jeans.

Patrick felt a strong connection to Black Elk Valley, a place of breath-taking mountain scenery, lush stretches of grass and a high-quality trout stream that had produced several state record fish in years past. The White River National Forest cradled the valley in peaks of pine and juniper, while the mountains fed the Black Elk River with numerous creeks rippling down through stands of aspen and spruce. The people who lived in the valley worked the land, raising cattle, sheep and horses. They grazed their livestock in the national forest in the summer and fall but had to move them to lower elevations in the harsh winter months and chilly spring. During this time, the animals survived on hay cut from the irrigated pastures running along both sides of the river.

Cattle and sheep weren't the only animals that moved out of the mountains when the weather turned. Every year, herds of elk and deer migrated out of the national forest and into the valley, seeking shelter and food once snow covered the peaks. The valley provided refuge for livestock, wildlife and the people who lived here. Patrick's job was to help ensure that the valley stayed this way, for all concerned.

As a private lands biologist, Patrick's position was unlike any other in the Fish & Wildlife Service. He didn't manage a wildlife refuge or enforce game laws. He didn't study the feeding and breeding habits of any animal or bird. He didn't even work on government-owned land. He focused on other people's land, working with private citizens to improve their grasslands and waterways for ranching and for wildlife.

Looking at his watch, Patrick stepped on the gas. He had a lunch meeting with Ms. Jessie and knew he'd best not be late. She was a busy woman and had little tolerance for anyone who threw off her schedule.

Jessibel Amanda Winde was the valley matriarch, alleged to be in her early seventies, but nobody knew for sure and no one had ever been foolish enough to ask her. "Age is immaterial," she would argue. "It's all in your head. If your ideas are old, you'll be old. But if you engage your brain and keep an open mind, then you'll stay sharp and vital."

In fact, she did defy age in spirit, energy and imagination. On any hiking trail, she offered stiff competition for people twenty years her junior. Her political views routinely crossed over party lines; she concentrated on truths, not dogma. Everyone in the valley called her Ms. Jessie, never Miss. She defended the spelling of her proper name Jessibel, explaining that her mother had loved the name but had not approved of the biblical character associated with it, so she had changed the spelling to avoid any unflattering associations.

Patrick wouldn't describe Ms. Jessie as a pretty woman. But with her bright white hair, piercing gray-blue eyes, weathered face and a slender six-foot frame, she was most striking. A fourth-generation rancher in the Black Elk Valley, Ms. Jessie not only knew the western cattle business inside and out, she also knew the family history of just about every person in the county. She was a powerful ally who cut him little slack, especially if he kept her waiting.

Patrick pulled into the cafe at five minutes before noon. He'd just made it. Ms. Jessie pulled up a minute later in her light blue pickup truck. Moving with the energy of a much younger woman, she made her way to the café door before Patrick had gotten out of his truck.

"Hurry up," she blurted, urging him on with an impatient wave. "We've got trouble."

CHAPTER FOUR

BY THE TIME PATRICK stepped into the coffee house, Jessie had already commandeered her seat in the second booth, giving her a clear view of the road and Patrick. The locals referred to it as Ms. Jessie's Perch and no one dared take that booth if any others were available. They kept it open out of respect for the valley's feistiest resident.

"That damned son of a bitch," she vented, skipping over any perfunctory greetings. "After all this time, I can't believe he'd try this. I could wring his neck!"

"Slow down Ms. Jessie," Patrick urged. "Who is this son of a bitch and why does he have you so riled up?"

"Eli McDermott, that good-for-nothing, drunken idiot who's never branded a cow in his life. He left town thirty years ago and we've all been better for it."

Patrick had never seen her so upset. Her eyes kept darting side to side and she rattled her spoon absent-mindedly. Her frazzled demeanor concerned him; she usually handled stress with an intense determination, a quick wit and a cool head.

"Did you say 'McDermott'? Any relation to the McDermott Ranch down the road from you?" he asked.

"By blood only, certainly not by experience," she spit out. "Eli inherited that ranch from his father, a real mean bastard." Her voice softened a bit as she looked out the window, drifting into memory. Then her lips tightened into a frown. "Eli cared more about drinking than ranching; he let the place go. Tom Payton has been renting his pastures for years because Eli wanted nothing to do with the ranch. Which was fine with me, just fine."

"So what's the problem now?"

"He wants to sell the ranch! That's my land!" She hit the spoon hard on the table. The waitress looked over in surprise. "He doesn't even have the guts to tell me himself. He sent a letter to Tom, with some absurd offer that Tom could never afford."

"I'm confused," Patrick admitted, distracted both by her strange behavior and by the grumbling in his gut. He needed some lunch. He flagged down the waitress, who approached hesitantly, her eyes on Ms. Jessie and the madly tapping spoon.

"I'll have the special today, Lynn. Thanks." He smiled at the waitress and gave her a reassuring nod. "Ms. Jessie will have her usual." Normally Jessie would have chastised him for placing her order, but today she was too preoccupied to notice.

"Why don't you just buy the land?" he asked.

"I wouldn't give that man a dime of mine, not now, not ever!" Hearing the bitterness in her voice, she caught herself and finally put down the spoon. Regaining some composure, she met Patrick's gaze. "And I can't afford to buy him out, even if I wanted to. That's the fact. Especially at the inflated price he sent to Tom. He must be in real trouble this time. Eli knows Tom doesn't have that kind of money, and he wouldn't be fool enough to pay it even if he did. No rancher would."

"Well, it doesn't sound like you have much to worry about," Patrick said. "If his asking price is too high, then no one will bite." Patrick wanted to ask the exact price, but knew it wouldn't be polite. He had learned early on that it wasn't considered good manners for an outsider to ask a rancher how many head of livestock he or she had; that was like asking how much money they had in the bank. You had to wait for them to tell you, if they ever did. Same thing applied to land prices. Selling land was sensitive business out here. Most ranches had been in the same families for generations. Selling land meant selling out. It also meant heartbreak for those who felt forced to sell because of financial hardship.

"You know as well as I do that this valley has just as many rich folks with vacation ranches as working folks." She shook her head. "I'm worried that some millionaire will move on it. Although some of them really do take care of their land, still there's no guarantee that they won't go bankrupt down the road and have to sell out, or just grow tired of the place. Or they die and their kids have no interest in ranching and just want to make a quick buck, so they look for a developer. We can't let developers get a foothold in here." She grew insistent. "If they do, it will only be a matter of time before they subdivide the entire valley. And I'll be damned if I'm going to let that happen in Black Elk Valley."

Patrick knew she was right. He'd seen development racing across the state like a cancer. Valley after valley transformed into subdivisions of expensive homes, each one vying for the best view of the mountains. And the irony was that these people paid exorbitant prices for a mountain view that, in his mind, was destroyed by the houses themselves. Each development bore the name of the wild things that they displaced—Eagle View, Pine Ridge, Cat-a-Mount Crossing. He bristled at the thought of this area falling prey to bulldozers. His conviction matched Jessie's in that regard. He would do all he could to keep development from this place.

"Would this Eli guy be interested in an easement?" Patrick offered. "I can get the paperwork rolling right now if he's willing. We can look at the land tomorrow and see if we can get the entire ranch to qualify."

Patrick knew how appealing an easement could be to a landowner, especially one in financial trouble. The U.S. Fish & Wildlife Service purchased the development rights to the land from the rancher in exchange for a payment for up to two-thirds of the purchase price. The rancher could continue grazing and haying the land. He just couldn't plow up the soil for any reason. The payment helped the rancher financially and guaranteed that the land would never be developed.

As the waitress put their lunch on the table, Patrick said that he hoped an easement would appeal to Eli McDermott, but Jessie shook her head. "Don't get your hopes up. Eli wouldn't let the government have a piece of land. He hates government boys just about as much as he hated his father. Doesn't like anyone telling him what to do, even when it's for his own good. Sometimes I don't know if he's supremely stubborn or just plain stupid. Maybe his father's beatings knocked all the sense out of him. The Eli I knew would just as soon spit on you as talk to you. Sorry, Pat." She eased the spoon into her soup.

"A lot can happen to a man in thirty years," Patrick offered. "Maybe he's changed. I'd like to talk to him at least to find out. I don't have anything to lose."

"I think you'd be wasting your time, but I won't stop you. Just take a bit of advice. If you ever deal with him face to face, don't do it when he's been drinking. He was the meanest drunk I've ever come across."

"Thanks for the warning, but I think I can take care of myself with an old man..." Catching his blunder, he said, "Ah, I mean a man who's not as young and in shape, you know what I mean."

"He's an old man, you can say it. But I can't imagine that the meanness has gone out of him," she said. "You're young and strong and I'm sure you don't lose too many fights. But, I'm telling you to watch yourself. You can't trust Eli McDermott. I learned that the hard way. Besides, I doubt he'd have the courage to show his face around here. He'll have his lawyer do all the work. You'll have to go out to Las Vegas, at least last I knew, if you want to try talking with Eli. Good luck finding the sewer rock he hauled his sorry ass under!"

Before Patrick could ask for clarification, Jessie got up, threw a twenty-dollar bill on the table, and said, "Lunch is on me. I gotta go." She left the coffee house before Patrick could even say "goodbye." Patrick stared after her, intensely troubled. Eli McDermott's letter had really unnerved her, and he sensed that her anxiety came not only from the potential land sale but also from Eli himself. He'd never known anyone to fluster her.

His curiosity piqued, Patrick began planning to locate Eli McDermott. He had to move fast; he wanted first crack at him before any developer wooed him with promises of big money. He also wanted to find out what this guy had done to Ms. Jessie years ago. *She's right*, he thought. *Eli must be really stupid. You'd have to be to cross a woman like Jessibel Amanda Winde.*

While Patrick ate his lunch, he tried to recall if Ms. Jessie had ever mentioned Eli. Nothing came to mind. In fact, he realized that she had never talked about any man being in her life. But she had been more than forthcoming about her family history, of which she was quite proud.

Patrick replayed the morning over a year ago when Ms. Jessie had told him the story of her family; it was the first time they'd met. He still cringed when he thought about the arrogance with which he had first approached her. He'd had only a couple of weeks in his new job as a private lands biologist when he had left a phone message for "a Mrs. Winde—My name is Patrick Duffy and I'm with the U.S. Fish and Wildlife Service's new program called Partners for Wildlife. I'm following up on the letter I sent describing the variety of programs we have to offer that could be quite beneficial to a rancher such as you. I would appreciate an opportunity to talk with you in person about the Partners program and how we can be of service to you." Even though he had come across like a used car salesman with that "have-I-got-a-deal-for-you" cockiness, Ms. Jessie eventually returned his call.

Patrick would never forget that first meeting. He'd gotten lost on the way to her ranch. He met her as she came flying out the door on her way to the stable. "You're late," she snipped. "Follow me." There was no hint of polite invitation in her voice.

For the next two hours, he tagged along behind Ms. Jessie, sweeping out stalls, getting water for the horses, repairing some loose boards, all the while listening to her lecture him about how messed up the federal government was, how the Forest Service didn't know what the Fish and Wildlife Service was doing and vice versa, how their policies contradicted each other, and how hard it was to run a ranch with such mixed messages coming from Washington. He tended to agree with most of what she was saying, and, had she been less combative and he less defensive, he would have told her so. But at that moment, he believed his best course of action was to keep working and to keep his mouth shut. That was, until her attacks turned personal.

"You can't just waltz in here and say, 'Hi, I'm with the federal government and I'm here to help you'," she scolded. "You're gonna get a backside full of buckshot before you ever get past the front door with an attitude like that. Who the hell are you anyway to tell us what to do on our land?" Then her demeanor softened a bit, but not her intensity.

"Look, son, we've been working this land a long time. We've invested our hearts, our sweat, our tears and our souls in this valley. We've buried loved ones here. We know this land, we're a part of it. And we don't take kindly to strangers thinking they know better than we do."

"But ma'am, sometimes we do know a better way to do things," he asserted, having taken about all he could. "Some of these guys run their operations in the exact same way their grandfathers did and won't change a thing, even though they're ruining their grass."

To his amazement, she had agreed. "But that's not the way to tell them. You've got a big chip on your shoulder that's getting in your way. You've got a lot to learn about dealing with people if you want to get anything done here."

And so began Patrick's education in the ways of working with ranchers in western Colorado.

"Let me tell you a little something about the people who live in this valley, Mr. Government Man." Her steely gaze had fixed on Patrick. "My great-grandfather was a prospector who combed the Rockies looking for gold. He never struck it rich, so eventually he and my great-grandmother decided to settle here in Black Elk Valley and start a cattle ranch. That was in 1881. By that time my great-grandparents had three children, but two of them had died of smallpox soon after they bought the place. For some reason, my grandfather didn't get sick. He was the only one left to help with the work.

"They nearly lost the ranch several times. Cattle got stuck in the mountains one year when the snows came early. Almost wiped out the entire herd. Then some years later, my great-grandfather came close to dying in a forest fire. He was trying to move the cattle out of the fire's path when his horse threw him and ran off. He broke his leg. Somehow his son, my grandfather, found him. Grandfather had been so focused on looking for wood to make a splint that he hadn't been paying attention to the tracks all around them. Before he knew it, my grandfather had gotten between a mother grizzly and her cubs. That bear took one swipe at him and probably would have killed him, but his dogs made such a ruckus that she finally let him be. She ripped his shoulder open clear to the bone. I can still remember tracing that scar with my fingers when I was a little girl. My great-grandmother was the one who ended up pulling both her husband and her son out of the woods and patching them up. I don't know how she kept the ranch going that summer while she played nursemaid, but she found a way."

Patrick recalled how Ms. Jessie had put her hand firmly on his shoulder and had shaken him. "The reason I'm telling you all this is so you get a sense of just how tough these people were who started these ranches. Life was hard here. They passed that toughness and that determination to survive on to their kids. They kept these ranches going, kept their families going by relying on themselves. They had no one else to turn to when things got hard or when work needed to get done. You'll find that same independence in the people living here today. And you'd best respect that."

Patrick had bristled under the implied rebuke, but he had kept his mouth shut. Something had told him to put his ego aside and pay attention. Jessie had continued her counsel but in somewhat kinder tones. "The first thing you need to do is get to know these people and let them get to know you. You have to build up some trust, show them you're willing to listen to them. That's the only way you'll even get a foot in the door out here." She had paused, then added, "They have to trust you."

For several months after their first meeting, Jessie had invited Patrick for dinner every Friday, and he had made a point of always arriving early. Despite her brutally honest guidance and stinging verbal reprimands, they quickly became friends and, eventually, allies. They needed each other. Jessie confided in him her fear that the wave of development sweeping over the state would one day hit her valley. And she wanted desperately to keep her corner of the world as it was. If this government program that Patrick represented could help her and her neighbors stay in the ranching business, maybe they could keep the developers at bay. This was her fervent hope and she had told Patrick she would do anything to help him succeed.

She had often invited ranchers from the valley to join them for Friday dinners. This gave people an opportunity to get to know Patrick as a person, not just as "that guy who works for the government." She encouraged him to participate in community events and church socials, which at times made him feel like he was running for political office rather than working as a biologist. But over time, some of the locals began to accept Patrick as "an okay kind of guy." Still, they scrutinized his every interaction, watching to see how he treated folks and waiting to see if this government program really worked as well as he claimed it did.

His opportunity to prove himself came when a sixty-two year-old rancher, Micah Donnelly, died unexpectedly from a heart attack. His son and daughter wanted to continue working the ranch, but they couldn't afford to pay the inheritance tax on the land. With some encouragement from Ms. Jessie, the son and daughter worked with Patrick to secure a conservation easement on the ranch. The payment they received helped them pay the taxes and keep the ranch in the family.

Everybody in the valley worried about the heavy burden of inheritance taxes. Consequently, the number one topic of conversation at the local sandwich shops and bars for a month was the Donnelly tragedy and Patrick's role in helping Micah's kids. Patrick earned a lot of people's respect that month. And yet he knew that this kind of trust would be continually tested with each and every interaction he'd have in the valley.

The waitress refilled Patrick's water glass, which brought his focus back to the moment at hand and back to the McDermott problem. He had to get to Eli before the developers and big money did. He needed an angle, a way of breaking the ice without having Eli want to break any of his bones. He took Ms. Jessie's warning to heart. He'd approach this McDermott character with caution. Patrick hoped that the deal he had to offer would be enough to keep Eli McDermott from selling his land to the highest bidder.

CHAPTER FIVE

SARAH CLOSED HER EYES and tried to find a comfortable position, but economy class airline seats were not designed to fit her five-foot-four-inch frame. She doubted if they made anyone's travel experience an enjoyable one. After shifting around and playing with different pillow placements, she gave up and ordered a vodka tonic. Relieved that she'd made it this far without angst, she hoped the drink would keep her calm during the flight. But a better distraction soon made herself known.

A small blonde-haired face popped up over the seat in front of her. "Hello," Sarah said with a smile. The little girl grinned shyly then disappeared. But not for long. The pixie face returned. "Well, hello again." A giggle, then another duck behind the seats signaled the beginning of a well-mannered game of Peek-A-Boo.

"Lillian, leave the nice lady alone," said the girl's mother.

"Oh, I don't mind, really," Sarah quickly replied. "Your daughter is delightful. Besides, it's good practice. I'm going to be an aunt in about four months. I can't wait."

Sarah wasn't sure she ever wanted children, but she loved the idea of being an aunt. She could play with the kids, spoil them just a little, then send them home and get a good night's sleep. And she knew Ruth would be a terrific mother.

The flight was only half full, so when Lillian asked her mom if she could sit with her new friend, mom and daughter were able to move into Sarah's row. As Sarah and Lillian squared off for thumb fights, her mom struck up a conversation and inquired about Sarah's travels.

"I'm a painter, a muralist. I've been commissioned to paint a number of murals at a ranch in the western part of the state. I'll be on site for at least three months, I think."

"That's so interesting. Did you get some kind of art grant to do this?"

"No, I was hired by the man who owns the ranch."

"Really? He must be loaded to afford an artist for a whole summer."

"He is rather wealthy, I know that. He comes from money and has also done quite well for himself as an investor. He lives in New York but spends a lot of time on his ranch in the mountains."

"If you don't mind my asking, how do you get a job like that?"

"Through my dad actually. Last summer, he got an invitation from one of his well-to-do business friends to go fly-fishing at this exclusive resort. Members-only kinda deal. Big bucks. Dad said it was the best fly-fishing he'd ever experienced. That's where he met the man I'm going to work for. He had just bought a ranch and wanted to do something unusual in the house he's restoring on the property. My dad suggested commissioning some murals and then told him about me. He liked my work, so here I am on a plane to Colorado."

"How cool."

"Momma, stop talking. I want to play with Miss Sarah!" Both women laughed at the little girl's outburst. They spent the rest of the flight playing games and telling make-believe stories.

Once they landed, Sarah offered to help the mom with her collection of bags. "When you travel with kids you have to bring so much stuff...games, food, a change of clothes," the mother groaned.

"No need to explain," Sarah assured her. "I've seen women traveling by themselves with just as much stuff."

"Thanks for entertaining Lillian and good luck with your murals."

Waiving goodbye, Sarah mumbled to herself, "I'm gonna need all the luck I can get."

Wrapped in a blue cotton robe, Sarah rubbed her wet hair with a towel. She loved the smell of clean skin after a shower, the sweet aroma of a fresh start, of possibilities. She sat on the hotel bed and picked up the phone. She wanted to let Ruth know she'd arrived safely.

"How's your stomach feeling? Ruth asked.

"Oh fine," she lied. "I mean, I'm feeling much better now that I'm out of the airports."

"What did you decide about tomorrow? Are you going to drive or are you going to send for your boss' helicopter? Does the guy really have his own helicopter?"

"Yes, he does. Amazing but true."

"Where does he land it?"

"He's got a landing pad at the ranch. He told me there's a local airport that he can use as well, but then someone from the ranch has to pick him up. So if the weather is good, he just flies right to his place."

"Sweet. You've got to get a ride in it sometime. How posh, dahling" her sister teased.

"I am tempted, but I really would like to make the drive if I can. It's so beautiful."

"You should be fine. But if you start to feel panicky in the mountains, pull off to the side of the road so you can breathe and center yourself."

"Thank you, Sister Shrink. I think I'll be okay." But the queasiness in her stomach said otherwise. "I'll call you tomorrow."

Sitting in the driver's seat of a dark gray Chevy 4x4, Sarah's hands fidgeted a bit as she grabbed hold of the steering wheel. This would be her first time driving in the mountains since her accident. Tilting the rearview mirror down, Sarah looked at her flushed face. "We'll be just fine," she told her reflection. With the engine idling in the parking lot, she picked up her cell phone and dialed her sister.

"Hi, this is Ruth, the walking incubator. I'm either in the bathroom or on my way to the bathroom, so please leave a message and I'll call you back sometime before this baby is born. Peace...*beep*."

God, I wish she wouldn't be so...explicit sometimes, Sarah thought. But then, that's how Ruth had always been: earthy, honest and funny.

"Hi, Sister o' Mine." She hesitated, trying to stifle the tears welling up.

"How're the incubator and the incubatee doing? Don't know if I'll have cell service once I get into the mountains, so thought I'd call to say hi. Nothing important," but the crack in her voice gave her away. "Gotta go, love you."

She hung up and impatiently dried her eyes. "I'll be fine. Don't think about it, just drive."

As she eased onto the on-ramp, Sarah spotted the sign to Boulder. She remembered her excitement nine years ago when she had first arrived in Colorado. She had never been to the state, had seen only pictures, and still she chose to attend the university in Boulder over Yale or Princeton, against her father's wishes. Remembering the disapproval in her father's eyes hurt her more now than it had back then. At the time Sarah had thought rebelling against your parents was the proper thing for a healthy teenager to do. But since she liked school, got good grades and loved her family, going to Boulder instead of an Ivy League school was as much rebellion as she could muster.

As Sarah merged onto I-70, she felt an urge to go back to Boulder, to drive through the campus, past the co-op, to see the run-down Victorian house where Blue had once lived. Would they all look the same? She wondered if her mural was still on the co-op wall or if someone had painted over it. She wouldn't blame them if they had. It had been her first and, in her opinion, was full of flaws. She quickly dismissed her impulse to visit old haunts. Even if buildings looked the same, the things that mattered had all changed. Blue wouldn't be there.

A flash of taillight red caught Sarah's eye and she slammed on the brakes, a bit harder than required. "I've got to pay attention to the road," she scolded herself. Traffic was heavy but moving.

On the west end of Denver, new construction dominated the hills on either side of the highway—three-story custom homes in various stages of completion. The extent of development took Sarah by surprise. She didn't recall seeing suburbs this far outside of Denver the last time she drove I-70. *Things do change*, she reminded herself. *We all do.* She wondered how Blue had changed. This kind of suburban sprawl infuriated him back then, and she felt sure it still would.

The last time she'd been in the mountains with Blue, they had had a fight. He had been studying black bears at a summer research camp between her sophomore and junior years. A harrowing encounter with a bear the year before had left her with an acute fear of the animal. Blue maintained she was paranoid; she felt he was insensitive. He couldn't understand why she wouldn't spend more time with him at the camp. She was too frightened to stay. Halfway down the mountain, she swerved to avoid hitting an old man on the road. She wrecked the truck and was knocked unconscious. She didn't come to until hikers came up along and found her. She spent several days in a Denver hospital, recovering from exposure and head trauma. Blue ended their relationship the week after.

The memory felt like a weight on her heart. Sarah opened the window to let the mountain air blow through her hair and the heaviness eased a bit. She turned her attentions back to the road. As her ears popped, she held her breath in anticipation of the transition from foothills to snow-capped mountains. The road crested one final hill, bringing the Rocky Mountain range into full view. The scenery left her awe-struck.

The masses of rock, the different layers of stone forming colored patterns on the face, all pushed skyward by some magnificent force, called her to follow their lead and look skyward. She could feel the immensity of the stone. In sharp contrast to the mutable landscape of the foothills, these rock masses seemed changeless. And yet she knew that even these towers continually eroded from the steady attention of water and wind. Still their infinitesimal alterations escaped detection, which only heightened her awareness of how drastically her life had changed.

Her college days had been filled with so many new experiences, mostly revolving around Blue. The innocent ecstasy of First Love, the challenges of a city girl learning to hike and camp in the mountains, the wonders of golden eagles soaring and of coyote choruses under a full moon, the invigorating freedom of making love in a sunny mountain meadow.

Would they still be together if.... "Don't go there," she reprimanded herself, feeling that old regret and the pointless questioning of "what ifs" welling up inside. "What's done is done." She put in a Mary Chapin Carpenter CD, turned up the volume and sang along.

As she reached the top of a rise, she spotted a buck deer lying dead on the side of the road. His head and neck were twisted grotesquely over his back; his glassy black eyes seemed to stare directly into the car. A shiver ran down her spine and her vision glazed with tears. In those lifeless eyes she sensed the dead place inside her, a part of her heart that still felt broken. In the routine of every day, she blocked out the void and lived a contented life. But here in these uplifted canyons of primordial bedrock, she felt exposed and vulnerable. "For god's sake," she chided herself. "I see road kill all the time back home and I don't fall apart. What's so different about here?" And while she couldn't explain it, deep in her gut she knew that being back in Colorado made everything different.

After an hour behind the wheel, Sarah finally felt more at ease. Her anxiety had subsided, much to her relief. She planned to stop in Glenwood Springs for lunch. Her favorite stretch of highway came just before the city, the drive through Glenwood Canyon. The four-lane, divided highway hugged the canyon walls and in many places ran above the Colorado River, not alongside it. The highway was an architectural achievement, but the canyon itself was far more impressive to her.

When she saw the exit sign for the town of Dotsero, she knew the canyon was coming up soon. She wished someone else could drive this stretch so she could take in the two-thousand-foot-high granite cliffs with their dark clefts and crevices, lone pine trees miraculously growing on stone and shimmers of waterfalls. She drove more slowly than the local drivers, soaking up as much of the beauty as possible along the fifteen-mile stretch. The road followed the Colorado River as it rumbled out of the canyon and into the town of Glenwood Springs. Sarah exited the interstate in the downtown area near the Hot Springs Pool and parked on the main street.

She found a small cafe with outside seating, ordered a sandwich and pulled out one of the books Mr. Tremaine, her employer, had sent her on Colorado sites and history. It was written by a Glenwood Springs native Jon Klusmire.

Perusing the index, she turned to the section on Glenwood Springs. She learned that the city has the world's largest natural hot springs pool, built in the late 1880s. "Doc" Holliday of OK Corral fame died and was buried in Glenwood Springs. Then a passage caught her attention:

> The town's most famous visitor was Teddy Roosevelt, who set up a western White House in the Hotel Colorado in 1905 and from which he went on a bear hunt in the nearby White River National Land Reserve. While he was out in the wilds he kept in touch with the White House via a telegraph line to the hotel and a

messenger who rode out on his horse every day to try to find the President.

"Guess Teddy's 'Walk softly and carry a big stick' took on a whole new meaning for those bears," she reflected.

A reference to "teddy bears" had her turn to another section in the book. "Teddy bears are named for Teddy Roosevelt. I didn't know that," she said as she continued reading.

> There are a couple of versions of the teddy bear myth. One has it that Teddy's daughter Alice was admiring the bears brought back by the hunters and decided to name one Teddy. A second version claims that the maids at the Hotel Colorado stitched together a crude little stuffed bear named Teddy and presented it to the President. Anyhow, a little marketing and hype later, the teddy bear was enthroned as an indispensable children's toy, a position it still holds.

Sarah thought about the Gund teddy bear that Ruth had given her when she had started having trouble with Blue. It was the softest, most cuddly stuffed animal imaginable. Sarah loved that bear. How ironic, she thought, that this stuffed toy had its origins here in central Colorado, the same place that had infused her with such an irrational fear of its real-life counterpart, a fear that eventually had driven Blue away.

Sarah wished she'd brought that Gund bear with her. While packing for this trip, she had resisted the urge to throw it in her bag, reasoning that adult women do not travel with stuffed toys unless as a gift for a child. So she had left the bear in her room, even though that creature brought her comfort during stressful times. Closing the tour book, Sarah prayed that teddy bears would be the only bruins she'd see this time, in the woods or in her imagination.

CHAPTER SIX

A FULL MOON DRAPED the mountain meadow in a bright shimmer. As Jessie and her horse stepped out of the trees and into the open, she stared appreciatively at the stunning scene—immense stone canyon walls rising above stands of pine and aspen and the glimmering river rumbling below. She dismounted and left her horse to graze while she walked over to a commanding rock that offered a panoramic view. Even at her age she did not stumble. Her feet knew every nuance of this path, every rock, exposed root, hole and turn. Weather permitting and sometimes to spite it, Jessie made this pilgrimage once a month to bathe in moonlight and reflect on her life.

Long ago she had found the perfect sitting rock, a red granite boulder with a slight depression that cradled her like a chair. She could sit there for hours and watch the full moon illuminate the landscape. On clear nights, the light was so bright, elk continued to graze until early morning rather than bed down after dusk. Coyotes yipped and howled more at this time, as though praising the return of its bright-white brilliance.

In the distance a calf mooed. "Tom's got his cows in the south pasture, I reckon," she remarked to herself. The calf annoyed her, because it was a reminder that this valley technically was not on her property; it belonged to the McDermott Ranch where Tom Payton leased land for his cattle. Years ago, this property had belonged to her grandparents and she felt the McDermotts never had a right to call it theirs. They didn't love the land the way her grandfather had. They always put too many cattle on the place and let them tear up the meadows and stream banks.

They only took from the land and never gave anything back. Jessie felt the anger building. They never deserved this place.

The calf mooed again as Jessie settled in to the well-worn seat on Full Moon Rock. She had to admit, since Tom had taken over leasing the ranch, the grasses looked so much better. He maintained the fences and was a fairly good rancher, although she could sense his whole heart wasn't in it. Still, he did right by the place, and she felt grateful that he worked the ranch now.

Jessie watched the moonlight dancing on the river, as water rushed endlessly over rocks. At first all she could hear was the running water. But soon, the initial hush that greeted her arrival modulated into sounds of animals scurrying, hunting, feeding and exploring. Tonight no wind blew, so she could tune into every rustle and flurry. She marveled at how sound became amplified at night. In the darkness, the smallest mouse can sound like a bull elk, especially when you're alone and frightened.

Jessie had spent her first night alone in this valley when she was twelve years old. Having been accused of being a sissy by the class bully, she had vowed to prove him wrong with her version of a coming-of-age initiation. Her mother understood her desire and had helped her prepare.

The moon had been full and the air calm that night, and she had been paralyzed with fright. Every sound had made her heart jump while turning her feet to lead. She swore she heard a huge bear barreling down the path to consume her and saw the round eyes of a mountain lion stalking her from a nearby tree. And she was sure she'd heard the faint mumblings of a crazy mountain man intent on causing her harm.

At the first hint of sunlight, her mom arrived as promised. Jessie couldn't remember who had been more relieved to see the other, although neither spoke of it. The dark circles under her mom's eyes told Jessie that she had worried about her all night.

Over a skillet egg breakfast, she had told her mom about her night. She talked about the bear and mountain lion as if they had been fact, although she omitted how frightened she had been. Her mom smiled and hadn't probed beyond the bravado. As they cleaned up camp, her mom had told her something she'd never forgotten. "Jessie, dear, I'm proud of you. It took courage to stay out here alone. I want you to know it's alright to be afraid. What we're afraid of always seems scarier at night. In the morning, we usually find that our worst fears are of our own making."

Jessie thought about those words now and wondered if this premonition that haunted her was of her own making. She sat on that rock in the stillness of midnight and cursed the creeping angst that once again weighed down her legs like lead. This night, she did not fear the sounds, the darkness or the animals living in the forest around her. She feared the future, a future full of changes that would take this valley from her, changes she wasn't sure she could stop. Unlike when she was twelve, Jessie knew this dread would not dissipate with the coming sunrise.

A flurry of movement brought her back to the present. Off to her left, she saw an owl catch a mouse in its talons and fly off on silent wings to consume it. She watched his flight until he disappeared into the trees. Only then did she turn back toward the river. A dark, hulking form stood behind a large spruce directly in front of her. She gasped before she could stop herself. The shadowy form stepped into the moonlight and moved towards her.

"Damn you, Duncan, don't sneak up on me like that," she snapped. "I thought you were a bear."

"You must be lost in thoughts tonight," the man said in his quiet, halting voice. "You always hear me coming."

He was right. She rarely let anyone or anything surprise her. She had let her guard down and kicked herself for being distracted. She couldn't afford to wallow in panic and she needed her wits about her.

"I heard you calling," he stated, "so I came." He spread out a small blanket and sat down.

Jessie had planned to visit him the next day but hadn't told him that. And yet he knew she needed to talk with him and knew where to find her. So he showed up. Long ago she stopped questioning him about how he was able to read her mind or sense her thoughts. Now she took it for granted. Duncan Hawk related to the world in a way she could only imagine. He knew about the goings on in the valley, even some things she didn't know, and yet he rarely came into town or visited with the other ranchers, except Jessie. Still, she was not his first source of information most times. He maintained that he learned things from the wind, the animals and the plants. Even the rocks seemed to talk to him. When they had first met years ago, he had tried to teach her, but she was never able to listen to the world as he did.

"Make yourself at home," she said, trying to salvage her composure.

"Eli has come back into your life and that disturbs you," Duncan said.

"So you've heard then. That bastard wants to sell the southern tract." She stood up and started pacing. "He wrote Tom a letter demanding a ridiculous price for the land. The coward, he didn't send me a letter. And I'm sure you didn't get one either. We need to figure out what to do."

Duncan sat without moving, his eyes looking out across the valley. Respectfully, Jessie took her seat and waited for his response. She had to temper her impatience whenever she talked with him. He never rushed into speaking, and she found that what he had to say was usually worth waiting for. Not that he always told her the truth. Duncan possessed a mischievous sense of humor often expressed at Jessie's expense, leading her down a path and zinging her before she even knew she was being had. But tonight, neither found any humor in Eli McDermott.

"It is good he has come back," Duncan began. He seemed to speak to the sky as well as Jessie. "It is time to put things right."

She waited, but he did not elaborate. "The only way he can make things right is to give me back the land his grandparents stole from my grandfather. They took advantage of a man down on his luck and then abused this place right in front of him."

"Down on his luck, yes, I see," he said, almost mockingly, "that must be what happened to my people when we lived here. The white man stole the Ute's land when we were down on our luck."

Jessie's face flushed. "I'm sorry, sometimes I'm an insensitive old woman. Forgive me. I know this land belonged to your people."

"Jessibel Amanda Winde, this land still is Ute land. It always will be," Duncan stated without malice. "These mountains, the rivers, the trees, the rocks, the animals, they do not forget who Creator blessed with this land. Only the people forget."

Of course, he's right, Jessie argued with herself. *The Utes had been living in Colorado since the Anasazi. They spent summers in this very forest for hundreds of years until the whites marched them out of Colorado and confined them to the reservation. But we can't rewrite history. White people have lived in this valley and worked the land for over one hundred years since then. I love this valley; it's my home. Then again, what the government did to the Utes was terrible and should never have happened. But it's not realistic to give all of Colorado back to them either.* There seemed no right thing to do or say, so she said nothing.

Looking at Duncan, she felt gratitude that he hadn't let the history of this valley and their ancestors interfere with their friendship. Duncan was a Northern Ute elder who never flaunted his heritage or publicly denounced the ranchers here. He kept to himself. Jessie knew that he was constantly watching and waiting, alert to every change in the valley, but had never interfered. She sensed he would step forward if the need were great enough. Maybe this was the time.

"Duncan, I think we can agree that we don't want Eli to sell any part of this ranch." She hesitated, waiting for some acknowledgement. He nodded his head slightly, so she went on. "And Eli cannot be trusted. He doesn't care about this place or anyone who lives here. He only cares about himself. He's a snake!"

"You did not always feel this way about him," Duncan said, leaving no room for denial. "The wound you carry still has not healed."

Frustration and anger radiated from Jessie's eyes, but she held her tongue. Duncan had more to say. "You may be right to call Eli a snake. Perhaps Eli carries the energies of Snake. Snake can shed its skin, start life again. Snake can be a healer. Maybe this is why he has come back."

With that, he stood up and folded his blanket. "It is best to let go of the pain from the past," he said in his soft, halting tone. "Otherwise it will only feed your fears and cloud your judgment. You may do things you will later regret." Duncan Hawk nodded his head as if in blessing and walked into woods.

Jessie seethed. Calling after him would do no good. He wouldn't respond. *He has as much reason to be angry about Eli as I do. He acts like nothing ever happened. How can Duncan be so detached?*

She was too angry to look for the wisdom in his words. All she felt was betrayal. She looked out across the meadow, the grasses glowing softly, as a dense cloud blocked out the moon and slowly swallowed the meadow in darkness.

"That bastard, he betrayed me once," she fumed. "I'll be damned if he'll do it again!"

At that moment, she wished she were an owl and Eli a mouse, so she could swoop down in deadly silence and squeeze his helpless body between her talons and peck out his eyes. The tears streamed down her faced as she pictured her revenge, wishing she could crush the dread rising inside her that Eli could again take from her what was most precious. The cloud passed and the returning moonlight comforted her.

When the morning sun finally painted the horizon in soft pinks, Jessie sat perfectly still, exhausted, drained—and resolute. Eli would never hurt her again. She tenderly called her horse to saddle up. She settled onto the graceful strength beneath her and clung to the soft mane for support all the way back to the ranch.

Duncan Hawk greeted the sunrise from the ridge above the canyon. Standing next to his horse, he offered prayers for the new day. A slight breeze caressed his face and teased his long hair as he finished. Then he mounted his horse and headed down the trail, stopping only when they reached the creek. As his horse drank, he watched the reflection of first sunlight dance and weave in the ever-flowing water, awakening the canyon from the shadows.

He pondered Eli's reappearance and his desire to sell the land. Eli had caused so much damage years ago; Duncan had no reason to welcome him back to the valley. And yet, he wondered if this was related to the work Spirit had called him to do? Maybe a catalyst, he sensed, but something was still missing. He must be patient and remain open to the path set before him. And he needed to heed his own advice so freely given to Jessie. He, too, must let go of painful regrets from the past.

So he sat up straight, breathed deeply and listened. He listened to the water, to the rocks, to the trees, to the wind. He walked a hundred yards down the path and turned off at the top of a rise. A huge boulder, once part of the towering cliffs around him, leaned up against the bank, providing a perch above the creek. Here he sat, tuning his ears and his heart to the sounds of the canyon. They spoke in different tones, touched him in various ways, but they all told him the same thing, affirming what Red Fire Woman had foretold in his vision.

The time has come. Be prepared. She is coming...to be redeemed.

CHAPTER SEVEN

As Sarah drove west from Glenwood Springs, the mountains gave up their bold colors of iron-red and charcoal black and replaced them with sandy tones of pale pink, yellow and white. At the town of Rifle, Sarah turned north. The stillness on the sparsely traveled highway lulled her into an appreciative silence. Forty miles later, she crossed the bridge over the White River and sighted a Kum and Go gas station and minimart, a jarring indicator of approaching civilization.

The Meeker welcome sign appealed more to her artistic sensibilities, a large wooden placard showing a dignified profile of an Indian man. "I wonder who he is? He's certainly not Mr. Meeker." She knew from her tour book that the town was named after the government man sent there to work with the Indians in 1878. She didn't have much time to ponder the question, however, before spotting a sign for the business district. Turning left, Sarah found the town one block in from the rural highway. The county courthouse, built with large blocks of salmon-colored sandstone from a local quarry, dominated the center of the square; local businesses, historic buildings and an elementary school built with the same rock lined opposite sides of the streets. The inconspicuous Veterans of Foreign Wars building hosted the only bar on the square. The business district extended a block or so before melding into neighborhoods of single-story homes.

Sarah parked on the street amid mostly mud-spattered pickup trucks. Leaving her bags in the car, she walked over to the Meeker Hotel. A community bulletin board by the front door advertised border collie pups, an auction of farm equipment, a church charity luncheon and the Fourth of July rodeo and music festival in Rangely.

Stepping into the lobby, she stopped just inside the door. "Wow." Two elk heads with enormous antlers commanded the entryway and Sarah's gaze. Amazed by the sheer size of head and headdress, she wondered aloud, "How can they carry around such huge antlers? They must have ridiculously strong necks."

"Those are record-size elk," explained the college-age desk clerk. "At one time I think they were the largest in the country. We have a lobby full of unusual mounts, mostly mule deer and elk, with a moose thrown in for variety. You're welcome to look around."

Sarah walked over to the clerk. "What makes them so unusual?"

"Their antlers mostly; some have tines that point down instead of up, others have abnormal shapes, most are just huge. They're fun to look at."

"I'll check them out, but first I'd like to check in," Sarah said, approaching the antique wooden counter.

"Cool," the clerk responded, delightfully surprised. "Do you have a reservation? Not that you actually need one this time of year."

"Not your busy season?"

"Nope. Things are pretty quiet around here until the Fourth of July. Then it slows down again until the end of August when archery hunting starts and the International Sheepdog Trials get started. We fill up then and business doesn't let up until after the hunting seasons end in November." The clerk smiled. "If tourists stop in here now, it's to look at the heads on the wall or to get a cold drink for the road. They don't usually stay the night."

"Well then, it sounds like I didn't need a reservation, but I know Hollis Tremaine made one for me anyway. I'm Sarah Cavanaugh."

"Oh yeah, I heard about you, I mean, from my boss. He said you were some famous artist or something. I'm Isabel. Nice to meet you."

"Nice to meet you too, Isabel. And for the record, I'm not exactly famous, but I am a muralist."

"How cool. Excuse me for asking, but what exactly is a muralist?"

"I paint murals, you know, paintings done on a wall. They are usually quite large and tell a story, depict a place, show some local history, that kind of thing."

"If you're interested in local history, the White River Museum across the square is a great place. And as soon as I finish your paperwork I can tell you a little more about the hotel…if you're interested."

"Thank you. I am." Sarah stepped into the rustic lobby of hardwood floors, brick walls, stained glass windows and leather upholstered couches and chairs made of rough-hewn logs. Antlers abounded—antlers formed bases for coffee tables, they floated overhead as light fixtures and they adorned a herd of beautifully preserved heads staring out from every wall. She loved the feel of the room, an odd combination of cozy and imposing. She envisioned spending an evening here, with a lively fire crackling in the cast-iron stove, a hot cup of coffee and her sketchpad. Having so many pairs of glass eyes watching overhead might take some adjustment, but she felt the room's antique warmth would more than compensate for the inanimate audience.

Isabel came into the lobby and eagerly offered her well-rehearsed two-minute tour-guide speech. "The town of Meeker was incorporated in 1885; it was the only incorporated town in northwest Colorado for the next twenty years. The Meeker Hotel was built in 1896, the first major structure in town. They used over 200,000 bricks to build this building; the walls are six-bricks thick. Up until a couple of years ago, all the rooms upstairs were bunk-type styles with only a couple of shared bathrooms. But you'll be staying in one of the renovated rooms. Don't worry, you've got your own bathroom."

"Good to know," Sarah said. "Are you from around here?"

"Sure am, although I go to school in Utah. I come back in the summers to work and to see friends. My folks have a ranch up river."

"Can you tell me a little bit about the valley then?"

"Sure. Folks up there are pretty much divided between sheep and cattle ranching. Originally it was all cattle. When sheep first came into the valley, I'm told things got real ugly for a while with feuds like you'd see in the movies. But we have a fairly amicable rivalry these days. My family raises sheep. You'll find a number of outfitters living in the valley too. Ya' know, guided hunts, mostly for elk and deer in the fall and winter, and fishing trips in the summer. Some guys rent out cabins or rooms in a lodge, some do horseback trips too.

"Then of course, there's the rich folks. We don't see much of them in town. They buy a big ranch and have a few local guys run it for them.

They come out a couple times a year, but they keep pretty much to themselves. I never see them in here."

The hotel phone rang and the clerk excused herself to answer it. Soon Sarah heard the bantering of good friends making plans for the weekend and knew that she had lost Isabel's undivided attention.

She picked up the key Isabel had brought to her and walked up the wide, wooden stairs, admiring the raw-log banister and enjoying the feel of varnished knotty bumps beneath her hand. She hoped, however, that the mattress in her room wasn't as rustic as the lobby decor. Her back was already feeling the aches from a long car ride, and she desperately wanted to get a good night's sleep.

The next morning, Sarah called Hollis Tremaine to let him know she had arrived in town. He apologized again for the need for her stay at the hotel and assured her that she could move into the guest cabin as soon as his daughter and grandkids went home in a week. He repeated how thrilled he was that the kids had wanted to extend their stay at the ranch. She told him that she would put her time in Meeker to good use and not to worry. She would come for dinner tomorrow night.

Sarah appreciated having some time on her own and spent the morning casually rummaging through the town's antique stores. She found comfort in old things. She wondered about the people who had owned them, marveled at the oddities that people collected and coveted the truly exquisite pieces that she couldn't afford.

Done with antiquing, she took a walk around the square and at the southwest corner, spied several old log cabin structures that intrigued her. On the door of the first one she found a small sign: "White River Museum." Remembering the clerk's recommendation, Sarah opened the door and walked in.

A petite, white-haired woman greeted her. "Welcome to the White River Museum," she said gently. "Have you visited here before?"

"No, this is my first time in Meeker," Sarah replied.

"You've just walked into the oldest structure in town. It was built in 1880 as an army barracks after they had some trouble with the Indians. Once the town got established, this became a private residence and then eventually was donated to the historical society for use as a museum. Please feel free to look around. I'd be happy to answer any questions."

"Thanks," Sarah replied, hoping she wouldn't dog her through the place, with a continuous curator chatter that could infect well-meaning museum volunteers. To her relief, the woman quickly disappeared, leaving Sarah to wander through the front rooms alone. Nothing unusual caught her attention, just typical pioneer kitchen displays and rusted farm tools. She moved into the center room that contained a large reading table and a number of books. Black-and-white photographs of early settlers lined one wall. The curator was reading at her desk.

As Sarah placed a five-dollar bill in the contributions box, she asked, "So, what are the highlights of Meeker's history?"

"Teddy Roosevelt spent a good deal of time here," the curator began. "He did a lot of hunting and fishing out this way. We host the International Sheep Dog Trials every fall; people come from all over the world to compete with their dogs. It's been a Meeker tradition for twenty years now. Meeker started out as a military post. Once the Indians moved out in 1881, then the ranchers came and settled the area."

"What Indians were those?" Sarah asked.

"The Northern Ute tribe, or the White River Utes. They were responsible for the Meeker Massacre, which is what this town is known for historically. After the massacre, the Indians were relocated to a reservation in Utah."

Sensing that Sarah had at least a mild interest in the topic, the curator quietly stepped into storyteller mode. "That's a photograph of Nathan Meeker," pointing to the portraits on the wall. "He was the Indian agent assigned to the White River agency in 1878. That's his wife Arvilla and his daughter Josephine."

"Is the town named after Nathan Meeker?" Sarah asked.

"Yes, it is. He lost his life trying to help the Indians here. He was working to get the Utes to adopt farming as a way of life. One summer he plowed up a meadow along the river where the Indians raced their horses. The Indians got upset and threatened Meeker and his family. Meeker called in military troops for protection. The Utes attacked the army and the people living at the White River Agency. They killed all the men in the agency, including Meeker, and then they kidnapped the women. Held them captive in the mountains for days before Chief Ouray, the main chief of the Ute tribes, negotiated their release. We have several books that cover the massacre, if you're interested."

"Thank you for the story," Sarah replied. The photograph of Nathan

Meeker held her attention, something about his face looked familiar and strangely menacing. His expression was passive, still she felt her body tense and her throat tighten. Why would she react so strongly to a picture? She turned around to find the curator watching her intently.

"I think I'll walk around a bit more," Sarah said, feeling self-conscious.

"Would you like me to show you where we keep the Indian artifacts?"

The curator led her past the Teddy Roosevelt photographs, guns and mounted heads of deer and elk he'd shot in nearby mountains. They walked over to a cluttered corner and stopped in front of a display case of arrowheads and other stone tools.

But before the curator could expound on the archeological treasures, Sarah stepped over to a larger glass case. "What a beautiful dress."

"The Ute women were known for their intricate beadwork and for their skill at tanning leather," the curator replied. "They made the softest skins. Colonists back east paid a lot of money for them in the 1800s."

Sarah wished she could try on the white buckskin dress that practically dripped with brightly colored beads. Equally ornate moccasins and leggings were also on display. "They would make any woman feel beautiful," Sarah remarked, although the mannequin that wore them was faded and chipped.

"Here are some articles about the massacre," the curator offered, pointing to the adjacent case. Sarah turned; her feet felt heavy. She could make out the headlines from old newspaper clippings—"The Utes Must Go!"—but the display case kept her from getting close enough to read the text. One article showed a photograph of an old Indian woman. "Chipeta, wife of Chief Ouray, died at age 81" read the caption. Again, Sarah felt a strange sense of recognition with this woman, even stronger than with Nathan Meeker. But Chipeta's gentle, weathered face made Sarah smile. *That's so odd*, she thought, *maybe I ran across these photographs in college*. And yet, she'd never taken a Colorado history course.

Her eyes moved to the silver belt buckles and beaded bags displayed below the newspaper clippings. She gazed at an Indian pipe. Carved animals and birds adorned the wooden stem attached to a soft red stone bowl. The museum label read "Peace pipe of Chief Colorow." The label offended her, but she didn't know why.

A chill ran down her spine when she caught sight of a simple necklace of beaded rawhide with a thick brown claw at least four inches long hanging from it. "What kind of claw is that?" she asked, as her left hand began to clench.

"I believe that is from a grizzly bear. The necklace was found in the White River Forest up river from here. It's kind of a mystery because we don't have any record of who donated it."

Sarah strained to hear what the curator was saying, but she suddenly felt dizzy and light-headed. She looked down to see her left hand shaking as though afflicted with a palsy.

"My dear, are you all right?" the curator asked with real concern. "Would you like to sit down?"

"Leave me alone," Sarah barked. "Stay away from me, just stay away." A buzzing began in her ears, like muffled drums, and rapidly swarmed through her head as the beaded necklace blurred into darkness.

CHAPTER EIGHT

THE POUNDING OF HIS FEET matched the frantic beating of his heart. Branches scratched his sweat-drenched face and blocked his view as he ran. Desperation pumped adrenaline through every muscle in his body. The sight of a huge grizzly rearing up on her hind legs jolted him to a stop. Her angry roar reverberated in his chest. Her yellow eyes burned into his as she threatened to attack. Fear rooted his feet to the earth. Then a gunshot fired and the grizzly staggered backwards. He started running again, as another shot ripped through the air and hit the bear. She fell to the ground, blood spurting across her face.

Anger replaced fear as he continued to run. An explosion offered brief warning of the bullet's crushing impact into his back that threw him to the ground. Gasping on his own blood, he looked up into the face of the dying grizzly lying directly in front of him. She stared at him with recognition. He watched the light fade as her amber eyes turned to glass. His body went into spasm....

Jason awoke to a searing pain in his back and fear pulsing through his body. He instinctively reached for a bottle. "Goddamn it! You mother fucker!" he shouted, at his nightmare and the absent whiskey bottle.

He got up and sat on the edge of his bed. Looking around the room, he tried to shake off the disorientation from his nightmare. The paintings on the wall and the view of the mountains through his window reminded him that he was in Colorado, in his uncle's home, not in his back-alley apartment in Nashville with its dirty linoleum floor littered with empty booze bottles, unpaid bills and crumpled up pages of bad song lyrics.

He made his way to the bathroom and splashed cold water on his face until his cheeks ached. He threw back his head to move his long black hair out of the way, then stared in the mirror. "Get a grip, man. It's just a goddamned dream." His hands had stopped trembling. Jason felt an overwhelming urge to feel the sun on his skin, so he pulled on his pants and boots and headed out the back door, hoping to avoid his uncle.

The nightmare wasn't new. Jason had endured this recurring specter from the time he'd turned fifteen. At age twenty, he'd begun having other disturbing dreams that he didn't understand. He had stopped telling his parents about them after awhile because they either laughed at him or lectured him about drinking too much, telling him the booze was making him crazy. But in fact, drinking was the only thing that seemed to keep the dreams and the voices at bay, at least for a time.

And alcohol had been easy for Jason to come by back then. He played guitar and sang in a rock n' roll band he'd pulled together with some friends. The band was good enough to get gigs in bars on a regular basis. Soon Jason spent more time on the road making music than he did back home in Utah on the reservation. When he wasn't singing, he was usually drinking, playing cards and getting into fights.

Fighting came naturally to Jason; he attracted trouble like metal to a magnet. He walked into a room with an air that challenged some idiot to cross him. Because Jason wasn't tall, people usually underestimated his strength. Every fool who wanted a piece of him found out the hard way that Jason was a muscular, mean son-of-a-bitch Indian who knew how to fight and win.

Unfortunately, Jason's last fight had landed him in jail and left him with an ugly gash on his forearm. He absent-mindedly rubbed that scar as he leaned against a large rock, staring up at the sun. The memory of that fight flashed through his mind.

He'd been living in Nashville for little over a year, trying unsuccessfully to sell his songs or his solo act. After a particularly tough week of steady rejection, Jason had lost himself in a four-day drunk. He'd gotten so out of control he never noticed that the guy who had grabbed him was wearing a badge. He'd nearly beaten the sheriff to death before somebody pulled him off.

Jason had hoped that his father would bail him out of jail. But no money came, just a note with some parental advice about how jail time might be good for him, give him time to reflect on how he'd screwed up his life and dishonored his family.

Consequently, Jason had been shocked when, three weeks later, the guard told him he had a visitor. He was even more surprised when he found Duncan Hawk waiting for him. Jason hadn't seen this tribal elder in years, but he immediately recognized him. He'd added a few pounds to his slender frame, and his once black hair was now peppered with gray. But Duncan Hawk still wore his hair in a long ponytail, and he still could look right through Jason and seem to read his heart.

The two men were not related by blood, but ever since Jason had been a small boy they had shared the emotional connection of uncle and nephew and referred to each other in those terms. Time apart had not changed those feelings.

Jason remembered the shame he'd felt as his uncle approached him. But Duncan hadn't driven from Colorado to Tennessee to chastise him. He had made Jason a take-it-or-leave-it proposition; Duncan would get him out of jail, but only if Jason agreed to live with him for four years, stop drinking and open his heart to his true path. Jason wanted out of jail, but he wanted no part of his uncle's proposal. Jason didn't like anyone telling him what to do. Duncan told his nephew that he had four days to think it over before he would head back to Colorado.

Before leaving, Duncan had said, "I know about your dreams. If you continue to ignore them, they will make you crazy." And for the next three nights, Jason woke screaming, unable to shake the image of the bloody bear and her dead eyes staring through him. On the fourth day, he agreed to his uncle's terms. That had been two years ago.

The sun washed over Jason's face as he pushed himself off the rock and hurried to the stables. He looked up to the top of the sandstone cliff just in time to catch a hawk circling on a thermal. Jason smiled to himself as he realized that he sensed hawks now before he saw them; he could feel their presence. When he'd first arrived at his uncle's mountain home, Jason would get angry whenever Duncan would tell him to "honor the hawk that is flying over you now." His uncle wouldn't be looking up at the sky; he'd be staring directly at Jason. And every time Jason would search the skies, he'd find the magnificent bird and curse under his breath. "How the hell can you do that? How did you know it was there without looking?"

All his uncle would say is, "Learn to listen, open your heart, and you will know Hawk."

Jason finally understood at least that part of Duncan's teachings, but so much of it still confused and eluded him. This morning, he was grateful for the hawk's greeting and told the bird so. His anxiety lessened. He stood in the sun's light and let its warmth wash through him.

"It is a good day for a ride."

The voice startled him. "Jesus, Old Man, don't sneak up on me like that. It's too early in the morning for your fun and games!"

Duncan didn't reply. Jason looked away from his steady gaze.

Having learned he could hide little from Duncan, Jason spat out, "It's back. My goddamned nightmare came back." Jason looked down at his boots as he kicked a rock across the corral. What he didn't tell Duncan was how badly he wanted a drink, how instinctively he had reached for a whiskey bottle when he awoke, how much he felt the seduction of losing his fear in a drunken haze. The intense feelings shocked him; he'd been sober for two years, ever since he first stepped onto this land. He'd suffered terribly the first few months, but eventually he had put the whiskey cravings and dependencies behind him, or so he thought. The bear dream had also ceased, but this morning both nightmares returned; Jason felt doubly shaken.

If Jason's news surprised Duncan, it didn't register on his face. Little seemed to rile his uncle.

"Has the dream changed?"

"Changed?" Jason's temper flared. "No, it hasn't changed. It's still the same shitty little show of blood and death." Duncan's question irritated him, but he didn't know why.

"There is a reason the dream has returned," Duncan said softly. "The task before you is to find out why. Find out what it tells you now, what it teaches you."

"It's telling me not to fall asleep, that's what it's teaching me!"

"You are a different man today; you are stronger. The dream has come back because you can handle it now. See it with new eyes. It holds power for you."

"Feels more like power over me... anyway, I'm heading out for a ride."

"Sit by the water, listen to its song. Ask Water to help you, ask Bear to help you. Then come back and we will talk together."

"Whatever." Jason tried to dismiss his uncle, unable to meet his eyes. Still fighting the urge to drink and the accompanying shame of his weakness, Jason wanted to lose himself in the mountains and put this morning's awakening behind him.

He rode west in the direction he'd seen the hawk fly. Sandy yellow cliffs lined with evergreens towered around him as his horse picked her way along the trail. Scrub oak and juniper grew in clumps on the arid soil. Small lizards scattered out of the way as he approached the fork in the path. Normally the shade of the river valley would call to him on warm days like today. But the chill in his bones persisted; he needed to feel the sun. So he chose the right fork that would take him atop the cliffs where the bighorn sheep come in the winter months. He didn't expect to see any sheep today, but he did need an expansive look at the land around him.

This trail quickly grew narrow and slippery for a mounted horse. Jason got off and walked the rest of the way to the top. The view never failed to impress him. In all directions, he marveled at the red and white ridges intersected by pine-green valleys, the crystal blue sky dotted with white clouds, the subtle gray-greens of sagebrush growing around him. A light breeze refreshed him as he caught his breath from the climb.

Finding a place to tether his horse, he walked to the cliff's edge. In his haste to leave, Jason hadn't said his morning prayers, nor had he honored the sun as it rose above the mountain peaks. Prayer helped ground him, helped him feel a part of something greater than himself. Hard as it was for him to admit at first, prayer helped him relate differently to the voices and visions that had once driven him to drink. And with Duncan's guidance, Jason had begun to make some sense of these experiences and started to trust these bits of intuition. Even his dreams had changed their tenor; they no longer taunted him. Until last night. The remembering caused a pain to ricochet down his back.

"Focus up, man," he growled.

Facing east, he began his morning prayer with a shaky voice.

"Spirit of the East, place of springtime and of Eagle, place of new beginnings, Spirit of the color yellow. I honor you."

He then turned to face the other three directions, at each offering a prayer. "Spirit of the South, home of summer and of Coyote and Mouse, place of heart truth, Spirit of the color red. I honor you.

"Spirit of the West, home of autumn and of Bear, place of great dreams and shadow, Spirit of the color black. I honor you."

"Spirit of the North, home of winter and of Buffalo, place of healing, blessing and death, Spirit of the color white. I honor you."

He then turned his face upward. "Father Sky, the Keeper of vision and protection, I honor you." As he touched the ground with his hands, he said, "Mother Earth, the Keeper of life and love, I honor you." Standing back up, he finished. "The Great Mystery, that which is unknowable, that which challenges me, teaches me and amazes me, I honor you.

"Creator, thank you for my life, for my path, for bringing me to this place. Help me always to walk with humility and gratitude on this earth. Help me to understand the challenges placed before me. Help me to see clearly what is now in darkness. And keep Old Man from harm, let him stay healthy so he can continue to give me shit. Guess I still need it. Thank you, Creator, for my life. Aho."

Jason sat on the ridge for a long time. While his body was quiet and still, his mind continued to race. He couldn't stay focused, his mind wandering back to his days in Nashville, of singing until sunrise, drinking a little past then, and waking in the late afternoon to another stiff drink. So much of that time felt foreign to him now, but his daydreams censored the cruel reality of that life and highlighted only the temporary peace that whiskey had afforded him.

"I'm not going back to that way of living; focus up, asshole." The water in his canteen tasted surprisingly sweet, so he took another swallow and concentrated on its coolness.

"Water, I need to be by water," he reminded himself. He stood up, offering thanks to the sun and to the earth, then walked back to his horse.

As they headed back down the trail, Jason welcomed the drop in temperature as the shade from the steep mountainside cooled his skin. Soon the song of water running over rocks greeted his ears. He didn't need to urge his horse to move faster; the promise of a drink put a trot in the mare's step. They came to a clearing in the trees where they could walk to water's edge. He tied his horse where she could reach both the creek and grass and then walked upstream a ways and lay down on a large flat rock. Jason felt the smooth stone against his back, closed his eyes and listened. His uncle's words came back to him. "Sit by the water, listen to its song. See the dream with new eyes. It holds power for you."

After a time, Jason allowed himself to think back on the dream. Had anything changed? Well, maybe. Feelings more than actions. He realized that he had felt anger this time, anger because someone had killed the bear. This time he wasn't screaming for himself, he was mourning this huge grizzly.

A hawk shrieked and Jason looked up to thank him for the affirmation. Yes, the dream had changed. "In the dream, I know this bear and this bear knows me," Jason spoke out loud. Before exploring that thought further, he slid into sarcasm. "Hey, man, that's only because I've had the damn dream so many times." But the snide comment didn't ring true. He pushed aside the doubts and focused once again on the creek. "That's why I'm angry. I was trying to save this bear; the bear wasn't trying to kill me. Someone else kills her and I'm trying to stop them." This discovery filled him with a sense of accomplishment. The dread he'd been carrying around all morning lifted. "Well, once again Old Man is right, damn him. There is more here than I thought."

A cloud floated in front of the sun as Jason's mood soured. "Yeah man, you tried to save that grizzly bear, but the fact is, you failed. She dies, just like all the other times. And I die too, or at least I feel like I do. So big fucking deal, now I know I'm dreaming about my own failures."

The sun came back out and shone once again on the rock where Jason lay. He allowed the running water to fill his head, lull him into a quiet place. As he drifted off, he thought, "Maybe Old Man will have a different spin on this. He usually does."

CHAPTER NINE

SARAH'S HEAD STILL HURT several hours after her fainting spell in the museum. The curator had insisted on walking her back to the hotel. The only way Sarah could prevent the desk clerk from calling a doctor was to accept her offer of bringing dinner to her room. Embarrassed, Sarah appreciated their concern but just wanted to be left alone. Popping a couple of aspirin, she picked up the phone and called Ruth.

The sisters had been close growing up but had let correspondence slide once they had gone away to college. After Sarah's car accident, they vowed not to let distance or busy schedules get in the way of staying in touch. Twice-a-week phone calls became part of their routine, and once Ruth returned to the Chicago area to set up her practice as a Jungian analyst, the sisters spent a lot of time together.

Whether over telephone lines or a cup of coffee, Sarah also got her fair share of free psychological advice and insight, lovingly veiled in sisterly concern, which she sometimes heeded but more often dismissed with a laugh. Tonight, she needed some of that advice and comfort.

Sarah felt a rush of relief when Ruth actually answered the phone. "I'm so glad you're home. I need to talk to you." Her voice caught.

"Hey, what's up? You sound a bit shaky."

Ruth's voice calmed her a bit. "I fainted today, in a museum. Out cold. Luckily someone was there to break my fall. Can you believe it? I actually fainted! Maybe coming back here was a mistake."

"How are you now? Did you hit your head?"

"I've got a nasty headache and I hurt all over. But the nausea's gone."

"Sounds like my first three months of pregnancy...uh, you're not pregnant are you?"

"Don't be ridiculous. I don't know what happened."

"Museums can be awfully stuffy, maybe you were reacting to some preservative chemical. What were you looking at when you fainted?"

Here she goes, thought Sarah, *out comes the analysis.* "What, you think this was a psychosomatic response to some old dusty artifacts? You know, you'd psychoanalyze a hangnail if I'd let you!"

Both sisters laughed. "So, what were you looking at?"

Knowing Ruth wouldn't drop it, Sarah tried her best to respond. "Some Indian stuff. You know, arrowheads, moccasins, drums, a beaded dress. Your basic Indian stuff."

"Hmm, what was the last thing you remember seeing?"

"There was this wood and stone pipe and...I don't know." Irritation crept into her voice. "Well, there was this huge bear claw on a piece of rawhide, a necklace of some sort. I remember feeling agitated as soon as I saw it. Go figure."

"Really. That's interesting."

"I know that tone in your voice. I don't think that had anything to do with my fainting. I probably got food poisoning from lunch."

"Uh huh, last I knew, food poisoning usually makes you throw up. I assume your meal is still intact."

Sarah didn't respond.

"Look, I'll make one observation and then I'll drop this, for now. You did say that the necklace had a bear claw on it. When you were with Blue, you developed a fear of bears. I'm sure you remember. So maybe that necklace touched something in you... or maybe you're just a bit touched in the head."

Sarah appreciated her sister's attempt at levity, but not her persistence.

"Just think about it. Maybe it has some significance for you that you're not seeing right now."

"Okay, whatever you say. So, how's the baby? And how are you?"

"This is an active little critter. She's kicking and rolling all the time, especially when I'm trying to get some sleep. I have to take a lot more insulin right now. Almost three times what I normally take, which is a real pain."

"Why do you have to take more?"

"Because the placenta produces certain hormones that actually block insulin. It's a bit of a struggle to get the balance right, but I'm figuring it out. The doctors say I'm doing a really good job managing my sugar levels, so that feels good."

"I'm sorry you have to deal with this diabetes bullshit on top of being pregnant," Sarah said. "It's not fair. I really admire you."

"Thanks, it pisses me off too. I get real tired of the shots. But it's better than the alternative." *Ruth, the eternal optimist,* Sarah thought.

"Call me tomorrow and let me know how you're feeling."

"Will do. Rub your belly and tell Baby it's from her favorite auntie."

Both sisters went to bed with the other on her mind and in her heart.

As Sarah slept, her dreams took her to a flower-filled meadow, where she lay naked in Blue's arms. He gently stroked her hair as he whispered, "I'll always be there to protect you." But when she looked at him, she saw a different face, a dark menacing visage staring back at her. Terrified, she broke free of his embrace and stood up to run away. She turned to find another figure standing directly in front of her—an old Indian man with wrinkled chocolate-brown skin that looked as though it had been weathered over a hundred years. He wore only a loincloth made of leather. Large brown feathers were tied in his long white hair. From his stern expression, she knew he wanted something from her. Then a gust of wind ushered in a rank animal smell; an immense shadow hovered over them as panic swept through her...

She woke sweaty and shaken, the shadow of the dream clinging to her. She tried to fall back to sleep, but as her eyes closed, a blackness threatened to envelop her. She gasped and sat up, shaking. "Dammit, not again. I can't go through this again." Unable to stay in bed, she took a long, hot shower and waited for the sun to rise.

CHAPTER TEN

SARAH'S MEETING WITH Hollis Tremaine was scheduled for eleven in the morning. She left the hotel early enough so she could drive at a sightseer's pace. According to the map, the road followed the main river all the way up the valley. Her turn-off came about halfway up.

On either side, tree-covered mountains defined the valley. The river ran on the right side of the road. The flat valley floor alternated between lush pastures and unmanicured fields decorated with sagebrush and wildflowers. In places, cottonwoods and willows lined the riverbanks, in others the view of the flowing water was unobstructed. Still damp from a morning rain, the landscape glistened in green.

"It's beautiful," Sarah said, feeling an instant affinity for the place and wishing she had a traveling companion to share it with. She noticed a fair number of houses along the road, but they became scarce as she traveled further from town. Along the way, she passed a variety of painted wooden signs for outfitters, vacation cabins, trout fishing, and horseback riding. She still had ten miles to go before her turn-off when she rounded a bend and got her first view of snow-capped peaks in the distance. "I wish Ruth could see this."

The road leading to the Tremaine's newly acquired ranch crossed over the main river and followed a smaller stream lined on both sides with pastures. The valley narrowed as the drive climbed in elevation. Sarah admired the stands of light-barked aspens that accented the otherwise dark green and brown hillsides of spruce and pine. Their leaves danced in the breeze, twirling and shimmering in the sun.

Pavement became gravel and fifteen minutes later she turned into the long, winding drive of the Double R Ranch. She drove underneath a weathered wooden archway, its cracked sign resting against one of the posts. Sarah could barely make out the faded "RR." A dusty, bumpy ride across potholed gravel eventually brought her to the main house.

"What a shame," Sarah remarked as she surveyed the structure. The two-story ranch house with a wrap-around porch was probably handsome in its day but years of neglect had stripped it of any charm. Shutters hung off rusty hinges, plywood boards replaced all the windows, and patches of naked wood could be seen through long cracks in the faded paint barely clinging to the house. Fortunately, the front porch floor and much of the railing had recently been replaced.

Sarah walked around the old house and then spied a cloud of dust on the road. Soon a shiny red pickup truck rumbled into view and parked next to hers. Two men got out of the vehicle and walked toward the house. They both wore the same refined, man-of-means face and carried themselves with a determined gait. The older man waved; the younger one just kept walking.

"They have to be related," Sarah thought, waving back.

With a genuinely warm smile, the senior Tremaine shook her hand enthusiastically. "Hello, Sarah Cavanaugh. Wonderful to finally meet you in person. Welcome to our little piece of heaven."

Sarah liked him immediately. His handshake was firm but not domineering. He looked her in the eye with respect, and his voice reflected the same sincerity that showed on his face comfortably creased with laugh lines. He dressed like a cowboy, with worn jeans, scuffed boots and a wide-brimmed hat broken in by many years of sun, rain and wind. His new Orvis shirt and Rolex watch reminded Sarah that he wasn't the real McCoy, but the dirt underneath his manicured fingernails told her that he was no stranger to the work required on a ranch.

"This is my son Nick," Hollis continued. "I wanted to show him what I've been doing with my latest acquisition."

Nick tipped his hat, but didn't offer his hand. "I see my father has better taste in artists than he does in ranches." His deadpan tone left Sarah wondering if he was paying her a compliment or taking a dig at his father. She noticed his eyes quickly dart up and down, checking her out through his designer sunglasses, but his face didn't register any reaction.

Hollis' son looked as though he'd stepped out of an L.L. Bean catalog. His khaki pants, linen shirt and Gore-Tex boots looked brand new. Only his black cowboy hat showed signs of wear. Nick's mouth seemed to frown by default, giving him an edgy pout that would make him irresistible to some women, Sarah thought. But not her.

"I know the house looks pretty bad from the outside," Hollis explained. "The good news is, she's structurally sound and we're really moving along inside. We're putting in the new windows this week."

"I'm glad to hear that," Sarah chuckled. "I have to admit, the exterior had me worried."

"Let me show you around. Nick, are you coming? You haven't seen what we've done in here. I think you'll be impressed," Hollis enthused.

Cocking his head, Nick did not try to hide his disapproval. "Father, I don't know why you didn't tear this place down. I think you're wasting your time restoring it. It would be a much better investment if you subdivided this property and built some modern cabins out here."

"Nick, we've been over this...."

He dismissed his father with a shake of his head and headed back toward the truck before Hollis could finish.

"I'm afraid Nick and I don't always see eye-to-eye on matters of real estate. He takes after his mother in that regard," Hollis said. "I hope you'll appreciate this little beauty."

They took twenty minutes to go through the house, careful to step over, around and under scaffolding, drop cloths, sawhorses and two-by-fours. "This will be absolutely stunning when you're done," Sarah proclaimed at the end of the tour.

"You mean, when you're done," Hollis corrected her. "Your murals in the great room will make all the difference, I'm sure. I think we're at least a month away from being ready for your talents here. You'll need that time to really get a sense of this place. There are so many things that can really grab your heart out here. I can't wait to see how these mountains inspire you."

"Me too," Sarah said nervously. "It's already starting to get to me, in ways I never expected."

They stepped off the front porch littered with sawhorses and turned around for one last look at the ranch. Hollis apologized for the delay in having her move up to the Flat Top Ranch where he lived. "I do hope the Meeker Hotel is treating you well. I'll have the Pine Cabin ready for you by the end of the week, once my family heads back to New York."

"Thank you, Hollis. The hotel is quite pleasant. Really. And I'm sure the ranch will be lovely too. I do hope your family is having a good time while they're here."

Hollis smiled. "You know, some do and some don't. I can't get enough of these mountains. I love horses, I love fishing, I love hunting and I love the view. I've got a granddaughter and a grandson, my daughter's kids, who enjoy this place as much as I do. But that love of the outdoors seems to have skipped a generation, I'm afraid. Don't know what I did wrong with my son and daughter. It makes me all the more determined to feed that fire in my grandkids as much as I can."

"I'd say your grandkids are lucky to have you." Sarah took a few steps to one side and almost landed on a dried out cow pie, which reminded her of an anomaly she wanted to ask Hollis about.

"I was wondering why I haven't seen many cows or sheep in these pastures. They're so lush; I thought they'd be full of animals."

"That's because we use the pastures to grow hay. We cut it and store it to feed to our livestock in the winter. We lease land from the Forest Service and run our cattle up in the mountains from early summer through first frost. That's where they do most of their grazing."

Sarah's rapt attention encouraged him to continue. "One of the reasons these pastures are so pretty is that we irrigate them. Plus, we've had good moisture so far from melting snow and spring rains, so I'm hopeful we'll have fine grass this season."

"Where do you keep your cows in the winter?" Sarah asked.

"We have to send most of them over to Utah because the winters can be brutal this far up the valley. Cattle don't do well in four to five feet of snow. We do keep about a fourth of the herd on another ranch we own closer to town. That place gets less snow because of its lower elevation.

"Nick is completing a project right now that should let us keep more cattle all year. You'll pass it when you come up to the Flat Top Ranch. He's built a large barn and indoor arena that'll be used for riding and training horses, and we should be able to keep a lot of cows in there if the weather turns nasty."

Hollis smiled with a father's pride. "Took me a bit by surprise, really, him finally taking an interest in something out here. Truth be told, I think some of my ranch hands gave him the idea, but no matter. He's running with it."

"Is Nick a developer by profession?" Sarah asked.

Hollis glanced over at the truck before answering. "Unlike my daughter Patricia who knew she was going to be lawyer when she turned ten years old, Nick wasn't born with that kind of determination. So you might say he hasn't really settled on a profession yet. His mother, my late wife, was afraid he'd grow up to be a professional playboy. There was a time when I thought she might be right. But he seems to be taking an interest in real estate these days, which certainly would have met with his mother's approval. She was a very successful commercial developer."

"Did you say 'late' wife?" Sarah asked, hoping she wasn't prying.

"Unfortunately, yes. She was killed in a car accident ten years ago, on Nick's twenty-fifth birthday," Hollis said. "That was a rough day."

"I'm so sorry."

"None of us were the same after that, especially Nick. It really tore him up for a long time. So, it does my heart good to see him taking an interest in something out here, even if we don't always agree on our taste in buildings."

As she and Hollis walked over to the trucks, Nick got out of the passenger seat and stood next the vehicle, watching them approach. He tipped his hat when Sarah bid him goodbye.

"I look forward to the next time we meet, Sarah Cavanaugh."

CHAPTER ELEVEN

PATRICK HAD AN APPOINTMENT to meet Tom Payton at the main house of the McDermott Ranch. He had called Tom right after his lunch with Jessie several days earlier because he wanted to walk the land before trying to contact Eli with the offer of a conservation easement. Since Tom was renting the pastures, Patrick figured he would be the best man to show him around.

The phone conversation had gone more smoothly than Patrick had anticipated. The hesitancy in Tom's voice resonated with a rancher's distrust of anyone who worked for the government. A call from a "fed," especially one from the U.S. Fish and Wildlife Service, usually meant trouble. They were always telling ranchers what to do and what not to do, where to graze livestock for how long. No one in the valley took kindly to government regulation.

Patrick sensed that the only reason Tom agreed to show him the ranch was because Ms. Jessie had already vouched for him. Patrick knew he would have to earn this man's respect; Ms. Jessie had simply gotten him a foot in the door.

As Patrick pulled up to the house, Tom got out of his battered white pickup truck that bore the faded lettering "Payton Electricians" on the doors. The men shook hands and exchanged cautious, polite greetings.

"Thanks for meeting me out here," Patrick said.

"I've got to check on some fencing up this way any how, so this works out for me."

"I'm glad to hear that," Patrick said. "I know this is a busy time for you and I really do appreciate your taking the time to show me around. And," he added, "I'll be happy to help with any fence repairs."

"Good, I was kinda' counting on that," Tom replied with a slightly disbelieving tone. "Leave your truck here and ride with me."

Tom Payton was a quiet man in his mid-thirties. A part-time electrician, he also held a part interest in his uncle's cattle ranch. A true handyman, he actually preferred working on a tractor to riding in the mountains with the cattle; his instincts lay more with the mechanical than the animal. Aware of this shortcoming, Tom read more than most ranchers about the latest recommendations for grass and cattle management. And he adopted many of them, usually with good results.

"I was admiring the pastures as I drove over here," Patrick said with honest enthusiasm. "I've seen a fair number of ranches in this valley and your grass is looking really good."

Tom allowed a quick grin to run across his face like a man not used to praise. "When my uncle first took over this ranch, the grass had really been beat up," Tom explained as they drove through a pasture. "Eli hadn't run the irrigation system in years. And yet he kept cows down here, so they just chewed up the place. Eli had no idea what he was doing, I can tell you that." Looking over his shoulder as if someone might be eavesdropping, he added, "Ah, but you didn't hear that from me."

"I bet Eli appreciates what you and your uncle have done with the place," Patrick said, trying to get a better sense of the landowner.

"He's never been back to see," said Tom. "I think all he cares about is getting his rent check on time. He's never asked about the place."

"How often do you talk with him?"

"Actually, I never do. We only hear from his lawyer from time to time," Tom explained as he slowed the truck. "Up 'til now, Eli's left us alone, and frankly, that's the way we like it."

Tom pulled up to a fence, stopped the truck and prepared to get out to open the gate when, to his surprise, Patrick beat him to it. Patrick deftly lifted the wire loop over the post and swung the gate open, waited for Tom to drive through, closed the gate and hopped back in the truck.

"I didn't know government boys knew anything about opening and closing gates," Tom said, careful not to show too much surprise.

"That's just some of my on-the-job training," Patrick offered, remembering how Ms. Jessie had called him out the first time they had approached a gate and Patrick had sat there looking at the scenery. "Are you gonna sit on that lazy ass of yours all day? This isn't a country club." She had informed him in no uncertain terms that if you were sitting in the passenger seat, you had gate duty. And you'd better make sure you closed them right, otherwise you had to round up cattle the next day.

Soon Tom and Patrick came upon some cracked fence posts and a stretch of barbed wire lying on the ground. They got out of the truck and Tom began pulling out equipment from the back. Patrick picked up some new fence posts, then took a moment to look around. The sun shone brightly on the mountainside, highlighting the red rocks exposed between layers of spruce and pine. White clouds framed the peaks as they moved along with the wind. "Man, this is beautiful country," Patrick exclaimed.

Tom barely looked up, his attentions given completely to the task ahead. "Yep, it sure is. Don't know if the cows appreciate it though." Patrick wasn't sure if Tom was trying to make a joke, so he just smiled a bit and stepped in to give him a hand.

"Have you had to do much fence work out here?" Patrick asked.

"This place was so run down when we got it. I bet I've replaced almost every foot of fence. I don't mind it, though. It needed to be done."

"How long have you been renting this land from Eli?"

"My uncle made the arrangement about a year before Eli left town, so just about 30 years, I guess."

"Did your uncle get along with Eli?" Patrick asked.

Tom finished pounding a fence post before he answered. "He never had much nice to say about the guy."

"Seems he isn't the only one who feels that way," Patrick said. "He certainly has Ms. Jessie all riled up."

"I can imagine." Tom didn't elaborate.

Not wanting to appear pushy, Patrick focused his desire for information into fence post repairs and waited to see if Tom would offer any more insights. Not until they'd both worked up a healthy sweat did the conversation continue.

"Sure would hate to see Eli sell off this place," Tom said, wiping his brow with a bandanna. "Even though we're renting the land, I feel responsible for it. Can't help but treat it like it was my own."

"Any chance that your uncle or another rancher would buy this?" Patrick asked, already knowing the answer.

"Eli's price is way too high. And beef prices are too low. It's not going to happen with today's market."

"Is this land crucial to your overall operation? I know your uncle's got a sizeable ranch."

"It's about one-fifth of our grass production, so it would hurt us to lose it, for sure."

"I'm hoping to interest Eli in a conservation easement as an alternative to selling," Patrick offered. "Like we did on Ms. Jessie's place. The government could write him a substantial check and he wouldn't have to do a thing."

"I don't mean any disrespect, Patrick, but I can't believe that the same federal government that rams regulations down our throats is now turning around and saying 'we'll help you.'"

"I've heard that before. Getting an easement doesn't make you immune to grazing regulations, government fees or government oversight," Patrick explained. "But this easement program is real; there are no hidden strings, no additional rules except one. You can't plow up the land. You can't build on it and you can't farm it. You have to leave it in grass or trees or a combination of both. You can continue grazing, cutting hay, irrigating pastures, raising horses, fishing, hunting, just like you're doing now."

"That sounds too good to be true," said Tom. "But you've convinced Ms. Jessie, and there's no rancher I respect more than her. So I'm inclined to give you the benefit of the doubt. Then again, it's not my land, so it don't much matter what I think."

"Well, any support is appreciated," Patrick replied. "Guess the million-dollar question is what Eli McDermott will think. Do you have any suggestions on how to approach him?"

"I'm afraid I can't be of much help since I've never met the guy," Tom admitted. "But I wish you luck."

The two men worked in silence for the next half hour, replacing fence posts and stretching barbed wire between them. After they'd finished and had loaded equipment back in the truck, Patrick still had questions nagging at him.

"Tom, do you think Ms. Jessie could afford to buy this place?"

"That's anybody's guess," Tom replied. "Depends on who you believe. Some folks think she's a millionaire and others think she's just squeakin' by. Fact is, folks don't know much about Ms. Jessie, but they sure love making up stories and pretending they're true. Guess she's sort of a legend round here. My guess is, half the stories are just that, stories."

"What do you think?" Patrick pushed.

"It's not my place to say. But, if she could, I'd think she would have, once she'd badgered Eli to lower his price. Maybe she's planning on doing that, I really don't know. She hasn't said anything to me."

Patrick saw it that way too, although he also sensed that her conflict over this land ran deeper than finances. Based on her reaction in the coffee shop, Patrick felt that Ms. Jessie would rather get kicked in the head by a bull than do business with Eli.

The road wound its way alongside Wapiti Creek. They rode over a small bridge and Tom slowed the truck. "This is the end of the property on the west side. I want to check the fence line on the other side of the creek," Tom explained. "The road's awfully narrow here, so we'll just pull into Mr. Hawk's drive. He lets me park here when I'm up this way."

They rounded another bend. A small mound of sun-bleached antlers was the only marker Patrick could detect for the well-concealed drive Tom pulled into. He parked a few feet further down in a grassy patch. Tom closed the truck door and headed back toward the road.

"Aren't we going to grab any tools from the truck?" Patrick asked.

"No need," Tom said as he continued on. "Ever since I took over the place, I've never found a loose fence post, downed wire, nothing along the fence between Eli's place and Mr. Hawk's. I'm sure that's Mr. Hawk's doing, although he never admits to it. So I come out here once a year just in case, but I've found hauling tools is a big waste of time."

"Is this Duncan Hawk's place?"

"Yup."

"I've never met the man," Patrick said, hoping to draw Tom into a conversation about him.

"And that's the way it will be until he decides he wants to meet you," Tom stated matter-of-factly.

"Why's that? Is he not very sociable?" Patrick asked.

"It's just the way it is with him."

Tom quickened his pace just enough to add finality to their conversation. Patrick wasn't sure if he was defending the man or was intimidated by him. Either way, his reaction stoked Patrick's curiosity.

Ms. Jessie had told him little of Duncan Hawk, and he'd found others even more reticent to say much, although the other landowners simply didn't know him. That wasn't the case with Ms. Jessie. He sensed she knew him extremely well. At first, Patrick suspected they might be lovers, but then he hadn't seen Duncan at any social function Jessie held or attended. Several times while pulling into her drive, Patrick thought he saw Duncan riding into the mountains. Eventually Patrick stopped speculating. Being out on his land sparked the questioning anew. *Ms. Jessie and her men,* he smiled to himself.

As the two men walked along the river, Patrick took in the stunning view. Wapiti Creek flowed out of a box canyon cut out of a towering beige fortress of rock. Patrick immediately wanted to explore the river as it wound its way between the mammoth cliffs. The fence line headed in that direction, stretching across the valley floor which was carpeted in soft grasses along the creek and quickly turned to a drier terrain of scrub oaks several hundred feet farther out.

A few horses whinnied from the pasture at the two men moving single file along the meticulously maintained fence. Eventually Patrick and Tom heard the quiet rumbling of the river. The fence line stopped at the bank. Patrick looked up the creek into the canyon that now was temptingly close.

"Ever hike up this little canyon?" Patrick asked.

"Nah, can't say I have. The cows never go up there, so I haven't had much call to either," Tom stated.

"Whose land is this on, Eli's or Mr. Hawk's?"

"Mr. Hawk's," replied Tom as he leaned against the corner fence post, testing its stability out of habit rather than necessity.

"I'd like to hike in there sometime. It's a beautiful canyon," Patrick said as they turned around and headed back to the truck. "Know how I can get a hold of Mr. Hawk?"

"No, I don't," Tom said. "If you're fixing to hike this canyon, you may just have to take your chances. Although I don't know why Mr. Hawk wouldn't like you."

"Thanks, that's reassuring."

They drove back to Patrick's truck in silence, a comfortable quiet shared between two men who had shared an afternoon of hard labor. When they reached the main house, they both stepped out of the truck.

"I never knew any government guys to get their hands dirty and help out like you do," Tom said with a smile and hearty handshake. "I guess Ms. Jessie was right, you are different."

"Thanks, Tom, I really appreciate you taking time out of your day to show me around. I'm glad I could be of some help, that's all. And if you can think of anything else that would help me with Eli, please give me a call." Patrick handed him a business card.

"If anything comes to mind, I will."

Getting into his truck, Patrick was tempted to drive back up the road to see if he could introduce himself to Duncan Hawk. But the sun would be setting before long, too late in the day for an unexpected visitor. He'd come back another time, after he'd figured out what to do about Eli.

CHAPTER TWELVE

SARAH APPROACHED THE DOOR of the White River Museum with apprehension. Three days had passed since her fainting spell, but her embarrassment had yet to subside. Unsettled by her bizarre episode, she needed to prove to herself that fainting had been a coincidence, not some kind of emotional reaction as her sister had suggested. She wanted to stand in front of the display without incident.

With the warmth of the midday sun on her neck, Sarah admired the beautifully restored log building that had once housed U.S. soldiers and that now harbored their memory. Tentatively, she turned the knob and opened the door.

The museum curator greeted her with a mixture of surprise and pleasure. "Ms. Cavanaugh, I'm so pleased to see you. How are you?"

"Oh, I'm fine, really. Thank you," Sarah replied self-consciously. "Sorry to have been any trouble before." Eager to move on, she continued, "I'm interested in doing some reading, bone up a bit on my history and was hoping you could recommend some books."

"Certainly, my dear. Please have a seat in the reading room and I'll pull a few things for you." The curator brought Sarah several books to peruse. "Take your time. I'll be around until five o'clock." She walked into another room, leaving Sarah to her research and her thoughts.

Relishing the quiet of the little museum, Sarah took a quick inventory of her body. She felt calm, no dizziness or headache. *You haven't gone back to the display yet*, she thought. *Of course you feel fine.*

Sarah decided she'd ease into the back room exploration after she'd read a bit. The curator had opened a book to a short narrative, entitled *Utes: Exit from the Land of Shining Mountains.* Sarah began to read:

The Ute Indians who roamed Colorado could always rely on one thing: safe haven in the mountains and valleys they called "the land of shining mountains." Ute bands roamed from the Great Plains into Utah and on the borders of present-day Arizona, New Mexico, and southern Colorado.

Before the Spanish brought horses into North America, the Utes scratched out a living much like the Paiutes, Navaho, and Apaches, with whom they shared their far-ranging domain. They relied on small-game hunting and gathering desert and mountain plants for subsistence.

Physically, the Utes were a stocky, powerfully built people with dark, bronze-colored skin. They would move their camps into the high country for summer hunting, but retreat to gentler climes to wait out winters. Their women's beadwork was, and still is, intricate, colorful, and refined into art itself.

The Utes also developed a rich ceremonial and spiritual life. They "knew" the bear and how to coax him from hibernation with the Bear Dance that signaled the beginning of spring. The Sun Dance, initiated in the middle of summer, was to ensure good hunting.

The Utes were also a playful people, and many of their dances—the Circle Dance, Coyote Dance, Tea Dance—were strictly social in nature. Social, but more serious, were the melodies from handmade flutes that a man used to attract his true love. All sorts of games occupied idle time, including stick dice, archery, ring spearing, juggling, wrestling, and foot races. Horse racing was without question the most popular sport and, unfortunately, contributed to the ultimate removal of the Utes from Colorado.

Spaniards spotted the Utes as early as the 1600s, and eventually arrived at an uneasy peace with them. The Spanish also provided the Utes with the horse, although that certainly wasn't their intention. The Utes became one of the first tribes with extensive herds, thus greatly increasing their mobility and heightening the respect given them by other tribes.

The Utes had few squabbles with the mountain men who arrived from the east in the 1830s. Many married Ute women and appreciated the Utes' knowledge of the land and how to live off it. But things changed when gold was discovered in the 1860s. As Colorado became first a territory and then a state, the drive to drive the Utes off their land intensified.

In 1878, Nathan C. Meeker arrived to head the White River Ute Indian Agency. He quickly decided hunting, racing ponies, and generally enjoying life wouldn't do for Utes. In modern jargon, he had no respect for the Ute's unique cultural or belief systems. Instead of free-roaming Indians, he wanted sedentary, Christian farmers. The culture clash made conflict inevitable.

When he suggested a good place to start the "civilizing" process was to forget about racing ponies and plow up the racetrack, the Indians refused in a manner Meeker thought a little surly. He called for some troops. To the Utes, troops equaled massacre, so they ambushed the troops, killed and mutilated Meeker and all the men at the agency, kidnapped Meeker's wife and daughters, held them for a week, and then released them unharmed. The politicians and public were outraged, the newspapers went nuts and soon the women's kidnapping became a lurid tail of horror at the hands of the redman.

"The Utes must go," became the cry of the day. And go they did, under Army escort, to reservations in Utah and southern Colorado on a trek they called the "Trip of Sorrow."

Sarah looked up at the stoic black-and-white portraits of Nathan Meeker, his wife and daughter staring out from the frames. They added a reality to the narrative that left her feeling uneasy. She noted that no photographs of Utes shared the space.

Something about this bit of history resonated with her, but she hadn't heard of the Ute people prior to coming to Meeker. Maybe Blue had talked to her about this on one of their mountain hikes. She recalled that he hadn't been particularly interested in history, so dismissed that possibility. Grappling for some rational explanation, she went in search of the curator.

"Excuse me, I was just wondering if there's been a TV documentary on the Utes or Nathan Meeker that I might have seen recently?"

"No. None that I'm aware of, although that's a wonderful idea," she smiled. "Are you finding the books of interest?"

"Yes, I am." Impulsively she added, "If you have them for sale, I'd like to buy a copy of each, please."

"Certainly. Let me take care of that for you."

While the curator wrote up the receipt, Sarah walked back to the Ute exhibit and dared herself to look into the glass case. Bracing for an undesirable response, she sought out the bear claw necklace. A tingling jolt ran down her left arm, as though she'd hit her funny bone. Her hand twitched involuntarily for a couple of seconds, then her first two fingers wrapped over her thumb and made a tight fist.

"What the hell," Sarah backed away from the case, staring at her left hand. She turned around at the unexpected sound of the curator.

"Are you okay, dear?"

"I think so," Sarah said, shaking her left hand, trying to ease the spasm. Her fist loosened. "I don't think I'm going to faint this time." She stuck her hand in her pants pocket. "Can you tell me the story of this necklace? It's so different from the beaded jewelry here."

"I don't know much about it, I'm sorry to say. That is a bear claw and the Utes had a strong connection to the bear. Perhaps it was a symbol of power, I don't really know."

"Is there someone else who might know more about it?"

"No one here at the museum." Responding to the disappointment on Sarah's face, she offered somewhat reluctantly, "There is a Ute man who might know, but he's not always very...how should I say...cooperative.

We invite him to speak at our festival every year and sometimes he shows up and other times he doesn't. We never know. Seems rather rude to me, but then I don't have to deal with him. My boss takes care of that."

"Why do you keep inviting him back if he's so unreliable?"

"He is very knowledgeable about Ute history and culture. And when he does show up, he's usually very pleasant," the curator said. "Besides, Duncan Hawk is the only Ute person around here."

"Is there any event coming up where I might be able to meet him?" Sarah surprised herself, not sure why she felt compelled to pursue this.

"Not until the 4th of July weekend, I'm afraid."

They walked back to the reading room where Sarah paid for her books. The curator mentioned two historic sites she might like to visit related to local history—a roadside display southeast of town near the original site of the White River Indian Agency and the Thornburgh historical site where the Utes and the soldiers fought. Sarah thanked her for the suggestions and promised she'd come back soon.

Sarah left the museum with mixed emotions—relief that she hadn't fainted and concern about the spasm in her left hand. She wondered if she was developing an allergy to artifacts and then decided not to give it any more thought. A soft breeze caressed her cheek and the afternoon sun warmed her face. It was a gorgeous day. As she walked past the brick courthouse, Sarah searched the square for an empty bench in the shade. Finding one to her liking, she sat down to continue reading about the Ute People and the land they once called home.

Two days later, Sarah drove out of Meeker with a road map and a growing sense of adventure. Once she turned onto Highway 15 driving north, she had the road to herself. She passed only a couple of homes, saw an occasional herd of grazing cattle and noted one parked pickup truck near a fence gate. Otherwise her only traveling companions were the open grasslands and the steady stream of wire fencing on both sides of the road, until she noticed the raven flying alongside the passenger window. The large black bird kept the same pace for a while, then flew ahead and disappeared.

A mile down the road, she spotted it again on a fence post. With a raspy squawk, the raven took to the air, flew past the truck and around a bend. Sarah and the raven repeated this pattern several times, giving Sarah the eerie feeling that the bird was somehow showing her the way.

Catching herself, she laughed. "If I think I'm getting divine guidance from an oversized crow, then I need to get a life." She looked at her dashboard. "And I need to pay attention to my odometer. I should be getting close." She glanced around for the raven, but her winged companion had flown from view.

The actual site was so inconspicuous she might well have driven past it. A patch of gravel served as a parking lot. A short path through prairie grasses took her to a fenced plot containing two cairns, markedly different in construction and age. The older one, a short, white stone obelisk, bore the carved names of soldiers killed or wounded in the six-day battle. The first casualty listed was Major T.T. Thornburgh. "So that's why the maps refer to this site as the Thornburgh historical site," she noted. "Guess it's not surprising that they named the battleground and the town after the dead white guys. To the victor went the spoils."

The modern cairn commemorating the Utes stood twice as tall and was made of stacked pieces of sandstone. Sarah read the sign etched in black slate:

> Let us not forget the Whiteriver Utes who gave their lives and those who were wounded in the battle at Milk Creek on September 29, 1879.
>
> Nathan Meeker, Indian Agent, did not understand the Utes and knew very little about their traditions and culture. Resentment toward Meeker's policy of farming resulted in a fight between Johnson, a Ute, and Agent Meeker.
>
> This was the beginning of the problems that ensued. Because of the battles at Whiteriver and Meeker, Colorado, the Whiterivers and the Uncompahgres were forced by gunpoint to the reservation in Utah, leaving behind their beautiful land in Colorado. However, the Uncompahgres had nothing to do with those events. Under the 14th amendment, their rights were ignored.

The cairns sat on a rise that offered an expansive view of Milk Creek winding through a valley dotted with freshly cut hay bales. Staring out on the pastoral scene, Sarah could not conjure up an image of the historic carnage that had taken place here. A breeze rustled the sagebrush, filling the air with a ruggedly sweet aroma. She breathed deeply. Folding her arms in front of her, she walked to the edge of the rise and watched the grasses swaying in the wind. She lost track of time in the solitude.

She didn't hear the sound of footsteps crunching on the gravel path until the breeze calmed momentarily. She turned quickly. *Who would be out here?* She searched the path but saw no one. *The wind must be playing tricks with me,* she thought. Still, she wanted to make sure, so she walked back to the cairns. Nobody. She looked out to the road and saw a pickup truck parked behind hers. *I did hear someone. Then where the hell are they?* She spun around and nearly ran into an Indian man standing directly behind her. Sarah froze.

The man stared back at her from under a black brimmed hat, a few small feathers in the headband fluttering with the wind. His expression betrayed no emotion.

"I did not mean to startle you." He spoke deliberately, softly.

"Well then you shouldn't sneak up on me," Sarah snapped, trying to recover from her adrenaline rush. "Where did you come from?"

"Not many people come out this way," he said. "It is a lonely place."

Still flustered, Sarah wasn't sure what to do. Here she was, in the middle of nowhere with a strange Indian man who seemed to appear out of thin air. Her big city instincts warned her to get out of there. "Excuse me, I was just leaving," she muttered as she turned around and started walking quickly toward her vehicle.

"You wanted to meet me," the old man said.

"Excuse me? What did you say?" She stopped and faced the stranger.

"You wanted to meet me. I am Duncan Hawk." Again his face held no expression she could read.

"Duncan Hawk? You're the man the museum curator told me about," she said incredulously. "Did she talk to you?"

He shook his head.

"If she didn't talk to you, then how did you know I'd be here?" Sarah's unease grew.

The Indian man seemed to ignore her questions. After a brief silence, he said, "Your name is Sarah. You come from the land of the Winnebagos and the Potawatomis, what you call Illinois. You have something to ask me."

Sarah's mouth dropped open. *How did he know that?* Then she noticed his necklace, a bear claw necklace. She couldn't take her eyes off of it, too stunned to speak.

"What did you want to ask me?" Duncan Hawk still did not move from where he stood.

"That necklace," Sarah stammered. "The necklace in the museum. It's almost a perfect match to the one you're wearing." She allowed her eyes to meet his. He grinned warmly in response.

Instinctively she smiled back and felt the tension in her shoulders loosen slightly. *Maybe he isn't going to hurt me,* she thought.

"I don't mean to stare, it's just that all of this has taken me by surprise, you, the necklace, your knowing who I am. Let's start over, okay? I'm Sarah Cavanaugh from Chicago."

"I am Duncan Hawk. I am from around here. Why are you interested in this necklace?"

She hesitated, trying to decide how much to tell him. "You'll probably think I'm a bit crazy here, but, uh, last week I was in the museum, standing at the Indian display. That's where I saw the necklace. I kept looking at it. I had a strong urge to hold it, and then I got very light-headed. The next thing I knew, I'd fainted. Very embarrassing." Watching his face, she saw no reaction, so she continued.

"Ever since then, I've been thinking about that necklace. I can't get it out of my mind. It's as though I'd seen it before, but I know that's impossible." She noticed Duncan's eyes shift to her left hand. She looked down to see her thumb and first two fingers squeezed tightly together, her hand shaking slightly. She tried to separate her fingers, but they would not release their grip.

"When did that start?" he asked without surprise.

"The first time I saw the necklace. My hand started shaking just before I fainted. And when I went back to the museum a few days later, my fingers started to clench like this." The returning twitch unnerved her. "What's going on?"

He reached over and touched her hand. The twitching stopped and her fingers relaxed.

"What did you do?" Sarah didn't know whether to feel relieved or frightened.

"I can tell you much about that necklace, Sarah. In time, you will tell me much as well. It is good we have met each other. You will come to my home and we will talk more about these things." Reaching into his back pocket, he pulled out a braided strand of green fibers about two feet long and handed it to her. "This is sweetgrass. Smell it and you will know where it gets the name."

She was immediately taken by its soothing aroma.

"Keep this with you until we meet again. At that time I will tell you more about it. Okay?" He laughed lightly as he walked past her. "Cheer up, Sarah. You look like you've seen a ghost. I'm really not that bad."

Before she could compose herself enough to reply, the wind picked up, teasing the braid in her hand. A gust snatched it from her, carrying it a short distance down the slope. She hurried after it and by the time she got back to the cairn, Duncan was nowhere to be found. The path was empty and his truck was gone.

If not for the sweetgrass clasped in her hand, Sarah would have thought her encounter with Duncan Hawk a hallucination. She turned around, looking in all directions for some trace of the man who had walked away just moments before. But Sarah stood alone on the rise.

She hurried to her vehicle, agitated and impatient to be gone from there. None of this made any sense. As she drove back to Meeker, she kept checking the rearview mirror, expecting to see Duncan Hawk's pickup truck following her. Instead, she just heard his voice in her head: "Keep this with you until we meet again."

She hadn't seen the raven sitting on the fence post or noticed it take flight once she'd pulled onto the road. The bird flew alongside just outside of view until Sarah turned onto the main highway. It shrieked four times and turned to fly back up the valley as another raven took its place, tailing her truck all the way back into town.

CHAPTER THIRTEEN

BUSINESS AT THE SPRINGHORN Mountain Lodge was light for a Wednesday night. Mostly locals, Patrick observed, and that's the way he preferred it. A few ranch hands swapping stories and drinking beers at the bar, families with young kids treating themselves to a steak dinner in the adjoining dining hall and visiting with neighbors not often seen because of the many acres that stretched between homesteads.

Every Thursday night, however, the scene would change with the arrival of the weekend tourists eager to get out in the fresh air, catch some fish, ride a horse or sit around all day on the front porches of rented cabins, looking at the mountains and drinking martinis. Tourists brought much needed revenue to this old-time outfitters' lodge. During hunting season, any place in the valley that had an extra bed was booked months in advance. Hunting, especially for elk, was big business here. But during the spring and summer months, local business owners relied on seasonal tourism and a growing interest in fishing to keep them solvent. And so, over the last ten years, this rustic hunting lodge had slowly evolved into getaway that gave city folks the impression of roughing it. The owner had even changed the name, from the Springhorn Hunting Lodge to the Springhorn Mountain Lodge, to appeal to this urban clientele.

The valley needed tourists, Patrick conceded, but they changed the dynamic of a place. In some bars, too many out-of-towners would eventually drive the locals away. He didn't want to see that happen here. He relied on Springhorn's, both for his job and his sense of belonging. Much of the valley's socializing, business transactions and tests of character took place here. Friendships and partnerships were won or lost during all-night bouts of shots and beer. So Patrick had learned how to drink like a local and had the hangovers to prove it. His reputation as "an okay guy, for a fed" was spreading through the valley. More folks would sit at the bar with him now and at least be sociable.

For the moment, though, Patrick had the corner of the bar to himself, which suited him. He had a lot on his mind and didn't want the distraction of social chitchat right now. Besides, he never felt alone in this old bar. A grand display of Colorado's game animals adorned every inch of wall space—mounted heads of elk, bison, big-horned sheep, mountain goat, and mule deer stared blindly at each other. Stuffed grouse with wings outstretched were frozen in mid-flight. Over the front door hung a large black bear pelt with an obligatory snarling display of teeth.

Patrick ordered a beer and stared into the glassy eyes of the large elk head hanging directly above the bar. Local legend had it that this elk was shot by Teddy Roosevelt during one of his many hunting trips in the White River National Forest. The bar owner's grandfather had worked as his guide and had personally dressed out the elk. Teddy kept the meat and gave the mount to his guide as payment. Every newcomer to Springhorn's heard that part of the story at least once. But the second part of the story Patrick had learned at the end of a particularly heated poker game with Albert, the bar owner, holding most of the cash. As a parting jab, one of the losers exposed the second part of the tale. Apparently Albert's grandfather had expected Teddy to pay him in cash, and when he'd learned of his actual recompense, had begun swearing at the President and was eventually thrown out of his own bar by the locals who had no intention of letting him offend the head of the country.

Patrick looked up at the elk as he put a couple of bills on the counter and picked up his beer mug. "To Albert's grandfather," he toasted, "Apparently, he never heard of 'Speak softly and carry a big stick'."

Ms. Jessie kept that Roosevelt motto on the wall next to her phone. But she hadn't been speaking in dulcet tones earlier this evening when she'd called Patrick. He definitely had heard the "big stick" in her voice as she barked orders at him. She had told him to put an easement proposal together for Eli's land, but under no circumstances was he to contact Eli until she gave the go ahead. When he'd asked her the reason for the delay, she became evasive, saying she needed to talk with Eli first.

Patrick asked about her earlier comment that Eli would never deal with the feds, and she snapped back, "When I'm through with him, he'll probably be begging you for a deal." As he pressed for more details, she cut him off and said she'd explain later. Patrick didn't like being dismissed, but he had held his tongue.

He'd come into Springhorn's upset about her need for secrecy. *After all this time, doesn't she trust me? What's she up to?* He raised his glass again to the imposing elk, "A toast to the mystery of Ms. Jessie."

"I worry 'bout my customers when they start drinking with the animals," the bartender teased.

"Well, Mrs. Shepard, you caught me there," Patrick said. "I was trying to keep my relationship a secret, you know how people talk!"

"Your secret's safe with me, honey," Mrs. Shepard winked at him as she pushed a lock of gray hair out of her way. In the forty years that she had worked in this bar, Mrs. Shepard had never missed a shift. A feisty woman, she always offered a compassionate ear, a kind word, and sparse advice. Patrick enjoyed her and was thankful that she liked him in return.

"What's so pressing that you need to consult Mr. Antlers?" she inquired quietly.

"I'm trying out my new sales pitch," he said, "and I figure he's in no position to say 'no'. I don't handle rejection well." Mrs. Shepard smiled.

"Actually, I'm putting together a proposal for a ranch out this way."

"What piece of property is the government fixin' to buy?" she asked.

Normally Patrick didn't discuss deals in progress with anyone other than his boss and Ms. Jessie, but he'd come to trust Mrs. Shepard. She was a good listener and not prone to gossip about her regular customers' business dealings.

"I'm not out here to buy up land," he assured her. "I know that's what folks think I'm doing out here. The fact is, I want the ranchers to stay on the land. I'm interested in buying easements, that's all."

"I know, I know. I just like to get you riled up. It makes those pretty blue eyes sparkle!"

"Mrs. Shepard, you're incorrigible."

She brought Patrick another beer and some peanuts. "I suppose you already know this, but I heard that Hollis Tremaine has hired an artist from Chicago to do some paintings for him. Murals, I guess. First it was the carpenters from Aspen who are doing the renovation, now this. I don't understand it. We've got locals who can do the work for half the price, I'm sure. But the rich guy always brings in outsiders. It just don't seem right, especially when people here need the work and can do it."

"I knew he bought the Double R and was fixing it up, but I hadn't heard about the artist. Sounds a bit extravagant, but then again, he appears to have the money to do whatever he wants," Patrick said. "What do you think about Hollis Tremaine as a landowner?"

"He's better than most wealthy folks, I guess," Mrs. Shepard said. "I know he runs a good cattle and hay operation on the Flat Top Ranch. He sure seems eager to buy up whatever he can though, and that makes me nervous. So far, he is working the land and not making too many changes. He's fixing up the buildings that are already out there. He hasn't built any mansions. Although, that horse barn did get a lot of folks riled up. I hear that's mostly his son's project. The local folks don't have anything good to say about his son, that's for sure."

"I've heard the same thing," Patrick said.

"What really concerns me," Mrs. Shepard said, "is when the stock market goes crazy again, and people like the Tremaines lose their shirts and have to sell investments. Then who knows what could happen to those ranches."

"That's where easements are really helpful," Patrick said.

"I suppose so," the bartender replied as she turned her attention to a couple of cowboys who had just come in.

Patrick had talked briefly with Hollis Tremaine many months ago. A pleasant man and very forthright, he had told Patrick to save his money for those people who really needed it, maintaining that he was a better conservationist than any government program could hope for. At first Patrick felt he'd received a gracious brush-off, but over time he'd found Hollis to be a man of his word. From all appearances, the Tremaine ranches were managed and maintained in accordance with good conservation practices. Patrick couldn't ask for much more than that.

All this talk about Hollis Tremaine led Patrick back to his current proposal for Eli McDermott. Before he left Springhorn's that night, he wanted to find out what Mrs. Shepard knew about Eli. She had lived in this valley all her life; she might have some insight that would be helpful. But he didn't know if she was aware of Eli's desire to sell part of his ranch, and the fewer people who knew the better. So he got his favorite bartender talking about the craziest characters she'd met in her career. When he asked about the legendary Eli McDermott, she shook her head slowly and raised her eyebrows.

"Now that's a good story. Eli was a sorry excuse for a man," she began. "Guess his daddy beat him a lot. Both of 'em had quite the drinking problem. Eli got into fights in town all the time. He had a short temper and a quick fist."

"Yeah, Ms. Jessie mentioned that," Patrick muttered.

"Ms. Jessie seemed to have a soft spot for Eli way back when. Kinda like an older sister or an aunt watching out for him while he was growin' up. When his daddy would kick him out of the house, he'd go stay with Ms. Jessie's family until things quieted down."

"What was his mom like?" Patrick asked.

"She took a trip to visit her family one year and never came back. Guess she couldn't take the drinking and the fighting. The ranch went to hell. His daddy was too drunk to care and Eli was too angry. When Eli was still a young man in his mid-twenties, his daddy died, apparently choked on his own vomit. Eli seemed to change after that."

"In what way?"

"He seemed to settle down a bit and even started to show some interest in cattle. Although folks thought he was doing that just to please Ms. Jessie. By then she had stepped in to help run the ranch. Which was probably a good thing, given as how Eli couldn't tell a stud bull from a milking cow. For a while, Eli seemed to calm down enough that folks around here thought he might have a chance at becoming a decent human being.

"But then, he got into a bad fight at a bar in town. Got tangled up with some local sheepherder who'd just come off the mountain for the winter. Sheepherders can be particularly surly and ready to raise hell when they've been in the wilderness for months on end. Anyway, Eli hurt one guy real bad, drove out of town that night and never came back."

"Can't imagine too many people were sorry to see him go," Patrick mused. "Except maybe Ms. Jessie. But then again, I can't imagine her putting up with anybody as troublesome and incompetent as he was."

"The only thing I can figure is that she loved the land enough to put up with the likes of Eli. You know, the McDermott ranch used to belong to Ms. Jessie's family."

"No, I didn't know that." Patrick sat up straight, wondering why she hadn't mentioned it.

"A bit of a sad story, actually," Mrs. Shepard said, as she poured him another beer. "Ms. Jessie's grandmother died giving birth to her mom. Her grandfather fell to pieces. He had such a hard time dealing with a newborn and losing his wife that he let his business slide for a couple of years. He ended up selling part of the ranch to pay bills. Eli's family bought it, but paid only half of what it was worth and then never took very good care of the land. Made for bad blood between the two families. I think Eli's mom was a distant cousin to Ms. Jessie's grandmother who died, or something like that."

"So, Eli and Ms. Jessie are related?" Patrick was shocked.

"Don't ever say that to her, young man. She'd never admit that. But if the story is true, then they'd be cousins of some sort."

"The plot thickens," Patrick said more to himself. "Is there anything else you can tell me about Eli?"

Mrs. Shepard paused for a moment, as though contemplating what to say. Leaning over the bar, she spoke in hushed tones. "Not many people know this about Eli McDermott, and those that do, rarely speak of it."

"You have my attention, Mrs. Shepard."

"They say that Eli McDermott is haunted by an Indian curse, and that Duncan Hawk put it on him years ago. Rumor has it that Eli's disappearance wasn't voluntary... that the only way he could escape the curse was to get away from here."

Although not one to believe in curses, spells or other hocus-pocus, Patrick still couldn't resist the intrigue. "What kind of curse are we talking about here?"

"I'm not an expert on this kind of thing, you understand," she looked over her shoulder, then back at Patrick. "They say he's cursed for grave robbing, disturbing their dead. The Indians don't take too kindly to that sort of thing, and I guess their spirits believe in revenge. Seems whoever comes in contact with Eli has bad things happen to them too. So don't go messing around with ol' Eli McDermott, young man. I wouldn't want to lose you."

CHAPTER FOURTEEN

DUNCAN HAWK SHIVERED under his sheepskin jacket. Even though it was early summer, a deep chill nipped at the heels of the setting sun. The cold rarely bothered him, but tonight it sent a dull ache down his back. Was this just his body aging or was this a warning of some kind? In either case, the sweat lodge that Jason was preparing promised to bring relief and clarity.

Duncan waited on the front porch on an old rocking chair, staring at the night sky. He watched the twinkling of the stars and sent his prayers toward the heavens. He prayed about the path that Spirit seemed to be calling him to take, the healing needed for the pains caused so many years ago. He prayed for vision because much of the road ahead still hid in shadows.

The fire outside the sweat lodge had burned down to a mound of searing hot coals, its fiery life still pulsing through the burnt wood as glowing orange-red light. Jason carefully scooped the heated stones from the coals, dropped to his knees at the low door and extended the shovel into the space to deposit the stones in a pit in the center of the lodge. The round structure stood less than five feet high, its dome-shaped frame made of willow boughs that were covered with canvas and blankets to block out all light. To enter or leave, one had to crawl on hands and knees. There was just enough headroom to sit upright; no one stood up to move around in the lodge.

As he carried stones from the fire to the pit, Jason recalled the first time he had done a sweat with this uncle over two years ago, remembering his own ignorance, his defiance. He had been three weeks into forced sobriety and felt like hell. His uncle kept inviting him to sweat, but he refused. He didn't need any of Old Man's spiritual cleansing bullshit. Duncan watched him closely in those days, and the few times his uncle allowed him time alone, a red-tail hawk always followed him, with its penetrating, golden-eyed stare. Jason used to think that the bird's appearance had been mere coincidence, but no longer. He still couldn't explain it, but he questioned such things less.

During his first sweat, however, he had fought everything. Duncan had explained to him that the sweat lodge represented the womb of Earth, a place for cleansing and rebirth and that you enter on hands and knees as a sign of humility and of connecting to all life. He had followed Duncan into the lodge and sat across the stone pit from him. Once Duncan had closed the canvas door, they sat in total darkness except for the orange-white glow from the stones. Duncan had poured water on the stones, creating a hot mist that soon had them drenched in sweat. Sitting cross-legged on the ground, staring into the stone pit, he had listened to his elder tell the story of how all people were born.

"In the beginning there was Darkness, Turtle and a Voice. The Voice said to Turtle, 'Bring me red clay.' Turtle gathered clay between his claws and brought it to the Voice. The Voice took the clay and made Earth. Then the Voice made all the animals. Turtle asked for people to be made. So Voice made a sweat lodge without rocks and put red clay dolls inside. The dolls remained in the sweat lodge all night. In the morning Turtle went inside only to find that the dolls were still not alive. Then Voice told Turtle to get a branch. Turtle found one and brought it back. Voice put the branch in the ground. It burst into flame. Voice instructed Turtle to put the burning branch into the sweat lodge. This brought the dolls to life. They became the People.

"This is why we return to the sweat lodge," Duncan had said in closing. "All people were born in the sweat, and we continue to be reborn here if we open ourselves to that blessing."

Jason had lasted only fifteen minutes during that first lodge. The imposing heat, the dark confinement, the spiritual intensity seemed to smother him. Instead of releasing trapped fears and nightmares into the sweat, he had held them close, and they tore at his soul. Duncan never reprimanded him for leaving; he had simply continued inviting him back, until one day, Jason felt strong enough to return. Slowly, he had let down his defenses and started to trust, first his uncle, then the mountains, and gradually more in himself.

Now Jason welcomed the opportunity to do ceremony. Tonight's was particularly intriguing. Old Man wanted to bring in all the stones at once and have only one round. Normally, a sweat ceremony was divided into four parts, where eight stones were brought in the lodge at the beginning of each round. Old Man said he would be seeking a vision in tonight's lodge as part of the preparation for another ceremony for healing the ancestors. Jason had no idea what that meant and planned to find out what he could once the lodge started. His uncle could be annoyingly cryptic at times. As he walked to the house to tell Duncan the sweat lodge was ready, he prayed that tonight would not be one of those times.

They removed their clothes and stood before the glowing embers. They burned sweetgrass and smudged themselves with the smoke. They offered prayers of gratitude, then Duncan went to the sweat lodge, kneeled at the entrance, offered a short prayer to Earth, and crawled inside. Jason passed in a bucket of water and a long bundle of sage before entering in the same respectful way. Then he closed the door and they began singing songs to call in the spirits. Silence followed. Duncan dipped the sage bundle into the bucket and then splashed the stones with water. They listened as the rocks whistled a steamy response.

"I have been called to do a healing for our ancestors." Duncan spoke with reverence. "Our ancestors had to endure much pain and suffering, and their tears continue to fall on us. Through prayer and ceremony, we can help them find peace. To begin, we need to ask the ancestors for a vision of how this healing is to take place. That is why we are here tonight. You have done well preparing this lodge."

"I am grateful to be in service to you, to this lodge and to the ancestors." Jason's curiosity was piqued. "How do you change something that's happened in the past? Do you actually travel back in time?"

"In physical form, we are limited. But Spirit can move through time in ways that we cannot."

Before Jason could ask for more of an explanation, Duncan continued. "I want to share with you a vision that came from The Ancient One. This was shown to me when I went to the memorial site at Thornburgh. I was taken into the forest, to the mouth of a cave where water flowing from it turned to blood." He spoke of his brief visitation from the Ute ancestor and the large grizzly bear near the cave. He described the woman who emerged from the cave. She had been beautiful once, but someone had brutalized the left side of her face, blinding her in one eye. "She spoke to me as though she knew me," Duncan said. "She commanded me to help her. But her message made no sense to me. And so I come here now to ask for a vision to show me how to heal her and the other ancestors she spoke of."

"Who is this woman, Old Man?"

"She is Red Fire Woman. Her story is too long to tell at this time."

"Can you tell me what the message was?" Jason tried to hide his impatience.

After a long silence, Duncan said, "She said she has to make amends, that I have to help her. We need to stop him from destroying the land."

"Who is she talking about?"

"I have no more answers for you. We need to ask the ancestors." Duncan threw water on the stones and started to sing.

A wave of heat hit Jason, making it difficult to breathe. He focused his attention on the pile of stones to distract him from the discomfort, watching their glow slowly fade from the added moisture as total darkness enveloped them.

Duncan felt the salty sting of sweat in his eyes and wiped his brow. Hoping that the ancestors were pleased with his songs, he now sat in silence. More water on the stones filled the lodge with a biting heat that seemed to steal the oxygen from his next few breaths. He struggled with the heat for quite some time before the vision came.

He saw himself dressed in his finest beaded regalia, eagle feathers in his hair, doing a dance for the ancestors along a small river. Red Fire Woman stood on the other shore. She looked angry, displeased with his efforts. He didn't know what he was doing wrong. Then Coyote came and stole his drum that was leaning against a tree. Duncan ran after Coyote through the forest. The trail led him up a hill. When he reached the top, he stopped and looked down into the valley. There was Coyote standing next to seven horses, each painted and dressed for ceremony, waiting for riders. Duncan recognized his horse and Jason's, but didn't know the other five. Coyote laughed at him and ran away. Duncan understood. He needed to find the people who belonged to these horses.

Otherwise, he would not be able to complete his ceremony for healing the ancestors. But what remained unclear to him was the reason why.

Duncan sang the closing songs, thanking the Spirits, blessing the earth. Then he told Jason to open the door. The men welcomed the burst of fresh air and the dissipating heat.

"Bring in some drinking water," Duncan said. "We will talk in here."

When Jason returned with a canteen, Duncan took a long drink and passed it back to his nephew. Then he told Jason about his vision but offered no interpretation. He needed time to contemplate the meaning before he would share his thoughts.

"Nephew, what did the Stones and Spirits show you?"

"I wasn't sure what to pray for, so I just asked how I could help you with this ancestor stuff. And if what I saw makes any sense to you, great. Because I have no idea what it means."

Jason took a sip of water before continuing. "I saw two hawks doing a courtship flight. One was red like the mountain cliffs and the other was pure white. They kept circling around each other, then one would dip down and the other would follow, all the time calling back and forth. Really beautiful.

"Then they locked talons and pulled in their wings and did that crazy falling thing. As they continued to fall, their wings caught fire. Just before they hit the ground, the birds released their grip and opened their wings. The fire disappeared. The red hawk soared back up in the air, but one of the white hawk's wings hit a tree limb and she fell to the ground. She kept flapping her wings but couldn't fly. The red hawk circled overhead and then landed in a tree. The white hawk started acting strange, like she was afraid of the red hawk that she'd just been courting. I could see it in her eyes. They were a brilliant green."

Duncan sat in silence, taking in all that Jason had shared.

"There's one more thing," Jason said. "I'm not sure if it's okay to say this in lodge, but that vision made me, well, horny. I know I should be feeling spiritual right now, but all I can think about is getting laid."

Jason looked embarrassed. Duncan liked seeing a bit of modesty in his nephew's tough persona.

"Good thing I'm not a woman or I'd have to fight you off." Duncan chuckled.

"Don't get weird on me, Old Man!" Then Jason laughed too.

"Laughter is good medicine," Duncan said, as he handed Jason his water bucket. "My elders taught me long ago that 'sacred' does not mean 'solemn'. It is good when we can laugh at ourselves, especially when we get caught up in trying to be too spiritual."

Jason took the bucket with him as he left the lodge. Duncan offered one more prayer of thanks and then crawled out into the night air.

With the ceremony complete, Jason went inside to sleep. Duncan sat on the rocking chair and watched the moon. The sweat had revealed much and left other things unclear. Spirit was guiding him in a way that was new to him. Did the white hawk in Jason's vision have anything to do with the green-eyed woman from Chicago? Was she the one Spirit had foretold would return? Did one of those horses belong to her?

He was too tired to ponder the visions any more that evening. Looking up at the moon, he began to sing a song with no words, only melody. "Songs to the Great Spirit do not need words," he remembered his father telling him so many years ago. "Spirit knows your heart." So Duncan sang from deep inside, sang all that weighed heavy on him until the yips and howls of a coyote chorus stilled his voice.

"Brother Coyote, you are Trickster. You show up to remind me that things are not always as they seem," Duncan said, closing his eyes. "Sing to me. Help me to understand."

CHAPTER FIFTEEN

MOVING DAY. SARAH threw the her bags into the truck and bid farewell to the Meeker Hotel. After the first three nights, the novelty of staying in this historic building had faded. She was ready for her own space and hoped that the guest cabin at the Flat Top Ranch would be a welcomed change. She was eager to get away from the town square too, but only because of the museum on the corner. Every time she saw the building, she thought about her fainting spell, her meeting with Duncan Hawk and her twitching hand. She was eager for less evocative surroundings.

Sarah headed up river into the valley, making note of various landmarks—the burned-out log cabin near the first big bend in the road...the turn-off to the Double R Ranch...the Springhorn Lodge where she'd had several meals and was surprised to find that the local girls waiting tables all knew who she was, "that artist lady from Chicago who's working for the Tremaines." And the latest addition to the valley, the new horse arena that Nick Tremaine had built.

Based on conversations with Isabel, the hotel desk clerk, Sarah learned that the construction of this building continued to be highly contentious in the community. The structure itself was beautifully designed and the colors blended into the landscape. But it was immense, the largest building in the entire county, slightly bigger than a football field. Nick Tremaine had not been required to get a building permit because he'd found a loophole that allowed him to list the arena as an agricultural building. Members of the planning committee felt he took advantage of the process in order to avoid scrutiny and regulations.

Just that morning, the local newspaper had run an article that quoted a committee member who argued that the building, just by its sheer size, should have been subject to zoning and building codes. The article questioned Nick's overall intentions for the use of the building, expressing concern that he would eventually turn it into a tourist attraction. Accompanying the article was a political cartoon suggesting that Nick had paid off members of the committee to allow his building to move forward despite the objections. Sarah decided to hold onto the newspaper and ask Hollis about it when his son wasn't around.

One mile beyond the horse arena, Sarah turned onto the road to the Flat Top Ranch. Her ears popped from the altitude. After another two miles of well-maintained fences, horses grazing on green pastures and idyllic river views, Sarah got her first glimpse of the ranch.

"This place is absolutely stunning," Sarah exclaimed as she drove up to the main entrance, boldly marked with a twenty-foot-high log archway. From the road, she could see one large log cabin and two smaller ones nestled in a backdrop of pine and aspen, each looking out on the meandering river. A large barn and corrals were located strategically so as not to block the priceless mountain views from the front porches. The long gravel road leading to the main house was freshly graded and the sun shone brightly in the sky as though scripted to create the perfect day.

Pulling into the circular drive in front of the main house, Sarah found a parking place next to a Jeep. She walked onto the expansive front porch where Hollis met her with a broad smile and welcoming handshake. "Did you have any trouble finding the place?" he asked, offering her a wooden deck chair.

"No. Not at all," Sarah replied, taking a seat.

"Splendid!" Opening the door, he leaned inside to announce, "Nick, Sarah Cavanaugh is here. Bring some iced tea, would you?"

Hollis sat down next to Sarah. "Welcome to the Flat Top Ranch," Hollis said, his voice bright with pride. "Let me tell you a little about the place. We're up around 8,000 feet here. And as you can see, we're right on the edge of the forest. Not too much farther up the road, the actual wilderness area begins. The mountains around here are called the Flat Tops because, up at 12,000 feet, they literally are flat on the top. Like plateaus. It's quite a view from up there. The landscape is much more open, all kinds of flowers, shrubs and grasses growing there, but not many trees." He paused, then exclaimed, "Isn't this beautiful country?"

"You took the words right out of my mouth," said Sarah, enjoying her employer's overt love of the land.

"We've got over 1,000 acres here of forest and pasture and one of the best trout streams around. Do you fish?"

Sarah shook her head.

"I'm surprised. Your father is quite an accomplished fisherman. I enjoyed meeting him very much."

"He absolutely loved it up here," Sarah said. "He talked about that fishing trip for months."

"If you ever want to give it a try, I'd be pleased to introduce you to the intoxicating world of fly fishing. But I warn you, you'll get hooked."

The front door opened and a petite young woman dressed for house cleaning stepped onto the porch with a tray of glasses and a pitcher.

"Bonnie, you didn't need to do this," Hollis jumped up and took the tray from her. "I asked Nick to bring out the drinks."

"I understand, sir," she spoke self-consciously, averting her eyes.

Sarah saw a brief look of annoyance cloud his face. "Thank you Bonnie. While you're here, let me introduce you to Sarah Cavanaugh. She's the artist from Chicago who will be staying in the Pine Cabin for the summer. Sarah, this is Bonnie James, my housekeeper and day cook."

The women exchanged greetings. Bonnie smiled warmly before hurrying back inside. Sarah wondered how many Tremaine family secrets that woman kept under her apron.

Hollis poured iced tea and handed Sarah a glass. "I am so excited to have you here. I just know the murals are going to be exquisite. I think the real challenge is going to be how you condense so much history and natural beauty onto just three or four walls!"

"That is the muralist's dilemma. I have to confess, that's one of the aspects that drew me to murals in the first place. I love painting stories."

"You'll find plenty of stories here, I assure you. No better place to start than this piece of land right here." Hollis gestured out to the mountains in front of them.

"Let me grab my notebook." Sarah hurried to the truck, grabbed her sketchpad from the front seat and returned to the porch. "Okay, tell me about your ranch."

"The first man I know of who owned this place raised sheep. We're talking maybe eighty years ago. When he got up in years, he fell off a horse and broke his back. Had to sell the ranch. The next rancher brought in cattle."

"Is that typical around here, to mix sheep and cattle like that?"

"In most places in the West, it's not. You tend to find one or the other. Early on, this valley was mostly cattle, but now there's a mix of cattle and sheep. I should point out that you rarely find both kinds of livestock on the same ranch. You're either a cattle rancher or a sheep rancher. I prefer cattle."

Hollis explained that the ranch again changed hands when a real estate executive acquired the land and turned it into a hunting and fishing retreat for him and business associates. He'd had no interest in ranching and stopped tending the pastures. The same was true for the three succeeding owners, all absentee landowners except for a month or two each year to fish and hunt.

"By the time I bought the Flat Top, no hay had been cut or cattle grazed on the land for nearly fifteen years. The only structure still in working order was the main house. I'm here to tell you, the place was a disaster."

"Sounds like the Double R," Sarah said, pouring more iced tea into both glasses.

"It took us fifteen months to get the Flat Top in working order."

In fact, Hollis had transformed it into a showcase of modern ranching. Every building had been restored, miles of fence line replaced, new irrigation pipes laid, the latest equipment purchased. He grazed a healthy herd of cattle and some world-class quarter horses. Hollis even brought in his own private fire truck and had county firefighters train his ranch hands how to put out forest fires.

Sarah put down her pencil and took a sip of tea when the front door opened and Nick made his appearance.

"Nick, there you are. You remember Sarah Cavanaugh."

The son stood in front of Sarah and extended his hand. "I never forget a pretty face."

His tone was charming, unlike the other day at the Double R when he seemed so standoffish. Maybe she had misread him. *First impressions can be deceiving,* she thought.

"Nick, why don't you show our artist-in-residence to her cabin? Sarah, make yourself at home in there. You are invited to have dinner with us tonight, and we can continue our conversation about the murals. Come by around seven for cocktails." Hollis handed her a key to the cabin.

"Thank you, Hollis. That's very kind. If you point me in the right direction, I'm sure I can find my way to the cabin. No need to trouble you, Nick," Sarah replied.

"No trouble at all, I assure you," Nick said. He walked over to his Jeep before she could counter. After a three-minute drive up the hill, she pulled into the small drive and shook her head in disbelief.

Nestled under two large pines on top of a small hill, the cabin that would be her home for the summer looked almost too perfect to be real. The pine logs gleamed yellow tan with no signs of weathering. The door and shutters had a fresh coat of red paint. Even the doormat looked brand new. Marigolds bloomed bright and cheery in window boxes, a luxurious porch swing swayed lightly in the breeze and hummingbird feeders hung all along the porch eaves.

"This is lovely," Sarah said as she stood in front of the cabin.

"Yes, I agree," Nick replied, looking directly at her.

"Is this where your sister and her family stay when they visit?" she asked, keenly aware of Nick's gaze.

He nodded. "I'm sure you'll find it will exceed your expectations." Nick walked toward the cabin and opened the door. "Look around. I'll get your bags."

Sarah hesitated. "No need, thanks. I can handle things from here." Nick had already moved past her and began unloading the truck. Realizing further protest was futile, she grabbed several bags and followed him into the cabin.

Her irritation turned to wonder as she walked through the doorway into an elegant kitchen even Martha Stewart would covet. This didn't look like any cabin Sarah had ever seen. Putting down her things, she wandered into the living room, with floor-to-ceiling windows, a stone fireplace and furnished with the finest antiques. Sarah couldn't believe how stunning this place was.

She turned around and nearly ran into Nick who was standing directly behind her. "Sorry, I didn't see you there," she said, then stepped back. "This cabin is quite something."

"Yes, it is."

"Thank you for your help." Sarah turned toward the kitchen.

"Don't you want to see the rest of the cabin?" Nick asked.

"I don't want to take up any more of your time. I'll find my way around." She walked into the kitchen and opened the door, intending Nick to follow.

He sauntered in and smiled. "Your bags are in the bedroom. If I can be of further service, please let me know."

"Thank you, Nick. I'm sure I'll be fine."

He moved slowly past her. "I look forward to seeing you at dinner."

Closing the door behind him, Sarah shook her head. He was a hard one to read, charming one minute and presumptuous the next.

Hearing him drive off, Sarah was now free to explore the rest of her new home and soon forgot about Nick. Every room, not just the living room, was furnished with antiques and yet every appliance was the most expensive technology available, from the Sub-zero refrigerator and convection oven, to a computerized shower system with surround sound, to a high-tech entertainment center with a fifty-inch wide plasma screen. The elegantly carved, handcrafted woods of the past and the metallic, micro-chipped machines of the future somehow blended in a way that celebrated the beauty and luxury of both worlds. Sarah thought the design was pure genius. And as Hollis had promised, the second bedroom had been converted into an art studio that exceeded her specifications, including the picture-postcard view.

Now I know what I'll do if I ever win the lottery, Sarah mused. She had just enough time to unpack and freshen up before dinner.

Her evening with the Tremaines began with cocktails on the deck, followed by a delicious elk steak dinner. Halfway through the meal, Nick left the room to take a phone call and never came back to the table. This gave Sarah and Hollis time to talk about his vision of the murals he wanted her to create. Local wildlife and landscapes, history, culture, he wanted it all. To Sarah's relief, he also was ready to give her the time and the opportunities to experience as much as she needed to. Her task was both daunting and exciting, and she couldn't wait to get started.

CHAPTER SIXTEEN

SARAH SPENT THE next week exploring the ranch, learning about the business of growing hay, raising cattle, and riding horses, mostly under Hollis' cheerful tutelage. Nick joined them on a number of occasions, although he rarely added much to the conversations. Even though he appeared preoccupied or uninterested most of the time, he always offered an appropriate response when Hollis asked him a question.

She noticed that Nick acted like a total gentleman in his father's presence. But when Hollis wasn't around, on days when Nick would drop by her cabin unannounced or when they met in passing at the stable, another side emerged, the one that seemed to be checking her out with an air of entitlement that left a chill in the air no matter how warm the temperature. As she explained to Ruth one night on the phone, his comments to her bordered on inappropriate, but it was more in the way he said things rather than the words themselves. "I can't come up with an example right now. It's more of a feeling I get. I'm always on edge when he's around. I don't like him."

"Glad to hear that not everything out there is idyllic," Ruth teased her. "After you told me about your little cabin and the gorgeous view, I was thinking you'd stepped into fantasy land. Sounds like Nick brings a little dose of reality to things."

"I suppose," Sarah sighed. "I just don't want him to make trouble. I think he's attracted to me."

"Ooh, that's awkward," Ruth said. "You could try dropping hints that you're gay."

"Very funny. You know I'm not a good liar."

Sarah tried to put concerns about Nick out of her head, as she settled in for an evening of sketching. Her studio was already overflowing with drawings; soon, every room in the cabin would have illustrations taped up on the walls.

Sarah finished hanging her latest sketches just as darkness was settling in. She frowned. Too many of her cowboys looked like Blue. They either had his eyes, his mouth, or his jaw. Some had all three. Being back in the mountains made it too easy to remember all of the reasons why she had loved him and to forget most of the hurt.

Pouring a glass of cabernet, Sarah wrapped herself in a soft wool blanket and went outside to the porch swing. She marveled at the stars glittering in the clear sky, realizing how much Chicago's artificial illumination robbed the Midwestern skies of this kind of light.

She thought about the first time she had made love with Blue on that camping trip. The sky had looked just like this. "I need to stop this silliness right now. I need to think about someone else."

Sarah went inside and into her studio. She pulled a few cowboy sketches off the wall and set about redoing the faces. Up until now, she had purposefully not sketched Nick; she didn't want to feed his ego in any way. But he had none of Blue's lovable qualities. Putting Nick's face to paper might just kill any romantic feelings that Blue's memory had kindled. So maybe now would be a good time.

She thought about Nick's eyes, hard, cold and insistent. Maybe she could make them more likable. But no matter how she tried, she couldn't soften them. They stared right into hers with an intensity that compelled her to tear up the drawing and throw it in the wastebasket.

That night she slept fitfully and was jolted awake by a nightmare—two menacing eyes surrounded by darkness. Her body ached with fright. She sat up and turned on the light. Slowly she felt her body relax. But then she became aware of the throbbing in her left hand. The palsy had returned, her thumb and first two fingers clenched in a tight ball, the whole hand trembling.

In the bathroom she ran hot water over her hand for ten minutes before it finally relaxed. Exhausted and upset, she was afraid to go back to sleep. She moved into the living room, lay down on the couch, still rubbing her hand, and waited for dawn.

Sarah dressed, ate an English muffin with peanut butter and drank several cups of strong black coffee. She was going to town, an hour's drive, to pick up groceries and a FedEx package from her sister with more art supplies and, she hoped, some of her famous chocolate chip oatmeal cookies.

Grabbing her purse, some cloth grocery bags and her sunglasses, Sarah stepped out into the crisp morning air that had not fully shed its evening chill. Realizing she'd need her fleece top, she turned back toward the cabin and spotted a piece of paper tacked to the front door. She read the note, written in a slanted, edgy print: *Sarah, Monday morning, 8 a.m. Follow this map. Bring sweetgrass. Duncan Hawk*

The hand-drawn map would lead her farther up river, into another valley east of the Flat Top Ranch. The meeting was three days away.

She stared at the summons, both annoyed and shaken by its terse tone. *When did he deliver the note? How did he get here?* She didn't remember hearing a vehicle. She looked around, wondering if the Indian was still nearby, but saw nothing unusual, so she went back inside to grab her fleece.

The gravel road, still wet from the heavy morning dew, did not kick up much dust as her vehicle crunched and rumbled its way along. With thoughts focused on Duncan's note, Sarah took the first turn too quickly, causing the vehicle to swerve a bit on the slick stones. She quickly let up on the accelerator and turned into the swerve to straighten out, just as she would on icy streets in the city. She slowed down at the next curve, but her mind still raced.

Should I go? What choice do I have? Sarah wanted to talk this over with Ruth to get some clarity...and some courage. She'd call when she returned from town.

The grinding of gravel gave way to the smooth hum of pavement as she turned west onto the main road. After several miles, she rounded a bend and quickly slammed on the brakes. Cattle sprawled all over the road. Cows and calves, too many to count, came walking slowly towards her. She saw a Flat Top Ranch pickup truck in the lead, with red warning flags sticking up on the hood. Sarah didn't know what to do.

The rocky wall to her right provided no shoulder to pull off onto. And she absolutely could not back up around that curve in the road, so she sat idling as the truck and cows approached.

A woman stuck her head out of the truck and waved. It was Shelly. She and her husband Tony managed the Flat Top Ranch. Sarah had met them earlier in the week and had spent a delightful afternoon with Shelly, listening to stories about the bravery and calamity that came with living in these mountains.

"Sarah, you look like a deer caught in the headlights. Don't worry honey, these cows are just a bunch of big old babies."

"What should I do? We don't have these kinds of traffic jams in Chicago," Sarah said. "We just paint statues of them and put them on the sidewalks."

"Drive straight and slow and they'll move out of the way."

"Really? Maybe I should just wait here 'til they've passed by."

"Don't be silly. You'll be out here all morning. They won't hurt you. I know they look intimidating, especially Joshua, that ol' bull, but they aren't that bright. Just don't honk your horn or turn on your windshield wipers. That'll upset 'em."

"Okay, I think I can handle that. Where are you taking them?"

"These cows just came in from Utah. We keep 'em there in the winter. Now we're moving them up into the forest for the summer."

"Did they walk all the way from Utah?" Sarah asked.

"No," Shelly chuckled. "They came by truck; we're walking 'em to a pasture along the creek and then later into the forest. Good luck on your first cattle run! Remember, don't honk your horn." Shelly waved and continued on her way.

"Time to get my Bonanza face on!" Sarah drove slowly toward the tide of bovine bodies, which started snorting and mooing and dropping cow pies in protest as she approached. She'd never been so close to a cow or a bull. She watched their eyes grow wide with confusion at the oncoming vehicle. They stepped left then right, then back again before trotting off to either side. Calves bleated, trying to follow their mothers in the melee. "Great, I'm going to separate a calf from its mom and get rammed by an angry cow! Wonder how that would look on an insurance claim."

One of the bulls stood his ground, staring through the windshield, frothing at the mouth and snorting. Sarah stopped the car, not wanting to provoke an attack. At that moment, the metal and glass of the truck did not seem sufficient protection against an angry bull with big horns.

To Sarah's relief, Tony came riding through the herd on a pretty black mare with one of his border collies at his side. He whistled and the dog pressed itself to the pavement, staring intently at the bull, which pawed the ground once, shook its head and reluctantly moved aside.

"Thanks, Tony. I thought I was done for," Sarah said, poking her head out the window.

"My pleasure, ma'am. We've had a little trouble with that bull. But the dogs are giving him a run for his money, so I'm sure he'll learn to behave. You shouldn't have any more problems getting through the herd." He tilted his head slightly and touched the front rim of his hat as Sarah drove by.

Tony was a tall, wiry man with the strength of a wrestler and the playfulness of a clown. Sarah thought he made the perfect cowboy— rugged, attractive but not handsome, capable, kind and a bit feisty. She recalled one of Shelly's stories about how Tony had, on a number of occasions, gone out early in the morning after a snowstorm and spent all day in the mountains on horseback, at his peril, to find a lost hunter before he froze to death, and then expected nothing more than a "thank you" in return.

I really should sketch him, if I can find a time when he's actually sitting still, Sarah thought. *I'm sure his face wouldn't give me nightmares.*

As she drove on, she wondered if she would be able to say the same thing about Duncan Hawk. Was it just coincidence that his note showed up the morning after her hand freaked out again? Or was he somehow responsible for the palsy? The only way to find out, she told herself, was to accept his early morning invitation.

CHAPTER SEVENTEEN

JESSIE WALKED OUT of the county courthouse with an old leather briefcase in one hand and a determined look in her eyes. She stopped, as she always did, to admire the fluid bronze statue of a border collie working several wide-eyed sheep, how beautifully the artist had captured the dog's fierce and focused intensity. Today Jessie felt just like that border collie, completely riveted on her mission. She would keep Eli McDermott from selling off part of the ranch. "If nipping at his heels won't work," she told herself, "I'll just have to go for his throat."

Jessie smiled at her analogy. In a sheep dog trial, any dog would be disqualified for biting a sheep. And a sheepherder would not tolerate violent behavior in a working dog. But she felt no compunction to play by the rules right now. She had too much to lose.

"He probably thinks there's no fight left in this old dog," she said to her bronzed counterpart. "But I'll show that sheep-brain that I've still got some bite."

Jessie cut across the lawn on her way to the Meeker Cafe, her favorite place to eat in town, not so much because of the food, but because of the way the cafe made her feel. She found comfort in buildings that had been around longer than she had. Fewer and fewer people met the criterion, which made it harder for her to pretend she wasn't aging. But when she stepped inside that old building, built before the turn of the century, with its black-and-white photos of the town's early days, she felt spry.

On her short jaunt across the square, she reflected on the morning's meeting with her attorney, Sally Grimm. The fact that Sally also happened to be Eli's lawyer might cause problems down the road, Jessie realized, but today she wanted to get some information and advice. At Eli's request, Sally had written the letter to Tom that gave him an opportunity to buy the land he'd been leasing for years. She confirmed that Eli was quite serious about selling and anxious to do so.

The two women had talked about Patrick's proposal for a conservation easement on the property. Jessie and Patrick were willing to write a letter spelling out the advantages for Eli—a substantial one-time payment up front which would still allow him to make money renting out the land. Sally could edit it to her style and send it out under her letterhead. She agreed to present the idea to Eli for his consideration, but both women suspected he would refuse the offer.

If Sally couldn't make him see reason, Jessie would have to take the next step on her own. She opened the door to the cafe and walked inside.

"Ms. Jessie, it's great to see you," chirped Elaine, a stocky, middle-aged waitress with large brown eyes and a charming smile. "If you can believe it, seems like everybody in town came in for lunch at the same time. We're full up right now, but a table should open up soon."

"Thanks, hon," Jessie replied, surveying the crowd. She knew the people sitting at the counter, all local folks. Many of the unfamiliar faces at the tables and booths looked like tourists. She was pleased to see the cafe doing so well, but felt a bit annoyed at having to wait. She hadn't eaten since sunrise and was hungry. She watched Elaine burst out of the kitchen with her usual exuberance and deliver a plate piled high with a hamburger and fries to a pretty blonde woman sitting in the back booth. The waitress stopped briefly to chat with the woman, then both of them looked up at Jessie. Elaine shook her head and shrugged her shoulders before walking up to Jessie with a tentative expression.

"The woman in the far booth there said you'd be welcome to join her rather than waiting for an open seat. I told her you were probably waiting on someone, but would ask you anyway," Elaine blurted out, anticipating a polite rejection.

Caught off guard, Jessie didn't reply at first, which Elaine interpreted as irritation. "Sorry, Ms. Jessie, I'll tell her no."

"Who is she?" Jessie interrupted. "Should I know her?"

"Uh, I don't think so. She's new in town," the waitress offered. "I think she's the artist who's working for Hollis Tremaine."

Jessie raised her left eyebrow, the only hint of surprise on her face. "Well, her invitation is very neighborly...do you know her name?"

"No ma'am, I don't. But she does seem quite nice."

Only then did Jessie look up and catch the woman's eye. They smiled politely at each other and Jessie nodded. "Thanks, Elaine. I will join her...and I'll have my usual."

As she walked to the back of the cafe, Jessie wondered if this woman was involved with the continuing development at the horse arena, a project she had opposed from the beginning. Jessie had the distinction of being the longest standing member of the County Zoning Commission and the horse arena's most vocal critic. She smiled at the fortuity of her unexpected lunch invitation and the possibility of learning more about the Tremaines' plans.

"Hello, my dear. My name is Jessibel Winde. Thank you for your kind invitation to join you."

"I'm Sarah Cavanaugh. A pleasure to meet you. And thank you for joining me. After the place filled up, I was feeling uncomfortable taking up an entire booth, especially when I saw you were waiting for a seat."

In the awkward silence that followed, both women looked at the plate of food in front of Sarah. Jessie spoke first. "Please, don't wait on me. Eat while it's hot. Elaine is bringing me something."

"Thanks. Help yourself to some fries."

"You won't find better fries anywhere," Jessie said. "Where are you from, Sarah?"

"I'm from Chicago, the northern suburbs, actually," Sarah replied. "Guess you can tell that from my flat, nasally 'A.' I'm not aware of it until I leave the Midwest."

"What brings you out to Meeker? Are you on vacation?"

"No, work. I'm going to be painting a number of murals at a place called the Double R Ranch."

"That's Hollis Tremaine's place. Are you working for him then?"

"Yes, I am. Do you know him?"

"I've made his acquaintance, yes. He's done some impressive work on the Flat Top over the years. Looks like he's starting on the Double R now, and that's good."

Sarah talked about her work as a muralist in Chicago, how her father's connection with Hollis had opened the door for this job and how she was now in the process of learning as much as she could about the area, historical and present day.

"I've lived here all my life," Jessie offered, "and I wouldn't live anywhere else." She gave Sarah a brief history of her family and of the valley. Polite conversation. Just enough to hold the artist's interest.

Jessie finished as Elaine delivered her lunch with an apology for the delay. "We are so crazy busy today. I don't know what's going on, but I hope it continues," she blurted out as she hurried back to the kitchen.

Halfway through her bowl of vegetable beef soup, Jessie broached what she thought could be a sensitive subject. "By any chance, are you going to be doing any work on the horse arena?"

"Not that Hollis has mentioned. I've got my hands full with the Double R. Besides," Sarah continued, "that seems to be his son Nick's project, and I'd prefer not to work for him."

Jessie nodded in agreement. Her dealings with the younger Tremaine had always been distasteful.

"I shouldn't have said that," Sarah said, regretting her unprofessional confession. "Hollis is such a great man to work for. I don't want to say anything negative about him or this job."

"Don't worry, dear," Jessie assured her. "Your feelings won't go any further than this table. It is interesting how different those two men are. Nick seems to take after his mother."

"Did you know her? Hollis told me she died in a car accident a number of years ago."

"I met Martha Tremaine once. And that was enough," Jessie said. "All business, always on the phone, seemed to be working constantly. The one and only time she came to the valley, Hollis had asked me to take her up to see Trappers Lake. Have you been to Trappers?"

Sarah shook her head.

"It's a must while you're here. One of the most spectacular lakes in this state. Let me share a little Colorado history with you. Back in 1920, a Forest Service employee named Arthur Carhart was sent up to Trappers to make a survey for construction of a road around the lake. Carhart was so moved by the beauty of that place that he recommended that Trappers Lake never be developed. The Forest Service took his advice and protected the area for all time," Jessie explained. "The modern concept of wilderness protection started right here."

"How far is Trappers Lake from here?" Sarah asked.

"Give yourself a couple of hours. The scenery is gorgeous for most of the drive. No reason to rush," Jessie smiled. "Unless you're traveling with Martha Tremaine. She couldn't get out of there fast enough. She was so upset that there was no cell service. As I recall, she had some real estate deal that was about to close and couldn't be bothered to hike even a few minutes to take in the best view. The drive back to town was most unpleasant. I think she was one of the most rude and driven people I've had to deal with. How Hollis ended up marrying a woman like that, I have no idea."

"My sister's a psychoanalyst and she's always talking about how opposites attract," Sarah said. "She says that principle alone keeps her in business because the long-term results in marriage aren't always pretty."

A busboy cleared away their plates and asked if either would like coffee. They both said yes, black.

"Jessie, why were you asking about my working at the horse arena?"

She took a moment before answering. "I like what Hollis has done on the Flat Top Ranch and how he manages his land, like a real rancher. The horse arena seems out of character in comparison."

"How so?"

"As you've probably noticed, it's the largest structure in the entire county. He let Nick build it on prime hay land along a scenic byway. And instead of bringing the idea to the county zoning commission, he found a way to exempt him from public scrutiny. Caused a nasty rift in the commission and in the valley. Created a lot of hard feelings."

"I read something about that in the paper when I first got here," said Sarah. "I don't know Hollis all that well, but he seems to love this place. And he talks a lot about conservation and open space. It seems strange that he'd be involved in something so contentious."

"As you already observed, Sarah, the main force behind the horse arena is Nick. But his father never opposed him. I don't know what to make of that."

"Well, Nick does seem to have a different view of things than his father does. He talks about how his dad would be better off putting up custom cabins on the Double R rather than restoring the buildings."

"I don't like hearing that," Jessie said with true concern. "That's the last thing this valley needs. May I ask, what was Hollis' response?"

"He seems disappointed that his son doesn't share his passion for restoration. But he also told me he's happy that Nick has taken an interest in things out here."

Jessie got quiet as her mind raced. Nick wanted to develop land in the valley and had the money to do it. She had to make sure he didn't find out about Eli wanting to sell. Sarah might be able to help her keep tabs on Hollis' son.

"Sounds like you have a lot of ground to cover for those murals you'll be painting. I would be happy to have you up to my place some time and show you around."

"Thank you!" Sarah replied. "That would be lovely. I'd enjoy that."

To her surprise, Jessie realized that she would enjoy it too.

She wrote down her phone number and address on a napkin, handed it to Sarah and then picked up both checks. Sarah reached out for hers, but Jessie stopped her. "It's the least I can do to say thanks for sharing the booth with me. And for such engaging conversation."

"You're very kind. Perhaps I can buy lunch next time." Sarah offered.

"I accept."

As they walked to the cash register at the front of the cafe, Jessie asked, "Where are you staying?"

"In a cabin at the Flat Top. Let me give you my phone number."

Sarah pulled out her sketchpad and tore out a page. Jessie caught a glimpse of some sketches. "Bring some of your drawings to dinner, would you? I would like to see your work."

"Thank you. I will." She closed the sketchpad quickly. "These are just doodles, really. I'd be pleased to show you more completed pieces."

Out on the sidewalk, just before saying their goodbyes, Sarah asked her new friend about one more thing. "This may sound strange, but do you know an old Indian man named Duncan Hawk?"

Jessie cocked an eyebrow. "Yes. Why?"

Sarah explained how she had met him at the war memorial and that they had talked about local history. She wondered if he could be trusted.

"What do you mean?" Jessie asked, slightly annoyed.

"You see, he invited me to his home, and I barely know the man. I'm not used to accepting invitations from people I meet in the middle of nowhere. He seems nice, but I just wanted to make sure he wasn't some local nutcase."

Jessie took a deep breath, curbing her instinct to defend Duncan's honor. "Young lady, Duncan Hawk is a dear friend of mine and a decorated elder of the Ute people. It is an honor to receive an invitation from him. You would do well to accept it and to treat him with the respect he deserves. This will be an experience you won't forget."

"I meant no offense. It's just that his invitation took me by surprise. But I feel much better knowing he's your friend."

The women said goodbye and Jessie walked to her truck. *Why is Duncan interested in this Chicago woman?* Maybe he was just being sociable, but that didn't sound like him. She wondered if he would tell her about his interest in Sarah Cavanaugh. Duncan Hawk maintained an air of mystery that frustrated her. It also made him quite captivating, even after all this time.

Duncan was the only man Jessie had ever known who both fascinated and intimidated her. He was also the only man who ever broke her heart.

As Jessie got into her truck, she found herself remembering their first chance encounter over forty years ago. She had come across Duncan on a trail near Trapper's Lake. Having stopped to rest her horse and take in the scenery, she hadn't seen him sitting next to the pine tree. When he spoke, she was so startled she spooked her own horse. Duncan helped her run down the mare before introducing himself. He explained that he was traveling through the Flat Tops looking for sacred sites that his ancestors had used. Immediately taken with his warm smile and teasing eyes, Jessie invited Duncan to dinner. His face turned to stone. "What kind of woman are you, asking a strange Indian to your home? Are you crazy?"

Jessie was taken aback. Had she offended him somehow? Fumbling for an apology, she backed up and walked towards her horse. But before she could take two steps, he began to laugh. "I accept your invitation!" She turned to see him smiling broadly. "I like a woman who isn't afraid of a wild Indian. The Spirits told me I would meet a friend today. The Spirits are always right."

Jessie willfully stopped the remembering there and turned the key in the ignition. *Had the spirits known we'd become lovers?* Jessie wondered. *Or that one careless act on my part would drive him away?* She sighed. That was a long time ago. But Eli's return to the valley was stirring up old regrets and heartache long forgotten, or so she had thought. "Damn him."

She had wrestled anew with those wounds at her last visit to Full

Moon Rock and had reclaimed some sense of peace with the way things stood between her and Duncan—a complicated friendship with occasions of sweet intimacy that had no regularity or reason. Long ago, she had come to trust that Duncan would always be in her life however the spirits guided him.

But today, Jessie worried that the trouble with Eli McDermott might push Duncan away as it had so many years ago when Eli had made such a mess of things. Back then, Duncan had stayed away for almost two years before giving her another chance to gain his trust and renew their friendship. She vowed not to let that happen again. Eli had already caused enough damage for one lifetime.

As she started her truck, she wondered again about Duncan's interest in Sarah and felt a twinge of jealousy. Where did that come from? "Jesus, Jessie," she scolded herself. "You're becoming an old coot. You've got more important things to worry about than a pretty young woman having breakfast with Duncan."

She thought of that border collie staring down the sheep. She needed that kind of focus right now to save the ranch from Eli's intentions.

CHAPTER EIGHTEEN

SARAH RUSHED TO get through her errands in town. Meeting someone who could vouch for Duncan Hawk made her feel better about getting together with him. Up until this point, she'd felt her situation had all the makings of a *Readers' Digest* cover story...naive woman, intriguing stranger, clandestine meeting, woman disappears, body never found. With Jessie's assurance, she was less apprehensive.

Before driving back up river, Sarah pulled out a map to locate the road where Duncan lived. His note listed a rural route number, but no indication of how far up the road he was. She decided to do some reconnaissance that afternoon so she'd know how to get there Monday morning. With the sun shining across a soft blue sky and a light breeze teasing the grasses, a drive through the mountains sounded like an ideal way to spend the rest of the day.

Like so many roads in the area, Rural Route 129 looked like a gravel ribbon following a river winding through a rocky canyon. Sarah passed several large ranches and numerous dirt roads heading into the forest that led to private cabins not visible from the road. She had driven nearly forty-five minutes before she began to wonder if she'd missed his place. It had been at least several miles since she'd seen any mailboxes and she'd passed a sign indicating that the national forest boundary was only a couple of miles away. She was just about to turn around when she spotted a pile of weathered antlers by the side of the road and a wooden sign to one side with the number she'd been looking for. She stopped to peer down the dirt road but couldn't see the house. Somewhat disappointed, she pushed aside the urge to drive down a ways to catch a glimpse. She made note of the odometer reading and the time it took to get there, then continued on, looking for a relatively straight stretch of gravel to turn around.

The road crossed the river, which this far up valley was only a couple of feet across. Just ahead Sarah found a wide shoulder on the opposite side to turn into. Much to her delight, a brilliant red patch of flowers decorated the rise. She turned off the car and got out to take a closer look. Clusters of trumpet-shape blooms adorned stalks easily three feet high. When she looked them up later, she learned these flowers were scarlet gilia, a type of phlox attracted to dry mountain soils. Sarah spotted a weathered trail sign halfway up the slope. Hoping to see more wildflowers, she got a hat and bottle of water from the car, locked her purse in the trunk, made a mental note to get a wildflower book on her next visit to town, and set out on a short walk.

She smiled at the hardiness of mountain flowers. Despite rocky ground, a variety of plants, most less than a foot tall, managed to bring delicate color and pattern to this hardened landscape—pink blooms of sticky geranium, yellow centers and white petals of cutleaf daisy and fiery red tufts of Indian paintbrush. Grasshoppers and lizards jumped and scuttled out of the way as Sarah walked among the rock piles and the twisted trunks of shrub oak and juniper. Intending to take only a ten-minute stroll, she became engrossed in the scenery and kept walking.

When the trail forked, she instinctively took the left bend that wound its way down into a box canyon. She welcomed the cooler air as she stepped into the shade of the steep rocky walls. The path narrowed, the vegetation grew denser and greener. Sarah noticed small white snail shells on the trail that crunched under her boots. Eventually she heard running water. The sound didn't surprise her. Somehow she knew where she was going, as though she'd walked this path many times before.

She quickened her pace until she reached the bank lined with stones worn smooth with time. The creek, nearly ten feet across, consisted of numerous rivulets flowing around, over and under boulders and rocky shelves, each current weaving in and around the others, resting in shallow pools, then cascading down ledges to the next passage through the stony obstacle course. The melodic rush of the water drowned out the bird songs that had serenaded her along the path.

Sarah had worked up a sweat on her hike and wanted to cool her feet in the water, so she found a flat rock to sit on and took off her shoes and socks. Though the sharp cold made her gasp, she plunged her feet back in and held them there until they turned numb. Refreshed, she made her way over slippery rocks to a shady spot along the bank. She leaned up against a tree and watched the ever-changing patterns of water on stone.

She tossed a few small rocks into the creek and watched them change color and come to life when the water blessed them. *So dull when they're dry,* she thought, *and so brilliant when wet.* She felt like these dry stones, without shine, without luster. *If only a quick dip in the water could restore me as easily as it does these stones.* But she knew it would take much more than that to put a spark back in her life.

When Blue ended their relationship, he broke more than her heart. His rejection made her question her sanity. She shut off her emotions so completely, she was afraid she'd forgotten how to feel.

Being back in the Colorado mountains made the memories of Blue hard to ignore. He had been a junior when Sarah started college, a wildlife ecology student with a particular love of bears. He had taken great delight in teaching her all he could about the animals and plants on long hikes through the forest. She had loved the long afternoons when they'd find a beautiful place to stop so she could draw. And make love. She had fallen in love with Blue in these mountains.

It was on just such an afternoon when she had encountered her first black bear. Blue had to point it out to her at first, moving through the trees on the far side of the meadow. Fortunately, they were upwind, so the bear couldn't pick out their scent. Unaware of the people watching it, the young male (Blue could tell just by looking at it) seemed in no hurry to leave the area, giving Sarah ample time to make many sketches of him turning over fallen logs in search of grubs and other food.

Eventually the wind had changed and the bear had started to sniff the air. Blue told her to freeze. At that moment, the bear turned to face them. Sarah felt the creature's brown eyes staring directly at her. Then, without provocation, it charged. She could still see that bear running in slow motion towards her and feel the pounding of her heart and the panicky numbness in her legs. For the first time in her life, she had known the cold grip of pure terror.

Blue jumped up and started to yell, waving his hands above his head.

The bear stopped and stood up on its hind legs to get a better look. Blue then picked up a large tree branch and continued waving and yelling. The bear grunted, as though amused, dropped down onto four paws and ambled off into the forest. Sarah wept with relief.

Shortly after that encounter, Sarah started having trouble sleeping. She would awaken in the middle of the night, filled with a sense of dread, as though she'd had a nightmare, but never remembering one. Out in the woods, she couldn't shake the sensation of being watched, whether by animals or people she was unsure. It became so distracting she could barely draw outdoors. She spent too much time looking over her shoulder or staring into the trees, trying to catch a glimpse of whatever she sensed was there.

Blue believed that a fear of bears was the cause of her anxiety and that she just needed to spend more time around them to get over it. But his strategy backfired. Her symptoms grew worse. Blue thought she needed psychological help, that she was becoming paranoid. She didn't believe she was. The conflict drove them apart.

Sarah picked up a small rock and threw it as far as she could, wishing she could throw away the memories as well and make them disappear into the running water.

The sound of scuttling rocks on the hillside startled her. She turned around to see what had caused the disturbance but heard no movement. *Probably a squirrel or chipmunk*, she assured herself. Even so, she picked up a large stone and held onto it. Its smooth, cool surface comforted her. So did the river's hypnotic music. Stretching out her legs, she closed her eyes and allowed the waters to sooth her into sleep and a dream.

She saw herself walking along the creek, watching butterflies dance in the sunbeams. She bent down to pick some yellow flowers. The angry buzzing of an agitated bee startled her. Then a shadow fell over the valley; she looked up and saw a dark cloud blocking the sun that sent a chill through her.

She heard a loud crashing sound. Panic pumped down her legs. She was running, running for her life, darkness crowding in around her. She could barely see the low branches that crossed the path, scratched her face...the pounding of hooves behind her...*keep running, keep running... don't let them catch me....*

Sarah awoke with a start. Scrambling to her feet, she hit her head on a low tree branch. Disoriented and in pain, she hurried along the bank, the same fear in her dream coursing through her, driving her to escape from this place. She turned onto the trail and then froze in mid-step before falling to the ground. Blocking the trail stood a dark Indian man with a large knife poised above her head.

"Don't move!" he commanded, as he looked down the trail. Then a perplexed look came over his face. "I heard you scream. I thought something was chasing you." He lowered his knife.

"Oh thank god, thank god," Sarah muttered. Her would-be protector offered her a hand and helped her to her feet. "I don't know what just happened. I was sitting by the river, then they were coming for me, I panicked. I don't know. I just had to get out of here...." Sarah looked behind her nervously, trying to figure out what was going on.

"Who's after you?"

"What? I don't know," she said. "I think it was a dream, I really don't know what I'm talking about. It seemed so real and then you jumped out of nowhere." Disoriented and embarrassed, Sarah wanted to get back to her car. "I need to get back."

"Are you okay?" he said suspiciously. "Are you on something?"

"I'm fine. And no, I'm not on drugs," Sarah said, stepping past the man. His level gaze unnerved her. As soon as she got to the first turn in the trail, Sarah started running.

The frightened woman inched past him and Jason resisted the impulse to touch her. He watched her bolt up the trail like a frightened jackrabbit, and soon he could no longer hear her footsteps. As he put his knife back in its sheath, a twinge of loneliness caught him off guard. He headed back to where he'd left his horse. A part of him wanted to follow that blonde woman with captivating green eyes who was trespassing on his land, although he wasn't sure what he'd do once he caught her.

CHAPTER NINETEEN

SARAH DIDN'T ALLOW herself to cry until she got back to the cabin and stepped into the shower. The hot water freed the tears to flow, slowly releasing the fear from the afternoon, letting the emotions circle around the shower floor and slip down the drain.

Exhausted from crying and prolonged wet heat, she reached for a towel just as a pain jolted up her left arm. Her thumb and first two fingers were clenched together so tightly, her knuckles had turned white and her ring finger and pinky felt numb. She shook her hand until the fingers released and rubbed her hand to relieve the ache.

"I don't know what's going on here," Sarah talked to her misty reflection in the mirror. "What's wrong with you?" The residual weakness in her hand made it difficult to hang on the towel as she tried to dry herself off. "I wish Ruth were here; she'd know what to do." Giving up on the towel, she put on a white terry robe and grabbed the phone.

Ruth picked up after the second ring. "Hey, Sister-O-Mine! How is life in the Flat Tops?"

"Better now that I'm talking to you," Sarah said, grateful to hear her voice. "How is your baby doing?"

"This little rascal is moving and kicking all over the place. She started just a few minutes before you called. Guess she knew it was you." They talked about the latest changes Ruth was experiencing in her pregnancy.

"Do you think this baby's going to be a girl?" Sarah asked. "You keep referring to the baby as 'she.'"

"I don't really have a sense of that," Ruth admitted. "But I refuse to refer to this little one as an 'it.' I guess it's my way of rebelling against the common usage of the pronoun 'he.' Our default setting is to see everything as masculine. Not that I have anything against the male gender. Trust me, I'm a great fan of those bearing the Y-chromosome. Still, I think it's healthy to put women out there more. 'She' is an underutilized pronoun and I'm doing my part to change that status."

"Trust my sister to make a cause out of everything, even a three-letter word." Sarah smiled. "What's next on your Vocabulary Liberation Front, the usurping of the word 'gay,' perhaps?"

"Very funny," Ruth replied. "Enough about me. How are you?"

"I was hoping you could tell me," Sarah said. "You wouldn't believe the last twenty-four hours I've had."

"I'm all ears."

Sarah explained about her trying to sketch Nick's face to help her break out of her fixation with Blue. And then how she'd had a nightmare about Nick's eyes. "They were the most sinister eyes I've ever seen. Just staring at me. Talk about getting the Evil Eye. And here's the even weirder part: when I woke up, my left hand was clenched and twitching. I was so freaked out, I couldn't sleep the rest of the night. Then, the next morning, I find a note tacked on my door from Duncan Hawk, telling me to meet him on Monday at his place. And to bring the sweetgrass."

Sarah paused. "So Ms. Psychologist, what do you make of that?"

Ruth hesitated. "It sounds as though you've stepped into quite the mystery, a delicious bit of synchronicity as we Jungians like to say."

"Synchronicity?"

"Synchronicity is the concept of 'meaningful coincidence.' Two apparently unrelated things happen that actually happen as they do for a reason, to get us to look at ourselves, see something we haven't before.

"In your case, you've got some connection with Indians, nightmares and the palsy in your left hand. And that Indian necklace. You had a fainting spell the first time you saw it in the museum and that's when your hand started clenching. Then you met an Indian man wearing the same necklace and your hand acted up again. He touched you and stopped the twitch. You have a nightmare about Nick and the hand problem comes back, followed by an invitation to meet the man who seems to be able to fix the twitching.

"These aren't random occurrences, Sarah. Something is going on here that you need to figure out. Your body doesn't lie. This clenching thing is your body's way of getting your attention. Find out what all these things have to do with each other and with you."

Sarah replied somewhat defensively. "Forget about the rich New York cowboy for a minute. What could an Indian and an old rawhide necklace possibly have to do with me?"

"I don't know. But it seems as though you're about to find out."

After a short lull, Sarah said softly, "There's more." She told her sister about her experience by the river, of her frightening daydream, and of the Indian with a knife who appeared out of nowhere.

"I can't get that moment, the way he looked at me, out of my head. I was so scared, I thought he was going to stab me. I couldn't get out of there fast enough. And yet another part of me didn't want to leave. How warped is that?"

"You really have stepped into something big here. When are you meeting with Duncan Hawk?"

"Monday morning. Do you think I should go?"

"Of course you should go. He sounds like the only one who can shed some light on the connection between the necklace and your hand twitching. He probably knows who the other man is too."

Sarah hadn't made that connection. "Damn, I hate it when you make so much sense," Sarah said. "I wish you could go with me. This should be happening to you, not me. This synchronicity stuff is vintage you."

"Well, it seems to me you were getting an inkling about this the first time you went to Colorado. I remember you telling me about your nightmares and weird vibes in the woods when you were dating Blue. Maybe that was a foreshadowing, of sorts."

"What do I do with that?" Sarah replied. "I was hoping you'd make me feel better about all this. Instead, you're freaking me out."

"Sorry, Sarah. There's something that you need to figure out. And it's going to keep showing up in any way it can to get your attention. You can't hide from it. And Duncan Hawk may hold the key."

The key to what, Sarah wondered. She was not at all eager to find out.

CHAPTER TWENTY

SARAH DROVE UP to Duncan Hawk's driveway ten minutes before eight on Monday morning, having barely slept the night before. She turned onto the dirt roadway and stopped, unsure about whether she really wanted to keep going, until she recalled her sister's encouragement from several nights before. Sarah put the truck in gear and wound her way through aspen groves until the drive ended in a large clearing.

Duncan Hawk sat in a rocking chair on the porch of a small wooden ranch house that was weathered but not neglected. A hitching post to one side stood empty, but fresh horse droppings indicated that it wasn't merely for show. Sarah parked next to the red Ford pickup on the opposite side of the yard. Duncan made no gesture of welcome or recognition; he just continued rocking slowly, a coffee mug in his hand.

Sarah hesitated. No one knew where she was. What if he wasn't as upstanding as Jessie Winde had claimed? She opened the truck door. *He doesn't look like an ax murderer. Besides I'm sure I can outrun him if I have to.*

"Good morning, Mr. Hawk," she called out, waving quickly. "I hope I'm not too early."

Silence greeted her in reply. Approaching the porch, she asked, "May I join you?"

He nodded.

She sat down in the second rocking chair. On the wooden table between them she noticed another coffee mug. "Coffee smells good. Is this cup for me?"

Again he nodded and kept rocking, his gaze fixed straight ahead.

"It's a beautiful morning. But it's quite chilly before the sun makes it over the mountains."

Duncan Hawk did not acknowledge her. Growing annoyed at the silent treatment, Sarah wondered if she'd done something to offend him somehow, but couldn't think of what that would be. After another attempt at polite conversation, she felt too uncomfortable to stay. "Sorry to have bothered you this morning, Mr. Hawk. I'll just be going."

"I was told that someone important was coming. I believe that person is you. Do you know why?"

Startled, Sarah said, "Excuse me?"

Duncan turned and looked at Sarah for the first time since her arrival. "I was told that someone important was coming. I believe that person is you. Do you know why?"

"I have no idea what you're talking about." Sarah resumed her place in the chair, looking quite puzzled.

Another silence hung over the porch like fog. Sarah resisted the urge to fill the void, waiting for her host to show some sign of life.

"Do you do medicine work?" He spoke in a soft, halting tone that resonated with purpose.

"I don't know what you mean by 'medicine work' but I'm sure I don't do it. Maybe you have me confused with my sister. She's a psychologist. Then again, you have no way of knowing I have a sister or what she does, so what am I saying?" Her discomfort was growing.

"All I know is that I fainted in the museum looking at some Indian artifacts. Then I developed this palsy in my left hand that seems to come and go. Then I ran into you at a war memorial, my hand started twitching and you made it stop. Then you disappeared. Somehow you found out where I'm staying, left a note on my door and here I am. Honestly, I have no friggin' idea what's going on!"

"You have a lot of passion, Sarah Cavanaugh," Duncan said. "I do not mean to make you so upset. I'm really not a bad guy." Then he laughed, bringing a warmth to his otherwise impenetrable face.

The tension in Sarah's shoulders and neck eased a bit as Duncan Hawk continued to smile at her, his dark brown eyes twinkling like a trickster who had just played a joke on someone. Sarah didn't know how to respond, so she just smiled back and drank some coffee.

"My people are the Yampa and Uncompahgre Utes. In times past, my people would return every year to the Flat Tops when the snows melted and Brother Bear called them back. They would travel along the rivers and across the meadows, enjoying the gifts of Creator. They lived here until the winter weather came. Then my people would leave the mountains until Bear called them back the next spring." He spoke with love and a touch of sadness in his voice, a sing-song quality that captivated Sarah and drew her into his story.

"My people are from these mountains." Duncan hesitated, his bright eyes dulling. "But we do not live here anymore. Only our Ancestors continue to walk here, lonely for my people to return and honor them. Do you know of my people? Do you know about the Utes?"

Sarah hesitated, unprepared for such a pointed question. "I'm afraid I'd never heard of the Utes before coming here to Meeker," Sarah confessed.

"I have been doing some reading...I picked up a few books at the museum in town...very sad what happened...the Meeker Massacre and all." Sarah couldn't detect any reaction in her host's face and didn't know what else to say, embarrassed by her ignorance.

Duncan nodded slowly. "Before we were forced to live on reservations, there were seven bands of Utes who traveled freely across Colorado, northern New Mexico and parts of Utah. The Capote and the Mouache bands lived in the southern mountains. Today they are known as the Southern Ute Tribe and live on the reservation in Durango. The Weeminuche lived in the west-central part of the state and now they are called the Ute Mountain Ute Tribe; their reservation is in Towac. The northern mountains were home to the Tabeguache, also known as the Uncompahgre, and the Yampa, or White River Utes. And the Uintah and the Grand River tribes lived in Utah.

"After the battle at Milk Creek, the northern Colorado bands were forced out of the mountains and made to live with the Utah bands. These bands are now known as the Northern Ute Tribe and live on the Uintah-Ouray Reservation in Utah."

"So then, you are from Utah?" Sarah asked, trying to keep all the names straight in her mind.

"I was born in Utah, yes." The weathered face of the Indian elder softened. "But my heart is here in the homeland of my Ancestors."

He paused and looked at his cup. "Do you like your coffee?"

"Yes. I like it strong." Sarah took a last sip. "It's so good, I'd like another cup, if there is any left."

An uncomfortable silence again fell on the porch. Duncan Hawk remained seated, looking out into the yard.

Duncan's erratic behavior confused her. Normal social chitchat seemed to turn the man to stone. *What am I doing wrong here?* Looking around, she spied a coffee maker on a cart near the door. The electrical cord ran into the house, causing the screen door to stand slightly ajar. Even though she was the guest here, Sarah found herself asking Duncan if he would like more coffee. He grinned broadly but did not look at her. He held up his cup. "Cream and sugar."

Duncan continued to grin as his bewildered visitor stood up and prepared the coffee. "We come from different cultures, Sarah. My people respect their elders in all things. The younger ones take care of the needs of the elders before their own. Keeping an elder's coffee cup filled is the most basic of courtesies."

So, that's what's going on, Sarah thought, as her face flushed. "I didn't know. I'm sorry." *Could this meeting get any more uncomfortable?*

He accepted the refilled mug without acknowledgement and waited for Sarah to sit down again before resuming his discourse.

"The Utes were the first Indians to acquire horses from the Spanish. The horse quickly became an important part of Ute culture. A man measured his worth by the number of horses he had and horse racing became a favorite pastime. My people became master horsemen. This made them all the more feared by our enemies, the Kiowa, Cheyenne, Arapaho, Comanche and Apache.

"In your books, I'm sure you read about how my people's lives changed once gold was discovered in the mountains of Colorado. This gold made white men crazy and dangerous. They eventually took all of our land, signing and breaking treaty after treaty." His voice trailed off. He sipped his coffee and sighed.

"There was a time when the United States government paid a bounty for the scalps of Indians...a bounty." The lilting sound of his voice remained constant as he spoke, though he stopped rocking in the chair. "Can you imagine?"

The inhumanity shocked her. She also felt politely chastised for things that she had no control over, atrocities perpetrated a long time ago.

"But that is not the story I want to tell you." He looked at Sarah. "The story I have to tell you is a story you will not find in any book."

Just then, they heard the steady percussive melody of trotting hooves on gravel. They looked down the driveway to see a dark-skinned man riding toward the house on a stunning bay stallion with black mane and tail. Slowing the animal as they approached the house, the man waved at Duncan, but frowned when he saw Sarah.

Her back stiffened as she recognized the face of the man she had collided with in the canyon the other day. Her heart beat faster as his rich brown eyes stared at her.

"I believe you two have met," Duncan said.

Moving closer to the porch, the younger man tipped his hat in greeting. "Not formally." He guided his horse to the hitching post, dismounted, gave him an affectionate scratch behind the ears and then strode onto the porch.

Sarah stood up and offered her hand. "I'm Sarah Cavanaugh. Nice to meet you under calmer circumstances."

"I'm Jason Little Bear," he said, shaking her hand, then turning his attention to Duncan. "Old Man, you never fail to surprise me. Just yesterday, I tell you about meeting a wild woman in the woods and now here she is, sitting in my chair."

Sarah couldn't tell from his inflection if Jason was irritated or pleased. But she backed away from the chair just in case.

"I amaze myself sometimes," Duncan replied, slyly.

"Are you two related?" Sarah asked.

"Jason is my nephew. He can be a bit testy at times, but don't let him scare you. He's okay."

"You're too kind, Old Man." Looking back at Sarah, Jason said, "Don't believe a word he says. He's just a crotchety old Indian who likes to impress pretty women."

Sarah smiled nervously and was relieved when Jason smiled in return. "Please have a seat," he said, pulling over another chair.

"I was just about to impress Sarah with a story," Duncan said. "You should hear it too."

Sarah adjusted her chair so she could see both men. Feeling uncomfortable with this second surprise encounter, Sarah wondered if Jason felt odd as well. She glanced over at him only to catch him looking at her. They both quickly looked away. Sarah stared at her hands in her lap. Jason stuck his hands in his pocket and looked over at his horse.

Sarah struggled against her impulse to study the man who had frightened her so in the canyon. Why was she attracted to him? He wasn't exactly handsome, and yet he was gripping somehow. He had that exotic appeal of someone from a different culture, but he wasn't debonair or even particularly friendly. There was little to recommend him, and yet she was fascinated and a bit intimidated.

Duncan started rocking gently and took a slow sip of coffee. Reverentially, he pulled out the old necklace that he wore beneath his shirt. A rawhide rope with yellow, red, black and white beads and a large bear claw hanging in the middle.

Sarah's throat tightened. She looked down at her left hand. It had tightened into a fist but it wasn't twitching.

Duncan took notice and asked, "Did you bring the sweetgrass?"

Sarah nodded.

"Hold it in your left hand. You will be fine."

Curious about the exchange, Jason watched as the blonde woman opened her purse and removed a large braid of sweetgrass, its soothing aroma permeating the air. She quickly brought it to her nose, inhaled briefly, then set it in her lap, her left hand securely wrapped around it.

"What's going on?" Jason asked.

"That is what we are trying to determine," Duncan replied.

"Could you be more specific?" Jason said.

Sarah stammered a bit. "Well, uh, I seem to have a reaction to this necklace and to one just like it in the museum. My hand gets this palsy. Your uncle says he knows how to make it stop. I know it sounds weird, but that's why I'm here."

Jason started to respond but Duncan cut him off. "The story that wants to be told is one that belongs to the bear claw necklace I wear. Both the story and the necklace were given to me by my grandmother. She told me that whoever cares for this necklace must also keep the story. Listen now to this story of Standing Bear and Red Fire Woman."

CHAPTER TWENTY-ONE

"RED FIRE WOMAN and Standing Bear lived during the time of great turmoil for the people; their story speaks of the last years the White River Utes lived in these mountains. Everything changed for my people when gold was discovered in the mountains. The year was 1859. As more white people moved onto Ute land, the government sent out Indian agents to help 'tame' the red man. They built an Indian agency in this part of Colorado in 1869.

"I give you the dates for reference, but when my grandmother first told me this story, she called this time The Winter of Broken Promises.

"The Winter of Broken Promises was very hard on the Utes living near the White River Indian Agency. They had not stored enough food for the long winter months. Too many of them believed the promise that the white man's government would send flour, sugar and meat on a great Iron Horse. But provisions never came that winter. Temperatures dropped so low, they say that a man's breath would freeze and fall to the ground as tiny pieces of ice. Terrible winds blew through everyone's soul and they suffered. People starved.

"So it was with great gratitude that they welcomed the Time of Spring Moon When Bear Awakes. The mountains once again came alive, offering the people food, hides and medicines.

"She first came to the Agency during the Time of Spring Moon. In her world, the year was 1871. Her people had named her Rebecca. She was 15 years old and had long, red hair and green eyes.

"Rebecca worked for the new Indian Agent who also had arrived that spring. His name was Littlefield. Unlike those who would come after him, Littlefield was a man of his word. He helped the Utes trade with the white man. He sent their elk and deer hides on the Iron Horse, the new railroad, for auction in Omaha and Chicago. Ute women were renowned for making the most soft and beautifully tanned hides in the western territories. When they came to the Indian Agency, they negotiated their trades with Rebecca. She always gave them a fair exchange. The people prospered for a time with this trade and their herds of ponies grew. Eventually, the women invited Rebecca into their social circles as one of their sisters.

"Rebecca did not talk much about her life before coming to the White River. All she shared with the women was that her mother was married to an officer stationed at Fort Steele in Wyoming. Rebecca had left the fort because of a soldier who had fallen in love with her. But she did not love him. This made the soldier very angry. He threatened her so she decided to leave the fort for her own protection. She missed her mother very much, but could not visit her as long as that soldier was there. That is all she spoke of her family. The Ute women found her story hard to believe. You see, in Ute culture, a woman owns the tepee. She would never leave her home or her mother because of a man. But they did not rebuke her. They let her be, trusting that Creator takes care of all things.

"The eldest woman healer in the tribe was named White Willow Laughing. She saw that Rebecca had the gift for listening to the plants and the animals. She began teaching her the traditional way of healing with herbs and other plants.

"At this time, Rebecca caught the attention of several young men who courted her. But when Standing Bear returned to the village after much time away, she soon lost her heart to him.

"Standing Bear was the son of White Willow Laughing. He was respected in the tribe because of a powerful gift given to him by Creator. He was the one who dreamed of Bear. Through these dreams, Creator called him to lead the oldest sacred ceremony of the Ute people—the Bear Dance.

"Bear is a powerful relative of the Ute people; we say Bear is our father's sister. We call ourselves the Bear People. Back at that time, both grizzly bears and black bears lived in these mountains. Every spring, when the first Thunder spoke in the sky, the Utes held a Bear Dance ceremony. This was their way of honoring Bear and of asking permission to enter the mountains, to share the abundance of the land after the snows had passed.

"This ceremony was given to the people many, many years ago after a young man went into the mountains in the late fall. He was caught by the winter snows, and a female grizzly bear allowed him to stay with her in her den. When spring returned and they came out of their deep sleep, the female grizzly taught the man how the bears dance with the oak tree...moving forward and backward, standing upright on their back legs. Then the bear told the man to teach this dance to his people. She instructed them to do this dance every spring, when they heard the first claps of thunder. Together the sounds of thunder and of the people dancing would help to wake the bears from their long sleep.

"So the man came back to his people and showed them all that the female grizzly had taught him."

Duncan Hawk paused to slowly sip his coffee. Then he began to sing in a low, growly tone, softly at first, then with more enthusiasm.

"You like that song, Sarah?" he asked.

"I'm not really sure," she said. "It's like nothing I've ever heard before. What kind of song is that?"

"That's a Bear Dance song. But it needs the morache, the instrument that really drives the song. Special songs, special instruments, only for the Bear Dance."

Jason offered more explanation. "The morache is a rasp made of notched wood. The musicians rest the rasps on top of a resonating chamber made of rawhide stretched across a hole in the ground. They run deer shinbones over the rasps to make music like a bear scratching against a tree. It's a sound unlike anything you've heard before."

"This is a dance Sarah would like, I think," Duncan said with a mischievous smile.

"Why is that?" she replied.

"Because the woman chooses the man she wants to dance with. And he cannot refuse her!"

Sarah glanced quickly at Jason and blushed when she caught his gaze.

"It is too late in the season to have the Bear Dance, but maybe I will show you the steps, so you can practice and be ready to pick your man next spring. You will need to have strong legs and comfortable shoes.

The dance lasts four days and on the last night, the dancing keeps going until someone falls down from exhaustion. It is a competition between the men and the women," Duncan said. "But, now I forget myself and the story. I will continue.

"Standing Bear made the Bear Dance happen for his people. At the end of the ceremony, he would offer healings to anyone in need. Then the people feasted.

"Standing Bear's dreams showed him when and where to hold the Bear Dance every year. They also told him how to hunt the bear to be honored. He had to follow the dream exactly. You see, through the dream, this bear agreed to give his life for the people. Killing the bear with respect, in a good way, brought the blessings of Bear to the Utes. All parts of the animal were ceremoniously honored, prepared and used.

"Standing Bear always pleased the Bear People and for this was much loved by his tribe. It did not take him long to fall in love with Rebecca. He courted her in the traditional way. He serenaded her with his cedar flute and seduced her with his sweet music. Within the year, Rebecca moved into White Willow Laughing's tepee as Standing Bear's wife. At that time, Rebecca was given the new name of Red Fire Woman because of the color of her hair.

"As a sign of his love, Standing Bear gave Red Fire Woman a bear claw necklace, the same necklace that has been entrusted to me. Standing Bear wore a similar one, also with a bear claw. He had made these two necklaces several years before when he had killed his first grizzly bear.

"Red Fire Woman followed the traditions and customs of a Ute woman. She learned how to set up and take down the tepee, how to gather food from the land, how to dress out the animals hunters brought home, and how to cook and preserve the meat. She learned how to tan leather, but her pelts never achieved the softness of those worked by White Willow Laughing and the other women. But White Willow Laughing did not concern herself with this. She knew her daughter-in-law's gifts lay in her connection to animals and plants.

"And so she focused on guiding Red Fire Woman in the healing ways. Much of her teachings took place in the menstrual hut. This is a place where women at the time of bleeding every month spent their days separated from the rest of the tribe. A woman at this time was very powerful; her menstrual blood could weaken men, especially the medicine men. Men were instructed to avoid women during this time and to avoid touching anything they handled or eating any food they prepared. The presence of a menstruating woman would disrupt sacred ceremonies. So women lived in seclusion during their bleeding time. White Willow Laughing attended to her daughter-in-law in the menstrual hut and mentored her in the ways of spirit and healing.

"My grandmother, at that time a young girl, also was learning healing ways from White Willow Laughing. She spent much time with both women. She had never seen a white woman before, but it did not matter to my grandmother. She came to love Red Fire Woman.

"Most of the people in the tribe looked past her heritage and accepted her as one of their own. Red Fire Woman lived as a Ute, so therefore she was a Ute. But some people did not approve of Standing Bear marrying a white woman. They wanted nothing to do with white people who continued to steal Ute land and spread disease. A few taunted Standing Bear for his choice in a wife.

"There was another who did not approve of this marriage—the soldier from Wyoming who was obsessed with Rebecca. Several times he traveled to the Indian Agency from Fort Steele, which was a three-day ride, looking for her. She did not want to see him and the Utes protected her. They pretended not to understand the soldier or sent him looking in wrong places. Each time he left angry, swearing that he would return and take her back with him. After two years, the soldier stopped coming and Red Fire Woman thought he had finally forgotten her. She came to find, however, that she was terribly mistaken."

Duncan paused, picked up his coffee cup, saw that it was empty and put it back down on the table with a grumble. "More coffee, Old Man?" Jason asked as he rose from his chair.

Sarah jumped up. "Can I help?" Jason nodded and the two walked into the house, taking the empty coffee maker with them.

Duncan noticed both the tension and attraction between the two. *She is quite pretty,* he thought, *especially her eyes. Jason obviously thinks so too.*

Duncan stood up and stretched, grateful to get some blood circulating in his legs. Too much sitting made his joints ache. He looked up at the billowy white clouds riding on the breeze and remembered back to the time over thirty years ago, when he had told this story to Jessie, hoping to impress her. It had done more than that. The story seemed to connect

Duncan to Jessie somehow and had ignited a passion that had been growing between them. He had trusted her with this sacred story, but then she had betrayed that trust and everything had changed. Was he making another mistake all these years later by telling the story to Sarah? Before he could contemplate the question further, Jason and Sarah returned to the porch with some cookies as well as coffee.

"We thought the storyteller might be getting hungry," Sarah said, handing him a plate.

Duncan grinned. "If you are trying to keep my energy up, I guess that means you want to hear more of the story." After savoring his snack, he continued with the tale.

CHAPTER TWENTY-TWO

"RED FIRE WOMAN DID her doctoring with the help of plants and herbs. Standing Bear worked his healing ways through ceremonies, including the sweat lodge. Unfortunately, the traditional medicine ways could do nothing against the diseases brought by the white man. The old teachings could not help the healers with small pox, tuberculosis, venereal disease or addiction to alcohol.

"Standing Bear and Red Fire Woman realized that they needed to bring a strong, new medicine to the tribe. So they traveled into the mountains, to the valley we now call Turkey Tail Creek, a place they visited every summer to gather medicinal plants and to watch the female grizzly that lived there. She was their teacher in the ways of spiritual doctoring. The summer before, she had showed Standing Bear her cave. This is where Standing Bear came to ask for vision and guidance.

"While Red Fire Woman set up a small camp and kept a fire burning to give him strength, Standing Bear fasted for three days and three nights inside the cave. During that time a female grizzly bear appeared in a vision and showed him a new way to run his sweat lodge, a way of doctoring that would work only for him, to be used only for the healing of the new diseases.

"The vision disturbed Standing Bear so much that he could not speak of it for many weeks after they returned. He knew his people would never accept this ceremony. It violated one of their basic beliefs. He did not know if he could do what Spirit asked of him. And yet as a healer, he could not ignore this vision; he had to trust it and walk through his fear.

"Later that summer, Standing Bear's favorite cousin, Yellow Eagle, returned to the White River Valley after more than a year's time. Yellow Eagle had been traveling with different Ute bands in the south and the east, seeing how white men were treating the people. His experiences had hardened him against the white man; his heart was full of fear and hate. He knew they could not trust the leaders in Washington to honor any agreements or to live in peace with the Utes.

"Yellow Eagle came back to warn his people about the dangers. He also had developed an addiction to whiskey. Yellow Eagle was an excellent hunter and proven warrior, yet he did not have the strength to rid himself of the craving. So he came to Standing Bear with a tobacco offering and a beautiful rug woven by the Navaho. He gave these things to Standing Bear and asked for a healing.

"Standing Bear could not refuse. He loved Yellow Eagle as a brother; they had grown up together. They had killed their first buffalo on the same hunt and had ridden into battle side by side against the Sioux. The time had come for Standing Bear to fulfill his vision. He would prepare the sweat lodge as Grizzly had shown him. He told Yellow Eagle to return in four days and that he must come alone.

"Red Fire Woman came into the tepee as Yellow Eagle was preparing to leave. At one time he would have greeted her with affection. But now he could barely look at her. His time among the whites had hardened him against her. Yellow Eagle made it clear that he saw her now as a white woman who could not be trusted rather than the wife of his cousin.

"Red Fire Woman hoped that, given time, Yellow Eagle would be her friend once again. But after she heard what Standing Bear needed her to do for the healing ceremony, she realized that might never be possible. Yellow Eagle held fast to the traditional ways. If he discovered the secret of the ceremony, he might feel he had been cursed instead of cured. He would be justified in killing them both for using such a medicine.

"Standing Bear told her that the ceremony was given to him by Spirit, so if they did it as he was shown, it would not bring harm. He also told her how to protect the secret so no one would find out. If the People did not know, they would have no reason to fear the healing."

Duncan paused his narration and looked over at Sarah. Her left hand clutched the braid of sweetgrass, and it trembled slightly. She caught his gaze and answered the question in his eyes. "I'm okay."

He nodded and continued on.

"This story does not reveal the secret of Standing Bear's sweat lodge. All we are told is that after the ceremony, Yellow Eagle no longer craved the firewater that made him crazy.

"The secrecy of the ceremony raised suspicions among those who did not approve of Red Fire Woman, but distrust soon turned into gratitude as loved ones returned from the sweat lodge without sign of the white man's illnesses.

"Standing Bear began these healings in the summer of 1876. That year Crazy Horse defeated Custer at the Little Big Horn. That same year the white man drew boundaries around Ute land; they called it 'Colorado' and their government declared it a state.

"During the winter of that year, once again, the White River Utes almost starved. Supplies promised by the white man's government never arrived. The food lay rotting in a warehouse in Wyoming because one of the government contractors had not paid his bill. Extreme hunger forced Standing Bear's people to travel off the newly defined reservation lands and move into southern Wyoming to hunt.

"The people suffered, and Standing Bear worried that the hard times his tribe faced were punishment for using the new sweat lodge ceremony. Red Fire Woman argued with him that Spirit would not give him a gift and then punish him for sharing it. And on most days, he believed her.

"Then one morning, when frigid winds ripped through even the thickest buffalo hides and hunger had weakened children into numbness, Yellow Eagle came to Standing Bear with a troubling vision. In his dream, Yellow Eagle saw people entering Standing Bear's sweat lodge. Yellow Eagle followed them in. But he found no one inside. In front of him were two doors. He crawled over to the first one and looked through. He saw his people at the Bear Dance. Women and men lined up opposite each other, stepping forward and back, forward and back, in time to the growling music of the morache. Then the cadence slowed, the singing changed to wailing. The dancers stopped and looked in disbelief. The musicians had turned into soldiers who were commanding them to keep dancing. Yellow Eagle watched as the people formed a long line and danced out of the oak arena and into the desert. The soldiers would not let them stop. The people finally fell down in the dust, exhausted.

"Yellow Eagle pulled back from the door, unable to watch the suffering and humiliation. Then he looked into the second door. There he saw Red Fire Woman sitting by a small fire. She smiled and invited him to join her. He came near the fire, but did not sit down. As he watched the flame, he noticed something flowing towards him from the fire pit. It looked like muddy water. He looked closer and realized it was blood running out of the fire. Horrified, he jumped out of the way. He heard Red Fire Woman laughing.

"Yellow Eagle ran back through the door and into the sweat lodge, which was now totally dark and full of searing steam. He woke from the dream before he could find his way out.

"Standing Bear talked to his cousin about this dream for many hours. Yellow Eagle believed that the vision was warning them about Red Fire Woman, that because of her, the people's blood would flow. She would bring soldiers who would lead them to their deaths. Hard as he tried, Standing Bear could not help his cousin see it differently. He could not convince him that the evil in the dream was actually the soldiers and the white man's illness, not the woman healer. His message fell on deaf ears. Yellow Eagle's heart had already hardened against Red Fire Woman. She was not Ute; she was white. And the white man was the enemy.

"Yellow Eagle reminded Standing Bear that the year Red Fire Woman had come to live with the Utes, they had suffered through a hard winter and the government had sent very little food. Now this year, the government was trying to starve them again. Yellow Eagle believed that this was not coincidence. He told Standing Bear to leave her. When Standing Bear refused, his cousin begged him to at least keep her away from ceremonies. White people should not know Ute ways, he argued.

"Standing Bear told his cousin he needed time to consider all that had been said. Before Yellow Eagle left, the two men smoked the Pipe together in silence. They did this to signify that they had both spoken the truth as they saw it, that they loved each other and respected each other.

"Troubled by his cousin's fears, Standing Bear struggled with what he should do. And then, Red Fire Woman had a miscarriage. Even though she had been only two months pregnant, she grew weak from loss of blood. Standing Bear could not risk any animosity against her when she was so sick. He decided to do as Yellow Eagle requested, at least until the next Bear Dance.

"By spring, Red Fire Woman had recovered her strength enough to join Standing Bear and a group of elders on a trip to the hot sulfur springs, in what is now called Glenwood Springs. The springs and caves were sacred; their hot waters brought healing and comfort.

"When the travelers reached the springs, soldiers blocked their path. They said the springs were for white visitors only. Standing Bear told them that Creator had given these healing waters to all people; soldiers could not deny them access. But the soldiers stood firm. They replied that the whites would not come if they had to share it with Indians. The Utes would have to leave.

"The warriors were outraged. Their ponies pranced nervously as the men moved in front of the women and elders. One of the soldiers called for the captain, then lifted his rifle in warning.

"Red Fire Woman pushed through the horses and stood at Standing Bear's side. She understood why Yellow Eagle hated the white man and why he distrusted her. She stood there trembling with fury and shame. She wanted to defy this captain somehow and defend the honor of her people. But when the captain stepped into view, she immediately regretted her brashness. Standing before her was the soldier who had desired her, the soldier she still feared.

"The captain recognized her immediately, but did not speak to her. His black eyes bore into her, never wavering from her frightened face as he spoke to Standing Bear. The captain said he would let the Indians use the hot springs if they would give him this white woman in exchange.

"Standing Bear lifted Red Fire Woman onto his horse. He told the soldier this woman was his wife. She was no slave. Then he asked Creator to curse these men who insulted them.

"Some of the warriors wanted to fight the soldiers but Standing Bear did not want to risk the lives of the elders who traveled with them. The soldiers already had guns drawn; they did not. The warrior in him wanted to smash the captain's face with his hatchet, but the healer in him ordered his people to leave without incident.

"The captain threatened to hunt them down and take the white woman by force, but Standing Bear did not give her up. Red Fire Woman spat on the ground and said she would never go with him.

"The captain replied with such fury that his curse still haunts this land.

"'I will make you regret this day, Rebecca. I swear I will destroy all that you love.' His voice became a hiss. 'Then I will destroy you!'"

CHAPTER TWENTY-THREE

SARAH FELT A CHILL ripple along her spine and a pain shoot up her forearm. Her first three fingers of her left hand contracted into a fist, pressing nails into flesh. She tried to shake out the hand, but the digits would not release.

"Are you okay?" Jason asked.

"I don't know," Sarah replied with an edge to her voice. Embarrassed by her actions, she covered her left hand with her right and held them tightly in her lap. She turned to look at Duncan with pleading eyes. "Why does this keep happening to me?"

"Where is the sweetgrass?" the elder asked quietly.

Sarah looked around quickly and spotted it on the floor near her chair. "I must have dropped it." She picked it up with her right hand and held it over her left. But the spasm did not let up.

Duncan removed his bear claw necklace and handed it to her. She hesitated, afraid to touch it.

"Take it," he insisted. "Put it on."

She had a sense that if she took the necklace, there would be irrevocable consequences. She wanted to refuse, but found herself reaching for it anyway. Once around her neck, the simple rawhide jewelry felt light in weight and yet heavy with old emotions from lifetimes ago. The first three fingers of her left hand closed around the bear claw.

"I'm so confused," she whispered.

Duncan nodded. His instincts had been correct. "This is not a gift. It is not yours to keep. But I want you to wear it until I finish the story."

He sat back in the chair and started to rock gently. He closed his eyes for a long time before he spoke again.

"When Standing Bear and his party returned to camp, he called a council meeting to discuss what had taken place at the sacred springs. Red Fire Woman was asked to tell them all she knew of this soldier.

"She told them his name was Ethan Amory. He was the solder who had come looking for her when she first arrived at White River. This man married her mother when Red Fire Woman was thirteen years old. Her mother was quite beautiful. Amory liked to surround himself with beautiful things. But he did not love her mother; he only wanted to possess her like a fine buffalo robe.

"Red Fire Woman did not want to leave her mother, so she traveled to the fort in Wyoming when the captain was transferred there. He became obsessed with Red Fire Woman, but she refused him. He became more insistent. He began threatening her. She knew she had to leave and wanted her mother to go with her. But her mother did not believe that the captain would be unfaithful to her. She called her daughter a liar. So, Red Fire Woman left alone, hiding in a supply wagon that was going to the Indian Agency in the White River Valley.

"Red Fire Woman said she believed the captain to be a dangerous man. She did not want any harm to come to the tribe because of her. The only way she knew to protect them was to leave.

"The council sat in silence for a long time, contemplating what Red Fire Woman had told them. They smoked the Pipe, asking Creator to help them see the truth.

"Yellow Eagle was the first to speak. He believed that the only way to keep the people safe was for Red Fire Woman to go back to her people. He warned that angry white soldiers were not warriors with honor. Remember the Sand Creek Massacre. The army pretended to talk peace with the warriors of the Cheyenne and Arapaho while they were butchering the women and children left unprotected in camp. Yellow Eagle told them about his vision. He believed it was warning them that Ethan Amory would bring such a massacre to the tribe if Red Fire Woman remained with them.

"Standing Bear spoke in her defense. He insisted that the people would never give one of their own to any soldier or warrior in exchange for peace. They defended their women and children.

"Yellow Eagle argued that she was not Ute and not worthy of their protection. Before Standing Bear could reply, the most respected medicine man in the tribe spoke. His name was Canavish. He was wise and so his words have been passed down with this story. He said, 'Yellow Eagle, I share your concern. You do well to remind us of massacres and the lack of honor in the white man's government. And Standing Bear also speaks true; we do not trade our people for peace. Red Fire Woman did not choose her mother or her father or her white ancestors. But she has chosen to live as a Ute woman. She honors our ways, she honors her medicine, she shares her gifts with all of us. Some of our brothers at this council have the blood of other tribes flowing through them. And yet, they live as Utes. We do not see them differently. We are all one tribe. Do not see Red Fire Woman any differently than you see these brothers.'

"Discussion continued long into the night until everyone in the council had spoken. The sun was rising when a final decision was reached. Red Fire Woman would stay with the people. Scouts would be sent out to watch for the soldiers. Tribal members would be warned to stay away from the hot springs.

"Ethan Amory did not come that summer. But the army did recruit Ute warriors to help the white man's government fight the Sioux. The Sioux were long-time enemies of the Utes. Some leaders warned against it, especially Yellow Eagle, but many young men were so restless and frustrated that they longed to fight.

"The warriors came back from the campaign with venereal disease and addiction to alcohol. Standing Bear and Red Fire Woman were forced to renew their sweat lodge ceremonies, despite Yellow Eagle's objections. The ceremony continued to heal.

"Even though the people fought with the white army against the Sioux, the government did not send enough food and supplies that winter. Again the people suffered.

"The next spring, in the year 1878, a new Indian Agent arrived. His name was Nathaniel Meeker. At first, he seemed to make life better for the people. Meeker got supplies and distributed them on time. He relocated the Indian Agency farther west and lower on the river where the winters were not so harsh.

"Meeker wanted the Utes to give up their lives as hunters and become farmers. He spent much of the year building a farm. Some of the people, including Canavish, showed some interest in farming, but most continued to hunt in the mountains.

"Yellow Eagle and others complained that Meeker was taking good meadow lands for his farm that the people needed for grazing their horses. But the elders said nothing at that time. Meeker did not appear to be a threat at first. His daughter Josephine spent much time with the children and caught the attention of more than one lovesick young man. Josephine and her father came to all of the horse races that year. Some took this as a good sign that Meeker understood how important horses were to men and how much all of the people enjoyed friendly competition, a serious wager and any game that made them laugh."

"Really?" Sarah interrupted.

Duncan smiled. "Are you surprised that Indian people know how to have a good time?"

"Yes, ah no, well, yes, actually," she said. "I actually hadn't thought about it much until now. But since you mention it, Indians always look so serious in the old pictures. I never saw any signs of games or gambling. So, no, I guess, it's not the image I have of Indians."

"Then a word of caution," Jason said. "Never make a wager with Old Man. He rarely loses a bet and I've never caught him cheating!"

"Duly noted," Sara replied, her mood lighter than a few minutes before. Her hand had relaxed completely, which let her relax a bit as well. "Are you a good game player too?" she asked Jason, a bit more flirtatiously than she had intended.

He replied in kind with a grin Sarah found enticing, "Depends on the game." Jason stood up and went into the house. He came back out with the coffee pot and filled his uncle's cup, smiled briefly at Sarah and then offered her a refresher. Sarah gladly accepted, even though she had barely touched hers. She was too engrossed in the story.

Once Jason sat back down, Duncan continued.

"Meeker did understand how much the Utes valued their horses, but he saw this as an obstacle to his plan of converting the people into farmers. He decided he must do whatever he could to get them to abandon their horses. He was stubborn and self-righteous.

"But he did not reveal the true nature of his plans until the next spring. So the people tolerated him. Some found his farming efforts more humorous than dangerous, but others distrusted everything about him.

"That summer, Yellow Eagle, Standing Bear and several other men traveled into the mountains with Canavish, the medicine elder, to seek a vision. On the third day of their fast, the men watched as the moon completely blocked out the sun. The medicine elder said it foretold of dark times for the people and for the men seeking visions. It took less than a year for Canavish's prophecy to unfold.

"Winter passed without incident. Red Fire Woman became pregnant again, but continued to go to the menstrual hut for the first three months. She did not want to tell Standing Bear until she felt confident she would not miscarry again. The women kept her secret. White Willow Laughing doctored her with herbs to strengthen her and the baby.

"Red Fire Woman did not miscarry. She finally shared the news of her pregnancy with her husband the night before he left to hunt the bear for the Bear Dance ceremony.

"The joy and promise of a baby filled his heart as he departed at sunrise to fulfill his obligation. He hunted for several days but no bear presented itself to him. For the first time, Standing Bear returned without a bear to bless the ceremony. The people held the dance anyway, because they needed to honor Bear to ensure safe travel into the mountains to hunt and gather food.

"But the dark times the sun and moon predicted had begun. It rained only once that spring. It did not rain at all after that. By July, hundreds of forest fires were burning across the mountains. Stories in the newspapers blamed the Utes, claiming they were deliberately setting the fires. They printed the headline, 'The Utes Must Go! The Utes Must Go!'

"News of this traveled back to the people on the White River. They were angry. Their distrust and fear of Meeker grew. Even Canavish, who had maintained a friendly relationship with the Indian agent, argued with him over land he was taking away from the horses for his farm.

"Finally, Meeker plowed up one of the best meadows in the valley. He told Canavish that the medicine elder had too many ponies and should kill them, so the cattle would have enough grass. Canavish exploded with rage and threw Meeker against a wall. Meeker responded by sending for troops from Wyoming. These events led to the battle at Milk Creek."

Duncan paused in his story telling and gently rocked in his chair. Sarah finally asked, "Milk Creek, that's where the Thornburg Memorial is, right? The place where I met you?"

He nodded. "You looked like you'd seen a ghost. I have never seen a lady jump like you did."

"What did you expect?" Sarah replied. "You popped out of nowhere!"

"I'm pretty dark skinned to be a ghost; maybe you thought I was the devil." He grinned, but only briefly. "There are too many ghosts in that place, too many...."

"How did you know I'd be there? Did your spirits tell you?"

"In a matter of speaking," Duncan said, but offered nothing more.

"Come on, Old Man, don't tease her," Jason said. The men exchanged glances.

"Your museum friend saw me in town and told me about you."

"Why didn't you say that before?" Sarah was surprised at how disappointed she felt with his practical answer.

"Old Man has a good bit of coyote in him," Jason said.

"What does that mean?" Sarah hoped it didn't mean he ate coyotes.

"Coyote is the trickster. He makes us think reality is one way when it's really another. Ultimately, Coyote teaches us to trust ourselves, but the lessons can be a bit challenging," Jason said. "That's why you've got to watch Old Man. He can be tricky."

"And now," Duncan interrupted, "this old coyote has a story to finish. The full telling of this battle and the events at the Indian Agency is best saved for another time. For this story, you need to know that Standing Bear and Yellow Eagle fought side by side and came away unharmed.

"Ethan Amory also fought in that battle. He too survived. But he did not return with his troops to Wyoming. He went looking for the woman he knew as Rebecca. Standing Bear had already sent word, through my grandmother, to hide Red Fire Woman in the mountains until he came for her. He had to attend to the wounded and the dead on the battlefield and could not intercept the captain.

"When Amory could not find her in the camp, he flew into a rage and demanded to know where she had gone. No one, including my grandmother, told him anything. A couple of young boys started taunting him, not realizing how crazy he was. Amory grabbed one of the boys and drew a pistol. He threatened to kill this boy unless someone took him to Rebecca. Yellow Eagle told Amory he would help him if he let the boy go. But the captain demanded that the boy come with them. Only when he found Rebecca would he give the boy back to Yellow Eagle. Yellow Eagle had no choice but to agree.

"He led the small group of soldiers east along the river and was never seen again. When Standing Bear learned of these events the next day, he took his two fastest horses and went to rescue Red Fire Woman. But he too was never seen again.

"Several days later, the young boy returned to camp. He told how Yellow Eagle had helped them find where Red Fire Woman was hiding and how the soldiers had captured her. Standing Bear had come in the middle of the night and set her free. But the soldiers soon discovered her missing and pursued them. The young boy was able to run away at that time. He did not know what had taken place after that.

"Two days after the boy had come back to camp, Amory returned to the Agency with Red Fire Woman as his prisoner. Two of his soldiers had been killed in the mountains. For several days, the captain kept Red Fire Woman locked up. White Willow Laughing demanded to see her, but the captain denied her and threatened to kill her if she tried. But my grandmother was able to sneak in once. She found Red Fire Woman severely beaten and barely alive. Two fingers on her left hand had been cut off. Red Fire Woman was so sick with fever that she could not tell my grandmother what had happened to Standing Bear.

"Soon after that, Amory took Red Fire Woman back to Wyoming with him. White Willow Laughing feared that she would die before ever reaching the fort. My grandmother would not know the fate of her friend for many years.

"Several months after the battle at Milk Creek, a band of Ute warriors searched the valley where they believed Red Fire Woman had been captured. They found the remains of a large grizzly bear. She had been skinned, a bullet in her skull. They also found two graves but would not open them to see who was buried beneath the stones. It is forbidden to disturb a burial site. The spirit of the dead will haunt you. The warriors believed that these were the graves of their brothers, Standing Bear and Yellow Eagle. But who had buried them still remains a mystery. The soldiers would not have done it. They never showed our people that kind of respect.

"When the warriors returned and shared what they had found, the people mourned the loss of Grizzly Bear. They mourned the loss of

Standing Bear, the Man Who Dreamed of Bear, and Yellow Eagle. They mourned the loss of their way of life. And many mourned the loss of Red Fire Woman too.

"Two years after the battle, the people were forced at gunpoint to leave their home in the mountains, just as Yellow Eagle had seen in his vision. The white man's soldiers made them walk many miles to the reservation in the Utah desert. Most of the people never saw their beloved mountains again.

"My grandmother told me that Red Fire Woman did return, years later. She lived in the cave of the grizzly bear and made the mountains her home. My grandmother would visit her when she could, but was never able to convince her to come back to the reservation."

"How terrible," Sarah said. "How did she survive out there all alone?"

Duncan gazed at the clouds. "I do not know. That is the end of the story that was given to me."

Fidgeting in her chair, she looked down at her left hand that gripped the bear claw firmly with her thumb and first two fingers. Her ring finger and pinky felt numb and useless. Then her stomach flipped as she recalled Duncan's narrative about Red Fire Woman's condition.

"Which two fingers were cut off?"

"I think you know the answer," Duncan replied.

Tears welled up in her eyes as she shook her head repeatedly in disbelief. She pulled the necklace over her head, but her fingers would not release the claw still in her grip. "Take this away from me. I don't want to have anything to do with it!" Duncan did not move.

Desperately, she looked at Jason for help, but he was lost in his own thoughts, staring into the woods.

She got up and stood in front of Duncan, her left hand outstretched. "Help me, please."

Slowly, he touched her hand and the fingers released. He gently picked up the necklace and placed it around his neck. Sarah sighed in relief once he tucked it beneath his shirt.

"Thank you for the story and for the coffee. But I really must be going." Sarah stumbled down the porch steps as she hurried to her truck. She prayed she wouldn't fall, her knees felt so weak.

Shaking, Sarah put the key in the ignition, but the truck would not start. Several times she turned the key and pumped the accelerator. The engine would not cooperate.

"You forgot this." Duncan's face in the window startled her. He handed her the strand of sweetgrass. As the soothing aroma filled the cab, she hung her head and started to cry.

CHAPTER TWENTY-FOUR

NICK STOOD IN FRONT of his magnificent horse arena and smiled to himself. Construction was almost complete; just some custom trim carpentry left to do inside and it would be ready for the private opening he had planned in September. He would invite some prominent horse breeders, as he had told his father. But he was also planning to invite potential investors who'd be interested in something more profitable than horses—million-dollar timeshares.

Nick's long-term plan was to create an elite get-away for the ultra rich who had a passion for horses. A select number of cabins would keep both demand and prices high. But for the time being, Nick would need to keep that part of the planning to himself. He had been more than fortunate in finding the section in the local building ordinance that allowed him to construct this arena without a permit. He wouldn't be that lucky again when it came time to build timeshare cabins on the property. That would raise all kinds of red flags, beginning with Hollis.

His father had no interest in exploring the development potential in this Colorado valley and Nick had failed to convince him otherwise. So had Nick's mother years ago when his parents first decided to buy a ranch in this valley. She had recognized that the real money to be made here was in development, not conservation. But his father seemed to fancy himself a cowboy and saw the ranch as a personal getaway. He felt the same way about the other properties he'd acquired over the years, including the Double R. Nick knew his father would never change.

What would Mother think of what I've built here? Nick wondered.

He liked to imagine her with a smile, telling him what a great job he'd done. But smiling had never come naturally for his mother. Neither had compliments or encouragement. An extremely driven and successful businesswoman, she had held expectations that often seemed impossible for Nick to achieve, so at a young age, he'd decided that it was easier to work at disappointing her. It was something he'd become quite good at.

Looking out across the grassy meadows behind the horse arena, Nick thought back to that time with a mixture of regret and resentment. After college, rather than going into business with his father, he had perfected his persona as an edgy playboy with a constantly revolving cadre of exotic women on his arm and in his bed. But all that had changed after a weekend of excessive partying landed him in the hospital with alcohol poisoning. He had almost died, and it had scared him enough that he took the advice from counselors in rehab to find something more worthwhile in life to pursue.

He had chosen real estate. Wanting to surprise his mother, he kept his ambitions a secret until he'd secured his real estate license, which happened a week before his twenty-fifth birthday. He was going to make the announcement at his party as soon as his mother arrived. But she had died in a car crash that night before he had had a chance to tell her. The next day, he burned the license and fell into a depression that dragged on for several years, until his father insisted that he come spend a summer in Colorado. One night, his father's ranch manager shared a dream he had of creating a horse training facility in the valley. Something about the idea resonated with Nick and he adopted it as his own.

Nick recalled the conversation he'd had with the ranch manager last week. He had told Nick how impressed he was with the horse arena and with how quickly he'd been able to get it built. Nick realized that he had his mother to thank for that, having gleaned a lot from being around her, especially with respect to negotiating and finding ways around building regulations and codes.

His mother's influence had served him well, and he acknowledged that he'd have to rely on it again. He needed to figure out whom he could influence or intimidate in the county government to minimize interference with his progress.

One thing he knew for sure: Jessie Winde from the planning committee would not be one of them. He was dreading this meeting with her. Even though the breeding barns and equipment sheds weren't part of the original plan, he hoped the committee would have no objection since they were considered agricultural buildings. Still, he sensed that this meeting with Jessie would be as unpleasant as previous encounters. She made no attempt to disguise her outrage at his addition to the valley.

Hearing the crunch of tires on gravel, he turned toward the road as two pickup trucks pulled into the property and parked next to his vehicle. He watched as the dark-haired man and the white-haired woman walked across the grass toward him. He recognized the private lands biologist that his father was so fond of. *What is he doing here?* Nick leaned up against the fence, letting them come to him.

"Hello, Mr. Tremaine, I'm Patrick Landwehr with the U.S. Fish and Wildlife Service," the man said, extending his hand. "I believe you already know Ms. Jessie Winde of the Planning Committee."

Nick shook Patrick's hand and tipped his hat to Jessie, who stared coldly in return. She made him feel like a little kid on his first day of school. He quickly looked back at the federal agent, hoping to finish with these two as quickly as possible.

"I hope you don't mind my barging in on your meeting with Ms. Jessie," Patrick said. "I was hoping to talk with you about the possibility of an easement...that is, after you two have completed your business."

Ms. Jessie didn't give Nick a chance to respond. "Members of the planning committee have looked over the preliminary plans you'd given to the building inspector and we've got some concerns, as you might well expect." The sharp edge to her voice put Nick on the defensive.

"Why is the committee going to be discussing the rest of this project?" Nick asked. "The building inspector already told me I don't need a permit because this is simply an extension of the plan already approved."

"Well, son, the planning committee has never approved an agricultural building the size of a football field before," Jessie said. "So some of us feel that your request for additional structures deserves more careful consideration than our easily assuaged building inspector is likely to give. I'm sure you can appreciate our position."

Again, Nick was taken off guard. He thought he had all the permission he needed. "Well, I hope you can appreciate my position as well. Surely the committee is not looking to hamper a man's ability to make a living."

"We've been ranching here a long time and no one's ever needed to keep his cattle this far up valley come winter," Jessie replied curtly. "There's plenty of winter pasture out west. I don't think your cows are gonna like staying up here when it's below zero, even if they are inside. And I don't think breeding barns for horses will make or break your dad's cattle business. So let's cut the crap."

Nick didn't like where this was going. He knew she had more clout than he'd like. He didn't want her meddling in his affairs any more than necessary, so he thought better of flipping her off and driving away. He'd be cordial, for now.

"As I'm sure you know, the main use of this facility will be the training of horses, which will be a new financial venture for us...and one that does not benefit from winter pastures elsewhere." His comments did nothing to soften the woman's stern visage.

"If you're training horses here, why now do you want to build breeding barns?" Jessie challenged.

"What's the point of providing top-of-the-line training if you have no control over the quality of animal that comes through the corral? This way, we can control the bloodline as well as the behavior."

"What kind of horses are you going to bring in?" Patrick interjected, staring hard at Ms. Jessie in an attempt to defuse some of the tension.

"Back east, we breed and train thoroughbreds. But, out here, we'll focus on rodeo horses. Our ranch manager assures me that there's a growing demand for them."

"You mean quarter horses. Not rodeo horses," Jessie quipped. "A quarter horse is a fine animal, a real working horse, not like those overbred, high-strung pedigrees you coddle back home."

Nick bristled, but he wasn't about to waste his time trying to educate this woman about the finer side of the equestrian world. "Well then, all the more reason you should be interested in my horse arena. It will be a real working horse's dream."

"You ever ridden in a rodeo?" Jessie asked.

"Certainly not." Nick was insulted. "Polo is my preferred equestrian competition. A bit more gripping than a cow-roping, I must say."

"Don't mean to cut short on the niceties here," Patrick interrupted. "But I do have another appointment after this. If you two don't mind, can I suggest we get to the committee's questions?"

Grateful to get back on track, Nick agreed. He took them over to a workbench where they could look over the preliminary blueprints. He spent the next twenty minutes fending off Jessie's barrage of critiques. She took copious notes. He had no doubt that she planned to be a thorn in his side.

Jessie ended the meeting as curtly as she'd started it. "That'll do for now. Pat, I'll call you later." She strode to her truck and drove off.

Nick shook his head and muttered, "What a bitch." He saw Patrick grin. "You weren't supposed to hear that."

"Ms. Jessie is definitely opinionated," Patrick replied. "Mr. Tremaine, I don't mean to take up much more of your time, but I would like to ask if you and your dad have talked about putting a conservation easement on the rest of this ranch? It might help some people, like Ms. Jessie, feel more comfortable about your overall intentions for the land. Which might mean they'll be more supportive of your project."

"I appreciate your concern, but I don't believe I need to cater to anyone on the planning committee. As for this easement idea, I don't like the government restricting my activities. Besides, the Tremaine family doesn't need federal handouts. Now, I really must be going."

"Of course," Patrick said. "If you're ever in Springhorn's, I'd like to buy you a drink. Tell you about some of the ranchers I'm working with. You might be surprised at how flexible an easement can be."

"Sure, that sounds fine," Nick replied, eager to end the conversation. It might serve to string the government man along for a while, especially if he had any influence with Jessie. Nick didn't want anything to derail his plans, especially an old woman with an attitude. Then another reason came to mind for being friendly with this biologist. Nick realized that he might have information on ranchers who were struggling financially and might be open to selling. "Patrick, my man, I'll be in touch."

Jessie sat on the bench in front of the Buford Store and waited for Patrick to arrive. She could tell by how he screeched the truck around the bend that he was angry. He parked the truck and started talking before he slammed the door. "Would you mind telling me what got into you back there with Nick Tremaine?" he demanded. "You practically cut off that guy's balls!"

"Meant to. Sit down and stop fuming." She motioned for Patrick to join her on the bench, but he remained standing. "I wanted him to know that he better watch out. Not every one on the planning committee is ready to turn a deaf ear to what's going on here."

"Well, you made that perfectly clear. I just don't want to get on his dad's bad side over this!"

"No reason to worry about that. Nick's angry with me. In fact, he probably thinks you're okay in comparison. I know what I'm doing."

"I hope so. Because I really don't think you can stop him at this point," Patrick continued, his anger still itching like a bad rash.

"Maybe so. But I am still going to demand some oversight on this thing. I don't want to give the Tremaines the idea that they can build whatever they want out here."

"But we don't want to tick them off so badly that they tell us to take a flying leap with the easements!"

"You're wasting your breath with Nick Tremaine. The only thing he sees when he looks at this valley is dollar signs...development dollars." Jessie spat out the words. "I'm guessing he's just waiting for daddy to die or lose interest in his ranching hobby, so he can build vacation ranches all along the river. So, forget about that easement. The crucial thing is to keep Nick from finding out about Eli wanting to sell that land."

"Not much we can do about that," Patrick said. "All Eli has to do is list it with a realtor, and we're screwed."

"We have to make sure he doesn't," Jessie said as though uttering a commandment. She put her hand on the biologist's shoulder. "Eli is here, in the valley, hiding out."

"What? How did you find out?"

"When I went to talk with the lawyer about the easement proposal, I noticed an envelope on her desk. It was addressed to Eli...at the Murphy cabin up along Big Trout Creek. You know, I think Sally wanted me to see that envelope, even though she had to make out like he was still in Vegas. Eli obviously doesn't want anyone knowing where he is. Which means he's scared. I'm guessing he owes someone a lot of money, someone who could easily kill him."

"You think he's in trouble with a mob in Vegas?"

Jessie nodded.

"Well, then maybe we should make sure their hit men know where Eli's staying. They could take care of our problem for us," Patrick offered, only half kidding. "They'd probably be more effective than that Indian curse that drove him out of here in the first place."

Jessie looked surprised. "Where'd you hear about the curse?"

"From Mrs. Shepard at Springhorn's," Patrick said. "I assumed it was some bartender story she made up."

"Don't make jokes about things you know nothing about," Jessie snapped. "There's nothing funny about that curse."

"Do you really believe that Eli was cursed?" he asked incredulously.

Jessie gave Patrick a hard stare, then looked down at her boots, measuring her words. "What if I do?"

Speechless, Patrick ran his fingers through his hair and sat down on the bench.

"What if I told you that I need you to believe it too? At least until we've dealt with Eli for good."

"You're kidding, right?"

"No."

Jessie was taking a serious risk. Could she trust Patrick to accept something he couldn't prove scientifically, that he'd have to accept on faith? Or should she tackle this on her own? She needed more time to consider her decision.

"Pat, how 'bout getting us some of Harry's bad coffee? My treat," she said, handing him a couple of dollars.

"Sure." He got up and went inside, slamming the door behind him.

That boy does have a temper, she noted.

Did she believe in this Indian curse? No one had ever asked her point blank like that. Then again, she'd never discussed it with anyone, except Duncan. He believed and that had been enough for her. But now she had to justify that feeling to a biologist who would demand concrete facts. What could she tell him?

She thought back to the time many years ago when Eli had betrayed her trust and turned both of their lives upside down. How she wished that she had never told him the tale of the Ute graves, a story that Duncan had shared with her in confidence. She had had no idea that Eli would go in search of those graves and then rob them. She remembered her horror when he'd shown her what he'd taken—the leather pouch, the necklaces, the feathers, the bones. She had insisted he return them. He had refused. Duncan had warned that he had angered the spirits. Eli had laughed at the old man's superstitions. But not for long.

First, Eli's father died, suffocating on his own whiskey vomit. Two days later, a black bear spooked Eli's horse on a steep trail. Eli was thrown and nearly fell to his death. The week after, his barn burned down. Then he started hearing voices singing, shrieking, whispering in a language he couldn't understand. Eli hid himself in the haze of a weeklong drinking binge, shooting at anyone who approached the ranch house. Jessie eventually snuck in a back window and found him passed out on the floor. When he came to, she convinced him that the voices would stop if he returned the items to the graves, which he promised to do. And for a time, he seemed to have appeased the spirits.

Jessie shook her head, trying to clear the difficult memories. She jumped as the screen door swung open and Patrick strode onto the porch. Could she convince him of this curse? She wouldn't tell him the location of the graves or whom they belonged to. But she could relate what happened to Eli. She took a deep breath.

"Patrick, I'm going to tell you a ghost story."

CHAPTER TWENTY-FIVE

JESSIE HATED TO start out the day with bad news. Picking up the phone, she could tell by the way Sally Grimm said "hello" that she had nothing good to say. Their brief conversation confirmed her suspicions. Eli refused to consider the easement and refused to talk with Jessie. There was nothing Sally could do to change his mind at this point.

His response didn't surprise Jessie, but it infuriated her, nonetheless. He would talk to her whether he wanted to or not. She had no desire to see him again, but she no longer had that luxury. Swearing under her breath, she grabbed her keys and stormed out of the door.

She parked her truck at the far end of the drive and stared at the cabin where Eli had taken refuge. She wondered what thirty years had done to him. Annoyed at the jitters in her gut, she slammed the truck door and yelled, "Eli, are you in there? It's Jessibel. Come out and show yourself!"

Silence.

"Damn you, Eli, get out here right now or I'm coming in."

No movement or sound came from the cabin.

Jessie walked up to the front door and kicked it with her boot. "Open the damn door, Eli. It's Jessibel."

Slowly the door swung back to reveal a grizzled, gaunt man trying to point a shotgun in her direction, but his hands shook too much to keep it steady. It took some imagination to find the man she'd known in the pathetic figure standing before her now.

"For God's sake, Eli, put down the gun before you hurt yourself."

"Jessibel Winde." Eli's voice cracked as he lowered the barrel. "I never thought I'd see you again. You're as pretty as I remember you."

"You always were a bad liar." Her voice softened a bit. "Come out on the porch so I can see your face."

As he shuffled into the light, a nauseating odor wafted out with him. "Jesus, when was the last time you took a shower? You reek."

He cleared his throat and hacked up a glob of spit that just missed her boot. Jessie stepped back, disgusted. They stared at each other for a few seconds, while she wrestled with conflicting reactions of anger and pity.

"What the hell's wrong with you, Eli? Hiding out like some recluse, telling Sally you won't talk to me, trying to sell my land? Why'd you come back here? Thought you were gone for good."

"Now, don't be mad, Jessibel. I had nowhere else to go."

She flinched. How many times had he said that to her as a young man whenever his daddy would kick him out or he'd be too drunk, or he'd gotten in a fight? Back then she'd always ask, "What happened?" Today was no different.

"I got in trouble. I owe people a lot of money. They're looking for me. They'll kill me if I don't pay 'em." Eli lowered his eyes.

"Who's after you?"

"A mob boss in Vegas."

"Is that where you went when you left town with my money?" Part of her had been determined not to delve into the past, to keep this conversation only about the ranch, but she couldn't stop herself, not with Eli finally in front of her after all these years.

"I didn't mean to take your money, Jessibel. But I had to leave town, you know that. I killed that guy. I had to use that money to live on."

"First of all, the sheepherder you beat up didn't die. And second of all, I gave you that money to pay the taxes so you wouldn't lose the ranch!"

"That's not how I remember it," Eli said. He started to pace.

"I'll gladly refresh your memory." Jessie fought the urge to deck him.

"Is that why you're here?" Panic tinged his voice. "Trying to get money out of me? Is that it? Well, get in line!"

"I'm here because I don't want you to do anything stupid. I won't let you sell the land." Jessie tried to remain calm.

"I've got to sell, I need the money! Why can't you understand that? That bitch Sally is the same way."

"Watch your mouth! If you'd get your head out of your ass and listen to her for a moment, you'd know that we can get you the money without having to sell."

Eli's eyes grew wide. "I'm not falling for your damn tricks. I'm selling and that's final!"

This was not going the way Jessie had intended, so she decided to take a more devious approach. She prayed that all the years of hard drinking hadn't damaged Eli's memory.

"Damn it, Eli. Just listen to me. You know you've got to be careful. You got on the bad side of the spirits once before. Remember? They hurt you. You don't want to risk that again. Selling is not the answer."

"Spirits? Don't talk to me about spirits! I don't believe in that crap any more." The distress in his face betrayed his words. He scuttled back into the doorway, ending the conversation the only way he knew how. Closing the door in Jessie's face, he yelled, "Keep your damn spirits to yourself and leave me alone!"

Two hours later, Jessie and Duncan sat at a table at Springhorn's, looking out on the river, waiting for their lunch orders to arrive. Jessie had finished telling him about her morning skirmish with Eli.

"It sounds like he wasn't that happy to see you after all these years," Duncan said with a grin.

"The feeling is mutual," Jessie said. Despite her anger, she couldn't help but smile herself. Duncan's impish expression was contagious.

"I need to come up with another means of persuasion, that's for sure. Have any ideas?"

"Maybe you should wear something a little more sexy next time."

"You're terrible." She enjoyed his humor, even when it was at her expense. The irony was, she had done that very thing to entice Duncan many years ago when they were both in their thirties. Without thinking, she said, "It did seem to work on you as I recall. But that was a long time ago." As soon as the words left her lips, she wanted to take them back.

To her relief, he said, "I remember. That was a good summer. So why don't you ever dress up nice for me any more?" His eyes twinkled.

Jessie couldn't tell if Duncan was serious or teasing. Most likely, it was a little of both. She decided to play along. "For the same reason you don't take me camping any more, I presume. I was a good cook with that dumpy camp stove."

"In the tent too," he said. "Listen to me. I sound like a dirty old man."

"You are a dirty old man."

"We did have some good times, Jessibel," Duncan said with sincerity.

Where is this coming from, she wondered? They had never really talked about their yearlong romance or why it had ended. Maybe it was Eli returning that stirred the memories. After all, Eli was the reason their relationship had fallen apart.

She looked at his face, worn and weathered, but still handsome. In an instant, she recalled in detail their first camping trip, every kiss, every caress. Back then, Duncan had been exotic, charming, mysterious, a visitor to the valley, looking for connection to a land where his grandparents had once lived. Duncan and Jessie had spent that summer together in the wilderness—camping, hiking, looking for sites that had been sacred to his ancestors. It had completely changed her perception of the landscape. Random piles of rocks she now recognized as trail markers, circles of stones as vision quest sites, wild plants as sacred medicine. Seeing the wilderness through Duncan's eyes made her love the land even more and helped her fall in love with him.

She believed he loved her, too. She remembered the night around the campfire when he told her the story of the white woman who came to live with the Utes. Red Fire Woman. And how she had fallen in love with Standing Bear and married him. Jessie had fantasized about her and Duncan being just like Red Fire Woman and Standing Bear, except that they would live happily ever after.

But then, she made the fateful mistake of telling the last part of the story to Eli one day. She had wanted to help Duncan find the graves and thought that some of the sheepherders who grazed flocks in the wilderness area might have seen them without knowing what they were. Eli overheard Jessie asking one of them if he'd ever come across old rock piles on the edge of a meadow. Eli asked her about it and she dismissed him, telling him to mind his own business. But he knew about Duncan and his interest in archeological sites. Eventually he figured out that she was talking about graves and confronted her. Caught off guard, she wasn't able to pull off a convincing denial. She had told him just enough of the story to appease his curiosity and, she thought, to instill a sense of respect for the graves. She made him swear that he wouldn't tell anyone about them. To her knowledge, he kept that promise. But Eli made it his secret quest to find the burial site. But not because he wanted to help her.

She could never forget the look of betrayal in Duncan's eyes when she told him about Eli's grave robbing. Soon after, Duncan left the valley and didn't return for almost two years. He said he needed to survey other parts of the state for sacred sites, but Jessie knew better. Her carelessness had driven him away.

"Yes, we did have some good times," Jessie said, as regrets threatened to undo her. "And I'm sorry for all the...."

"No apologies," Duncan interrupted. "We both could have handled things differently. Life has a funny way of playing out sometimes. And look, here we are after all this time. Still friends. Close friends."

"True. And I want to make sure we stay that way now that we have Eli to deal with again," Jessie said.

The waitress brought lunch and refilled water glasses. They ate in silence for a while, which gave Jessie time to wrestle with how to present her plan to frighten Eli.

"Is lunch that bad?" Duncan asked.

"No, why?"

"You're frowning. If it's not the food, then maybe it's the company."

"No, no. I'm just...I have an idea I'm not sure you'll like, but I want you to hear me out, okay?"

Duncan nodded. "If it has to do with sexy clothing, I will like it."

"I'll keep that in mind." This unexpected flirtation pleased her but she doubted it would continue once she shared her request. "We need something that frightens Eli more than the mob to keep him from selling the land. And the only things I can come up with are the spirits. They got his attention before and he listened. Maybe they can do it again."

"Eli angered the Spirits before. I don't see how he's doing that now."

"You don't think selling land to a developer is enough cause!"

"I don't speak for the Spirits, Jessibel." His voice hardened a bit. "And neither do you."

"Of course, you're right. But, what if Eli *thought* the spirits were angry? That might be all we'd need."

"How do you propose to do that?" Duncan leaned forward, his eyes no longer playful.

He listened without expression until Jessie finished her explanation. "I don't know that the Spirits need any human intervention on their behalf. Or if they would welcome it." His voice sounded grave. "I caution you. Misrepresenting the Spirits could have consequences for you. Be completely clear about your intentions here. Make sure your actions come from love and not anger or spite. Or greed."

"Do I have your permission to try this?"

"It is not mine to give. Only the Spirits can do that. You would do well to ask them. But I will pray for you, Jessibel."

Later that evening, Jessie sat at her kitchen table, staring out of the window, waiting for the sun to sink below the tree line. She toyed with a cup of coffee that had gone cold an hour before. Patrick had reluctantly agreed to help her, but not because he believed in the curse. That didn't matter, she reassured herself. He didn't need to. It was Eli who still needed to believe. She stood up, walked over to the sink and poured the coffee down the drain.

She wished Duncan had given some kind of verbal support for her plan. Then again, if he truly opposed her actions, he would have said so. Leave it to Duncan to be cryptic just when she needed clarity.

First she washed the mug, then her hands. It was time. She poured a tall shot of tequila. Not the sipping kind. She needed something raw and burning in her gut for this type of work. Duncan would disapprove of mixing alcohol and spiritual work. But, she knew of Central American cultures where tequila was treated as sacred. So to be safe, she said a quick prayer before downing the shot. As she headed into the root cellar with her kerosene lantern turned up high, she sang a song Duncan had taught her years ago. A Ute prayer for protection.

CHAPTER TWENTY-SIX

PATRICK ARRIVED AT Jessie's place at eight in the morning, just as her phone message had specified. He found her in the kitchen hovering over a cup of coffee. The bags under her eyes spoke of a long night with little sleep, although her face looked more worried than weary.

"I know you don't believe in spiritual stuff, but I need you to promise me that you'll do exactly as I say," Jessie said, pointing to a red cloth bundle on the side table near the door. The bundle was surrounded by sage leaves. "It's important that you show respect for these objects even if you don't feel it. I'm not playing around here."

Patrick drank his coffee while he listened to her explicit instructions and then repeated them back to her, word for word, several times upon her insistence.

"You've got it," she said. "The weather should be clear tonight. See if you can deliver this before sunrise. And then report back to me."

She stood up and stretched. Before she handed him the red parcel, she lit one of the sage leaves and fanned the smoke all around his body. She called it 'smudging' and told him it would help protect him.

"Don't unwrap this until you're ready to use it," Jessie said sternly. "Remember now."

"I know, treat it with respect. I got it."

"Good. I'm going to see about some sleep. Thanks, Pat. Be careful."

He waited until the moon rose high enough in the sky to help light his way before heading out. As instructed, Patrick waited until he'd reached his destination and parked the truck before opening the package. The contents disturbed him. The talisman consisted of a large white tail feather splattered with blood, with a thin bone and hair tied to the quill.

"Shit, that's a bald eagle feather!" He could lose his job if he was caught with an eagle feather in his possession. And the bone looked like it could be human, from a hand. Patrick caught himself mid-thought. Ms. Jessie must have used a black bear bone. The bones in a paw are remarkably similar to those in a human hand. He quickly put the talisman back in the cloth bag as though someone might be watching him, even though it was three o'clock in the morning and he was alone on a back road in the forest.

He left the truck and walked about a half mile to reach Eli's hideaway. The cabin was dark, no truck or horse on the property, no smoke from the chimney. Only the sound of erratic heavy snoring gave Eli away. His instructions were to place the talisman in plain sight so Eli would see it when he woke up that morning. Patrick hung it on the hitching post, then found a thick stand of spruce up the side of the hill to hide out and keep watch.

As dawn crept in, Patrick could make out the run-down log cabin that sat near the creek. It was concealed from the dirt road by a profusion of wild rose and serviceberry bushes. An old wooden sign, too weather worn and full of bullet holes to be legible, swung by a nail from a post near the road. Patrick doubted if anyone had lived there, even during hunting season, in many years. A perfect hideout, he had to admit, until today.

Patrick had a clear view of the front porch and the old hitching post where the talisman hung. Ms. Jessie had insisted that Patrick leave no sign of human involvement in its placement. "I want him to believe the Spirits floated in there to deliver it." An easy task for Patrick. His years as a field biologist and hunter had given him exceptional tracking skills; he could walk the woods as quietly as a mountain lion and leave no trace.

The sun rose high enough to peak over the mountains and still there was no sign of movement from Eli's cabin. A cow elk and her young calf stepped out of the forest and drank from the creek, then grazed for a time. Suddenly the cow's head sprang up, her full attention focused downstream toward the road. Patrick followed her gaze but saw nothing.

A minute later, he picked up the faint rumble of tires, but by then the elk and her young one had retreated into the trees.

Soon a green Cherokee van pulled into the drive and parked in front of the cabin. A slim woman dressed in khaki slacks and a crisp white shirt stepped out of the van with a briefcase in hand. She stood on the edge of the bushes and shouted, "Mr. McDermott, hello? It's Sally Grimm."

No reply. She took another step but appeared reticent to walk up to the door. "Mr. McDermott, are you there? I've got your supplies."

Undetected, Patrick moved closer in the hopes of hearing the conversation that might ensue. After another long silence, the door slowly opened and a hand popped out, waving the lawyer forward. She took a few steps, then stopped. "Mr. McDermott, please come out on the porch and let's talk like civilized folk. No one followed me, I assure you."

The door swung wider and a man emerged, quickly glancing left and right as though expecting an ambush from either side of the cabin. Then he looked at Sally and again waved her closer.

So that's Eli, Patrick noted. He was shorter and more frail than he'd expected. He looked like a man on the run, with a scraggly gray beard, dirty jeans and denim shirt on a gaunt frame, hunched with fear as much as age. His hands trembled slightly and his eyes continually darted from side to side. A pistol was tucked in the waistband of his jeans.

Sally put a brown grocery bag on the porch but she stayed at the bottom of the steps. *She probably wants to stand down wind of him,* Patrick mused. It looked as though Eli hadn't seen a bar of soap for way too long. Probably smelled a bit like road kill.

Eli grabbed the bag. "You didn't forget the whiskey, did ya?"

"It's there."

"Good. Found someone to buy my land?" Eli croaked out, with a voice raspy and raw as though he had just come out of hibernation.

"Not exactly," Sally began, hesitating slightly. Her concerned look indicated she didn't think Eli would like what she had to say. "I would like to just go over what I presented to you before. I don't think you were, well, in the clearest frame of mind last time we talked."

Drunk most likely, just like he will be again soon, Patrick thought. He was pleased with the way the lawyer explained the conservation easement he had put together.

Eli listened without interruption until she got to the dollar amount.

Then he exploded. "The hell you say! That's not enough, I already told you that!" He ranted for a good five minutes before Sally tried to gain control of the conversation.

"Mr. McDermott, that's the dollar amount we had agreed to."

"The hell it is!"

"Let me see if the dollar amount is negotiable. Although this really is a good deal, Mr. McDermott...Ms. Jessie thinks so."

Eli paused, his face softened. "Ms. Jessie?" He spoke her name with a reverence that surprised Patrick. Then Eli began mumbling. Sally seemed confused and finally asked Eli what he was saying. In response to the interruption, he resumed his tirade about how the government was trying to screw him out of the money he rightly deserved.

Sally reassured him that she would check into a higher price. Please consider this offer, she'd get back to him as soon as she had more information. Please try to calm down. Goodbye.

She stepped away, appearing hesitant to turn her back on the man. Once she got to the safety of the bushes, she spun around and hurried to her van, climbed in and locked the doors before making a hasty exit.

Patrick saw now what Ms. Jessie had warned him about. Eli was crazy. But a crazy man who seemed to have a soft spot for Ms. Jessie.

A breeze through the front yard caused the feathered talisman to float and twist on the post. It caught Eli's attention. He froze in mid rant; his eyes grew wide and his hands began shaking. He stared transfixed until the winds calmed. Then he slowly pulled his pistol out of his waistband. With shaky steps, he descended the three stairs and then spat on the ground. The shots, loud and rapid, made Patrick jump. Eli fired at the feather as if to annihilate it. But the wind picked up again, letting the talisman dance between the bullets. The shooting and the breeze stopped at the same time. The feather rested against the post, unharmed.

Eli grabbed a rusted pitchfork and frantically jabbed at his inanimate enemy until it fell to the ground. As though possessed, he trampled the feather and bone into a mangled mess.

Patrick watched in amazement. Ms. Jessie's trick was turning this old fart inside out. Eli fell to the ground and didn't move for several minutes. Eventually the old man struggled to his feet, stumbled into the cabin and slammed the door behind him.

CHAPTER TWENTY-SEVEN

JASON DROVE INTO the Flat Top Ranch and followed the road past the main house to the guest cabin where he parked next to Sarah's truck. He knocked on the door. "Why the fuck am I so nervous?"

It had been several days since Duncan had shared the story of Standing Bear and Red Fire Woman. And then this morning, Old Man told him to pay Sarah a visit. "I'm not your errand boy" had been his first reply. But disrespecting elders was the alcoholic in him speaking, not the sober nephew. After a terse apology and a shower, Jason found himself standing in front of Sarah's door. And it was hard to deny that he was actually eager to see her.

Over the last two days he'd found himself thinking a lot about her. Jason had known plenty of pretty women in his life. Always one to admire the view, he rarely developed any serious interest on first meeting. So he wondered why he felt so drawn to Sarah. Maybe because it had been so long since he'd been with a woman. There hadn't been anybody since he'd gotten sober. Back in Nashville, he'd slept with so many women he couldn't remember them all. Didn't help that he had been drunk most of the time and couldn't remember his own name after a bottle of whiskey. Jason certainly recognized the sexual attraction Sarah stirred in him, but her appeal ran deeper than that.

The door opened. "Jason. Hello, uh, what are you doing here...I mean, I had no idea you were coming...sorry, let me start again. Hello. How are you?"

Seeing her flustered made his nervousness vanish.

Sarah invited him into the kitchen and immediately began apologizing for how she looked, how the place looked, then excused herself to pull herself together. "I wasn't expecting company."

Jason told her to take her time and helped himself to a cup of coffee. She didn't have to make herself up for him. He liked her tousled hair, sweat pants and flannel shirt. As he walked into the living room, he found himself wondering what she might look like without the sweats and flannel but stopped in mid fantasy when he saw all the drawings covering the room, taped on walls and windows, strewn on the table and couch. Portraits of Duncan, Jason, and a woman with long, unruly hair. He admired the work. Not only did she draw accurately, she also captured an energy that was palpable. He couldn't help but feel a bit flattered.

"You weren't supposed to see all this," Sarah said as she came up behind him. She had combed her hair and changed into jeans and a green shirt that brought out the color in her eyes.

"You've been busy, I see. They're very good."

"You really think so? These are just roughs." Sarah quickly picked up the drawings on the couch and table and motioned for Jason to sit down. She kept looking at the others on the wall, as if contemplating how to take them down without looking too obvious.

Jason assured her, "Relax, please. No need to straighten up. I understand the creative process. You should have seen the mounds of crumbled up paper in my apartment when I was trying to write music. This looks neat in comparison. Leave 'em."

"Okay." She sat in a chair by the window. "So, you're a song writer?"

"Used to be, in another life. Maybe I'll get back to it again, we'll see." Jason quickly changed the subject. "How are you? That was a pretty bizarre experience you had the other day. Old Man wanted me...uh, actually I wanted to see how you were doing."

"Thank you. That's kind of you...and Duncan. I really have no idea how I'm doing. Nothing like this has ever happened to me before. But, as you can see, I can't get the story out of my mind." She pointed to another series of drawings on the floor by the fireplace of characters dressed in traditional buckskin and old army uniforms.

"It's the strangest thing," Sarah almost whispered. "Whenever I start to draw that captain, my left hand spasms like it did the other day, except not so violently. I can get it to relax. But still, it's freaky."

She picked up a sketch of Red Fire Woman and studied it as she spoke. "Duncan said some things to me when I was sitting in my truck. I was so upset, I don't think I understood what he was trying to say. He mentioned something about the spirits of ancestors wanting to get our attention. He thought that was why my hand reacts the way it does. He said he thinks the spirit of Red Fire Woman needs my help." Sarah glanced over at Jason. "Does this make any sense to you?"

Jason caught a glimpse of fear in her eyes and had to resist the urge to comfort her. "I'll tell you what I know, but that isn't much. There is a Ute belief that the pain and suffering of people who have died can continue to cause problems for future generations. So, there is a ceremony that people can request for their ancestors to help bring them some peace. Old Man says he is being asked to do this healing ceremony for the ancestors in the story he shared with us. He's been asking the Spirits for guidance, but doesn't seem to have a clear sense of it yet. He didn't share anything specifically about you or Red Fire Woman."

"I've never heard of a ceremony to heal ancestors," Sarah said. "And I still don't understand what this has to do with me. As far as I know, Red Fire Woman isn't a relative of mine, so why would I respond to anything about her past?"

"I don't have an answer for you." Jason shrugged his shoulders, wishing he had more to offer her.

"I have a sister back home," Sarah said. "She's a psychologist with a spiritual bent. She knows about the problem I've been having with my hand and when I told her about what happened when Duncan told us the story, she started to wonder if this had something to do with reincarnation."

"What do you mean?"

"Well, after I told her about how my left hand reacted to that necklace and about Red Fire Woman having two fingers cut off on the same hand, she thought that coincidence might be some kind of indication that I had been Red Fire Woman in a past life. My sister believes in reincarnation. I'm not sure what I believe."

"Not sure what Old Man would think of that either," Jason said. "There's no reincarnation in Ute beliefs. Is there any chance that Red Fire Woman is a blood relation, through some distant cousin or something like that?"

"I'm ashamed to say, I don't know much about my family history. I suppose there's a slim chance, but I'd have do some genealogy research to know for sure."

Sarah looked down at her hand, then stood up. "Are you hungry? I was just going to make some eggs when you showed up. I really need to eat something, and you're welcome to join me."

Jason wasn't particularly hungry, but he wasn't ready to leave either, so he accepted. "As long as you've got more coffee."

While Sarah busied herself in the kitchen, Jason looked through the drawings on the floor. He picked up one of a snarling grizzly standing on its hind legs. Even though the animal wasn't fully rendered, the sketchy image reminded him of his nightmare. The bear in Duncan's story had been shot in the head. So was the bear in his dream. *Are the stories of Standing Bear and my nightmare somehow connected? That's too fuckin' weird.*

He dropped the drawing and turned toward the window, only to see a sketch on an end table of a hand, with the thumb and two fingers clenched, the ring and pinkie fingers severed. Next to it was a portrait of a woman, her eyes hauntingly blank, as though she had nothing left to live for. He couldn't stop staring at the face; his heart knew that kind of despair. He had been born with it, but it came through him as anger. His mother said he started fighting in the womb, kicking her so hard she'd lose her breath.

Why was he burdened with such dark feelings? His life hadn't been that tough growing up, not compared to what his ancestors endured. *Ancestors...is this what Old Man is talking about? Am I somehow carrying the emotions of my ancestors?*

Sarah called from the kitchen. Jason decided to keep these thoughts to himself for now, until he had more time to digest their implications.

During breakfast, Jason asked Sarah about her commission with the Tremaines and about life as a muralist. She seemed eager to talk about her work, almost relieved. Jason found himself engrossed. The more she talked, the more relaxed she became and the more enticing Jason found her. Not just physically. He was drawn to her like a hawk is to the wind.

"Enough about me," Sarah concluded as she removed dishes from the table. "It's your turn. Tell me something about Jason Little Bear."

He winced. He didn't like talking about himself; there wasn't much to feel good about except being two years sober. He had talent as a songwriter and singer, but had managed to drink away any Nashville breaks that had come his way. He developed a nasty reputation in the music business that he couldn't overcome no matter how many good songs he wrote.

He pushed back his chair and then turned toward the kitchen door. He heard a truck pull into the drive. "You've got company," he said, with both relief and annoyance at the interruption.

Sarah got up and looked out the window. Jason saw her body stiffen. "What does he want?"

Before Jason could ask who he was, Sarah opened the door and started to step outside, but was stopped by the sudden appearance of Nick Tremaine on the porch. Jason knew he was Hollis' son, had seen him in town, but had never been introduced. Not interested in meeting him now, Jason quietly retreated into the living room.

"Hello, Sarah. There's a strange truck in the drive. You must have company," Nick announced as he stepped past her into the kitchen without waiting to be invited in.

"Nick. What can I do for you?" Jason heard the tension in her voice.

"I stopped by to inform you that Tony and the boys are moving cattle in the forest tomorrow or the next day. Father would like you to go with them." Nick started walking into the living room. "I have to return to New York tomorrow for business, so I won't be able to escort you."

Sarah hurried behind him. "Thank you. Now if that's all you needed to..." She nearly bumped into Nick who had stopped walking and was staring at Jason. Neither man spoke.

Sarah made hasty introductions.

"Jason Little Bear, I haven't seen you around before. Are you one of the new summer hires?" Nick's unctuous tone accentuated his insult.

"Hardly." Jason clenched his fists, fighting the urge to punch the arrogant bastard.

Sarah stepped in between the two men. "Nick, please tell Hollis I'd be happy to go with Tony on the drive. If that's all, let me show you out."

"I also came by to see how your ideas for the murals were coming along." Nick walked over to the coffee table and picked up a few sketches. He frowned as he examined them. "I see you're focusing on ancient history at the moment. How quaint." He stared at Jason, then back at her.

"Don't forget about the cowboys, Sarah. They did win the war and conquer the red man," he said, tossing the drawings back on the table. "Cowboys have owned this land for generations and still do." His eyes moved slowly around the room, taking in her sketches on the wall. "But, I'm sure you'll figure that out." Ignoring Jason, he grinned at Sarah with a coolness that lingered even after he'd left the cabin.

Jason was seething, but knew enough to check his temper. He didn't want to jeopardize Sarah's job. "If I ever meet that son of a bitch in the forest, I can promise you the coyotes will eat well that night!"

"I am so sorry. I can't believe how rude he was!" Sarah sat down on the couch. "What does he have against you?"

"You mean, aside from me being an 'Injun'?"

"How can he be so prejudiced?"

"You don't get it, do you, Sarah?"

"Get what?"

"The prick is jealous. He has a thing for you."

"I think he's too full of himself to have a 'thing' for anyone else." She sounded as though she was trying to convince herself as much as Jason.

"Watch yourself around that city-ass cowboy. I don't trust him."

"I will."

"If he ever gives you trouble, let me know and I'll take care of him."

Sarah smiled. "My hero. You do have a thing for coming to my rescue, even when I'm running from my own nightmares."

Recalling their first encounter in the canyon, Jason said, "Having seen how fast you can run, you just might be able to take care of yourself!"

"You scared the crap out of me that day," Sarah said.

"You never did tell me what you were running from."

She told him about falling asleep along the river, about her sense of being pursued, the panic she felt when she woke up. "I could have sworn someone on horseback was after me. So I just ran...right into you."

"Does this happen to you often," Jason teased.

"Yeah, actually it's a new technique I've developed for picking up strange men in the woods. How's it working so far?" she teased back.

Jason wasn't ready to let her know just how well it was. "Well, given all that's been happening lately, do you think that nightmare has anything to do with the story of Red Fire Woman?"

Sarah sighed. "I'm not sure what to think...about any of this. I'm afraid of what it all could mean. This isn't what I signed up for. I just came out here to paint."

"I usually hate it when people say 'I know what you mean', but in this case, I do," Jason said. "Comes with hanging out with Old Man. Weird shit always happens around him."

He saw the concern in her eyes. "However, things do seem to make sense...eventually."

"Your pep talk needs some improvement," Sarah replied. "And I need a cup of coffee. I'll be right back."

She returned with two mugs and handed one to Jason who was sitting on the couch. "I'm curious about something," she said, settling into the armchair. "Why do you call Duncan 'Old Man'? It seems a bit disrespectful and yet that's not how you treat him."

"I've been calling him that since I was a kid. His favorite cousin used to call him Old Man. The cousin was Blackfoot, from the Siksika tribe. In the Blackfoot stories, Old Man is a revered character. In some tales, he's the creator of all things and in others, he is the human who learns important lessons on behalf of his people. I believe his cousin started calling him Old Man as a joke because he thought my uncle had too high an opinion of himself when he was young. But, I didn't know that at the time. I just thought it was a cool name and started using it."

"Does anyone else call him that?" Sarah asked.

"Not that I know of. But, speaking of Old Man, he wants you to come sweat with us."

"Sweat, like in work out?"

"No, a sweat lodge ceremony."

"Sorry. Of course," she said. "I don't know what to say."

"'Yes' would be a good choice."

"Will you be there?"

"Yes."

"Will there be other people there?" She fidgeted in the chair.

"No, just the three of us. And whatever spirits decide to join us."

"When is this ceremony going to happen?"

"He didn't say, but probably in a week or so. He'll let us know."

Jason could read her emotions from the subtle changes in her face. He liked that about her. He wanted to ease the furrows in her lovely forehead. "I can't say you'll have nothing to worry about, but I can assure you that you'll survive."

"That's reassuring," Sarah replied, playfully slapping his knee. "FYI, pep talk number two was even worse than pep talk number one."

"Give me a chance, I'm just getting started," Jason replied, pleased to see Sarah smiling.

He returned her smile, wondering if she sensed that he was talking about more than just pep talks and sweat lodge ceremonies.

"I'm nervous about going, especially after listening to Red Fire Woman's story," she said, picking up a pencil and a sketchpad. "Go sit by the window, will you? The light is good and sketching helps calm me down. And then please tell me everything I need to know about this sweat lodge ceremony."

CHAPTER TWENTY-EIGHT

"IT'S BEEN A WEEK since Eli received his little surprise," Jessie said, looking across the kitchen table at Duncan and Patrick, her reluctant allies in this subterfuge. This was the first time these men had met. Jessie had been trying to get the two of them together for months, but Duncan hadn't been willing, until now. They were both men of the mountains, completely at home in the wilderness, but such opposites in how they related to that world, she noted. The young biologist and the aging Indian. She felt grateful that they were both here to help her and wasted no time in getting to the point of their gathering.

"The good news is Eli is scared. He won't even come out of the cabin to talk with Sally. She stopped by several times and got nowhere."

"Does she know he's still alive?" Patrick asked. "He might have died from fright or overexertion. He went ballistic over that talisman."

"She heard him moving in the cabin. That old bastard is still alive."

"Well, if he's not talking to his attorney, then he's not signing an easement either," Patrick remarked. "So where has this gotten us?"

"It's a first step," Jessie assured him. "If he's afraid of the curse, then I'm hoping that he'll be too afraid to actually sell the land. And that he'll see the easement as his only hope to get the money he needs and not upset the spirits."

Patrick rolled his eyes, but caught himself when he saw Duncan frown.

"You don't believe in Spirits," Duncan stated.

"Can't say that I do. Never found any need, I guess." Patrick shifted uncomfortably in his seat.

"You are a man of science. And yet, you are a man of the forest too. You know the animals, you know the plants. When you hunt the elk, you look into his eyes as he takes his last breath. There is a part of you that has touched that elk's spirit. He is more than fur and meat and antlers. Your heart knows this."

Jessie watched Patrick's expression shift from irritation to surprise.

"I respect the life of the animal that I kill," Patrick said. "But I don't think that equates to believing that animal has a spirit."

"But what do you feel, in that moment? Don't use your mind to answer. There is a different kind of knowing. Perhaps next time you go hunting, you will feel the spirit of that animal offering itself to you."

"Perhaps you will come hunting with me this year so you can show me what you're talking about."

Duncan nodded. "Jessie, think I can teach this scientist how to hunt like an Indian? Now that would be something!"

"If anyone can, you can," Jessie replied, hoping for Patrick's sake that these two would get together again. He could learn a lot, but he'd have to set aside his black-and-white view of the world in order to see things from Duncan's unique perspective.

Jessie stood up and walked over to the window. "The other person I wanted to talk to you both about is Nick Tremaine. If he finds out about Eli, I know he would make an offer. Nick wants to develop out here. So far, Eli hasn't posted the land with a realtor. He's too cheap to pay a commission. But we can't assume he won't," she continued. "That's another reason we need to keep Eli holed up in his cabin. I don't want him talking to anyone in town."

"I have a good relationship with all of the realtors," Patrick said. "They let me know as soon as any new properties are listed. So far, nothing from Eli."

"The question is what realtor does Nick have in his back pocket?" Jessie wondered. "That's what worries me. I'm sure he must have an in with someone."

Neither man replied.

"Well, I'm working on my own insider, you might say," she said. "Hollis has hired an artist from Chicago to do some work at the Double R. She's staying at the Flat Top. I made her acquaintance in town. She said that she'd met you, Duncan."

"Sarah Cavanaugh. Yes, we have met. A most intriguing woman," Duncan said, but offered no further explanation.

"It seems that Sarah isn't too fond of Nick. I'm taking her riding later today to see the big aspens. I'm hoping she'll be willing to help us keep tabs on him."

Jessie was just about to ask Duncan what he thought of Sarah, but he never gave her the opportunity. Instead, he got up and thanked her for the coffee. To Patrick he said, "Come visit me. We can hike the canyon you are so eager to explore. And we can talk some more about the Spirits." Then he walked out of the kitchen door.

"How did he know about that? I asked Tom Payton about that canyon weeks ago," Patrick said. "Is he always so...abrupt?"

"Duncan's always been a succinct...and full of surprises," she replied. "Have you met Ms. Cavanaugh?"

Patrick shook his head.

"I think you might like her. You're welcome to join us."

"Thanks, Ms. Jessie. But I've got a meeting. Maybe another time. Appreciate the coffee and getting a chance to finally meet Duncan Hawk. Well, I'd best be going too."

As Jessie cleaned up the coffee mugs, she remembered Duncan's face when she'd mentioned Sarah Cavanaugh. He seemed to like her. What wasn't there to like? She was attractive, intelligent, and pleasant. But she sensed that there had to be something more to hold Duncan's attention. He had called her "intriguing". Jessie wanted to find out why.

Sarah patted the soft, chestnut nose of the horse she was going to ride. The mare had gentle looking eyes.

"Her name's Molly. She'll give you a nice ride." The tall, slender man holding the bridle smiled so warmly, Sarah liked him immediately. "And I'm Karl. You've got a beautiful day. The upper meadows are blooming with all kinds of wildflowers now. Ms. Jessie will give you a fine tour."

"Thanks," Sarah said, taking the bridle cautiously. "Even though I've been riding a bit at the Flat Top, I still don't feel all that comfortable around horses."

"Give it time. By the end of the summer, you'll probably be a natural," Karl assured her. "Or you could give our mule a try, but I wouldn't recommend it!" They walked Molly over to the lodge where Jessie was talking with a woman whose smile was as genuine as Karl's.

"Sarah, I'd like you to meet Mona," Jessie said. "She and Karl own the Ute Lodge."

"Great to meet you," Mona said with a sparkle in her voice. "Ms. Jessie tells me you're an artist. I'd love to see your work some time."

"Thank you." Sarah felt an instant rapport with her.

"Karl, I sure appreciate you letting us take your horses up to see the big aspens," Jessie said. "Saves me having to haul my trailer over here."

"Our pleasure," Karl said. Sarah could tell he meant it.

While Jessie and Karl continued talking about horses, Sarah turned to Mona with a question. "I'm curious. Your place is called Ute Lodge, but I don't see any lodge here. Only these lovely cabins."

"That's because the lodge burned down a while ago, before we bought the place. The previous owner never rebuilt. We've got plans to build one in a couple of years. Karl's been cutting logs for it from the forest."

"Do you rent these cabins all year round?"

"We're a two-season place. We get the summer vacation folks starting in early June and then we start filling up with hunters come fall. Winters are too tough out here for most tourists. This isn't ski country."

"You've got such a beautiful place here," Sarah said.

"You're welcome any time," Mona said. "Karl and I love to cook, when we've got time. We'll have you over for elk steaks real soon. Ms. Jessie, you know you're always invited too."

"I wouldn't miss your elk steaks for anything," Jessie said.

Molly was indeed gentle and Sarah adjusted to the saddle after about twenty minutes. The trail through the forest was particularly steep and narrow, so the two women could not ride side-by-side, which made conversation difficult. Sarah didn't mind the silence; she needed to concentrate on riding for the moment.

The forest was thick with pine and fir trees. She was surprised by the patches of tall ferns, which she associated more with wetter climates, and was equally taken with the large amount of dead timber on the ground. She wanted to stop and paint the contrast between the lacy fronds of the lush green plants and the cracked, stripped poles of gray wood.

Jessie stopped when they reached a meadow and twisted around in the saddle. "How are you doing?"

"Better than expected," Sarah replied. "Wow, Karl was right. The flowers up here are gorgeous."

"They are. About another ten minutes before we reach the aspens."

"I'd like to stop and take some reference photos, if you don't mind. They'll help me with my painting later."

"Take your time. I'll wait over here in the shade."

The sun felt good after the cool of the forest. Sarah was pleased to see how many flowers she remembered. All of those hikes with Blue and his constant quizzing about species names had stuck with her. She stopped herself from replaying sweet memories and came back to naming flowers. Soon her thoughts took her in another direction. *I bet Jason knows all these plants, and the trees too,* she mused. *I'd like to go for a ride with him and spend some time in this meadow, perhaps on a blanket....*

"Sarah, look up, to the east." Jessie's voice broke into her fantasy. Soaring overhead was a golden eagle, its huge wings outstretched.

"Oh my. How magnificent!" Sarah said softly.

"It's always a good day when you get to see eagles flying," Jessie said, her gaze still skyward.

Sarah caught a softness in Jessie's face that reminded her of how a mother looks at a baby. *She loves everything about these mountains,* Sarah realized. *She belongs here.*

When the eagle glided out of view, both women resumed their ride until the trail entered the forest again. The large aspens lay ahead. In the shade of the trees, Sarah dismounted and stretched sore legs.

"A bit stiff?" Jessie asked.

"Yeah, I am."

"Well, I think you'll find these trees are worth the aching muscles." Jessie took the lead rope of both horses and tied them to a tree.

As soon as Sarah caught sight of the white aspens, she forgot about the pain. She stood in front of the closest one and placed her hands with reverence on the soft bark. The tree was so big, she couldn't wrap her arms around it and had to crane her neck to see the lowest branches. This giant was easily five times wider than a normal aspen. The deep, dark fissures in the bark spoke of its age. "I feel like I'm in the presence of something ancient and holy."

Jessie smiled. "You are, my dear. You are. Glad you feel it too. I was hoping you would."

Sarah saw that same softness in the old woman's face. "This may sound weird, but I wonder what these trees would tell us if we just sat here long enough to listen."

"Nothing weird about that to me," Jessie replied.

"That's what I try to do when I paint. I listen. With both my ears and my eyes, hoping that my fingers can capture the truth of what I'm experiencing. I'd have to spend a lot of time here to truly draw these trees. I would love to do a painting of you with one of these aspens."

"A portrait of two old-timers, is that what you're suggesting?"

Fumbled for a reply, Sarah feared that she might have inadvertently insulted her.

"I'd be honored," Jessie said, "just so long as you make the aspen look much older than me!"

The aspen grove contained ten titans and a few that had already died and fallen over. The women walked from tree to tree sharing a sense of awe and reverence. Eventually they sat down on one of the large logs and shared a drink of water from Jessie's canteen.

"Did you ever meet up with Duncan?" Jessie asked. "You had mentioned receiving an invitation from him when we met in town."

"Yes, I did." Sarah wasn't sure how much to reveal about her visit. "It was lovely."

"Lovely isn't a word one would normally use to describe time with Duncan. Fascinating, frustrating, different, but not lovely!"

"You got me there. We drank coffee on his front porch and we talked some about the history of his people. Then his nephew Jason joined us and Duncan told us a rather long and very sad story."

"What story did he tell you?"

"He called it the story of Red Fire Woman and Standing Bear, I believe. Do you know it?"

Jessie looked annoyed. "Why would he tell you that story?"

"I don't really know why he shared it with me." Sarah lied a little, not wanting to go into her twitching hand or the bear claw necklace.

She mentioned Jason's invitation to the sweat lodge ceremony in the hopes that Ms. Jessie had been to one and could give her advice on what to expect, but she wasn't forthcoming. She just said, "It's an honor to be asked," then stood up and walked over to the horses. "Come on, we should be heading back."

On the edge of the forest, Sarah spotted a raven that seemed to be staring at her perched in a pine. The bird uttered a gravelly caw as they rode by into a meadow delicately painted with the reds, pinks and purples of wildflowers. Here the path became wide enough to ride next to each other.

"How are things going for you at the Flat Top with the Tremaines? Have you started painting?"

"I'm not painting yet. The ranch house isn't quite finished. Besides, I'm still in the preliminary stages. I've been doing a lot of sketching and I've got some good ideas." Sarah hoped she sounded more confident than she felt about her progress. She'd been so taken with her sketches of Red Fire Woman's story that she hadn't put much time into the overall mural concept.

"What does Hollis think or have you shown him anything?"

"Hollis is great. He seems to like anything I do...." Sarah's voice trailed off.

"But," Jessie prodded.

"Nick is another story."

"Isn't he though," Jessie agreed. "Does he have much to do with you? I thought you said he was preoccupied with the horse arena."

Again, Sarah wasn't sure how much to confide in her newfound friend. "Officially no. But he certainly is opinionated about many things. Very pro-cowboy and fairly anti-Indian, I've come to find out."

The meadow trail led to the edge of a cliff that overlooked a long stretch of the valley, including the horse arena.

"What a view," Sarah proclaimed.

"I used to love coming up," Jessie said. "But not so much now. Imagine how this valley would change if more of these beautiful meadows got bought up and turned into vacation homes. I'm not afraid of many things, Sarah, but that thought terrifies me."

"I understand."

"I thought you might," Jessie said. "Anyone who listens to trees before she paints them must truly appreciate the natural world."

They stood in silence for a time, enjoying a breeze that complemented the summer sun.

"Sarah, I have something to ask you, a favor if you will. I think Nick is looking for land to buy in the valley. I wanted to ask if you have heard about any prospects he might have? I guess I first need to ask if you would be willing to tell me if you knew?"

"Ms. Jessie, I certainly understand why you'd ask. I'm not sure how to respond. I have no allegiance to Nick and frankly I don't really like the man. But I do work for his father."

"Hollis doesn't want to see this valley developed any more than I do," Jessie stated.

"Then why wouldn't he keep his son from doing so?"

"That I can't answer. Somehow he seems blind to his son's ambitions. That's why I'm asking you. Sarah, there are two kinds of people who buy in this valley—those who love this place the way it is and those who want to change it. Take Karl and Mona. They bought the Ute Lodge a few years ago. They really appreciate the forest and want to protect it. Their business attracts people who want a wilderness experience."

"I can see that," Sarah said.

"I just want you to know that anything you might share with me, I would keep in confidence. The Tremaines wouldn't know that you talked to me. I promise you that."

"I can tell you that Nick has not discussed any new deal with me. I'm not sure that he would."

Sarah took one more look up and down the valley. She'd come back here to paint. She wondered if Hollis would mind if she left out the horse arena in her paintings. It would feel good to get back at Nick after he trampled her work the other day. Then again, his sudden anger concerned her and she wasn't eager to experience it again anytime soon.

As the horses made their way down the trail, a raven flew past them and into the trees where the meadow met the forest. The big black bird stayed ahead of them, just out of sight, until Sarah and Jessie rode through the gate to the Ute Lodge.

CHAPTER TWENTY-NINE

EVERY NIGHT SINCE Jason's visit, Sarah fell asleep wondering what it would be like to kiss him. She found herself blushing sometimes while sketching his likeness. Before leaving the house this morning, she tore up one she had drawn of him naked, embracing a woman who looked a lot like herself.

Sarah was eager to see him again, perhaps too eager, she thought. Knowing how emotionally transparent she could be, she prayed that Jason wouldn't pick up on her growing infatuation—that is, of course, unless he felt the same way.

Ruth had long ago dubbed her "the against-all-odds romantic" because of her less than compatible choices in men over the years. Jason had all the trappings of a repeat performance, although he certainly was more intriguing than the others, and so more certain to fail, if it even ever got started. Her rational assessment of the situation did nothing to temper the electricity that ran through her when she caught sight of him on the side of the road.

He had invited her to join him on a hike today in the box canyon where they had first run into each other. He waved as she pulled up.

Their greeting was friendly but awkward. She didn't know what to do with her hands, a handshake was too formal and a hug too intimate, so she stuffed them in her pockets. Jason, she noticed, was holding a cowboy hat in his hands. While she pulled her gear together, he asked if she had had any more visits from Nick.

"He's been gone for several days," Sarah explained. "You know, I didn't realize how uptight he makes me until he's been gone. I'm still upset with how he treated you the other day." She slammed the door a bit too hard.

"I'd stay far away from him," Jason said in all seriousness as he put on his hat and then turned toward the forest. They didn't speak much until they reached a fork in the trail.

"What's up that way?" Sarah asked, pointing away from the river.

"That path will take you to the top of the canyon. It's quite the view. Maybe for another time," Jason said. Sarah liked the promise of another hike together. "What I want to show you is in the canyon."

Stopping at the spot along the river where they'd almost collided a few weeks ago, they took in the view of the waterfall and had a drink of water before continuing on.

Sarah wondered how she would feel coming back here, if the panic would return. As they walked further into the canyon, she found herself enjoying the view and the company too much to give it more thought.

"We've got to cross the river up here," Jason said. "There are plenty of rocks to step on, but you're still gonna get your shoes wet. Sorry."

"What is it that you want to show me?"

"You'll see. Give me your hand." His hand felt warm around hers. As he pulled her onto the large rock by the bank, she reached out her other hand for balance. He grabbed that one too. They stood so close her body tingled. Slowly she lifted her head and looked into his brown eyes. The depth she saw there made her catch her breath. Then her foot slipped, throwing her off balance but Jason's tight hold kept her from falling and pulled her even closer to him. For a time, they stood perfectly still, bodies almost touching as the water rushed around the rock they stood on. Jason's voice broke the delicious tension. "Let's get across before one of us ends up in the river." Reluctantly, they let go of each other's hands and carefully hopped from stone to log to stone before reaching the other side of the river.

"We're close now," Jason assured her. "Come on."

She felt a cold flow of air as they stepped out of the trees and stood at the mouth of a cave cut into the canyon wall. The roughly rectangular opening reached nearly six feet high and four feet across.

"Can we go inside?" Sarah asked.

"In a minute."

Jason set down his pack and pulled a small leather pouch from a pocket. He opened it and took a pinch of something out of it and held it in his left hand as he spoke softly with words she didn't understand. He moved his cupped hand up and down and all around his body before sprinkling the material on the ground. Then he turned to face her.

"Before we enter the cave, I needed to..."

"Ask permission to enter." Sarah felt compelled to finish his sentence.

"Yeah. How did you know?" Jason was taken aback.

And so was Sarah. "I have no idea. It just came out of my mouth."

She stepped closer to the entrance and said, "This is the cave from the story about Red Fire Woman, the grizzly bear's cave. Isn't it?" Her next steps were wary.

"That's what Old Man says. Did he already bring you here?"

"No. I've never been here before." *But then,* she wondered, *why does this place feel so familiar?* She couldn't tell from the frown on his face if Jason didn't believe her or if he was just as confused as she was.

"We're going to smudge with sage before we go in," he said as he pulled a small branch of the herb from his hatband and lit it. "Sage cleans you up." The sweet and rugged smell delighted her as she drew the smoke towards her with the same hand motions Jason used. Soon her whole being was quiet.

They stepped into the cave. Enough sunlight made its way inside for Sarah to see all around the space. The seven-foot ceiling sloped downward toward the back, like a funnel. She could make out a hole at the far end, perhaps leading to another chamber. The floor was sandy with very few rocks.

"Is there more to the cave," Sarah asked, pointing at the hole, "through there?"

"You're observant," Jason replied. "Yes, there's a smaller room back there. I'm told that's where the bears hibernate."

"We're not going to run into a bear now, are we?" Sarah looked around, a bit uneasy.

"No. They don't use this much except during the winter," he reassured her. "I haven't seen any signs of activity here in a long time."

"No fresh scat?" she asked, playfully.

"Scat. Listen to you." Jason looked amused. "That's not a word I'd expect to come out of an artist's mouth."

"I dated a wildlife biologist once. I heard the word all the time."

"Are you still dating this biologist?"

"No, that was back in college." Sarah replied, pleased that he wanted to know. Taking a chance, she asked, "Are you dating a biologist?"

"No." He might have been blushing, but she couldn't tell in the dim light. Then he smiled and her heart skipped a beat. As they looked into each other's eyes, the cool air suddenly felt warm and still. *Is he going to kiss me? God, I wish he'd kiss me. What am I saying?* Sarah looked away first.

Jason took off his hat and sat down on the ground, gesturing for her to join him.

"I hope you don't mind if I'm direct with you." Jason began.

Sarah nodded, her mind racing. *Here comes the brush off. He's probably married with kids back home some place. Or a girl friend he's crazy about.*

"Ever since I first ran into you, I've felt such a strong attraction to you. Not just sexual. You're a very attractive woman, don't get me wrong. But I don't let my prick run my life." He was looking at her with an intensity that was both exciting and intimidating. "I can't stop thinking about you. There's some connection here I don't understand. Something I've never felt with a woman before. And it's taking every ounce of energy I have right now not to kiss you."

Sarah wasn't sure what to say. Then again, words weren't exactly called for, but she was too nervous to lean over and kiss him. "You definitely are direct."

He looked away.

"And I like that."

Jason fidgeted with his hat but kept his gaze lowered.

"What I mean is, I've felt something too. When your uncle was telling us that story. This may sound weird, but I felt like you and I were in it together somehow. That sounds totally stupid, doesn't it?"

Jason met her eyes again. "No, it doesn't."

He leaned over and kissed her. His full lips caressed hers gently at first. Then he pulled her to him and kissed her deeply, tongues lightly touching. She ran her fingers through his silky hair as he cradled her face in his hands. Each kiss became more intimate and passionate, making them hungry for more.

Jason pressed his body against hers until they were lying down on the cool sand. She loved the feel of his chest on hers, his hand caressing her neck and shoulder, his lips exploring hers. While the rest of her body was eager for his touch, she wasn't ready to give herself completely to this man she barely knew. Not right away. And yet, she wasn't sure how long her resolve would hold. With each new kiss, her desire grew.

Then she heard buzzing, like a huge bee flying near her ear. She pulled away and started swatting around her head. Jason looked surprised. "What's wrong?" he asked, breathing heavily.

"Something's buzzing around my head. Can you see it?" The humming got louder.

"There's nothing there. I don't hear anything." Jason sat up. "Sarah, what's going on with your hand?"

Her clenched fist was twitching violently, shaking her entire arm. Jason put his hand on her forearm, but it didn't stop the spasm. The noise in her head grew deafening.

"Jason, what's happening? I can't see you...." Sarah watched as his troubled face faded into blackness.

"I don't remember much except that I passed out again, just like in the museum." Sarah fought back tears as she tried to recount to a very concerned looking Duncan Hawk what had happened back in the cave. "I'm not even sure how I got here."

"Jason said you were unconscious for a few minutes before he was able to revive you. He burned a lot of sage in the cave to help you." Duncan smiled softly. "You were able to walk back to the truck, with a lot of help. Once he got you here, you slept for over an hour."

He looked down at her left hand. It was still tightly clenched and twitching slightly. "You slept, but your fingers did not."

Sitting up, Sarah found herself on a small cot covered in some kind of soft animal pelt. The room was small and dark; a few Indian weavings hung on the wall. The strong smell of sage and cedar hung in the air.

"Where's Jason? Is he alright?"

"He is fine. He went to clean up."

"I am in your home?" she asked tentatively.

"Yes. This is where I do some of my doctoring."

"Doctoring? Does that mean you're a medicine man?"

"A medicine man is powerful." He sounded hesitant. "I just do what Spirit shows me, a little doctoring. Not really a medicine man."

Sarah started to move off the bed but Duncan stopped her. "We still have some work to do here. You asked me if I could stop your hand from making that fist. I think we need to see if I can. Okay, Sarah?"

"Okay." Her stomach felt queasy. "What are you going to do?"

"You don't have to be afraid. Nothing will hurt you."

Sarah wanted to believe him, but she still found herself sliding back into a corner and pulling her knees up around her chin.

"Why does my hand behave like it's Red Fire Woman's hand? I never even heard of her until you told me that story!"

"I do not have an answer that I think you will understand," Duncan said. He picked up a stool, placed it near the cot and sat down. "In my tradition, we believe that we carry the suffering of the people who lived before us. Those wounds will continue to cause pain in the present day unless we can heal them. We work with the Spirits to make this happen."

"How exactly? Do you travel back in time?"

"No time machine, if that is what you mean. In the Spirit world, time works differently. Healing energy can go where it is needed, as long as our intentions for the healing are clear and good."

"Are you saying that you actually change the past?" Sarah leaned forward in anticipation.

"So many questions." Duncan stood and put the stool back against the wall. "I do not always have the words to explain what happens with the Spirit medicine. What I can tell you is that this healing can change the present. I hope you will experience that."

Sarah stretched out her legs as she considered what Duncan had said. "Does that mean that you think Red Fire Woman is my ancestor?"

"It would appear so." His inflection left room for doubt.

"What about reincarnation? Do you think it's possible that we're connected that way?"

Duncan looked puzzled.

"I mean, do you think that I was Red Fire Woman in a past life?"

"I do not know about past lives," Duncan said. "Is this white man's medicine?"

"I'm not sure whose medicine it is. But my sister sure thinks it's real.

She works with spiritual stuff too, but from a psychological point of view. Reincarnation, as my sister describes it, is the belief that your soul can have many lifetimes, that after you die, you can be reborn in another body. Your soul gains new experiences from every lifetime, and you keep reincarnating until you've learned enough, I guess. It seems to make more sense when she explains it."

"What is your sister's name?"

"Ruth."

"Ruth. I will pray for her, just like I pray for you. And maybe one day, Ruth will come to the mountains and tell me about this reincarnation medicine. For today, we will do it the Indian way, okay?"

"Okay." Sarah had no idea what she was agreeing too, but what choice did she have? She wanted to make the twitching stop and sensed that no conventional doctor would have a clue about how to treat this. And even though she was apprehensive about what an Indian healing session would entail, she felt oddly at ease with Duncan. He seemed genuinely concerned about her.

"Would you like some water before we get started?"

"Yes. I'd also like to use the bathroom."

Duncan pointed her in the right direction and said he'd get the water.

She literally ran into Jason in the hallway. After the initial surprise, he hugged her tightly and spoke softly in her ear. "How are you? You gave me quite a scare." She welcomed his strong embrace and let him go only when she heard footsteps behind them.

Her mouth felt dry. Before she could say, "I don't really know,' Jason spoke up. "Hey Old Man, she's looking much better. What did you do?"

"Answered a lot of questions," Duncan said with a frown. Sarah worried that she'd upset him somehow. But then he smiled. "She asks about so many things, I almost forgot about doing any doctoring."

"Do you need any help from me?" Jason asked.

"I do not know. She seems to faint when she is around you. Not sure if that is good medicine or not," Duncan replied.

Sarah blushed, suddenly self-conscious. Jason stuck his hands in his pockets and looked down at the floor.

"Come nephew. You can drum for me."

The three walked back into the healing room and Duncan slowly closed the door.

CHAPTER THIRTY

SARAH WAS INSTRUCTED to lie down on the bed. A scented cloth was placed over her eyes as she heard Duncan tell her to relax, but her heart raced. A slow, strong drumbeat filled the small room and reverberated in her chest. After a few minutes, she became aware that her pulse had slowed to match that of the drum. She smelled the pleasant scent of sweetgrass burning, then the sharper aroma of sage. Soon the air felt thick with smoke, yet she had no trouble breathing. Apparently neither did Duncan, who started to sing in his native tongue, the melody sometimes at odds with the beat and sometimes right with it.

The singing and drumming continued without break, eventually filling Sarah with a sense of peace. She had images of walking in a mountain meadow splashed with colorful wildflowers under a bright sun.

Without warning, the mood changed. Her heartbeat, now indistinguishable from the drum, began to quicken. Clouds darkened the sky. Tranquility turned to fear, desperation. But not for herself. She was trying to save someone...the man she loved. She was running, crying, fighting...dying....

When she opened her eyes, she saw Jason's face lined with worry. He helped her sit up and then hugged her tightly.

"Sarah, I'm so sorry you had to go through that. Are you alright?"

She gently pulled back from his embrace. "I don't know." Disoriented and fuzzy headed, she looked around the room. "Where's Duncan?"

"He went out to pray." Jason didn't elaborate. "I think you could do with some fresh air. Can you stand?"

Sarah swung her feet around to the side of the bed and stopped. "Ooh, I'm dizzy. Give me a moment."

Eventually the two made their way onto the porch. The sun was setting. Sarah sank into the rocking chair, exhausted.

"I'll get you a sweater and some water," Jason said.

"I'd rather have a shot of tequila." Sarah smiled weakly.

"I bet you would." He kissed her forehead and headed back inside.

Rocking slowly, she listened to the creaks from the floorboards and tried to remember all that had taken place, feeling as though she'd woken up from such a deep sleep that the dream was eluding her. But it hadn't been a dream, not exactly. More like living through a memory, as observer and participant. Even that didn't quite describe what she had just experienced. Maybe Jason would have a better way of explaining it.

"Here ya go." Jason handed her a sweater and a glass. "Do you remember anything that happened to you during the healing?"

"It's all so confusing," she began, wrapping the soft covering around her shoulders. "I saw myself running. I had the sense that I was trying to help someone. A man, someone I loved. I felt a lot of fear and then things got dark. I don't have any images for this next part. I curled up and put my hands over my head, as though I was trying to protect myself. I didn't feel anything, but my body was reacting as though I was being beaten. I didn't actually feel afraid and yet I knew I was. This sounds so bizarre," she hesitated, but Jason encouraged her to continue.

"Eventually I had a sense, or an image, or I made it up, I don't know...I saw a man in a long coat hovering over me, hitting me. At one point, I saw a black horse rearing above me. I thought it was going to crush me with its hooves. Then everything went dark again. I felt my left hand make that fist. I don't know what happened after that."

"Old Man did a lot of doctoring for you," Jason explained. "Can't tell you exactly what he did. But he was praying a lot. Finally your body relaxed and you seemed to sleep. He told me to sit with you until you woke up. He doesn't want you to drive home tonight."

Sarah bristled a bit. She didn't like being told what to do, but another part of her was relieved, wanting to spend the evening in this rocking chair, with Jason near by, reassuring her that she wasn't out of her mind.

"Can you remember any other details of your vision?" Jason asked gently. "What did you look like?"

Sarah thought for a moment. "I'm not sure if Duncan's stories are influencing my imagination, but the woman who I saw had long, dark red hair."

"You said the man was wearing a long coat. Can you describe it?"

"It was a dark color...and it had large brass buttons." Sarah's mind went back to the Meeker Museum displays. "It was a military coat."

"Sarah, this isn't coming from your imagination. That's not what happens in a healing," Jason looked stern. "You had a vision. Trust me, I was watching you. That was no make-believe thing."

"You mean I saw something that is going to happen, like a premonition?"

"Not exactly. I think you saw something that happened in the past."

Sarah shook her head in disbelief. "Do you think that the woman I saw was Red Fire Woman, you know, because of the hair?"

Jason nodded. "And the man was probably Ethan Amory."

A sense of dread hit her so quickly she almost dropped her water glass. Closing her eyes, she started rocking more quickly. "He was the one. He was the one." She groaned as the mental picture flashed before her. "He was beating her. She was trying to hold onto something precious. He wanted it and she wouldn't let go. He couldn't pry her fingers open. She fought back. Then he did it...he pulled out a knife...and cut off her two fingers. He cut them off! But she wouldn't let go."

Sarah was sobbing uncontrollably. Jason eased her out of the chair and held her close, trying to comfort her. She pressed herself against him and didn't let go until her tears stopped. Slowly, she released her hold and looked up at Jason. He kissed her softly and moved a strand of hair from her face.

"That bastard." Anger replaced her anguish. "How could he have done that to her? He had such hatred in his eyes."

"Do you know what she was holding in her hand?"

She spoke without even thinking. "The bear claw necklace. I didn't actually see it in the vision, but I know that's what it was. Remember when Duncan was telling us the story and he handed me the necklace, after my hand was twitching so badly? I put the claw in my left hand and it stopped moving. But my fingers held onto it, like it belonged there. Red Fire Woman was protecting Standing Bear's necklace."

A sharp breeze blew across the porch and Sarah shivered.

"Let's get you inside. It's getting cold," Jason said while guiding her toward the door. "I'll light a fire and we can wait for Old Man to come back. We'll see what he has to say about all this."

Sarah stopped just before the door. "Why is this happening to me?"

"I have no fuckin' idea."

She felt tears welling up again as she followed him into the living room and settled into the couch. "I'm scared."

He left what he was doing by the fireplace and sat down next to her. "What are you frightened about?"

She took a deep breath, weighing the risks of sharing her past with him. Ruth was the only person she'd ever confided in about Blue and what had happened to her in the mountains. What if Jason reacted the same way Blue had to her story, or worse yet, what if Blue turned out to be right? What if the hand twitching, fainting spells, nightmares and visions were all signs that she was simply crazy?

Seeing the concern on Jason's face gave her the courage to continue. "I lived in Boulder for a couple of years when I was in college. That's when I was dating the wildlife biologist. I had some weird things happen to me back then that really messed me up and I feel like it's happening all over again, but in a different way."

As Jason listened intently, Sarah told him about falling in love with Blue, about the black bear that had charged her in the woods and how Blue had protected her and turned the animal away. Then the nightmares had started, as did her extreme fear of bears. "It's hard for me to put into words, but I felt as though the bear that had attacked me in the forest was out there looking for me, just waiting for another opportunity to get me. Blue thought I was losing it. He insisted that if I just spent enough time in the woods studying bears with him, I'd get over it. But that only made things worse."

Sarah bit her lip, watching Jason for any reaction, but his concentrated gaze hadn't changed. "Go on," he said gently.

"We had a fight when I'd come up to visit him at this research camp way up in the mountains. I knew I couldn't spend another night there, so

I decided to drive home, even though it was going to get dark soon and the dirt road was not safe, lots of potholes and hairpin turns. You know the kind of road I'm talking about. Anyway, I was halfway down the mountain, and this old man comes out of nowhere and steps right in front of me. I swerved to get out of the way and crashed the car. By some miracle, I hit a tree. Otherwise, I would have gone over the edge. It was a really bad accident. I was knocked unconscious. I hurt my back. Some hikers found me and got me to a hospital.

"I was able to get a message to Blue and he came down to be with me. But when I told him what had happened, he didn't believe me. He broke up with me after that."

"What was so hard for him to believe about your story?" Jason asked, a tinge of anger in his voice.

Sarah sighed. "The description of the man who stepped out in front of me. I saw an Indian man, very old, long white hair, wrinkled dark brown face. He was practically naked; all I could see was a leather loincloth. He had feathers in his hair and red paint on his face. He looked like he'd walked out of a history book. Blue thought I was hallucinating. He made me feel like I was a nut case."

Her voiced cracked. "I thought that was behind me. But here I am again, having weird experiences that make no sense. Maybe I am crazy."

Jason took her hand and gave it a reassuring squeeze. "If you're crazy, then Old Man and I are crazy too. Your boyfriend didn't understand the power of visions and dreams, Sarah. That's all. There's nothing wrong with you. He just didn't get it. But I do, or at least I'm starting to."

Filled with relief, she wrapped her arms around him. "Thank you," she whispered.

"You're not going through this alone. I'm a part of this too." Jason spoke softly in her ear. "I've got some things I haven't shared with you, some visions of my own. Now it's time I did."

While he finished building a fire in the fireplace, he told Sarah his recurring nightmare about the grizzly bear, about how both he and the bear are shot and killed. "In the dream, I'm not dressed in modern clothes," he explained. "I'm dressed in buckskin like my ancestors wore in the 1800s."

"So, what do you think it means?" Sarah asked, unsure if she was prepared for the answer.

"I'm wondering if somehow I've been dreaming about Standing Bear, even though it feels like it's happening to me. We know they found a dead grizzly near the grave where Standing Bear was supposedly buried." He touched her cheek. "And if you're related to Red Fire Woman and I am related to Standing Bear, maybe that would explain in part why I am so incredibly attracted to you."

He kissed her neck. "We'll figure this out together, I promise."

As she pulled him closer, she prayed fervently that he wouldn't break that promise.

Sarah woke up with a start, confused about where she was, but the sound of Jason's gentle breathing quickly reminded her. They had fallen asleep on the couch waiting for Duncan to return. The anticipation of his appearance was the only thing that had kept passions in check and most of their clothes in place.

The picture window looked out onto a dark sky that hinted at dawn's imminent arrival. Trying to stretch the kinks out of her neck, she stood up, careful not to wake Jason. Then she heard a rustling in the kitchen. Quietly she walked over to the door to listen and heard Duncan's voice muttering in Ute. Relieved, she slowly opened the door. The old man was filling a water bottle. An opened backpack lay on the table.

"Glad you're back. We were worried about you," Sarah said, her voice quivering a bit with emotion.

Duncan did not turn around.

Thinking that he hadn't heard her, Sarah repeated herself a little louder. Duncan walked over to the table without any kind of acknowledgement of the woman talking to him.

"Duncan, are you alright?" Sarah asked, stepping in front of him.

No reply. He didn't meet her gaze as he zipped up the pack.

The door swung open and Jason came into the room, looking half awake with tousled hair and his shirt unbuttoned. "Old Man, where have you been?"

Duncan swung the backpack over one shoulder, looking past Sarah as though she wasn't there and briefly addressed his nephew. "I am going to the circle to speak to the Spirits." Then he turned around and walked out the front door.

Sarah looked to Jason for some kind of explanation. She wasn't sure if the lump in her throat came from anger or hurt, but she knew she'd cry if she tried to speak.

"What did he say to you?" Jason asked, irritation in his voice.

She just shrugged her shoulders as the tears came any way.

"Hey now, what's this?" Jason said. "What's going on?"

"I don't know. He wouldn't speak to me, he wouldn't even look at me. I have no idea why. At first I thought he hadn't heard me. But then I realized he was ignoring me."

Jason wrapped his arms around her. He felt so good, so strong and reassuring. Needing a tissue, she reluctantly stepped out of the embrace. "Did I do something wrong, something to offend him?"

"Not as far as I can tell," Jason replied. "Old Man can act strangely at times. I have no idea what might be bothering him."

"What did he mean by 'going to the circle to talk to the spirits'?"

"He's going to a vision quest site; it's a circle of stones in the wilderness. Usually he fasts while he's there."

"How long will he be gone?"

"Probably three days."

"Three days is a long time to go without food," Sarah replied. "Is that okay for him to do at his age?"

Jason laughed. "Don't let him hear you say that. He'll be just fine. He's been doing this all his life." Then his tone darkened.

"What I don't get is why the sudden need to leave. A vision quest is something you plan and prepare for. You don't just decide at the last minute to go unless there is some emergency. And if there were, he'd tell me about it before going out. He's never done this before."

Jason emptied yesterday's coffee grounds from the coffee maker and ran water to fill the pot. Sarah took the coffee out of the cupboard and handed it to him.

"Do you think this has something to do with the healing...with me?" Sarah asked.

"I guess, but then why wouldn't he talk to you or me about it? That doesn't make sense," Jason said. "Then again, every time I think I've got Old Man figured out, he does something that throws me for a loop."

Sarah put two coffee mugs on the table and sighed as the comforting aroma of coffee filled the room.

"I hope he'll be alright," she said. "I just wish I knew what I'd done. It was like he was hurt or offended. I could feel it."

"Don't worry about it, Sarah. You haven't done anything wrong. Whatever it is, he'll tell us only when he wants to. All we can do is hold him in prayers while he fasts."

With mugs of hot coffee in hand, they stepped outside to greet the dawn. Despite Jason's reassurance, she couldn't shake the dread that she was responsible for Duncan's odd behavior. A hummingbird buzzed past her head on his way to the bird feeder. She watched it hover and feed, its wings beating so fast they blurred. Even this delightful creature couldn't lift her mood. She felt lost and confused. And a little scared. She'd call her sister as soon as she got back to her cabin.

CHAPTER THIRTY-ONE

DUNCAN SADDLED UP his horse and rode into the mountains. He knew that Jason understood, or at least accepted his sudden departure from the house. But Sarah was different. Duncan saw the hurt in her face, yet he couldn't find the words to tell her why he had to leave.

As he entered the forest, his own anger and confusion resurfaced. In all the years that he had been doctoring people, he had never come so close to losing his composure as he had with Sarah. What had come over him? As a healer, he was supposed to be like a hollow bone, allowing Spirit to work through him. The healer remains detached and open to any instructions from the spirit world.

But half way through the ceremony, as he watched her body writhing in apparent pain, he was suddenly overwhelmed with concern and affection for the woman on the healing table. He nearly forgot the words to the songs. Duncan had to fight his emotions to regain that healer's calm, and the experience had left him shaken and unsure.

What troubled him most was that these feelings for Sarah remained, no matter how much he tried to suppress them. They touched a deep lifelong desire, a sense that destiny had selected one woman for him, and that she was out there somewhere waiting for him. When he had first met Jessie years ago, he'd thought that she was the one. But his love for her did not survive his rage over Eli's desecration of the graves and Jessie's unintended complicity. She had meant no harm in telling Eli parts of the story of Standing Bear and Red Fire Woman. Still, the consequences of her actions had been devastating. Looking back now, he wondered if he had been too harsh. It had taken him several years before he reopened a friendship with Jessie. At various times over the past twenty years, he had followed his affections and become intimate again, but the nagging twinge would eventually return, that she was not his soul mate. And they'd go back to being friends.

During the healing session, he had been overcome with the yearning for that kind of partner in his life and found himself utterly captivated by Sarah. But that made no sense to him. He was too old for such emotions. She was young enough to be his daughter.

After several hours of riding, Duncan reached a small meadow protected on three sides by massive walls of stone. At the far end was a large circle of stones, nearly twenty-five feet across. Overgrown with grasses and sagebrush, this vision quest site was almost invisible to the untrained eye. But Duncan could feel the power of this place; he felt his ancestors and the weight of their prayers, their anguish and triumphs that had played out in this sacred circle.

When Duncan first entered the meadow, he got off his horse, opened his tobacco pouch and took a large pinch of tobacco in his left hand. He offered his own prayer.

"Spirits of this land, of this sacred circle, I am Duncan Hawk. My ancestors are buried in these mountains. I am of these mountains too. I ask for safe travels in this place. I also ask your permission to pray with my relations, these stones in the sacred circle." He sprinkled the tobacco on the ground and waited until he felt an answer, a welcoming from the land and the spirits. He walked his horse the rest of the way.

He set up a meager camp. Had he been back on the reservation in Utah, this vision quest would have looked quite different. A medicine man would be with him, helping him to attain his vision. They would hold a sweat ceremony to cleanse his spirit, smoke the sacred pipe to bless him, and his family would prepare a welcoming feast for him upon his return. But here in Colorado, so far from his tribe, Duncan had to improvise and simplify. As he had come to learn, the only thing that the Creator really required of him was his willingness to trust and surrender himself to the spirit world.

He walked into the center of the circle, placed a blanket on the ground and sat facing west, so he could watch the sun disappear behind the mountains. He wrapped a second blanket around him to ward off the ensuing chill. In the dusky light, he looked at the stones in the circle and spoke a greeting to each one of them. About the size of small watermelons, the stones looked neglected and forgotten. For over a hundred years, no one had come to pray in their presence; the people had forgotten where to find them until Duncan had discovered the site ten years ago. He had made a pilgrimage to the circle every year since, always to honor the ancestors and several times to seek a vision.

Duncan raised his hands to the sky, asking for understanding and guidance. Why did his heart ache for this woman from Chicago? How was he to help heal the wounds of his people, of Standing Bear and Yellow Eagle? What did Red Fire Woman require of him? He prayed long into the night. Eventually he heard brother coyote begin to howl. It sounded like he was laughing.

CHAPTER THIRTY-TWO

As soon as Sarah got back to her cabin at the Flat Top Ranch, she took a long, hot shower with a quick cold rinse to finish. Her body felt refreshed but her mind remained muddled, still struggling to make any sense out of the last day or so. She made a pot of coffee and called Ruth while waiting for it to brew.

"It sure sounds like you're dealing with a past life here." Ruth didn't waste time getting to the underlying issue after nearly an hour of her sister's retelling of the cave adventure, the healing session, making out with Jason on the couch and Duncan's baffling behavior. "From what you've described, I'm wondering if your body was actually reliving experiences that Red Fire Woman went through, including having her two fingers cut off. I bet that's why your left hand has been twitching and clenching so badly. It's probably triggered by situations or objects that have some connection to her."

"That's freaky." Sarah shuddered at the notion of a dead person somehow affecting her body. "What am I supposed to do with that? I'd like to have my own reactions to things, thank you very much. Duncan said this healing was going to take care of my hand twitch, but he ran off without telling me if it worked. Maybe he wasn't able to do anything for me. Or maybe he made things worse and that's why he left." Sarah's shoulders tightened.

"Or maybe he wanted to give you and Jason some time to be alone, you know...."

"Ruth! You can't be serious."

"No, I'm not. Just trying to make you smile. You sound so stressed about all of this."

"I am." Sarah's voice cracked.

"Sorry I can't be there to give you a hug. But I do have something fun to tell you. I did some digging around into our lineage. It doesn't look like we had any relatives who lived in Colorado at that time, so that kinda nixes the idea that you're related to Red Fire Woman. But I did find a fascinating little bit of synchronicity that you're going to love."

Sarah begged for a minute break so she could get rid of the two cups of coffee she managed to drink even while talking almost non-stop.

"Okay, I'm back. What did you find out?"

"You remember that Grandpa used to work for Thomas Edison? It was his first job out of college. He sold Ediphones."

"Of course. I love that picture Mom has of Grandpa with Edison and the other salesmen." Sarah made a mental note to ask her mom for a copy of that photograph.

"Turns out that Thomas Edison has a connection to your Red Fire Woman story, although it's a small one. In 1878, Edison actually met Nathaniel Meeker on a train to Wyoming. Edison was traveling there to build an observatory in Rawlins so he could study the total solar eclipse that happened that September. Meeker made note of the meeting in his diary and was none too impressed with Edison. Meeker was a renowned teetotaler and a conservative and so was quite disappointed to learn that this brilliant young scientist had the disgusting habit of chewing tobacco!"

"How funny," Sarah said. "That must be the eclipse that Duncan mentioned in his story. The Utes took that as an omen of bad times to come. And they were right. It's wild that Grandpa worked for a man who actually met Nathaniel Meeker," Sarah continued. "If this past life thing is true, I theoretically could have met Edison too, as Red Fire Woman. Too weird for me."

"But fun to think about," Ruth added with genuine enthusiasm.

"What am I supposed to do with all this past life stuff? I can't change the past, so what good is it to know all this?"

"According to your Ute friends, you can change the past. They seem to think they can do something about the wounds of their ancestors. I'd love to learn more about that, so make sure to fill me in once you find out how they do it."

"I tell you, Ruth, you're the one who should be going through this, not me!" Sarah replied.

"You get all the fun." They both laughed.

"To get back to your question, there are a number of ways that I work with my clients when past life stuff comes up," Ruth said. "Some find that there is a quality or attribute from the past life that they need to cultivate in this lifetime, so making that connection allows them to fully embrace and develop that trait. Sometimes, a past life comes into our awareness because there may be karma at work, a need to make amends or balance the scales. Here's an example of what I'm talking about. Let's say you killed somebody in a previous lifetime. The rule of karma could have you taking care of that person in another life to balance things out. In your case, I'm wondering if there may be something you are supposed to do that will somehow right a wrong that Red Fire Woman was responsible for."

"I don't know what she did wrong," Sarah said. "It sounds like she was more the victim in this story."

"But we don't really know what happened in the mountains, according to Duncan. We don't know how Standing Bear and Yellow Eagle died, or if they are actually the ones buried in the graves."

"You don't think she had anything to do with their deaths, do you?" Sarah asked, incredulous.

"Not directly, But Ethan Amory wouldn't have pursued the Utes into the mountains if she hadn't been with them."

Before Sarah could respond, she heard a knock on the door. "I gotta go. I think Jason's here. I invited him for dinner and I look like a mess."

"Dinner? It's not even three o'clock your time. Well, I'm sure you two will figure out something to do in the meantime." Sarah could feel her sister's lovingly wicked smile across the phone line.

"I'll call you tomorrow and we can continue this conversation. Love you," Sarah hung up the phone and sprinted to the door.

Her hand froze on the doorknob as she looked out the window. The man outside was not Jason, but since he was facing away from her, she couldn't tell if it was Nick or Hollis. As she opened the door, the man turned and Sarah breathed a sigh of relief. Hollis tipped his hat and smiled broadly.

"Good afternoon, Sarah. Sorry to come over unannounced, but Nick is just getting back from New York and I wanted to invite you over for dinner tonight."

Sarah wondered if she should cancel her evening with Jason, but she really didn't want to. "Hollis, that's so nice of you, thank you. But I've already made plans for tonight."

"We'll miss your company. Glad to see that you're making some friends out here."

"Thanks for understanding." Sarah immediately second-guessing her decision to decline, but Hollis already had moved on.

"I'm eager to see how you're coming with your sketches. Can we have a meeting tomorrow, around nine, to go over what you've got so far?"

"Absolutely. I'd like that."

"Have a good evening, Sarah."

As she closed the door, her stomach flipped. Nick had returned. What would he do if he saw Jason driving over here? Would he come over and give them a hard time again?

Maybe she should call Jason and offer to bring dinner over to his place. She picked up the phone, then put it back down, sensing that he'd be furious if he thought Nick was intimidating her. She didn't want to give him a reason to confront Nick. She felt trapped. All she could do was hope that Nick wouldn't notice Jason driving up.

Sarah spent the next hour pulling together her portfolio of selected sketches to show Hollis. Overall, she was pleased with the variety of work she had created and was eager for his input. Looking at her edited collection of historical images, she hoped he had a more open-minded opinion of the Utes than did his son.

Jason arrived without incident. They sat on the deck overlooking Lodgepole Creek that flowed through the ranch's meadowlands. Fortunately, her cabin was completed hidden by trees, so no one at the main cabin could watch her from a distance. They couldn't see Jason's truck in the driveway or observe them on the deck, sitting at a square table with place settings for two. Still, she felt a bit distracted with one ear alert to the sounds of anyone approaching.

"Would you like some wine?" Sarah asked, ready to pour a lovely cabernet she'd discovered the week before, a recommendation from the owner of the local liquor store in Meeker.

"Would love to, but no thanks," Jason said.

"Are you a beer drinker? I didn't think to ask you before. I'm sorry."

"Actually whiskey was my drink of choice. The operative word here being 'was'. I like the stuff too much. Water will be just fine."

Sarah hesitated. She had set out only wine glasses and was uncertain if she should pour herself a glass.

"Please, don't hold back on my account."

"Is it...uh...uncomfortable to be around people who...."

"Who drink? No, it only makes me uncomfortable if I'm making you feel self-conscious." His earnest gaze eased the awkwardness a bit.

"Got it." Sarah filled her glass a third less full than usual. "Help yourself to some salad while I get us some water."

She hurried into the kitchen. Placing two glasses and a water pitcher on a small tray, she shook her head. Jason doesn't drink. *Why didn't I know that?* Then again, she hadn't spent that much time with him, certainly not in a typical dating kind of situation. But the intensity of the experiences they had already shared made her feel an intimacy with him that wasn't based in familiarity. *Was that a good thing or a dangerous thing,* she wondered? *He has a problem with alcohol, so what other skeletons might be in his closet?* She pushed the doubts aside. *I want to enjoy myself tonight.*

Conversation flowed smoothly during dinner. They talked about favorite foods, movies, musicians, painters, books and vacation spots, delighting in each other's company as well as the food. Sarah did allow herself a second glass of wine.

Once the sun went down, the drop in temperature demanded either the donning of a fleece and hat or a migration inside. Jason suggested they move into the living room. "I have something to share with you."

Once inside, he offered to make a fire and then suggested they sit on the floor. He pulled a variety of things out of a leather bag and placed them on a red cloth—several round stones, two black feathers, a piece of brown fur and a stick stripped of its bark. The beauty of that natural collection inspired Sarah to pick up her sketchpad and start drawing.

"Always the artist, aren't you?" Jason said with admiration.

"Can't help it, especially when I'm surrounded by so many good looking things," she replied, looking right at him. He held her gaze so long, she stopped sketching and blushed. "Tell me about your treasures."

"I can only tell you about the ones that I brought. Later on I'll be eager to learn as much as I can about the one from Chicago."

Sarah put down her pencil and paper and leaned in a little closer. "You got my attention."

"Remember when we were waiting for Old Man to get back after your healing and you asked about the phrase he used, 'I do this for all my relations?' I said I'd explain it some time. Now feels like a good time."

Sarah frowned. "I sure wish I knew why he wouldn't talk to me."

"Don't worry too much about it. He gives me the brush off so many times and then comes around." Jason reached for her hand, held it tenderly for a bit, then slowly released it. "It's just his way."

He looked over at Sarah and was struck by the beauty of her eyes. The green color reminded him of another pair of eyes, those of the white hawk he'd seen in his sweat lodge vision that had been courted by a red hawk. The white hawk had injured her wing, and the vision had ended with the white hawk extremely frightened of the red hawk. Jason hadn't met Sarah yet when this vision had come to him. But being here with her, he had no doubt about its significance or about its warning of potential harm to her.

"Earth to Jason." Sarah touched him on the arm. "It seemed like your thoughts took you somewhere else just now."

"Sorry. I was looking at your eyes and it reminded me of a hawk I'd seen a while ago. A beautiful bird."

"I'm flattered, I think. No one's ever compared me to a bird before," Sarah said. "Do hawks have green eyes?"

"No, not really," Jason said, not ready to disclose his vision to her until he understood it better. "A story for another time. Let me get back to telling you about all my relations."

He put another log on the fire. "My people believe that we are related to all things, not just to other Utes or other people, but to all living things, including the animals, plants, rocks, waters and mountains. Everything is connected through the Sacred Hoop of Life."

"That must make family reunions quite interesting," Sarah grinned.

"Yeah, especially when you're serving one of your relatives for dinner," he quipped. "Seriously, though, that is why we always show respect for any animal that we kill. We ask that animal's spirit to make a sacrifice for us and we give that animal our thanks. We offer tobacco in gratitude. When we do ceremony, we acknowledge that connection when we say, 'I do this for all my relations.' We can't have a sweat lodge without the stones and the wood, without the fire and the water, the earth and the air. We can't live without them either."

Jason picked up one of the large black feathers and handed it to Sarah. "This is Raven. Raven is one of your allies. Good medicine for you."

"How do you know that?" Sarah asked, gently stroking the feather.

"Raven told me. Do you remember the raven that followed us back from the cave after you fainted? It was screaming the whole time we were hiking back to the truck. She was definitely watching out over you."

"I don't remember that at all. Then again, I don't remember much after I fainted." Sarah started to give the feather back to Jason.

"No, that feather is for you," he said.

"Thank you." She turned the feather over in her hands, admiring its simple beauty. "That's really strange about the raven in the canyon. I realize that I've been seeing a lot of them. Well, not a lot, actually. I usually see just one, but it seems to follow me everywhere. It can't be the same one. I mean, I saw one at the Thornburgh Memorial when I first met Duncan. And whenever I go over to the Double R, there's one hanging out in a tree nearby. Same thing when I went for a horseback ride with Ms. Jessie. A raven kept showing up. It's strange."

"No, not strange. Raven is your protector. So, of course you would see her around you. Next time you see her, talk to her. Tell her 'thanks'."

"You're being serious, aren't you?" Sarah asked.

Jason nodded.

"Do you have a protector?"

"Yes, red-tailed hawk."

"That fits you." Sarah smiled as she ran the feather along her forearm then brushed Jason's arm with it. "Do ravens and hawks get along?"

Jason closed his eyes and sighed. "In nature they don't. But I think you and I could work on a peace agreement."

She tickled his cheek with the feather; he gently grabbed her hand and pulled out the feather. He drew it down her neck, the tip stopping in the cleavage between her breasts. She felt a rush of warmth spread across her body. He kissed her lightly on the lips.

In a soft voice, he said, "We'll definitely come back to feathers. But now let's talk about trees."

He handed her the feather and picked up the white stick. He talked briefly about the power of trees, about all the gifts they provide, from medicine and food to shelter and fuel for the fire. He gave her the aspen stick stripped of its bark.

"It's so smooth, almost silky," she said, running her hands along its length. "I've never felt wood like this before."

"You do that very well," Jason remarked. "I've never been jealous of a stick before."

Sarah smiled as she continued to caress the piece of aspen. "Hmmm, we might just have to see what we can do about that."

Jason picked up a round stone and rubbed it along her calf, brushing the edge of her jean skirt. The coolness complemented the sultry glow she felt everywhere else.

"Stone people hold the oldest memories, the most ancient wisdom."

Sarah placed her hand on his as he continued to roll the stone over her other calf and up along her thigh. Almost breathless, she managed to ask, "What kind of stone is this one?"

"A seduction stone." He kissed her ear, then her neck. He took the stone and rubbed it softly against her cheek, then across her lips. His lips followed the stone, kissing her fully on the mouth. He placed the stone in her hand as he reluctantly pulled back.

"We have one more relation to meet." He lifted her tank top and placed a deliciously soft piece of fur on her stomach. "Do you know where this came from?"

She relished the sensation on her skin, and was in no hurry to pick it up and identify its original owner. "I'm not sure the tummy touch is enough to help me determine the species. I think further exploration is in order before I can figure it out."

She slowly pulled off her top and unhooked her bra. The beaver fur made her nipples hard as it slid over her breasts. Jason wrapped his arms around her, running the pelt along her spine. Sarah sighed and pressed herself against him. He kissed her deeply and then inquired, "Now about that stick...."

CHAPTER THIRTY-THREE

DUNCAN SPENT HIS second day and night in the vision quest circle in prayer without receiving answers, just continued mocking from coyotes at night. On the following day, he woke in the darkness, as he did every morning, just before four. He groaned as his body protested from sleeping in the cold on unforgiving ground. Standing took considerable effort, as did his first steps. Movement would warm him. The sky was clear, the stars still glistened as though touched by the dew that dampened the grass. He breathed in the hard cold air and started walking. On most mornings, he would walk around his ranch or down the road, but he needed to stay within the confines of the prayer circle, so he shuffled around his stony circumference in a sun-wise direction and thought of his grandmother.

She used to take her prayer walk, as she called it, every morning. She had told him that the veil between the worlds, the physical and the spiritual, was thinnest just before dawn. It was a good time to talk to those who had departed this life and a good time to hear what Spirit wanted to tell you. After she passed away, Duncan began his ritual of morning prayers predawn and sometimes he would feel her presence with him and they would talk. He wanted to talk with her now and so he gently called out her name. He felt nothing so kept moving, accompanied by a touch of loneliness.

He brought an image of her into his mind, her beautifully wrinkled face and nearly toothless grin. Despite the hardships life had thrown at her, she loved to laugh and played practical jokes on young and old alike. She also made a fry bread that made his mouth water.

But she was most often remembered as an exceptional storyteller, the best in her tribe. Every time she recounted the story of the forced march out of their mountain homeland into the deserts to the west, Duncan could feel the pain and heartbreak of every Ute in her voice.

She told Duncan about celebrating the Bear Dances when her people still possessed the Bear Medicine. And how those powers left after Standing Bear was killed. She insisted that no one since had had the ability to shapeshift into bear and learn from bear in that way.

The concept of shapeshifting had fascinated Duncan, even as a young man. As he understood it, a medicine man could become so attuned to an animal that the animal's spirit would move into the person and speak through him. Or, in rare cases of deepest spiritual connection, the holy man would actually change into the animal for a time. Through that magical transformation, great healing and wisdom was received and shared with the people. Duncan had never met anyone who had physically shapeshifted before, but he believed it was possible because his grandmother had told him so.

She had been a young girl when Red Fire Woman came to their tribe. Because she was Standing Bear's niece, she spent much time with White Willow Laughing, learning the medicine ways at the same time as Red Fire Woman. His grandmother was the last of his people to see Red Fire Woman before the soldier took her away. She became the guardian of Red Fire Woman's story and when his grandmother neared her death, she passed that responsibility on to Duncan.

This morning, Duncan needed her to tell him a different story, one that explained the confusion he felt about Sarah, the blurring of the past and the present, the healing that needed to take place. He stopped in front of an old pine tree growing on the inner edge of the circle and felt a warm breeze brush his face. As he walked slowly around the trunk, he saw her, more mist than substance and yet her energy was unmistakable. She took the chill out of the air. Smiling, she said nothing.

"Thank you for coming, Grandmother," Duncan greeted her with love and awe. "You told me so long ago that there would come a time when I would tell the story of Red Fire Woman and Standing Bear to someone not of our people, and that the rest of the story would be revealed. You said that there would come a time to wear the bear-claw necklace, that I would be called on to help heal the wounds of my ancestors. That time has come."

The ghostly image just nodded.

"The woman Sarah. She has a strong connection to Red Fire Woman that is clear to me. It may not be by blood. They may not be related. She asks about past lives and reincarnation. You taught me about the ways of healing our ancestors but nothing about living more than once on this earth. And yet, Grandmother, there is some part of me who knows her in a way I cannot explain. The wind spoke to me of her coming before I met her. I have feelings for her that I do not understand."

Duncan had conducted many ceremonies for the ancestors and helped others bring healing to their lineage. He had never had a sense of knowing someone from before, nothing that ever hinted of past lives. But his dealings with Sarah were different. Was it because she wasn't Ute?

"Grandmother, can white people heal their ancestors like we can? Or do they need to do this in a different way? Can you tell me that?"

In response, she opened her shawl to reveal two dolls. One looked like Sarah. It had a silvery cord tied around its waist. The cord was attached to the other doll that looked like Red Fire Woman. As Duncan watched, the faces on both dolls began to blur. When he looked again, the body of each figure wore the face of the other. His grandmother grinned as she closed her shawl, hiding the dolls from view. Then she turned around and when she faced Duncan again, she was holding a package in her arms, wrapped in fur. Duncan recognized it as the medicine bundle she had given him the day that she had died. It was Red Fire Woman's medicine bundle, a collection of tools and sacred objects that had been given to her for healing work. Duncan had put it away for safekeeping and had not thought much about it because it contained woman's medicine. He was not allowed to open it or use it in any way. His grandmother started laughing as though she'd just told a funny joke and then she was gone. A stiff breeze sent a shiver down his back.

Duncan sat down on the ground and leaned against a tree. He pulled out his tobacco pouch and rolled a prayer cigarette in a cornhusk wrapper. He offered the tobacco to his grandmother's spirit, thanking her and praying to understand all that she had shown him—the meaning of the silver cord that connected Sarah and Red Fire Woman and what he needed to do with the medicine bundle. The smoke of his prayers rose in the air as greeting to the sun's rays glowing behind the mountaintops.

His grandmother had promised years ago that the rest of the story would be revealed. But how would that happen? Duncan suspected that she knew what had happened in the mountains, how Red Fire Woman had been captured, how Standing Bear and Yellow Eagle had died, what had happened to Red Fire Woman after Ethan Amory took her away. After all, she had remained friends with Red Fire Woman until her death. Over the years, Standing Bear's wife must have confided in her. But every time his grandmother told the story, she maintained that no one but Red Fire Woman knew what had happened and that she had refused to speak of that time to anyone.

Duncan stood and stretched, welcoming the sun's warmth on his face. Maybe the rest of the story would come to him in a dream or a vision inside the sweat lodge. What needed immediate clarification, he realized, was how to resolve his unwelcomed reactions to Sarah, something his grandmother's visitation did not address.

He sat down in front of a large basalt stone on the west side of the prayer circle. "Stone Mother, I ask that you help me. Why am I suddenly so drawn to this woman? She is clearly not for me and yet my heart aches. I feel like Coyote has played a terrible trick to teach me something. But what? I do not want to feel this way. I need the strength and wisdom of Stone to help me."

He spent the rest of the day in prayer, focusing his awareness on connecting to the rocks in his prayer circle, inviting the spirit of Stone to enter his heart and mind, asking to experience its strength and endurance as his own and to know their wisdom gathered from eons of existence. As the sun set, he finally felt his body grow heavy and dense and his thoughts slow to the pace of water eroding bedrock. In that moment of stillness, a vision came to him of a beautiful cave lined in crystals, a sanctuary that would hold emotions he needed to contain until he found answers to their meaning. He could leave his unexplained heartache in this place, so it would no longer overwhelm him. He thanked the stones for this place of healing.

By the next morning, Duncan felt grounded and clear enough to return home and explore the next piece of this mystery as a healer, despite the questions that still haunted him.

CHAPTER THIRTY-FOUR

SARAH SNUGGLED UP against Jason on the couch in his living room, savoring his body heat and the warmth from the fire crackling in the fireplace. Summer evenings in the mountains felt more like early winter, but it was not the airy chill that drew her closer to him.

"How did your meeting go with Hollis this morning?" Jason asked while gently rubbing her shoulder.

"Overall, good. But Nick was there. The odd thing was, he was paying me compliments, acting like a total gentleman in front of his father. He was a completely different guy from the one you met, although he did manage to get in one dig about my Indian collection and then shot me a look that made my skin crawl. As soon as Hollis looked over, he switched right back to being charming. It's almost like he's got a split personality."

"I'd like to split his head open. I don't like the idea of him living so close to you."

"Me either. I do keep my door locked. Anyway, enough about Nick. Thank goodness Hollis is a normal guy. He liked most of my sketches and gave good feedback on the ones he didn't. I can tell he has a pretty clear idea of what he wants and yet he seems to be open to my ideas too. That's really quite remarkable for someone as wealthy as he is."

"What do you mean by that?"

"Most super-rich people I've worked with seem to pride themselves on firm opinions and have really bad taste in art. Hollis is different. He seems to value my expertise and doesn't see me as a minion who he's paying to bring his divine vision into the world."

Jason got up and put another log on the fire. "And his taste in art?"

"He liked the sketches I did of you and Duncan." She smiled.

"Well then, he must have impeccably bad taste in subject matter," he teased as he bent down to kiss her, "but excellent taste in artists." She reached up to meet his second kiss and pulled him onto the couch for a deeper embrace.

"I told him a little bit of the Standing Bear story and he was interested. I didn't go into too much detail, but I'm glad he wants some history in one of the murals. Guess that means that I'll need to make many, many more sketches of you."

Jason appeared more interested in exploring her neck than in replying. She relaxed into his affections, until he started unbuttoning her shirt.

"What if Duncan comes home?" She placed her hand over his.

"We'll hear his truck." Kissing her hand, he returned to the buttons.

"He took his horse, remember?"

"Right." Jason looked playfully at her. "We can go back to my room."

"We could." She kissed his cheek. "But I'm not sure how that solves the 'what if Duncan comes home' issue."

He looked puzzled.

"I don't know that it's the best thing right now, for Duncan to find us involved. He's already mad at me; no reason to get him more upset."

"Why would sleeping with me make him upset?" Jason asked.

"I don't know, but it just seems like it would." Her instincts told her that Duncan may not be ready for his nephew to be her lover.

"When it comes to Old Man, I guess anything is possible, but I'm willing to take the chance." He pulled her up as he got off the couch.

"I'm not sure I am...yet," she said. "Let's clean up the dinner dishes and we can discuss it."

Jason gave her a tender peck on each breast and then picked her up and carried her into the kitchen.

"You're playing 'hard to say no to', aren't you?"

"How am I doing?"

Real good, maybe too good, she thought to herself.

While they washed and dried dishes, Sarah talked about her last phone call with Ruth, about her suggestion that Sarah and Red Fire Woman might be connected through a past life and that there might be some kind of karmic payback at work here.

"For the sake of argument, let's assume that the past life thing is possible," Jason began. "And that you were Red Fire Woman in that past life. What good does knowing that do you?"

"According to Ruth, I'm being made aware of this connection because there may be something I'm supposed to do that will make up for something Red Fire Woman did. Righting some kind of wrong, if that's how karma works. The question is, what did Red Fire Woman do that was so terrible? From Duncan's story, it sounds like she was a victim, not a perpetrator of anything."

Jason was quiet for a time while he made coffee. "Maybe we should look at it a different way. Rather than what she did wrong, maybe the question is, what was allowed to happen because of her actions?"

"Give me an example," Sarah said, looking at the coffee pot. "You're making decaf, right?"

"You are such a lightweight," Jason teased. "You know, Indians don't drink decaf. But for you, I've made an exception." He held up the newly opened bag like a love token.

"You're too good to me. Thank you." She gave him a quick hug. "You were saying."

"If Red Fire Woman hadn't come to live with the tribe, would Standing Bear and Yellow Eagle have died? Ethan Amory wasn't intent on killing them. He wanted Red Fire Woman."

"True. But somehow it feels like there should be something more specific than that." Sarah took the cream out of the refrigerator. "I don't know, maybe there was something she could have done that would have spared their lives somehow."

"Good thought, but how would we ever know? Old Man's story didn't go into what happened in the mountains."

"I wonder if that's what I'm supposed to figure out." Sarah rubbed her left hand out of habit.

Jason poured two cups of coffee, dressed his with sugar and cream, and handed the black one to Sarah. "The other thing we don't know much about is the sweat ceremony that she and Standing Bear conducted. According to the story, they did something that normally would have been taboo."

"Do you have an idea what it was?"

"I hadn't given it any thought. But I bet Old Man has." He sipped his coffee. "I think that would be something to pursue whenever we get around to doing a sweat. We should ask the spirits about this and see if we get any answers."

"Oh fine, don't put too much pressure on me," Sarah said only partly teasing. "I've never been in a sweat ceremony before, and now I'm supposed to have spirits talk to me too! I was already nervous about this. Thanks a lot."

"Don't worry, I'll be there with you. You can always hold my hand," he said, taking hers and kissing her palm. "I won't let anything bad happen to you."

"Promise?"

"I promise."

They walked back into the living room and settled into the couch.

"While we're entertaining the possibility of past lives here," Sarah hesitated, feeling a little anxious, "where does that put you? Do you think you could have a past life in this story too?"

Jason took his time before replying. "As I said before, anything is possible. Hearing Standing Bear's story helped me see my nightmare in a different way. I took that to mean that he and I are related. Then again, maybe I was Standing Bear in a past lifetime. Who knows."

"Tell me your dream again. I remember some of it, but I was pretty shaken up when you told me the first time."

"It starts off with me running. I used to think I was running away from something. But then I realized I was running toward something. And I felt I was being pursued. Then I see this huge grizzly bear rear up in front of me. The bear gets shot, then I am shot. We both fall down and I watch the life drain out of the bear's eyes as it dies."

"Do you die in the dream?"

"I have the sense that I am dying."

"Where are you shot?"

"In the back."

"Hmmm." Sarah picked up a pen and started drawing stick figures on a small piece of paper.

"Are you running towards the bear or away from it?"

"Towards it. Why?"

"Well then, how did you get shot in the back?" She turned the paper around so Jason could look at it. She had drawn two stick figures and a bear on one side and a bunch of stick figures on the opposite side. "I know what you've told me is a dream, but I'm assuming that it is related to the story, since everything these days seems to be related to the story. And if that's the case, then the dream is telling us something about Standing Bear. But it doesn't make sense."

"What do you mean?"

"Take a look at this sketch. It's a likely scenario for the confrontation in the mountains. In Duncan's story, Standing Bear rescued Red Fire Woman from the soldier's camp. The soldiers came after them. I'm making an assumption here, but I'd imagine that Red Fire Woman and Standing Bear would be standing near each other, facing the soldiers. We also know that the bear got shot. The only ones who would shoot the bear would be the soldiers, right? So how does Standing Bear run toward the bear but get shot in the back by a soldier. Are you with me?"

Jason nodded. "You've got Standing Bear and Red Fire Woman and the bear facing off against the soldiers."

"Exactly. So, if Standing Bear is running toward the grizzly, the only person standing behind him would be Red Fire Woman. And there's no way she would have killed him. So who shot Standing Bear?"

"Maybe a soldier snuck up behind them somehow."

"That's possible."

Then Jason shook his head and stood up. "On second thought, that seems unlikely. I've been up to the gravesite where this took place. The trail leading to the meadow is too narrow. No one could have gotten behind them. Standing Bear would have seen anyone coming up that trail. And the terrain on either side is too steep for someone to sneak up on them without making a lot of noise."

Sarah caught her breath as a terrible thought surfaced. "What if Red Fire Woman shot him by mistake? Maybe she was aiming at a soldier and hit him instead?"

"I'd hate for that to be true," Jason said. "You'd have to be a pretty bad shot to make that mistake. I have no idea if she would have known how to handle a gun. But since we're speculating, we need to consider all possibilities. I don't think this is the most likely scenario though."

"I hope you're right. That still leaves us with the question of who shot Standing Bear." Sarah paused, then hesitated. "What about Yellow Eagle? Could he have shot his cousin?"

"Why would he do that?" Jason seemed slightly annoyed.

"Because he felt cursed from the sweat ceremony?"

"I think you're fishing," Jason said. "It had to have been a soldier."

Jason picked up the stick figure sketch and stared at it while slowly pacing the floor. Sarah got up to go to the bathroom. On her way back, she heard flute music, a sad, halting tune. Jason was sitting on the floor with a long wooden flute to his mouth. She stood in the doorway listening. When the last breathy note had faded, she spoke gently. "That was beautiful."

"Thanks. I tend to think better when I'm playing. My guitar's in my room, so I picked up the flute. It's been a while."

"Couldn't tell by the music. It was lovely. Play something else."

"Are you asking me to seduce you?" Jason's eyes twinkled.

"What do you mean?"

"The traditional way for Ute men to court their women is by serenading them with flute music."

"That's right. In the story, that's how Standing Bear won Red Fire Woman's heart." Sarah smiled.

"Although Yellow Eagle was the one known for his flute playing. He must have broken a lot of women's hearts, because the stories of his music are famous. Every flute player on the reservation knows about Yellow Eagle. Standing Bear was probably a novice compared to him. But let's see what I can do." Jason played another melody, a bit brighter than the first one.

Sarah's knees weakened, forcing her to sit down. Her body recognized this song, and yet she had never heard it before. How could she have? When he finished, she wrapped her arms around him.

"Guess it really does work." Jason laid down his flute and returned the embrace.

He led her down the hall to his room and guided her to his bed. As she lay down, he slid a CD into the player. He pulled off his shirt and his pants and lay down next to her, with the seductive sound of Indian flute music to serenade them.

As the sun disappeared behind the mountains, Duncan rode up the drive to his home. Sarah's truck was parked by the barn. Despite his best efforts, he felt his heart quicken. She was here to see Jason. *As it should be,* he reminded himself. As he stepped onto the porch, he heard flute music coming from the house. A courting song.

Leading his horse to the corral, Duncan felt as lonely as the stones in his prayer circle and just as old.

CHAPTER THIRTY-FIVE

IT WAS DARK BY THE TIME Jessie and Patrick set foot on Duncan's porch. They waited anxiously for a reply to their knocking. Silence.

"Maybe we should have called first," Patrick said, walking over to a window and peering in.

Jessie knocked again, trying not to pick up on Patrick's edginess. He was apprehensive about Duncan's reaction to the news. "He's here; give him a moment. His hearing isn't what it used to be." She made note of the truck by the barn. He had company. She hoped they wouldn't be interrupting anything, but the reason for their call was urgent.

Soon after her third rap on the door, it swung open and a weary looking Duncan Hawk signaled her in with a brief hand wave. He did not react when Patrick stepped through the doorway after her.

"Sit." Duncan instructed them.

"We're sorry for coming here at such an hour," Jessie began. "Something's happened that you need to know about."

"So important it could not wait until morning?" Duncan muttered.

Patrick blurted out, "Would you like us to go?" Jessie shot him a look.

"Make us some coffee and then we can talk," Duncan said as he picked up his backpack and turned toward the hall. "I have been in the forest and have to unpack my things. Jessie knows where everything is."

That explains why he looks like he hasn't showered in days, she thought. Jessie waited for him to get out of earshot before telling Patrick where to find the coffee to make a fresh pot.

"He really moves in his own little world, doesn't he?" Patrick said.

"It's not a little world," Jessie scolded. "He'll surprise you with what he knows. Don't underestimate him. He likes his coffee strong."

"How is it that a Ute elder lives up here?" Patrick asked. "Land is expensive and I know the government didn't leave any of this to the tribe. No disrespect here, but you don't see too many Indians owning prime mountain real estate in Colorado."

"True," Jessie replied, irritated with the question because it brought up her own inner conflict about owning land that once belonged to Duncan's ancestors. "A man named Barney Filmore used to own this ranch. His grandfather was a trapper who married a Paiute woman. Barney's grandmother died when he was very young but he always talked about her, seemed obsessed with his Indian heritage. When Duncan first started coming to this valley almost forty years earlier, he spent a lot of time looking for sacred sites in the mountains. He met Barney and they became friends. Barney insisted that Duncan stay at the house whenever he was in the area. Duncan told me that Barney would drive him nuts, constantly asking him about Indian culture and history. Even so, he liked Barney; he even did a couple of ceremonies for him. When Barney died, he left the ranch to Duncan."

"How did Barney's family feel about that?" Patrick asked.

"There was no family, at least as far as I know," Jessie said. "Duncan became his family."

"Maybe you can get Jessie to leave me her land when she dies too."

Jessie and Patrick turned around to find Duncan in the kitchen.

"You startled me," Jessie said. He looked so tired.

"Patrick," Duncan said, "what do you think of this new kind of easement? The white people can live on the land until they die and then their land comes back to the Utes."

Patrick hesitated, unsure if he was kidding.

Duncan laughed. "I've frightened our biologist here. He thinks I'm a crazy savage coming to take his land!"

Patrick grinned half-heartedly. "You had me going there. I can run your idea past my boss and see what she thinks."

"Good," Duncan said. "I'm ready for my coffee. And then you can tell me why you drove over here in the middle of the night."

Jessie was anxious to share their latest dealings with Eli, but knew better than to rush Duncan into conversation. She and Patrick listened patiently while he told them about the animals he'd seen while camping. Jessie wondered if he had gone on a vision quest. Why else would he have gone out by himself for days? She knew it was inappropriate to ask, so she made small talk instead.

Patrick fidgeted in his seat, got up to wash out his mug, then put more coffee in it. He wasn't used to Indian elder time. Jessie tried to catch his eye, but Duncan was finally ready to hear what they had to say.

"Patrick, I am boring you with my stories. You are a biologist; you see animals all the time."

"Oh no, sir, not at all. I mean, about being bored. It's just that I'm more concerned about what happened today…."

"Did you find yourself a spirit?" Duncan asked, teasing the biologist.

"Uh, no."

"We've got a problem with Eli," Jessie interjected, signaling Patrick to take his seat.

"You have always had a problem with Eli," Duncan stated kindly.

Jessie bristled. "We may have pushed him over the edge."

She poured Duncan another cup of coffee before continuing. "Patrick put out another spirit warning for Eli after our meeting in my kitchen. I got the idea of prodding him a little bit, you know, in the direction of the easement idea."

An uneasy silence filled the room as Jessie gathered up the courage to continue. "So I attached a note to this one. It said, 'Give back what you have taken. Leave this land to the Spirits and you will be set free.'"

"Did you write it in Ute?" Duncan couldn't hide his amusement.

Jessie was too preoccupied with the story to appreciate the jest.

"He didn't respond to the note the way I thought he would." Jessie looked over at Patrick. "Tell Duncan what happened."

"At first he got real quiet and then he started to shake so hard, he dropped the note. I thought he was having a seizure. He stumbled into the cabin and I didn't hear anything for a while. Then he came out, got in his truck and drove off. I had quite a hike back to where I'd hidden my truck. I'll spare you the details, but I was able to follow his tire tracks to the turn off into your valley. Good thing he stayed on gravel roads and we'd had some rain. I found his truck parked at a trail head about a mile west of your ranch."

"I know the place," Duncan said, his face now serious.

"It took me about an hour to catch up to him on the trail. He was pacing and muttering at a spot where the trail splits."

"By the beaver dam." Duncan added.

"Yes. So you know where he was?"

Duncan nodded.

"He had something in his hand, something small, wrapped in cloth. A couple of times he held it up and yelled, 'Is this what you want?' Then he'd go back to pacing and muttering. Seemed like he was trying to build up enough nerve to go down the trail to the right. Finally, he started walking that way. I waited a bit before following. The trail ended in a meadow. I saw him at one end. He was acting crazy, pushing through the grass, like he was looking for something. I snuck around to get a bit closer and then climbed a tree so I could watch what he was doing.

"He got to a pile of rocks and started yelling again. 'Don't hurt me. I'm putting it back. You motherfuckers, leave me alone.' The guy seemed to be having a nervous breakdown or something. He started throwing rocks off the pile. I couldn't see from where I was, but I'm assuming he put that bundle inside..." Patrick looked at Duncan, who hadn't moved since the story began, "...inside the grave. I didn't know that's what it was when I was there, but Ms. Jessie told me later."

Patrick cleared his throat. "As Eli started putting the stones back on the pile, the weather changed, faster than I've ever seen it, even for these mountains. A huge dark cloud moved over the meadow; it felt like dusk. Thunder cracked so loud overhead, I almost fell out of the tree. Then we got hit with wind gusts, must have been twenty miles per hour. No rain, but the lightning was intense. So I got out of that tree. I was sure that lightening was going to hit something.

"Next thing I know, Eli is running down the path, looking like he'd seen a ghost. I know this sounds weird, but it's as though that black cloud followed him. By the time I got to the grave, the sun was shining and the wind had stopped."

"What did you do when you got there?"

"I saw that Eli hadn't finished putting back the stones. There were still a few scattered around. I hope this was okay, but I put them back on the pile. I meant no harm, only respect."

Duncan just grunted. Patrick looked at Jessie for an interpretation of his response. She nodded for him to continue.

"I headed back down the trail and caught sight of Eli where it split. But instead of going back toward the truck, he bolted down the other fork. As you already know, that trail feeds into your valley, so I finally got a chance to hike it, although not in the way I'd prefer. It took Eli hours to make it back to the road. He stumbled around like a drunk man, tripping on rocks, getting snagged in branches. I had parked my truck down the road from his, so I was able to follow him to make sure that he got back to his cabin."

Jessie watched Duncan's face for any sign of emotion. A boulder had more expression. "Duncan, I'm so sorry," she blurted out. "I never thought Eli would have the guts to go back there. I'm sick about what he did to the grave. I had no idea he still had something from there."

Duncan didn't say a word. Jessie was prepared to wait out his silence, but Patrick looked anxious. She stood up. "Patrick, let's give him a minute. Come with me."

She led him down the hallway into the living room where she took a seat on the couch. Patrick paced in front of the fireplace. "Man, that guy is hard to figure out. I mean, Eli didn't really do any damage, did he? He returned whatever he took, so that's good, isn't it?"

"In the Ute tradition, disturbing a grave is never good."

"Do you think he's mad at me for putting those stones back?"

"I have no idea," she replied. "But I'm sure he knows you had the best intentions. Nothing you can do about it now, so stop worrying."

Patrick didn't look comforted, but he stopped pacing. "Do you think Eli is scared enough now that he'll sign the easement?"

"I sure hope so. Then again, maybe we've pushed him too far and he's losing his mind."

"Well, that may not be all bad," Patrick said. "If he cracks up, he won't be in a position to sell. I'm pretty sure you have to be of sound mind to enter into legal contracts."

"If Nick Tremaine ever finds out about this, I'm sure he'd have a lawyer who would find a way around that," Jessie said.

Patrick nodded in agreement. "Did I tell you that Hollis asked me to spend the day with that artist he's got living at his ranch? He wants me to take her out into the forest and teach her some ecology."

"Really?" Jessie said. "When are you going with her?"

"Day after tomorrow."

"Make sure you don't mention anything about Eli or the ranch to her. I don't think she'd say anything to Nick, but we can't take any chances."

A woman's voice startled them both.

"Don't worry. I won't."

Jessie and Patrick immediately turned around and saw Sarah standing at the end of the hallway.

"Ms. Jessie, I didn't mean to eavesdrop on your conversation, but I was, uh..."

Just then Jason came walking up behind her, his long hair loose, wearing only a pair of jeans. As he caught sight of Sarah, he said, "Hey, there you are. I was wondering where you'd gone."

Sarah nodded her head in Jessie's direction just as Jason stepped into the room and realized they were not alone.

"Ms. Jessie. Patrick. What a surprise. No offense, but what are you doing here?" Jason walked over and shook both their hands.

"Hello, Jason," Jessie said. "We came to talk with Duncan."

Jason looked around the room.

"He's in the kitchen," Jessie's mind was racing. *What is Sarah doing here? Don't be stupid; you know why she's here. Just look at Jason's face. She knows about Eli. Damn it!*

"Old Man finally made it back. Good," Jason said. "How did you know he was home?"

"Actually, I didn't know he'd been gone until we got here. It's a long story," Jessie said as she turned and walked back into the kitchen to avoid further conversation. The others followed her.

They found Duncan still sitting at the table, eyes closed, speaking softly in Ute, as though in prayer. Jason waited until he'd finished before touching his shoulder and greeting him in their native tongue. As they talked together for a time, Patrick and Sarah introduced themselves.

"How funny, Hollis had just mentioned you and our field trip and here we run into each other like this," Sarah said, trying to restore a sense of normalcy to an uncomfortable situation.

"Quite the coincidence," Patrick replied.

Jessie tuned out the conversations as she tried to figure out how to proceed. It was obvious that she was not going to get any reaction from Duncan tonight. What a mess. She hoped he was not too upset and she prayed that Sarah would not mention any of this to the Tremaines.

Just then Duncan stood up and the room grew still. "I need to do ceremony for the Spirits of the ancestors who have been disturbed today. All of you are going to assist me. We leave for the meadow tomorrow at three o'clock. We will take the horses." Not waiting for a response, he walked out of the room.

Jessie wasn't sure who looked more confused, Patrick or Sarah. "I'll explain on the drive back," Jessie assured her biologist friend. "Looks like we'll see you both tomorrow. Good night."

As she stepped into the cold night air, Jessie thought about Sarah standing in the kitchen, her hair mussed, leaning up against Jason. She felt a twinge of longing knot in her stomach. She had never stayed the night at this ranch; Duncan had never invited her to. Over the years, when affections would rekindle and they would share intimacies, they did so only in her bed or on camping trips. But never here. And for years, she found that arrangement had suited her. But seeing Sarah and Jason together in the kitchen flustered her. Jessie wanted more from Duncan. She wanted him to look at her like Jason looked at Sarah. *You're a crazy old woman,* she told herself as she drove off. *As crazy as old Eli.*

CHAPTER THIRTY-SIX

THE DAWN LIGHT CAST the landscape in a soft glow that brought out the beauty in every living thing—blades of grass, aspen leaves twirling in the morning breeze, the marmot scurrying for cover as Sarah's truck passed by, the shiny black of the raven that flew past her window. She drove slowly, soaking in the images, the colors, the composition. Replicating this dawn palette would be a challenge when she started painting her murals, which made her eager to get back to her cabin so she could play with the colors in her sketchbook.

Hoping her early return from Jason's would allow her to slip past the main cabin undetected, she pulled into the long drive to the Tremaine ranch. As she topped the rise, her throat tightened. Hollis and Nick were standing on the deck. Hollis waved to her. She felt compelled to pull in. *How do I explain where I've been? What do I tell them? Think, Sarah.*

"Good morning, young lady!" Hollis always sounded so happy and welcoming. "Out for an early morning drive?"

"Why, yes, I was." A raven landed on the corner of the deck railing. Sarah looked at the bird, which triggered a memory of her conversation with Jessie on their recent horseback ride. "Ms. Jessie had suggested that the best time to see elk along the river was right before dawn."

"Right, she is," Hollis said with enthusiasm. "Should be mostly cow elk with their calves. How many did you see?"

"It was hard to count them, but I did see a bunch. Their fur looks lovely in this light," Sarah hoped she sounded convincing. The raven bobbed up and down, as though in agreement with her.

"Splendid," Hollis said. "Did you say you met Ms. Jessie?"

"I did. Yes. We ran into each other." Sarah listened to her own voice, as if it was a separate person, wondering what she would say next. "In fact, she was with the biologist you wanted me to meet. Patrick, I believe is his name. Turns out, he has some free time this afternoon, so we're going to have our ecology lesson today rather than tomorrow. Funny how things work out."

"Yes, funny," Nick said. "I didn't hear you leave this morning. You must have been in stealth mode."

Sarah avoided eye contact, afraid he was not buying her story.

"Where is our fine government friend going to take you?" Nick seemed to be daring her.

"I'm meeting him up along South Elk Creek." Sarah kicked herself. *Why'd I tell him that? I should have made up some place. He knows that's near Jason's place. You dummy.*

"Well, perhaps I should come along," Nick said. "You never know, maybe I could learn something."

Sarah felt trapped in her own deception. How could she refuse? She couldn't have Nick come with her to Duncan's ceremony by the gravesites. The raven started to caw.

"Any other day, I'd say that would be a fine idea," Hollis said. "But we've got the irrigation contractor coming this afternoon and he needs to talk with you about the horse arena."

Sarah let out a sigh. The raven cawed louder, which made Sarah grin. The bird sounded like it was scolding Nick or laughing at him. Nick must have thought so too, because he picked up a stone and threw it at the bird. The rock missed its target and the raven flew off in the direction of Sarah's cabin.

"Hollis, I hope you don't think me rude, but I'd like to get back to my place so I can capture some of the images from this morning while they're still fresh in my mind."

"I'd love for you to have breakfast with us, but I understand that the art comes first. That's why you're here, after all," Hollis said. Sarah wanted to hug him for being such a kind man and for keeping Nick at bay, at least for today.

As she drove the short distance to her cabin, Sarah congratulated herself on her quick thinking. Not only had she come up with an explanation for her early morning return to the ranch, but she also had a story for where she would be this afternoon. The raven, perched on the porch swing, greeted her with a raucous chorus.

"You know, maybe Jason's right. Maybe you are my protector, Raven. You do seem to be hanging around. Hold on a minute." Sarah went into the cabin and brought out some sunflower seeds that she threw on the ground near the spruce tree. The large black bird flew over and eagerly started eating.

Much to her relief, Sarah didn't run into Nick while leaving the Flat Top Ranch later that afternoon. She arrived at Duncan's place a few minutes before two and spotted Jason in the horse corral, brushing a small nutmeg-colored mare.

"She looks just the right size for me," Sarah said.

"That's what I thought, too. And she's really gentle, so you should have an easy ride."

"Thanks," Sarah said, slipping between the railings. She put out her hand and the mare sniffed it, then shook her head as if to say, you can pet me now. Sarah complied by scratching behind her ears.

"She likes you already," Jason said. "Me too." He put his arm around Sarah's waist and slowly kissed her. She wrapped her arms around his neck, and melted into his embrace until the mare whinnied and jabbed her nose into Sarah's shoulder.

"Ow. That hurt," Sarah said.

"Molly does like being the center of attention. You can keep petting her while I get her saddled up."

"Will do." Sarah liked the feel of her soft nose against her palm. "Well, Molly, I should have brought you some carrots. Next time."

When Jason returned from the tack shed, Sarah told him about her encounter with Hollis and Nick that morning and her quick thinking. She also mentioned the raven that seemed to be following her.

"I told you Raven was good medicine for you," Jason said.

"Duncan told me the same thing about sweetgrass."

"We get our medicines from many sources. You're no different."

"But I am," Sarah said. "I'm not Ute. Doesn't all this talk of medicine and animal protectors apply only to native peoples?"

Jason tightened the cinch on Molly's saddle and tied her to the railing. "Not in my book, it doesn't. I don't think Old Man sees it that way either. The way he taught me, we're all related. That includes people of all races. We all come from this earth, our Mother. So do the plants and animals, the rivers and the mountains. I think a bird or a plant can bring you medicine as readily as it does me. The important thing is being aware of the gifts being offered. Not everyone grew up believing this stuff. I sure didn't and I'm an Indian. But Old Man can be persuasive, if you know what I mean. So, if you're learning about these ideas now and can open to them, the medicine should work for you as well as it does for me or Old Man."

"I'll give that some thought. How is Duncan this morning?"

"Haven't seen him. He's been in his healing room all getting ready."

"Do you know what's going to happen at this ceremony today?"

"I don't. But don't worry. Just do what he tells you and you'll be fine. Help me get these other two horses ready to go."

By the time they had finished with horses, Duncan stepped outside, his face stern, and motioned for Jason to come over.

"I'll wait here," Sarah said, not eager for another icy reception.

Duncan handed saddlebags to his nephew and then sat down on the porch. A few minutes later, Jessie and Patrick arrived with a horse trailer in tow. Sarah watched as they unloaded horses already in bridle and saddle. Everyone converged in front of the house and exchanged greetings, then waited for further instruction.

"Let us go," was all Duncan offered. He signaled Jason to follow behind him.

Jessie rode over to Sarah as they moved down the long drive to the road. "Sarah, we didn't get a chance to talk last night. I don't know exactly what you overheard."

"I apologize for not letting you know I was in the room sooner." Sarah said. "Guess I wasn't sure what to do. But I won't say anything to Nick or Hollis, I assure you."

"Thank you," Jessie said. "What did Duncan tell you about Eli?"

"Nothing, really. He talked a bit with Jason and then went to bed. He told Jason that Eli had robbed some Ute graves a long time ago and had recently gone back and disturbed them again. I guess Patrick saw him do it? Jason said Eli owns a ranch around here but hasn't lived in the valley for years now. That's really all I know."

"Did Duncan tell you whose graves they were?"

"No. Do you know?"

Jessie raised her eyebrows, curious as to why Duncan hadn't told her that the graves were related to the Red Fire Woman story, but didn't answer Sarah's question. "Once again, I need to insist that what I'm about to tell you is kept in the strictest of confidence."

"Of course."

Reluctantly, Jessie gave Sarah the abridged version of the Eli saga, beginning with his original robbing of the graves, the series of disasters that plagued him after that and his eventual realization that his misfortunes were most likely caused by Indian spirits haunting him because of his grave robbing. She explained about how he ran off to Las Vegas once fear got the better of him. Then, his unexpected return a month ago and his desperation to sell the land in order to pay off gambling debts and Patrick's attempt to get him to take a conservation easement instead. And her efforts to scare Eli with reminders of spirit curses to keep him from selling. She ended with a description of his breakdown by the graves the other day.

"I don't need to tell you again, but I will any way," Jessie concluded. "If Nick finds out about Eli wanting to sell, I'm afraid we'll lose that land to the worst kind of development and I'll do anything to make sure that doesn't happen."

"I understand. I was wondering, what is a conservation easement? I've never heard that term before."

"Patrick is the best one to explain that to you." Jessie called out to him and told him to switch places with her.

"Good talking with you, Sarah."

Sarah could tell from Jessie's tone of voice and forced smile that she was uncomfortable sharing this story. Sarah would not betray her trust.

Patrick smiled warmly as he waited for her horse to catch up to his. "So, Ms. Jessie says you want to know about conservation easements. You've come to the right place."

Sarah listened intently. He spoke with a nice combination of conviction and instruction.

"Can't see why Eli wouldn't go for an easement," Sarah said off-handedly. When Patrick stiffened, she immediately added, "Don't worry. Ms. Jessie and I talked about all of this. I won't say anything to the Tremaines about Eli."

"Thank you."

Slowly his furrowed brow softened. "So, you're, uh, friends with Jason and Duncan, I take it."

"I guess you could say that." Sarah blushed a bit.

"Then, do you know what Duncan has in mind for today? I asked Ms. Jessie and she either didn't know or wasn't too keen on sharing."

Sarah shook her head. "I have no clue what's going on. Guess we'll find out soon enough. But since we've got some time, how about giving me your ecology talk while we ride? I'm not sure I'll be able to meet you tomorrow. It's a long story and I won't bore you with the details. But I'd certainly appreciate your taking the time today, if possible."

"I'd be happy to."

As they made their way down the forested trail, Sarah took in everything Patrick had to say about shrub oaks, lodgepole pine, wild turkeys, bighorn sheep, fire hazards, beetle infestations, logging, ranching, coyotes, bears, mountain lions and everything in between. She noticed Jason checking on her with frequent backwards glances throughout the ride. The thought that he might be a little jealous pleased her. She wasn't aware of her sore knees or rear end until the procession stopped and she dismounted at the entrance to a mountain meadow.

Duncan spoke to the group for the first time since the ride began. "The place we are entering is sacred ground. We have come to honor the Spirits of the land and the Spirits that have been disturbed in their resting place. Enter this space with respect for both the living and the dead. Leave your horses under those trees. Jason, bring my saddlebags."

Jason walked over to Sarah and took her horse. "Have a nice talk with the fed?" he asked, kissing her on the cheek. She started to answer, but he didn't wait for one.

Sarah remained on the trail, while the others tethered their horses under the aspens. She observed Duncan as he took out his tobacco pouch from a larger beaded satchel and reverently sprinkled some on the trail. He looked up to see her watching him.

"I am making an offering to the Spirits of this place," Duncan said, "telling them who we are, asking them for permission to enter here."

"Who is buried in the graves that are here?"

"You tell me, Sarah."

Before she could ask him what he meant, the others joined them.

Duncan instructed them to form a circle while he pulled a long sweetgrass braid from the satchel, held it up to the sky and then touched it to the ground. He held a lighter at one end until it caught flame. Shaking the braid gently, it began to smolder. "We will ask for the blessing from sweetgrass to begin our ceremony." Duncan walked around the circle, inviting everyone to put out their hands and draw the fragrant smoke towards them. The group received the offering in solemn silence.

After Duncan finished with the blessing, he instructed them to follow him down the trail, the burning sweetgrass braid still softly swaying in his left hand. After a few minutes, he led them into the grass and stopped at the side of a rock wall. Smaller rocks were strewn all along the base. Had she walked past this on her own, she would not have seen two stone piles, distinguishable only by the slightly more uniform way the stones were placed on top of each other. Jason had to point them out at first, but then she saw them clearly. Two graves. Her limbs suddenly felt heavy and the joints in her fingers started to ache. She wanted to sit down, but she didn't wish to appear disrespectful.

Duncan instructed them to move back a few feet, giving him room to walk in front. She watched him, standing first at one grave and then the other, chanting in Ute, burning sweetgrass, offering tobacco. It was like watching a dream; she felt disconnected from the people, from her own body. Tears streamed down her face as grief overcame her. When Jason asked if she was alright, she couldn't answer him.

Fighting an urge to throw herself on the stone pile, she grabbed onto Jason instead. Images came to her, like flashes of insight, of dragging a limp male body, of a long stain of blood left behind in the grass, wailing, piling up stones until her fingers bled.

In the distance she heard someone calling her name. Slowly her eyes focused. Duncan stood directly in front of her, his brown eyes boring into hers. He wore the bear claw necklace and she instinctively reached for it with her left hand. He put his hand over hers and gently pried her fingers from around the large claw. His face carried the same anguish that ripped at her heart. She began to sob. Duncan held her awkwardly for a moment and then pulled away.

"Take this tobacco and offer it to the Spirits." He placed a large wad in her left hand.

Trying to stifle tears, Sarah placed the tobacco over her heart and held it there. She didn't know what to do and yet she did. She started to speak softly, in a halting fashion, as though struggling for each word. Her ears did not understand her speech, but in her mind she knew she was offering prayers to the spirits of the departed...to the spirits of the two men she had buried here so many years ago. Standing Bear and Yellow Eagle. No, Red Fire Woman had buried them. The lines began to blur in her mind. Frantic, she looked around for help. Her heart calmed when she caught sight of Duncan. *He's alive!* Then she stopped herself. *What am I saying? That's Duncan. And I'm Sarah. I am Sarah.*

She saw the others offering tobacco under Duncan's guidance, each one stealing glances at her with worried expressions. She looked at the tobacco still clenched between her fingers. She kept staring at it until she felt Jason's hands on her shoulder.

"Sprinkle it on the ground and then come sit down. You look pale." She did as she was told and then collapsed on the ground. Jason took her hands in his. "Where'd you go? You looked like you were in a trance."

She still felt disconnected, unsure of where she was or who she was. No words came. Someone passed her a canteen of water and she drank. The cold refreshment helped her focus and a bit later she felt strong enough to stand. Seeing the concern on everyone's face made her feel self-conscious and silly. She managed "I'm okay," but it didn't change the way they looked at her.

"Let's get you home," Jason said as he started to walk back toward the horses. She began to follow. "No, Sarah, you wait here. I'll bring Molly over to you."

While the others joined Jason, she found a log and sat down. But then something shiny caught her eye, a few hundred feet beyond the graves. It glistened in a way that beckoned, "come look at me." Still unsteady, she slowly walked over to see what it was and found a stone with a large piece of quartzite that reflected the sunlight. As she bent down to pick it up, she heard a deep growl that made her knees buckle. Looking around, she saw movement in the grass but got a clear view once she stood up. Running towards her was a huge black bear, saliva spitting from its mouth. She screamed, desperately wanting to run, but her feet were frozen in place. All she could do was watch as the bear slowed its charge, then reared up on its hind legs, roaring. She fell to the ground and curled in a ball, covering her head with her hands.

Trembling uncontrollably, she braced for the pain of teeth and claws against flesh. The growls grew more ferocious, she heard footsteps of people running, then voices.

"She's got a cub in the tree."

"I've got a shot. I can take her."

"Sarah, don't move."

"Don't shoot, don't shoot!"

Then Duncan's voice, low and steady, chanting, singing, stilled the others and grew closer. The bear's growling turned to grunts; padded feet hit the ground, rustling and sniffing coming towards her. Hot, musky breath on her neck. *Oh my god, it's going to kill me!* The heavy weight of a paw on her arms. She saw the blood dripping on the ground before she felt the pain sear through her forearm. A raven started shrieking. She heard Duncan chanting and grunting. She gritted her teeth for the next assault, but it never came. The bear suddenly moved away, its husky panting replaced by Duncan's steady tone, now right by her side.

"Sarah, you're safe. Get up slowly." She felt his arms helping her stand. The bear had torn two long scratches in her left forearm that bled profusely. "She could have taken your arm off if she wanted to," Duncan said. "But she did not." Sarah found little comfort in that. Duncan gave her a folded bandana and told her to keep pressure on her wounds.

"What happened to the bear? Why didn't she...." Sarah couldn't finish the thought. Duncan pointed toward the east where she saw the bear walking away with a cub by her side, turning around every few steps to watch the humans.

Duncan put his arm around Sarah to help her walk back to where the others waited transfixed, unable to fathom what they had just seen.

Jason was the first to break the silence. "Sarah, are you alright?" She just nodded. He started to move towards her but Duncan shook his head and he backed off, confused.

"I've never seen anything like that before," Patrick said. "It was like you charmed that bear. It was going to kill her and then it just backed off. How did you do that?"

Duncan didn't answer. He directed Sarah over to the horses before he had her sit down. His demeanor told the others to keep their distance.

"I have no idea what just happened," Jessie said. "And I wouldn't have believed it if I hadn't seen it for myself."

Jason paced, staring at Sarah and his uncle, frustrated by his rebuff.

"Jason, did you know that Duncan had this gift?" Jessie asked.

"Gift? What do you mean?" Jason was in no mood for conversation.

She ignored his brusque tone. "His ability to talk with bears."

"Ms. Jessie, are you serious? You think he actually talked to that bear?" Patrick asked.

"You saw it for yourself," Jason said. "There's no scientific explanation for it, if that's what you mean. Shit, Old Man told me that our people lost their bear medicine when they left these mountains. But I'll be damned, it sure looks like he found some of it today."

Sarah listened to what the others were saying, while watching Duncan rifle through his saddlebags. The throbbing in her arm was making her nauseated. "Is that what really happened? Did you save me by talking to that bear?"

Duncan pulled out a small bag and signaled for her to remove the bandana compress. "This salve will stop the bleeding, help with healing." She flinched as he treated her wounds.

"Duncan, please answer me. Why didn't that bear kill me?"

"Because she recognized you. She saw your medicine. She scratched you as a way of honoring you, marking you."

"I don't understand," Sarah said. "How can I have bear medicine? Bears terrify me. I thought raven was my medicine animal."

Duncan smiled briefly. "Raven is your protector. Bear is your medicine. You will understand in time. We will sweat together. In four days. Then we will talk about this. We will also talk about the vision you had today. "

"My vision?"

"Red Fire Woman spoke through you, honoring the dead."

Sarah thought she was going to throw up. "How did you know?"

"She told you who was in those graves."

"Yes," Sarah whispered. "Standing Bear and Yellow Eagle. She buried them herself."

"So she was the one," Duncan said. "She must have had time before the soldiers caught her. What a strong women she must have been."

"Didn't you know that she buried them?" Sarah asked.

Duncan shook his head. "There are parts of this story that are not known. But with your help, Sarah, I believe more will be revealed."

"I don't know anything," Sarah said. "None of this makes sense to me. Don't you see?"

"I have seen much today." Duncan said, placing a hand gently on her shoulder. "And I have received a great gift. I am grateful to you."

"Why me?"

"You always ask so many questions and do not make time to listen." He removed the bear claw necklace he wore and placed it around Sarah's neck, then turned around. As he walked toward the group, she heard him say, "Four days."

CHAPTER THIRTY-SEVEN

SARAH ENJOYED A GLASS of cabernet on the deck, watching the late afternoon sun shining on the rugged profile of the Flat Tops. Three days had passed since her all too personal encounter with the bear. Her arm still ached, but the wounds had scabbed over. Duncan's ointment proved to be nearly miraculous. She would have two long scars that would draw attention, and she wasn't sure what story to tell any one who might ask about them. No one would believe what really happened. She still didn't.

A raven landed on the railing and cocked its head in her direction. "Hello, Raven." Sarah reached into a sack and threw some seeds on the deck for the curious bird. The offering was quickly consumed. Since this raven looked like every other raven she had ever seen, she chose to assume that this was the same bird that had been keeping her company over the last three days, even though adopting a human was not exactly typical raven behavior. From her internet search, she had learned that ravens are considered to be one of the smartest of all birds. "So why are you hanging around with me, if you're so clever?" The bird flapped its wings and cackled in response. "You agree with Duncan, I see. You think I ask too many questions too." The bird bobbed its head up and down. "Everyone's a critic."

She started to wonder if the bird really did understand, but then caught herself and took another sip of wine. "Duncan may be able to talk with bears. But I certainly can't talk to birds. Listen to me. I sound like a whacko." She threw more seeds for her feathered friend and then turned her attention to Duncan's other comment about her helping to bring parts of the story to light. What more could she possibly add to a story that she'd only heard about through him?

She hadn't had much time to ponder this over the last few days. She had met Hollis at the Double R Ranch to see how construction was progressing. They would be ready for her to start on the walls in about ten days. She made sure to wear long sleeves to cover up her scratches. Fortunately, the wounds did not interfere with her drawing, so concealing them ended up not being a problem.

She and Hollis had pored over drawings and the main mural was starting to take shape in her mind. Inspired, she had immersed herself in sketches, stopping only to eat and talk on the phone with Jason before going to sleep. Even her evening wine breaks at sunset had been more of a scene study than relaxation. She was pleased with her progress.

She was also growing more nervous about the upcoming sweat lodge ceremony, despite Jason's attempts to ease her fears. She was just as concerned about Duncan's behavior towards her as she was about the ceremony itself. Jason's admission that he didn't understand his uncle's aloofness only added to her anxiety. It didn't help that her sister was away at a retreat for the week and not readily available. Sarah would have to muddle through the next few days on her own.

Finding some solace in the scenic view from the deck, she began mulling over the story of Red Fire Woman and Standing Bear and any possible connection it had to her life. As she recalled, the sweat lodge had played a prominent role in the story. Standing Bear had been given some new direction about how to run his lodge, with Red Fire Woman's help, that brought healing for diseases that had shown up courtesy of the settlers. But they had to keep it a secret because something was done in the ceremony that was strictly forbidden. How could it be so wrong if it helped all those people? Even Yellow Eagle had been cured, but then he had turned on her and wanted the ceremonies stopped.

Yellow Eagle intrigued Sarah. Next to Red Fire Woman, he was the most complex character in the story. He loved his cousin, Standing Bear, but came to hate his wife. He condemned the very ceremony that had healed him. He had fought with the white man's army against the Sioux and had seen their power. He probably knew the futility in resisting the white man and yet he went to battle against them anyway. What a conflict of emotions.

Sarah doodled on a sketchpad. It helped her think. What if the conflict ran even deeper? What if Yellow Eagle believed that his cousin favored his white wife over the safety of his own people? How would he have reacted? She wondered if that would have driven him to kill his favorite cousin. There was no way to know for sure. She crumpled up her doodle page and threw it on the ground.

Sarah decided to take a shower and clear her head. She walked into the bedroom to undress and get a change of clothes. Digging around in her dresser drawer for a pair of jeans, she uncovered a red bag. Slowly she picked it up and put it on top of the dresser. The bag held Duncan's bear claw necklace. She had buried it in the drawer the night she came back from the canyon and hadn't looked at it since. It frightened her. It had some power over her, and even though its effects appeared benevolent—her left hand had not gone into spasms once since she'd received the necklace—she didn't like anything having control over her, especially an inanimate object.

Touching the bag, Sarah felt drawn to pull out the necklace. What would happen if she did? She had handled it only in Duncan's presence.

Oh, come on, she chided herself. *It's just a necklace, for crying out loud. You're acting like this is an Indiana Jones movie!* Shaming herself into a burst of courage, she pulled it out of the bag and felt the smooth rawhide string against her fingers. The four-inch long grizzly claw was framed on either side by large colored beads of yellow, red, black and white. When she put it on over her head, the claw slipped between her breasts.

Looked at her reflection in the mirror, she noted the contrast between the elegant satin bra and panties and the earthy rawhide necklace. Not exactly Vogue cover material, she had to admit. The necklace felt good against her skin. Red Fire Woman's necklace.

If Ruth is right about this karma thing, that my connection to Red Fire Woman has to do with righting a wrong from her life, what exactly am I supposed to do to make that happen? Sarah wondered. *It's not as though I can bring the Utes back to Colorado or bring Standing Bear back from the dead. What can I possibly do to make amends for a white woman who fell in love with a Ute during a bad time in history?*

Before she could find out whether the necklace would mysteriously answer all of her questions, she heard a loud knocking at the door. Pulling on jeans and a tank top, she headed into the kitchen. Shelly Banks, the ranch manager's wife, stood on the front step.

"Hey, Sarah! Glad you're home. Tony and I are roasting a couple of lambs and wanted to have you down for dinner."

"Thanks. I'd love that," Sarah said. "Give me about fifteen minutes and I'll be over."

"Come hungry!"

Hollis had raved about Tony's roast lamb when she first arrived, said it was the best in the valley, so Sarah was excited to finally taste it for herself. Hurrying to get ready, she ran a brush through her hair, put a long-sleeved shirt over the tank and grabbed a light jacket. She remembered to pull out a bottle of wine to bring along. She was halfway to their house before she realized she was still wearing the bear claw necklace, but it was too far to turn back. She tucked it under her top and hoped no one would notice.

As she passed by the corral, one of the horses whinnied and Sarah stopped to pet her. She was starting to feel a bit more comfortable around these big, beautiful animals. Then the horse's ears perked forward and her head started to bob, eyes wide. Sarah felt a hand on her shoulder and jumped as the horse snorted and backed away. Turning around, she came face to face with Nick, who smelled of alcohol.

"Nick, you scared me. Don't sneak up on me like that," Sarah said.

"But it's such a pleasure to run into you," he said, leaning towards her. "I've been looking for you."

"Why? What do you want?" Sarah folded her arms self-consciously.

"Is that an offer?" Nick sneered, stepping inappropriately close.

Sarah backed up and bumped into a fence. He had her trapped. "No, it's not." Her pulse quickened.

"I've found that women usually mean 'yes' when they say 'no'. It's a weakness of the gender." She could feel his breath on her face, their bodies almost touching. He was staring at her cleavage.

"I assure you I mean what I say. And I'd appreciate your backing up," Sarah stated as firmly as possible.

"Do I make you uncomfortable? Artists can be so high strung. You should really learn how to relax." He leaned in and spied her necklace.

"What little treasure are you hiding here?"

Sarah grabbed the bear claw, in a futile attempt to hide it.

"It's nothing."

"If it's nothing, then you won't mind my looking at it," he taunted.

"I do mind. And I want you to back off."

Rather than stepping back, he started to reach for the necklace. Sarah exploded. "Keep your goddamned hands off of me!" She pushed him away with such force, he stumbled backwards.

"You little bitch!"

"Leave me alone!" Sarah said, her right hand now balled in a fist and her left hand grasping the bear claw.

He took a step towards her, his eyes dark with anger.

"Stop right there or I'll scream."

A disturbing calm came across Nick's face. "High strung and feisty. And·a screamer too. Does your redskin boyfriend make you scream?"

"Move out of the way," Sarah tried to hide the tremor in her voice.

"Aren't we all worked up over an ugly Indian necklace. Did your boyfriend give it to you? Looks like his style. Tacky."

Sarah heard the barn door open behind her and prayed that someone would see them and come over. Nick looked up, frowned and backed away. "We'll finish this another time."

She turned around to see Tony waving at her. *Saved by the handsome cowboy,* she thought, as she waved back. She leaned into the fence, her body still trembling. In her left hand, she clenched the bear claw like a vice, feeling as though she would protect this necklace with her life. Much like Red Fire Woman had done a long time ago, and she had paid dearly for it.

CHAPTER THIRTY-EIGHT

JESSIE HAD AGREED to meet Duncan at Full Moon Rock in the late afternoon. This was the first time she'd seen him since the ceremony at the gravesites and the unbelievable encounter with the bear. Her horse whinnied as they reached the meadow. A whinny in reply told her that Duncan had arrived ahead of her. She found him sitting on the large piece of granite, his gaze fixed on the rushing river below.

"Well, my friend," she began. "Perhaps I need to start calling you the Bear Whisperer."

"Yes, that could be good. Then maybe someone will write a book about me, Robert Redford will make the movie and I will get rich." Duncan's sparkling eyes complemented his smile.

They sat in silence for a time, listening to the wind and the river.

"Do not speak about what happened with the bear," Duncan said. "What you saw was sacred, a gift from Creator, not to be discussed."

"I understand," Jessie said, even though she didn't. "Would it be alright if you and I talked about it now? While no one's around?"

"What do you want to say?"

"For starters, I'd like to know what really happened. Did you talk to that bear? Or did you think that by acting crazy, you'd scare her away?"

Duncan took his time in answering. He spoke so softly she could barely hear him. "Yes, I did. The Bear Medicine has come to me. A piece of it anyway. I was told that it had died with Standing Bear. When my relatives were moved out of the mountains, we lost that kind of connection to Bear."

"That's incredible," she said, trying to comprehend the implications of this revelation. "I must say, I'd have a hard time believing this if I hadn't been there. Are there other surprises that come with this bear medicine?"

"To the Utes, Bear is our brother. Those who held that medicine could communicate with the bears, would get teaching from them. Bear first taught my people what foods were safe to eat and what was not. Bear showed us plants that could be medicine for us. And some medicine men could even become Bear."

"You mean shapeshift?"

Duncan nodded.

"I've read about shapeshifting but never thought it was actually possible." She scrutinized Duncan but saw no sign of Trickster in his face. "Assuming this can happen, why would a medicine man need to actually become a bear?"

"Bear has healing power." Duncan said. "In ceremony, a medicine man can do great things as Bear, can heal illness and bring blessings to many. At one time our most powerful teacher was Grizzly Bear. But they do not live in these mountains anymore."

Jessie felt his sadness. "Do you think this ability coming back to you has something to do with the ceremony you did at the graves?"

"Yes. And with ceremonies yet to come. That is why I asked you to meet me here. To discuss a healing ceremony that will require you and the others to participate."

Confusion clouded her face.

"I will try to explain," Duncan said. "We will walk in the meadow."

They followed the path for ten minutes or so before Duncan spoke again. "You remember when Eli first disturbed those graves?"

"I'll never forget it," Jessie sighed.

"Then you will remember that one of the pieces he stole was this necklace." Duncan pulled on the rawhide string around his neck to reveal the large bear claw.

"I thought Eli returned that!" Jessie was shocked.

"I did not trust him to do that. I made a copy, like the one in the museum. I gave him an imitation to rebury. Spirit told me then to keep the necklace in a safe place until the right time. Now is that time. I am being asked to do a healing for the ancestors. I realize now that it is not just up to me. I trust you remember the story I told you years ago about Standing Bear and Red Fire Woman."

"Yes, of course I do. He made two bear claw necklaces, one for him and one for Red Fire Woman." Back then, Jessie had secretly hoped that Duncan would make such a necklace for her, but that had never come to pass. The memory still stung.

"You remember well. I had a vision just before Sarah Cavanaugh arrived in Meeker. In the vision, Red Fire Woman told me she needed my help to make things right, to heal the wounds from her time, for Standing Bear and for all the people."

"What do you mean by healing your ancestors?"

"We believe that through ceremony and prayer, we can bring harmony to the Spirits of those who have gone before us. We do this for those who have suffered or struggled, who did not die in peace. I do not know if I can explain it any more than that. But the healing that was spoken of in my vision is different. Something must happen in the physical world as well and that Sarah is a part of the healing."

"I was wondering when you'd get around to Sarah," Jessie said. "Jason seems quite taken with her."

Duncan looked away, absorbed in thought. Jessie wondered if she had said something inappropriate, but she had only stated the obvious. She was just about to break the silence when Duncan cleared his throat and lifted his gaze.

"I have come to realize that Sarah is related to Red Fire Woman, not by blood but through their spirits. She has been called here to the mountains, to learn the ways of the Spirit path, to be a healer in her own right, just as Red Fire Woman was. But, before she can do this, she must take part in a healing of the past, something yet to be revealed."

"If Red Fire Woman is not a blood relative of Sarah's, what exactly is their relationship?"

Duncan walked over to an aspen log that had long been stripped of its bark and sat down. He motioned for Jessie to join him.

"I do not know for sure. I understand some people believe in reincarnation. Perhaps that is what is at work here." A grin spread across his face. "Maybe that's how it is with white people. You have to come back again and again because you cannot figure out how to live in a good way. The Creator takes pity on you and keeps giving you other chances!"

"I suppose the Utes always get it right the first time?" Jessie bantered. "No need for second chances?"

"Now you're catching on. I always knew you to be a wise woman."

"If you always get it right the first time 'round," Jessie replied, not to be outdone, "then why the need to heal your ancestors?"

"Hah, you have me there," Duncan said. "Like I said, a wise woman."

"Do you think there is any validity to reincarnation and past lives?" Jessie asked. "For white people or for Utes?"

"I believe that is something Spirit wants me to explore," Duncan said, his expression turning solemn.

"Well, if Sarah is who you say she is, then given her affection for Jason, does that mean that he is somehow related to Standing Bear? Is their relationship part of this healing you're talking about?"

"Enough with the questions!"

Duncan's sudden annoyance surprised her. *What's wrong with him? Maybe he doesn't approve of his nephew's choice in women.*

It took a few moments for Duncan to regain his composure. "I had a vision several weeks ago. Red Fire Woman sent Coyote to me. Coyote showed me seven horses decorated for ceremony. At the time, I only recognized my horse and Jason's. The message from the vision was that I needed to find out who belonged to the other horses because they all must be part of this healing for the ancestors," Duncan said, his tone flat with no hint of previous playfulness or irritation. "I now know that Sarah is one of the riders. When I did ceremony in front of the graves, I sensed that in some way, we had been there before. I believe that two of those horses in my vision belong to you and Patrick. That leaves two horses still without riders. I will ask Spirit about this in the sweat lodge tomorrow."

Duncan's conversation left her with more questions than clarity, but she refused to be rebuked again, so remained silent.

Without warning, he stood up and started walking back toward Full Moon Rock.

Jessie took a few deep breaths and then picked up a stone that fit nicely in her palm and hurled it over the cliff. "That man tries my patience!" A chipmunk sitting on a nearby rock chirped in response, then darted off.

She almost ran into Duncan on a curve in the trail. He had stopped and was staring at the river. He turned to face her.

"Jessibel, I do not mean to be so gruff with you. Spirit seems to be testing me in ways I do not understand."

"Funny, I feel the same way." She stepped a bit closer and they embraced, a tender hug and a peck on the cheek.

"Duncan, is there anything I can do to help you?"

"I do not know." He hugged her again. "My grandmother used to say that the answer to any question usually comes when you are not trying to find it. Or after a meal of elk burgers and potatoes."

"Duncan, you used to be much smoother at inviting yourself to dinner. Follow me back to the house and I'll fix us some dinner. Maybe with the help of your grandmother, some answers will find their way into the kitchen."

CHAPTER THIRTY-NINE

THE CRESCENT MOON SHONE dimly in the sky, standing vigil as the morning sun pushed away the shadows and brought a shimmer to the dewy grass. The glint of hummingbird feathers flashed in the sky and the red-shafted flickers chirped a welcome to the day. Jason experienced none of this even though he had risen before dawn and was leaning up against a large spruce, facing east to greet the sun for morning prayers. A vice-like headache blurred everything, except for the even stronger agony of wanting a drink. He fumbled with his lighter, eventually lighting the sage smudge stick and allowing the breeze to blow smoke over his trembling body. Its soothing smell gradually brought some relief to the pain in his head and the weakness in his spirit. He slumped to the ground and bathed himself in the smoke until the sage smudge was consumed.

For the past four mornings, Jason had struggled, a flashback to his first days of sobriety. But he hadn't had a drink for two years now. *What the fuck is wrong with me?* He wondered if his addiction was kicking up because he was opening his heart to Sarah. Did he have to shut down all of his emotions to keep this craving at bay? That thought made him even more upset. He pleaded with the sun to shed some light on his turmoil, but no insights came. He prayed that he would find some relief in the sweat lodge ceremony. He couldn't take much more of this.

The headache and whiskey cravings had started the morning after Sarah's encounter with the bear. He was too ashamed to tell her or Duncan, but he sensed that Old Man knew. Fortunately, Sarah had been so busy with her work that she hadn't had time to see him. Their evening phone calls brought him some comfort, just hearing her voice. Still, he was anxious about today. He wasn't ready for her to see his vulnerability or weakness. Besides, he knew Sarah was counting on him to help her through the sweat.

He rubbed the back of his head, the pain now a dull ache. His eyes scanned the sky until a familiar shape caught his attention. "Hello, Brother Hawk." He spoke to the large bird perched in a pine on the edge of the forest. For a moment, their eyes met. "I will need your strength and vision with me today." The hawk lifted off, flew over the sweat lodge site and circled several times before heading to the valley to hunt. Jason stood and offered a pinch of tobacco in gratitude for the bird's blessing. He scattered the tobacco at the base of the tree and headed into the house for some much needed coffee.

Duncan had already made a pot and was sitting at the kitchen table when he greeted Jason. "Today is a good day for ceremony."

"You know best," Jason said. "I'll make us some eggs." He worked in silence, uncomfortably aware of his uncle's eyes on him.

When Jason brought food to the table, Duncan nodded his thanks and asked for more coffee. The two men ate breakfast without speaking. Jason wondered about his quiet demeanor. Before ceremony, he usually would be giving instructions on how to build the fire, how many stones he wanted. But he seemed as preoccupied as Jason this morning.

Jason cleared the plates. "When do you want me to start the fire?"

"Wait for Sarah. You can teach her how to build a fire. We will need thirty-two stones." Duncan stood up and walked out of the room.

Jason split wood for the next hour until he heard a truck coming up the drive. Putting down his axe, he headed toward the front of the house and quickened his pace when he caught sight of her. Sarah smiled, looking as lovely as the sunrise. And she felt just as warm. He held her tightly, then kissed her.

"It's really good to see you," she said.

His deep kiss in response conveyed how happy he was to see her.

"I'm nervous," she said. "I'm glad you'll be there. Otherwise, I don't think I could do this."

"You'll be fine," Jason said. Stepping toward the truck, he offered to help her unload.

"How is Duncan today? I hope I don't get the silent treatment again."

"Don't worry about it. He's usually in a good place when we sweat."

"You could sound a bit more convincing and I'd feel better," she said, taking a hard look at him. "Are you okay? You seem, I don't know...."

"I didn't sleep well last night, that's all. I've got a bit of a headache. I'm fine." He opened the passenger side door. "Let's grab your stuff and go build a fire."

For the next two hours, Jason taught Sarah what he could about the sweat lodge ceremony, starting with the fire. "Duncan refers to it as Grandpa Fire. It's a relation, just like everything else. Once the fire is lit, do not step between a person and the flame. You don't want to cut anybody off from their connection to the fire."

He showed her how to use the logs to make a platform and how to place the stones on top. Duncan wanted thirty-two stones, each the size of a melon. There were four rounds to the ceremony. He would bring in eight stones each round. The number was significant. Everything was done in multiples of four because four honors the four seasons and the four directions.

They piled more wood and kindling around the stones and then offered tobacco to the pyre, honoring Grandpa Fire. Once the wood was lit and burning on its own, they sat down and drank some water.

Jason had never taught anyone how to do ceremony. He was surprised at how much he knew about the symbolism and the spiritual connections that went into it.

It wasn't lost on Sarah either. "This is quite the involved process," she said. "And we haven't even gotten to the lodge part of things. How long will it take for the fire to heat the stones?"

"Two to three hours. Feel free to add more wood when needed."

They stared at the flames for a time. "I love fire," Sarah said. "It's hypnotic. I could tend a fire all day."

"Well, you're a quick learner, like you've done this before." Jason said.

"I have a good teacher." She gave him a quick hug.

"Maybe. Red Fire Woman was the fire keeper for Standing Bear, you know. You may come by this naturally...from past experience, as your sister would say."

She frowned. "I've been trying not to think about that. I feel like Duncan expects me to tap into her life story somehow and I have no idea how to do that. Do you?"

"Not really. But I do know that Spirit can reveal many things in ceremony. We'll just have to see what happens. Try not to worry about what Old Man expects."

"Easier said than done. Where's Duncan? Doesn't he help set up?"

"He leaves this part to me. Although he's usually out here by now, singing to the fire. He must still be saying prayers or harvesting sage. He'll be along. Are you ready to cover the lodge?"

Sarah nodded.

They removed blankets and cloth tarps from a stand-alone shed and carried them over to the lodge frame, a round domed structure nearly four feet high and about ten feet across. It was made out of eight saplings anchored into the ground, each bent toward the center and tied together with the sapling opposite it. Two horizontal rows of smaller saplings, two and three feet above the ground, wound around the perimeter. A shallow pit had been dug in the middle of the lodge to hold the heated stones. The structure stood to the west of the fire pit, about twenty feet away.

"The frame is so beautiful," Sarah said. "It's a shame to cover it up."

"Guess it would be hard to keep the heat in if we didn't," Jason said lightheartedly.

It took them about twenty minutes to place the tarps and blankets over the frame and to create an opening on the east side that faced the fire. Jason noticed that Sarah seemed to relax more and more as they worked, while he grew more uneasy, partly because he wanted to make sure she made it through the ceremony. But there was more, something deeper and dark, almost a dread of what was to come.

Sarah was focused on sketching the covered sweat lodge when Duncan walked up behind her. "Are you going to draw me too?" She dropped her pencil in surprise.

"Duncan, hello. I would love to sketch you, if you'd let me." She wondered if Jason had told him about the many attempts to depict his likeness that already filled her sketchbooks and studio walls. Many looked just like Duncan, but none captured his enigmatic personality.

"Not today. We have ceremony." He walked over to the fire and offered tobacco. He looked back at Sarah. "You built a good fire."

"I just did what Jason told me to do," she said. "I really liked doing it."

Duncan nodded and then pointed at her arm. "Are you using the medicine I gave you?"

"Yes, it's amazing." She rolled up her sleeve and peeled back the bandage to reveal long red scratches that had completely scabbed over. "Should I be worried about them in the sweat lodge?"

"No. The Spirits will help them heal even faster."

"What about me? Will I be okay?" Sarah tried to sound casual but the edge in her voice betrayed her.

Duncan put his hand on her shoulder and looked at her with sad and demanding eyes that could see through her, touch her fears, test her spirit. She held her breath, waiting for him to reassure her that all would be well, but he said nothing, keeping to himself whatever he had sensed from peering into her.

Duncan took a few steps back. "I need to talk to the Fire. Go tell Jason it's time to get ready." He turned to face the flames and started singing.

Shaken, Sarah fought the urge to run back to her truck and drive away. What had she gotten herself into? Duncan was holding something back, something about her. She saw it in his eyes.

Jason arrived with an armful of wood that he placed on the pile near the firepit. Looking over at Sarah, he frowned. "What's wrong?"

"Maybe I should go," Sarah said.

"Why? Did Old Man say something to upset you?"

Sarah shook her head.

"Then what's going on?"

"Nothing, I guess. Just nervous." She reached out and he took her hand. "I don't have anything to worry about, do I?"

"You'll be fine. I promise." He gave her hand a squeeze.

"Duncan said we should get ready for the ceremony," Sarah said, trying to regain her resolve.

"Then let's go back to the house and change."

Jason held on to her hand as they walked. "I've got to ask you kind of an embarrassing question. I need to know if you're on your moon, you know, got your period. Guess I should have asked you earlier, because if you are, you really can't be doing ceremony."

"Don't worry. I won't get my period for another five days or so."

Jason was relieved. Old Man would never let him live it down if he messed up that one.

"Can they really tell? If a woman doesn't say anything, what would happen?"

"Trust me, the medicine men, they know. I've seen them stop a Sun Dance ceremony because a woman in the crowd was on her moon. He had the dancers step out of the arena until she left. They say a woman is too powerful when she's menstruating; she can make men sick if they are doing ceremony."

"Have you ever experienced that?" Sarah asked.

"No, can't say I have. But that's the way I've been taught by Old Man. So I honor his ways. You should, too."

When they reached the house, Jason offered to get towels and drinking water while she changed. He traded his worn blue jeans for a pair of baggy shorts and his boots for sandals. He changed T-shirts, choosing one from an old 4th of July powwow held in Utah. He wore his hair loose.

He found Sarah on the back porch, dressed in a colorful cotton sundress, her hair pulled back in a ponytail. She clutched a small red bag in her left hand. She was pacing.

"Is this alright?" She pointed at her dress.

"Looks like what I've seen other women wear. You look beautiful."

They held hands and together walked back to the sweat lodge. A raven flew overhead and started to caw. "There's your raven, watching out for you. That's a good sign."

"If you say so," Sarah said. "I'm starting to like her."

The raven landed near the sweat lodge where Duncan was waiting for them. He greeted them this time with a burning strand of sweetgrass. He invited them to bathe their bodies with the smoke. "It will clean you up, get you ready for ceremony," he said.

Duncan pointed at the red bag in Sarah's hand. "Good. You brought it. Put it on the bench." Jason saw another red bag already there. Duncan smudged the bags with the sweetgrass and muttered some words that Jason could not make out. Then he opened both bags and removed the bear claw necklaces that Standing Bear had made for himself and Red Fire Woman. They looked almost identical, except one bear claw was shorter than the other. Duncan handed the shorter one to Sarah and told her to put it on. Jason started to reach out his hand for the second, but Duncan didn't offer it to him. Instead, he put it on himself. Duncan said, "It is not your time."

Jason didn't understand what that meant. It seemed clear from his dreams that he was connected to Standing Bear. Why was Old Man messing with him?

For the first time that day, Duncan looked directly at Jason. The elder's eyes were heavy and his face tense. "Are you okay, Old Man?"

"All is good. Let us begin." Duncan picked up a long bundle of sage and his rattle and waited while Jason lifted up the blanket covering the door to the lodge. Duncan bent down and crawled inside.

"Sarah, you come in next. Bring a towel to sit on," Jason said. "When you enter, the tradition is to say, 'I do this for all my relations'. Sit down to the right of the door."

Jason grabbed a pitchfork and dug out the first stone from the fire. Balancing the scorched stone on the tines, he carried it over to the door, bent down and placed it in the shallow pit. He repeated this seven more times. Then he grabbed the metal bucket full of water and a couple of towels and entered the lodge. He passed the water bucket and a towel over to Duncan, who sat in the back of the structure. Jason and Sarah sat across from each other. He smiled at her, trying to reassure her. "It'll be okay," he said quietly, wishing he was sitting next to her, but Duncan had been clear about where he wanted them to be.

"Close the door," Duncan said.

Jason pulled the blanket over the opening, bathing the lodge in total darkness. His hands began to shake and his head to pound, just like the first time he ever entered a lodge. *Get a grip*, he told himself. *Listen to the music.* Duncan was rattling and singing an invocation song, calling the Spirits to join them in the lodge.

Jason thought about Sarah. *I've got to be here for her. She's counting on me.* That realization calmed him enough to ease his desperate desire to leave the lodge and lose himself in drink.

The door closed and Sarah caught her breath as fear flashed through her body. She grabbed her knees, forcing her legs to remain in place, fighting the instinct to flee from the heat of the stones that hung heavy in the air, pressing against her. Closing her eyes made the darkness seem less oppressive; this was a blackness she knew. She rocked back and forth, trying to calm down until she smelled sweetgrass burning. She stopped and opened her eyes to see the stones glowing a fiery red where pieces of sweetgrass smoked on top of them. This gave off just enough light to ease her distress. She breathed in the sweet smudge and let the tears flow.

"I can get through this, I can get through this," she spoke in a whisper while Duncan sang and rattled. She heard the sizzling of water hitting the stone pile and immediately felt the wave of wet heat assault her. Three more times, water sputtered into steam and the rising temperature made it difficult for Sarah to catch a breath.

"Sarah, just breathe normally," Jason said gently. "Put your face closer to the ground; it's not as hot."

She laid down on her side and found the heat less oppressive. The earth felt cool and comforting. Sarah remained there for the rest of the round, curious about the meaning of the songs and prayers that continued non-stop. Duncan spoke only in Ute. If she ever made it through this ceremony, she would ask Jason for an explanation. But right now all she could concentrate on was keeping the claustrophobia in check by calling up images of blue skies and sunshine.

Duncan's voice fell still and she heard a rustling as Jason pushed against the door, slid outside, then lifted up the blanket, letting in a blessing of fresh air and light. "Oh, thank god!" she exclaimed, then clamped her hand over her mouth. Embarrassed by her outburst, she glanced briefly at Duncan, who was trying not to grin. "Sorry."

"You can step out if you need to," Duncan replied. "Get a drink of water. And put more wood on the fire."

She crawled out, remembering to say "for all my relations" as she passed through the doorway. Her knees wobbled a bit as she stood. Wiping her hands on her wet dress, she accepted the canteen Jason handed her.

"How are you doing?"

"I survived, that's about all I can say. Tell me it gets easier, please."

"Well, it's going to get hotter, I'm afraid. But you've made it through the first round. That's always the toughest part, being new to this whole thing. And remember, if it gets too much for you, just say you need to leave. I'll let you out, no problem. Really."

Jason pulled eight more stones out of the fire, and one by one, put them in the lodge pit. Sarah added a few logs to the flames and then they both went back inside.

He started to close the door, but Duncan stopped him. "In the first round, I was inviting all the Spirits to be with us, making them feel welcome, asking for their help and blessings. I burned sweetgrass to honor them. Now, I offer cedar. Cedar brings protection." He burned small pieces on the stones, filling the space with a fragrant smoke. "In this second round, I will call in the ancestors who want to come for healing. I will call in Standing Bear, I will call in Red Fire Woman, I will call in Yellow Eagle, I will call in Grizzly Bear, I will call in any other ancestors from that time. I will ask them to reveal to us what we need to see so we can help them heal."

"Is there anything specific that you want me to do?" Sarah asked.

"I do not know how Spirit speaks to you, Sarah. Ask to be shown." Duncan picked up the long bundle of sage that had been soaking in the water bucket. Then he signaled Jason to close the door.

Sarah caught a glimpse of Duncan flicking the sage over the pit, throwing water on the stones. Her heart beat faster as the heat and darkness descended, but she didn't panic. Her body quickly became drenched in steamy heat. She wiped perspiration from her face in a fruitless attempt to keep sweat from stinging her eyes and the scratches on her arm. Her left hand brushed up against the necklace. She took the claw in her left hand and held it against her heart. The songs and rattling lulled her into a meditative state for a time.

Duncan put more water on the stones and in response, a warmth began to spread between Sarah's legs that had nothing to do with steam. *Oh, no, this can't be happening.* Sarah moved to her knees and felt another rush of unwelcome moisture. *I can't be bleeding. It's too soon.* She pushed her towel between her legs, praying that her flow would stop.

What should I do? What will this do to Duncan? To her dismay, the singing stopped abruptly. She cringed, afraid of what would follow. After an interminable silence, the rattle started again and Duncan continued praying in his native tongue.

Sarah exhaled. *Maybe I can get out when the door opens without anyone noticing. What do I say about why I'm not coming back?* Then more blood flowed. Frantically, she reached around in the dark, needing to find the extra towel Jason had brought in. She heard him moving toward the door as her hand touched terrycloth. She threw the towel over her lap just as the door opened. She turned toward Duncan, who was staring at her. Overwhelmed with embarrassment, Sarah stammered, tears coming instead of words.

Duncan raised a finger to his mouth. "I know. You may stay."

A mix of shock and relief replaced her stress. *My god, he really can tell that I'm menstruating. Jason was right. But then why is he letting me stay?* She looked over at Jason. He stared at the ground, anger etched his face into a severe frown that alarmed her. *He must know, too! He probably thinks I lied to him.* She wished she had never agreed to do this ceremony and prayed she could disappear that instant.

Duncan seemed not to notice Jason's silent rage. "Bring in some drinking water for us. And a few more towels. And when you are ready, bring in the rest of the stones. We'll have only one more round." Jason crawled out of the lodge without a word. Sarah wondered if he would ever forgive her.

Duncan sprinkled tobacco on the mound of new stones in the center of the lodge. A pungent, earthy aroma permeated the space. "I offer tobacco as prayers of gratitude. Much was revealed to us, challenging things about the past. In this last round, we offer thanks to the Spirits for all that they have brought to us. We also ask for their help to show us how to bring them healing in this time."

Duncan nodded to Jason and they were once again wrapped in darkness. Once his eyes adjusted, he saw the red glow of the stones, pulsing with heat. "Grandmother Stones, thank you for all that you have made clear to me. For this new power that flows through me. For the healing that is to come."

As he splashed water on the stones with the sage bundle, Duncan still could not believe what he was feeling. When he was in ceremony, open to spiritual messages, he could always tell when a woman near him was on her moon time. His Spirits had warned him when Sarah started to bleed. He had sensed it in his body. But instead of his power being drawn out of him, as in times past, he felt stronger and his inner vision became clearer. He could "see" the spirit of alcohol that still clung to Jason. And in amazement, he watched as the spirit of the disease was removed from his nephew's body and transformed into white light.

Duncan continued to sing and pray until another vision began to take shape. It was a continuation of the vision his grandmother's spirit had shared with him. Again, he saw the two dolls that looked like Sarah and Red Fire Woman with the silver cord running between them. Then his grandmother showed him another doll, one that bore Duncan's face, with its own silver cord wrapped around it. In the vision, he took hold of the cord and followed it through the woods until he came to the edge of a clearing. The silvery tether led into the clearing. With great reluctance, Duncan stepped out of the woods to see who was tied to the other end of the cord. The revelation filled his heart with a distress that would find no solace in the light of day.

CHAPTER FORTY

THE HOT SHOWER FELT like a gift from heaven. As Sarah washed away the sweat from her arms, her face, her back, her belly, her breasts and the blood from between her legs, she had a sense of returning into her body. Her surreal experience in the lodge had left her frazzled and emotionally raw—from the claustrophobia in the first round to the panic and shame of her period starting, to Jason's anger and her worry that he was upset with her. If Duncan hadn't shown that brief moment of compassion in the lodge, she would have fallen apart.

Sarah willed the steamy shower to rinse away her doubt that she had done something wrong. She had no way of knowing that the sweat would cause her to start her period early. Or had it really started? When she got out of the lodge, her flow had stopped. She was not even spotting now. *It must have been a weird reaction to stress,* she decided as she turned off the water and grabbed a towel.

By the time she dried off, she finally felt more relaxed. She sat on the edge of the tub, wrapped in towels, wanting to make the moment last. She made no effort to move until there was a gentle rap on the door.

"Sarah, is everything alright in there?" She heard no edge in Jason's voice. Maybe he had forgiven her.

"Yeah, sorry for taking so long. I'll be right out." She opened the door, expecting to see him, but the hallway was empty. He wasn't waiting in his bedroom either. She took her time getting dressed, hoping he would show up. After a few minutes, she heard the shower turn on. *Maybe he doesn't want to see me until he had cleaned up as well,* she thought. *Or maybe he doesn't want to see me at all.* She walked quickly past the bathroom door and made her way to the kitchen.

She found Duncan sitting at the table, sipping a cup of coffee. An oblong bundle wrapped in buckskin lay in the middle of the table. Duncan, his salt-and-pepper hair still wet from a shower, greeted her with a request for more coffee. She refilled his cup, poured herself one, then sat down, trying all the while to not stare at the strange package.

"How did you like the sweat lodge?" Duncan looked out the window.

"I don't know what to say, actually. I'm so sorry. I had no idea I would...you know...start to, what's the term you use? Start my moontime in there."

"Yeah. Things do seem to happen when you're around, Sarah."

She waited for a reprimand but none came. For a time, the ticking of the wall clock was the only sound in the kitchen, aside from a clanking spoon and the sipping of coffee. Sarah finally cleared her throat, but had no idea what to say.

"You did well today. The Spirits showed us important things about the ancestors and their story." Duncan sounded like a schoolteacher. "Did you have any visions?"

"No." Sarah felt as though she had failed the test. "Not unless you count seeing my life flash before my eyes. I was so scared that first round, all I focused on was making it through. In the second round, I didn't feel so panicky and was starting to relax. Until...Then all I could think about was how I could get out of the lodge without either of you knowing."

"That still leaves the last round."

"I kept wondering why you let me stay in the lodge and if you were going to get sick or something. I saw how angry Jason was with me. But after a while I found myself thinking about the fire, imagining myself building the fire, talking to it and singing to it. That's really all I saw. Not exactly a vision."

"Your first sweat ceremony and already you are an expert on visions?" Duncan said. "If you remember the story, Red Fire Woman always tended the fire for Standing Bear's sweat lodges. I imagine she talked and sang to Grandpa Fire, just as you saw. And in those special healing ceremonies for the white man's diseases, Standing Bear was required to do something that was forbidden. Spirit showed us today what that was."

Duncan looked straight at Sarah. Suddenly self-conscious, she couldn't hold his gaze. "My period," she gasped.

"Yes. Red Fire Woman must have tended the fire when she was on her moontime. She fed Grandpa Fire with some of her blood. The spirit of her blood came in with the stones to help with the healings."

"That's incredible." Sarah wrestled with the ramifications of what Duncan was saying. Was the bleeding she experienced just a coincidence, or was it truly a vision? Was Red Fire Woman communicating somehow through her? Was there healing power in menstrual blood?

"Is that really possible?"

"I saw it working. I watched as your blood healed Jason. The spirit of alcohol left his body and was transformed into light. It will not come back to him as before. I have never seen a healing like this."

"What do you mean?" Sarah struggled to understand.

"A disease is like any living being; it has a spirit. When the spirit of the disease is stronger than the spirit of the person, the disease has power over that person. In a healing, we ask the disease to leave the body. I have seen the spirit of alcohol leave Jason before, but it was always hovering around him, waiting for him to weaken so it could come back. But this time, that spirit was healed and became light. It is gone from Jason forever."

"Does he know this?"

Duncan nodded.

"Then why is he so angry? I would think he'd be thrilled."

"You should ask him."

"Please, Duncan. Can't you tell me more than that?"

He took a sip of coffee. Sarah's eyes wandered to the buckskin bundle and felt a desire to pick it up.

"Jason saw other things in the lodge besides his healing," Duncan said. "Challenging things. He must be the one to tell you."

"Do you know what he saw?"

"I could feel the power of his experience but was shown nothing."

Sarah wondered how long it would take Jason to have any kind of conversation with her, much less talk about what he saw in the lodge. He was proving to be as difficult as Duncan. Her fingers gingerly touched the long fringe that adorned the buckskin package in front of her.

"Do you like it?"

Sarah pulled her hand away, feeling like a kid who was caught with a hand in the cookie jar. "It's beautiful."

"That bundle is for you. It is Red Fire Woman's medicine bundle."

Sarah had no idea what a medicine bundle was.

"Go on. Pick it up. It won't bite you," Duncan said.

She slowly reached for it. The leather was surprisingly soft to the touch. Then she remembered what Duncan had told her about the Utes being known for their remarkable leatherwork. She fingered the beaded leather tie wrapped around the package but was reluctant to open it.

"What is a medicine bundle? And why are you giving this to me?"

"A medicine bundle contains sacred objects that a medicine man or woman uses when doing ceremony and healings. Bundles are passed down from healer to healer. Only the person who cares for it may open it and use the tools inside. That is a very basic explanation. I am passing this to you because you and Red Fire Woman are relations. The sweat ceremony made that clear."

"Relations? What do you mean? That we are relations as in 'she is my relative' or as in 'past life' related?" Sarah asked. "My sister did some research and couldn't find any relatives who had lived in Colorado."

"I guess you have your answer then," Duncan said.

"Do you *really* believe that? When we talked about this before my healing, you didn't seem to give much credence to reincarnation."

"I had a vision in the sweat that showed me some things about what is possible with what you call reincarnation. The path of past lives can be difficult...and painful." Duncan's voice caught. He looked out the window for a bit and then cleared his throat. "There is still much for me to learn about this path. But what I do know is that Spirit has shown me that this is your connection to Red Fire Woman. This is why you have come to these mountains and why I must give you this medicine bundle."

"I don't know how to respond to all this," Sarah said. Even though she had been toying with the possibilities in her head for a while, she was taken aback to hear Duncan say that she may have actually *been* Red Fire Woman. He had been so vague before. "And I certainly don't know what to do with the bundle. I don't want to sound disrespectful, but I can't accept this gift."

"It is not a gift, Sarah. It is your calling, your medicine. You cannot refuse your medicine."

"My medicine? I have no idea what that means. And I'm pretty sure I don't want it even if I did." She shoved the bundle towards Duncan.

"This is not for me. I cannot use it." He gently pushed it back. "Take this bundle home. Let the sacred objects speak to you. They may teach you. Remember, you must treat this with respect."

Sarah sighed. She knew there was nothing to be gained by refusing him, so she picked up the bundle. It felt heavier than before, weighed down with responsibility she did not want.

"Do you have a medicine bundle?"

"I do," Duncan said. "It was given to me by my grandfather."

"Did he teach you how to work with it?"

"He taught me some things, but mostly the medicine taught me, just like it will teach you."

Duncan's vagueness was frustrating. "How did you get this bundle?"

"Red Fire Woman entrusted her bundle to my grandmother, who cared for it until she got too old. That is when my grandmother gave it to me, along with the bear claw necklace. She told me that Spirit would find the woman who belonged to the bundle and necklace and that I was to keep them safe until that time."

"And you believe that woman is me?"

Duncan nodded. Sarah frowned.

"Do you know what's inside?"

"I have never opened it."

Before Sarah could ask another question, Duncan stood up. "I am going to bed. I hope you sleep well." He walked out of the room as Sarah wished him a hasty good night.

She took the coffee cups over to the sink and washed them along with the coffee pot. The shower was no longer running and she wondered where Jason had gone. Maybe he could explain this medicine bundle thing to her. Her curiosity was piqued about the contents, and yet she felt that by opening it, she would be agreeing somehow to become its caretaker. And she was not ready for that.

Still, she did not feel right leaving it on the kitchen table, so she took it with her and headed back to Jason's room. She found him sitting on the bed, wearing only a pair of jeans, his Indian flute in one hand. She stood in the doorway but he did not respond.

"May I come in?"

Jason nodded, but didn't look up. She sat down next to him, wanting desperately to have him hold her. "I'm sorry if I did anything to upset you today."

"What do you have to apologize for?" His voice was barely louder than a whisper.

"For bleeding in the lodge. I can't explain it. But it's stopped now." She felt her throat tighten. "I don't know what happened."

Jason glanced at her, then turned his attention back to the flute. "I didn't know."

"I thought that's why you were mad at me."

"I'm not mad at you, Sarah."

"Then why are you so upset?" She touched him on the shoulder. His muscles were tight. When he didn't answer, she swung around and kneeled down, facing him. "Jason, look at me." She gently put her fingers under his chin and lifted his face. His eyes glistened with tears. "What's wrong? Please talk to me."

"I don't want to lose you." Jason pulled her close and held her in a fierce embrace. Then he kissed her hard, with a desperate passion that startled her. As he drew her down on top of him, Sarah let go of her angst and surrendered into the moment. Tonight she didn't need words; his hands and lips told her how much he wanted her. Any concerns could wait until morning.

CHAPTER FORTY-ONE

SARAH WOKE TO THE SUN streaming in through a crack in the curtains. Rolling over, she found herself alone in the bed, the sheets still warm. Jason could not have gone far. She had to hunt a bit to find her clothes that had been strewn in all directions the night before. Savoring the memory of his body pressed against hers, she was reluctant to dress, hoping to hear his footsteps in the hall, eager to make love again. Looking around for her second sock, she spotted the medicine bundle on the desk, next to Jason's flute. *I'll deal with that later,* she told herself.

After freshening up in the bathroom, she followed the smell of coffee into the kitchen. Jason wasn't there, so she poured herself a cup and was about to look for him at the stable when he came through the door, a frown on his face.

He responded to her "Good morning" with a hasty peck on the cheek and a kick to the kitchen chair. "Damn him!"

"What happened?" Sarah watched her romantic morning vanish before it ever got started.

"Nothing I want to talk about right now. Let's go get some breakfast. I need to get outta here."

They drove to the Springhorn Lodge in silence, listening to a CD of Lyle Lovett singing sad Texas ballads. As Jason parked the truck, Sarah finally found the courage to speak. "I am not going to sit through breakfast not saying anything to each other. Either you agree to talk to me or you can eat by yourself. I need to know what's going on with you."

"I know. I'm being an ass. Let's grab some food and then we can drive up Aspen Creek Road. There's an overlook up there I want to show you. We'll talk up there. Okay?" He gently kissed her on the mouth.

"Fair enough."

After a quiet breakfast and an hour ride, they sat on a picnic table overlooking a breathtaking view of the Flat Top Mountain range. At an altitude approaching twelve thousand feet, the cool wind made Sarah wish she had brought a fleece. Jason put his arm around her, but that only warmed one side. At any other time, she would have relished the scenery, but she felt like Jason was using this as a distraction, and she was tired of waiting. Giving the mountains a respectable amount of reverence, Sarah suggested they talk in the truck so she could warm up.

"Duncan told me that you had a healing in the lodge yesterday," Sarah said, reaching the end of her patience.

"Yes, I did."

"Will you tell me about it?"

Sarah listened as he reluctantly told her about his recurring struggles with alcohol and how the past few days had been extremely grueling for him to stay sober.

"I had no idea," Sarah said. "Why didn't you say anything?"

"Because I didn't want you to know, that's why."

His brusque tone hurt and it showed on her face.

"Sarah, I'm sorry. I didn't want you seeing me as weak."

She hugged him and asked him to continue with his story.

He explained that during the sweat, he felt something shift inside of him, the craving totally disappeared, as though it had been pulled from his body. When he'd first gotten sober several years ago, he found the sweat helped him stop drinking, but the desire for whiskey never really left. In this ceremony, the experience was totally different. Alcohol no longer had any hold on him. He was completely healed.

"That's wonderful," Sarah said. "Duncan thinks my bleeding had something to do with your healing. He said that was the secret that Red Fire Woman and Standing Bear had to keep from their people."

"Yeah, Old Man told me the same thing. Kinda blew my mind. Back home, being on your moontime around ceremony is strictly forbidden. I think people on the reservation would freak out if I told them what happened to me. It must have taken a helluva lot of courage for Standing Bear to offer that ceremony."

"Are you ashamed about being healed in this way?"

"I don't know how I feel about it, actually. I'm grateful, for sure. But it's a bit shocking because of what I'd been taught. The only shame I feel comes from being an alcoholic, and all the stupid ass shit I've done because of it." Then he fell silent.

"Duncan told me that you saw other things in the lodge besides your healing."

"Old Man should mind his own business," Jason snapped.

She leaned over and kissed his cheek. "What's wrong? I thought that the main reason we did this sweat was to find out more about Red Fire Woman and Standing Bear. Why won't you tell me what you saw?"

"Okay, okay. Just promise me, you'll...I don't know...just promise me that you won't overreact."

"I promise. Now stop stalling."

Jason fidgeted with his truck keys, took a big breath and began. "I was shown what happened to them in the mountains with Amory and the soldiers. As I'm sure you remember, Standing Bear had sent Red Fire Woman into the mountains to hide after the battle because he'd heard that Ethan was looking for her. And that Ethan had threatened to kill a young boy unless someone showed him where he could find her."

"Yellow Eagle offered to take them in exchange for the boy's life."

"Yes, but the soldiers wouldn't set the boy free until they had captured her. So Yellow Eagle had no choice but to take them to her."

"I remember. Go on."

"Well, I was shown that after Red Fire Woman was captured, Yellow Eagle did try to save her, but not in the way you'd expect." Jason turned the key in the ignition enough so that he could open his window to let in some fresh air.

"Jason, how did you 'see' all this? Was it like a dream or did you hear it being told to you like a story?"

"More like a dream, I guess. Although at times, I felt like I was actually there. It's hard to describe."

She reached over and squeezed his hand.

"Yellow Eagle convinced the soldiers to set up a camp in a meadow and to let him go ahead to find Red Fire Woman and bring her back to them in exchange for the Ute boy. When he found her, he climbed a tree and watched her for most of the day, struggling with what he should do."

Jason shifted in his seat. "This next part of the vision I actually felt more than I saw. I could tell how confused he was. He hated Red Fire Woman for what her people had done to his. Plus, he felt messed up from the healing in Standing Bear's lodge. I didn't understand why he felt this way in the vision, but now I realize he must have figured out the secret of the menstrual blood. That's why he believed that he'd been cursed by the ceremony. He would have been banished from the tribe if anyone had found out. And yet, underneath all of his anger and resentment, I could sense that he actually loved Red Fire Woman too. He hated her and loved her at the same time."

"How sad," Sarah said.

"The story doesn't get better. Yellow Eagle finally showed himself to Red Fire Woman and told her why he had come. He explained about the soldiers and Ethan's obsession for her, that the captain would kill anyone who tried to protect her, including Standing Bear. She begged Yellow Eagle to help them. He told her that she was putting her husband's life at risk, and that the only way to save Standing Bear was for her to leave him and to go with Yellow Eagle. He would take her far away where they couldn't be found."

"Why would she need to leave Standing Bear?"

"If Red Fire Woman was captured by Amory, Standing Bear would try to save her. But Yellow Eagle knew there were too many soldiers. Standing Bear didn't stand a chance. Even if he somehow managed to kill Amory in the mountains, the government would send more soldiers to take revenge on the tribe. Yellow Eagle wasn't willing to risk any of his people to save Red Fire Woman."

"Then why was he willing to leave everything to be with her?"

"Yellow Eagle believed he was cursed by the sweat ceremony and couldn't return to the tribe. He told her that he'd take care of her out of respect for his cousin. Yellow Eagle warned her that the only way to keep Standing Bear safe was to never return to the tribe."

"What kind of choice was that?" Sarah demanded. "She couldn't abandon the man she loved!"

"Maybe she should have," Jason said. "Because Yellow Eagle was right. Red Fire Woman refused to go with him. She was sure Standing Bear would save her and that Ethan Amory would be sent back to Wyoming and never bother her again. Yellow Eagle was forced to take

Red Fire Woman prisoner and deliver her to the soldiers. Standing Bear did eventually come for her and they escaped, but the soldiers caught up with them. As you know, they ended up in that meadow where the graves are and where you met the bear."

"Did you see what happened to them, how they died?"

Jason opened the truck door and got out. He started walking down the gravel path to the overlook, so Sarah jumped out and followed him. The wind had died down and the sun shone brightly, making the temperature almost pleasant. She caught up to him at the railing and put her arm around his waist.

"What is it that's so hard to tell me, Jason?"

"Do you really believe in this past life stuff?" he asked. "Is that why you're with me? Because you believe we were lovers in another lifetime?"

"The idea of past lives is the only thing that helps me make sense out of everything that's been happening to me since I got to Meeker. So, I guess so."

"But is that why you're attracted to me? Because you loved me once as Standing Bear?"

"Yes, I mean, I don't know. I'm not sure we really would have met if we hadn't met before, so to speak. What does this have to do with the rest of the story?"

"Never mind."

"Jason!"

"Let me finish telling you this and you'll see," Jason said, his voice heavy with dread. "The soldiers had them trapped in the meadow. Standing Bear was figuring out a way for them to escape when the grizzly came into the meadow. He tried to warn the bear about the soldiers, but didn't have time. Someone fired a shot at the bear that missed. The grizzly turned toward the sound and snarled. Standing Bear needed to create a distraction, so he and Red Fire Woman started shooting into the trees where the soldiers hid. This drew fire in their direction, but it also riled up the bear, which was about to charge. Standing Bear started running toward the grizzly to chase it away, but that made him an easy target for the soldiers. Amory bolted from the trees and shot Standing Bear in the chest and legs. Standing Bear fell to the ground. Amory was going to finish him off when the grizzly attacked. With one swipe of her paw, the bear sent Amory flying. But she didn't have long to live. One of

Amory's soldiers shot her in the head and brought her down. Standing Bear struggled to his feet, but then two shots rang out. One killed Standing Bear."

Jason shifted position, kicking a random stone with his boot.

"You said there were two shots," Sarah said.

"Yeah, the second one killed Yellow Eagle."

"Yellow Eagle? How did he get there? Didn't he return to the village with the boy?"

"No. Red Fire Woman's refusal to go with him pushed him over the edge. Still, he knew he'd done the wrong thing when he handed her over to Amory. He pretended to leave with the boy, but came back once he knew the boy could find his way back. Yellow Eagle had hoped to catch Standing Bear to warn him, but he had rescued Red Fire Woman and was gone before Yellow Eagle could help him.

"So, Yellow Eagle followed the soldiers to the meadow, snuck up behind one small group of them and killed one. Then the grizzly came into the meadow. He watched Standing Bear run towards the bear and get shot. Yellow Eagle jumped up and ran toward them, trying to save them. But he was shot just before he reached them."

Jason turned to face Sarah and pulled her close as he whispered in her ear. "He was shot in the back. Just like in my dream. He watched the life drain out of the grizzly's eyes, just like in my dream. Standing Bear was shot in the chest. Yellow Eagle was shot in the back. I wasn't Standing Bear in that lifetime, Sarah.

"I was Yellow Eagle. And I betrayed you."

CHAPTER FORTY-TWO

THE EMERGING IMAGES on the wall looked more like ghosts, outlined in pencil without much detail, their stories just beginning to emerge. Seeing her vision taking form both excited and challenged Sarah because it tested her artistic ability to convey so much emotion and relationship in one piece. The composition of the mural, how the characters interacted with each other, was key; the details would simply fall into place once the foundation was established.

She had spent the better part of the morning sketching a portion of the wildlife mural and needed to take a break. The elk, with his expanse of antlers, provided a nice balance to the impressive wingspan of the golden eagle in flight. The mountain lion lounging in a tree and the howling coyotes had a convincing energy about them, but the bear was giving her problems. Every time she started to sketch, the scratches on her arm began to burn and her thoughts jumped back to her bear encounter and to everything else that transpired after that—the sweat, the stories, the revelations, the unanswered questions...and her bewildered heart.

She stepped out onto the front porch of the main house on the Double R Ranch, grabbed the railing with both hands and slowly stretched out her back. The house was unfurnished, but Hollis was thoughtful enough to have a couple of rocking chairs and a small table on the porch. The kitchen remodel was not complete yet but the space did have a working refrigerator, a few cups and glasses, a coffee maker, and a microwave, which allowed Sarah to work all day without leaving the site, if she remembered to pack a lunch, something that slipped her mind this morning. The rumbling in her stomach told her she would need to make a trip to Springhorn's.

The rocking chairs looked like the ones on Duncan's porch, only newer. She realized that every rocking chair she'd seen in the valley looked just like these and wondered if the chair maker was a local. She also wondered how Duncan and Jason were doing. She hadn't seen either in days and phone calls with Jason had been brief. She told herself it was because she was so busy with her artwork, but the truth nagged at her. She was avoiding them.

In last night's conversation, Jason had asked if her feelings for him had changed. She insisted they hadn't, that she just needed to focus on the murals right now. But was that really how she felt? As though nothing had changed? She simply didn't know. Some of the allure seemed to have worn off. But maybe that was just disappointment at learning that Jason might not be her soul mate from another lifetime. He was exotic and mysterious, but was he someone she truly loved?

She didn't like to think of herself as prejudiced. Still the fact that he was an Indian and a recovering alcoholic troubled her now. They came from such different cultures and experiences, could this really work?

When she had mentioned this to her sister the other day, Ruth had thought she was joking. But when she'd realized that Sarah's concerns were real, she'd done what she always does, give really good advice.

"Listen to me. You never know what is going to work until you give it a try. If you run away after the first disappointment, you'll never know. Not to bring up a touchy subject," Ruth continued, "but at one time you thought Blue was the perfect guy for you. And he ended up thinking you were loony tunes. But with Jason, he understands all the supernatural stuff you're going through and seems to love you all the more for it. So, who's to say what will work out and what won't."

Her sister made some sense. Blue never put any stock in her premonitions or intuition. He dismissed her feelings as being hormonal and eventually rejected her for being nuts. Jason, she admitted, helped her make some sense out of the craziness.

What will happen once we figure out the mystery of Red Fire Woman? Can we make it last?

Frustrated with the doubt and the indecision, she stood up to go back inside. The sound of a truck on gravel made her stop and turn around.

She prayed it wasn't Nick. A white Blazer with a U.S. Fish & Wildlife Service logo on the door pulled up next to her vehicle and parked.

Patrick got out of the truck and waved. "I was passing by and saw your truck here, so I thought I'd stop by and see how you're doing."

"This is a surprise," Sarah said.

Patrick walked right up onto the porch. "How's your arm? That bear must have given you some nasty scratches."

She pulled up her sleeve to reveal two long scars, red and bumpy.

"Wow, those are healing fast."

"Duncan gave me some salve that seemed to do the trick. They only hurt on occasion."

They talked for a short while before Sarah invited him inside. "I'm wondering if you could help me with something I'm working on. I'd appreciate a wildlife expert's eye. If you wouldn't mind."

Patrick agreed and followed her into the great room where photographs, sketches and doodles covered just about every flat surface available, from the folding table and chairs to the walls. He glanced quickly at the reference material and then gave his full attention to the emerging mural on the main wall.

"They're rough still. I'd welcome your feedback," she said.

"These are very good. I like them." He hesitated. "But it seems like you're having some trouble with the bear."

Sarah appreciated his honesty. "You'd think I could draw this from memory, but my eyes were closed the entire time."

"That must have been very frightening," Patrick said.

"At the time, I was terrified. But now the entire day seems more like a dream. Maybe I'm still in shock, I don't know."

"It sure seemed surreal to me. I had my gun drawn when Duncan told me not to shoot and started chanting. I've never seen an attacking bear calm down so quickly. It's almost as though that bear was listening to him. I've heard stories from old-timers about mountain men and Indians who had a way with bears, but I never gave them credence, until now."

"Thanks for trying to help me. I don't understand what Duncan did either, but I'm grateful it worked."

She picked up her pencil and started sketching on a blank piece of paper. "Duncan told me that the Utes are connected to the bear. The animal is very important to their culture."

"They have an intelligence, that's for sure," Patrick offered. "You can see it in their eyes. If you can capture that, then you'll have the essence of the bear. In fact, bears are remarkably similar to humans. A skinned bear looks a lot like a person."

Sarah shivered. "That's creepy."

"And fascinating. Their diets are like ours. Anything a bear can eat, we can. And things that are poisonous to them will hurt us too. Bears use certain plants for healing, the same ones we use today. So, you can be sure that early humans learned a lot by watching bears."

Sarah nodded. "I can see even more why the Ute people would feel connected to them, call them 'teacher'." She thought about Standing Bear and what the story said about his relationship to the grizzly that was killed. Maybe it wasn't so far fetched that they actually had a bond. "Would grizzly bears have lived up in that meadow where we were?"

"Most likely," Patrick said. "Perfect habitat for them. Colorado had grizzlies up until 1952 or so. That's when the last one was killed in the state. Ranchers didn't think too highly of them; neither did developers."

"What, so they just shot them all?"

"Pretty much. The black bear population has expanded since then, filling the void." Patrick moved closer to see what Sarah was sketching. "The bear is looking better, but I'm not so sure about that biologist."

Sarah blushed and tried to cover up the page. She'd started out drawing a grizzly face but then found her sketching Patrick's as well. "Sorry, old artist's habit. Drawing whatever's in front of me."

"Don't apologize, please. I'm flattered." Patrick grinned. "Maybe you'd let me buy you lunch and you could keep sketching."

Sarah's stomach grumbled loud enough for both to hear. "Guess I can't say I'm not hungry. But I can't be gone too long. I've got to keep going with this. I'll leave the sketch pad here."

They took Patrick's truck. Based on the clutter in the passenger seat that he had to clear out, it was obvious he had not planned on taking her or anyone else to lunch. "Sorry, this is my office as well as my truck," Patrick explained.

"No problem, I understand." Sarah got in and buckled her seatbelt. "How is your work going? Any progress with Eli?"

"No. We can't get him to consider the easement. You haven't mentioned anything to Hollis or Nick, have you?"

"No. I told you before I wouldn't say anything."

"I'm sorry. Of course you did. It's just that this is so important, any slip could be bad."

They drove down the long drive and pulled onto the county road.

"Where is the land that Eli is selling?"

"When we get to Springhorn's I'll show you on a map. But the back end butts up to both Ms. Jessie's and Duncan's properties. The meadow where the graves are is on his land."

Sarah had no idea. Duncan and Jason wouldn't want that land to be sold either. She wondered why neither had mentioned anything about it.

"Turns out, Ms. Jessie's family used to own the McDermott Ranch," Patrick said. "Eli's land was originally part of the Winde ranch, but Ms. Jessie's grandfather had been forced to sell that parcel."

"Can't she just buy it back?" Sarah asked.

"She says she can't or won't, I'm not sure which."

"And Duncan? He can't buy the land either?"

"If he can, he hasn't said anything to me or Ms. Jessie."

"Isn't there someone else who could buy it, someone who would be open to the easement idea?" Sarah was thinking of Hollis.

"No one comes to mind." He looked at Sarah. "I'd consider Hollis if he didn't have a son named Nick. Please, don't even think about it."

They drove in silence for a time until they turned onto the main road.

"On the ride up to the meadow, Ms. Jessie gave me a quick rundown on the story about Eli," Sarah said, "but I have to confess, I don't remember much of it now. Why is Eli hiding up here?"

"The story is he's hiding from a mobsters he owes money to. He thinks they'll kill him if he doesn't pay up," Patrick said.

"Why was he messing around with those graves?"

"Didn't Duncan or Jason talk with you about this? You seem to be, well, close."

"Duncan Hawk is the most perplexing person I've ever met. Let's just say he hasn't been all that communicative lately. So, you'd have my undying gratitude if you could fill me in about Eli."

"And Jason?" Patrick asked.

Sarah blushed. "Well…"

"Got it. None of my business. Here's what I can tell you about Eli." Patrick shared what he knew, including his role in setting out the talismen that got Eli so worked up and Ms. Jessie's explanation of the spirit curse that supposedly had plagued him in the past.

"Doesn't sound like you believe in this curse," Sarah said.

"Can't say as I do. But Eli seems to and I guess that's all that matters."

The Springhorn Lodge came into the view. He slowed the truck, preparing to turn into the drive.

Something was nagging at Sarah about the nature of the curse. "Patrick, it sounds like all of the bad things happened to Eli years ago when he first robbed the graves. But now that he's returned what he's taken, what is he afraid of?"

"As I understand it, Eli has been warned that if he sells the land, the spirits will be angry with him."

"What's the reason he won't sign the easement?"

"He said it wasn't enough money to pay off his debt, but I didn't believe him. He hates the government, basically. Doesn't trust 'em, thinks he'll get screwed."

"Is he more afraid of the spirits or of the mob?"

"That's a good question. He is acting so crazy now, I think he's afraid of everything."

Sarah let the question ruminate in the back of her mind over lunch. It wasn't until she'd returned to the Double R to resume work on the mural that a spark of inspiration hit. *Maybe there's a way to have the curse take a different turn, so that Eli would have no choice but to protect the land.*

CHAPTER FORTY-THREE

RUTH RETURNED SARAH'S phone call the next morning. "You had lunch with Patrick? Really. Tell me more." Ruth had her gossip voice on. "Does Jason know about this?"

"Slow down, it was just a lunch. Business. That's all."

"He's not the reason you're getting cold feet about Jason?"

"No, not at all. Patrick is cute, I'll admit. But, I'm not interested."

"You sure? You've been attracted to biologists before."

"Yes, I'm sure. And I'm not exactly getting cold feet. I'm just being cautious, I guess. I don't know what's really real, sometimes."

"Ooh, the baby just kicked me. I think she's saying hello to you."

"Rub your belly and tell her it's from me. I wish I could be there."

"Me too. Sarah, my office phone is ringing. I've got to take it. I'll call you right back. Don't go anywhere."

Nice timing, Sarah thought. *I was just getting to the important stuff.*

A raucous cackling from the back room broke her train of thought. Sarah got up to investigate and found a raven at the bedroom window, pecking the screen and flapping its wings, like it was attacking something.

"What's with you?" Sarah asked. She noticed the medicine bundle sitting on the dresser just below the window. She walked slowly into the room. The black bird quieted only once she placed a hand on the medicine bundle.

"Is this what you want?" Sarah picked it up to show the raven. The bird cawed and flew off. "Guess not."

Sarah sat down on the bed, cradling the buckskin package. She still hadn't opened it. Intrigued by the raven's odd behavior, she took the bundle out on the porch and see if her feathery friend showed up. If so, she would open it. If not, she would wait. A year ago, such cockeyed logic wouldn't have made any sense to her, but it did these days.

Armed with a few pieces of bread for the raven and some iced coffee for herself, she sat down in a rocking chair on the deck and placed the bundle on the side table. Rethinking her decision to bring food—how would she know if the bird showed up because of the bread or the bundle—Sarah was about to take the offering inside when the raven flew by and landed on the table. It pecked gently at the beaded tie.

"Okay, okay, I get it." She playfully waved her hand at the bird, which hopped onto the railing. The buckskin opened to reveal a shiny brown animal pelt that wrapped around the rest of the contents. It was beaver, just like the piece Jason had brought over when he taught her about all her relations. Brushing her hand against the fur sent a rush of excitement through her body, evoking the exquisite memory of his caresses.

She folded back the fur and found a small leather-bound book, along with a few stones, a rattle, and leather pouches containing dried herbs. Gingerly, she picked up the book and opened it. The pages were filled with handwriting, the ink faded but legible. It was a journal. Turning to the first page, she confirmed what some part of her already knew.

This was written by Red Fire Woman!

"Look what I found," she exclaimed to her raven, who cawed and bobbed its head with approval. She broke up the bread and placed the pieces on the railing. "Look at me. I'm celebrating with a bird."

While the raven finished eating, Sarah sat down with this view into the past—actual words from a woman she never knew but felt so connected to. It sat in her lap for quite some time while she contemplated what she might find inside. A dull ache in her left hand brought her back to the present. Looking down, she saw her hand twitching, the thumb and two fingers curled up. *Not again!*

Remembering her work with Duncan, she went into the house, found the strand of sweetgrass and brought it outside. She lit one end and smudged with the smoke, savoring the aroma. She smudged the bundle and the diary too. She tried blowing smoke over by the raven, who would have none of it, and then rubbed the burning end against the railing to put it out. Her hand relaxed. Then she began to read.

When Sarah looked up from the pages, the late morning sun that had brightened the deck was now behind her, warming the back of her head. A distant buzzing caught her attention. "My phone. Ruth!"

Sarah jumped up and ran into the cabin, managing to answer her phone just in time.

"Where have you been? I've been calling you for the last couple of hours." Ruth sounded worried.

"I'm so sorry, but you'll forgive me when you hear what I've been doing...reading Red Fire Woman's journal!"

After a quick explanation of how she had come by this treasure, Sarah tried to sum up what she'd read so far.

"The first entry is dated Coyote Howling Moon, 1892. That's eleven years after the Utes were relocated to Utah. She wrote this for whoever would receive her medicine bundle. She wanted that woman to know the truth about her life, what happened to her. What she felt responsible for. It's an incredibly detailed accounting of her life. I'd read parts to you, but it's a slow go. Her handwriting is not great and her phrasing is kind of odd at times. So, I'll give you the highlights."

"I can't wait to hear."

"She starts out with a confession of sorts, that she feels responsible for what happened to the Ute tribe she lived with. She's wondering if there was something she could have done to save them. To save Standing Bear and Yellow Eagle. She talks about the grizzly bear too. Asking all of them to forgive her. Then she describes how she came to live with the Utes. Get this, she had a relationship with Yellow Eagle before she met Standing Bear."

Sarah paused. "When Jason told me about his vision from the sweat lodge, he said he had a sense that Yellow Eagle loved Red Fire Woman but didn't understand why. Now we know. Unfortunately for Yellow Eagle, Red Fire Woman fell in love with Standing Bear, and according to the diary, he didn't fight over her. I don't know if that was part of their tradition, or if he was just a nice guy. She wrote that Yellow Eagle loved and respected his cousin enough that he stepped away. He went to fight the Sioux with the white man's army and started drinking whiskey."

"Poor guy," Ruth said. "That's no reward for being chivalrous."

"I agree. Yellow Eagle seems to get the short end of the stick in this deal." Sarah cleared her throat. "So, what does that mean for me and

Jason? If we're somehow following in the footsteps of our past lives, I mean. Jason now believes that he's connected to Yellow Eagle, not Standing Bear. Maybe that's why I've been questioning how I feel about him. And maybe I'm taking all of this way too literally."

"I'm not so sure you're destined to repeat history," Ruth said. "Otherwise, what would be the point of living more than once? You're supposed to be learning lessons and making different choices, according to karma philosophy. So, don't feel like you're trapped by the past."

"I guess that's good news," Sarah voice wavered. "Before we get sidetracked with that, let me tell you about what else I read. Her story of being captured was almost the same as what Jason saw in the sweat."

"Go on." Ruth was riveted.

"She described the soldiers forcing the Utes into Utah after the Meeker Massacre. The army made them walk all that way. She said that Ethan was one of the soldiers on that march and that he boasted about shooting anyone who fell behind. He gloated about the white people taking over Ute lands. Red Fire Woman felt responsible for Ethan's atrocious behavior because she said everything he did against the Utes was to punish her because she loved them."

Sarah got up to pour herself a glass of water. "Ethan is one sick asshole, let me tell you. What he did to Red Fire Woman is unbelievable. After the fight in the meadow, she escaped and hid from the soldiers. She watched as they carried Ethan out of the meadow and head back down the trail. He was wounded. She thought they would take him back to the agency and leave her alone. She thought she was safe for a while. The next day she buried Standing Bear and Yellow Eagle as best she could. Even though she knew she should get away, she was too exhausted and couldn't leave the meadow.

"Ethan sent several soldiers back into the mountains to capture her. They found her sobbing by the graves. She wasn't able to fight them off. I'd forgotten this, but she was pregnant at the time. She wrote that the soldiers could tell she was pregnant. But that didn't stop the bastards from raping her before they brought her to Ethan."

"How awful," Ruth said. "That hits too close to home right now."

"I can imagine. I hate to tell you, but it gets worse. The soldiers made her walk most of the way back. They finally gave her a horse after she'd fallen and couldn't get back up. When they arrived at the agency, a soldier pulled her from the horse and threw her on the ground. She wrote that she could barely move. She looked up to see Ethan riding towards her on a black horse. She made special note of his long soldier's coat. He made the horse rear right above her and she was afraid it would crush her. But the horse backed up before its hooves hit the ground. Part of her wanted to die then, but she was carrying Standing Bear's child, so she knew had to find a way to live."

Sarah quickly wiped away a tear before it fell on the fragile pages.

"Ethan took her to a cabin and tied her to a bed. Of course, he raped her. Red Fire Woman begged him to stop so he would not hurt the baby. He went into a rage. He said that she was carrying the devil's child and slapped her across the face. She spat at him. He just kept on hitting her. She was able to get her left hand free. She wrote that the only weapon she had was her necklace. She grabbed the claw and started stabbing him with it. He tried to pry the necklace from her but she wouldn't let go."

"When she wouldn't give him the necklace, he pulled out a knife and threatened to cut off her hand. They struggled, he grabbed her wrist, but she pulled back. Instead of cutting through her wrist, he hit her two fingers instead. Her pinky and ring fingers. That's all she remembered because she fainted.

"When she came to, her hand was bandaged, with the claw still in her grasp. She described a frightened young soldier who was watching over her. He warned Red Fire Woman to do whatever the Captain said. He told her to give him the necklace. Otherwise, he was afraid the Captain would kill her.

"Ethan returned. He was drunk. He told the soldier to leave the room. Then he started ranting about Red Fire Woman living with a red devil, having his child. From what she wrote, it sounds like he went psychotic because he started telling her how beautiful she was, how he had wanted her from the first time he saw her. How she haunted his dreams. He accused her of running away to live with animals. Then he hit her so hard, he broke her jaw and her cheekbone. He called her a whore, unfit to be a mother. He pulled her from the bed and threw her on the floor.

"Then the bastard started kicking her. He kept on kicking her while she screamed. The soldier finally came in and pulled Ethan away from her. But it was too late. She said she felt the blood flowing out of her and knew her baby was dying. She wanted to die. Then she passed out."

Sarah sighed. "That's as far as I got before you called."

"Oh my," was all Ruth could say.

"There's more, but I'll read it later. This is so disturbing, I'm not sure I want to know the rest. My guess is, there's no happy ending. I think I need some wine."

Both sisters took a short break to grab something to drink and process what they had learned.

"I'm still shaking," Ruth said. "It's horrible what happened to her."

"She certainly was made to suffer. Seems like she already paid her karmic debt, don't you think?"

"Speaking of that, you were going to tell me about your recent brainstorm." Ruth sounded eager to change subjects.

"Yes. Two things came to me, actually."

Sarah went on to share her conversation with Patrick. "I think Hollis would be the perfect person to buy the McDermott property from Eli. And yet, there is no way to keep that from Nick and no way to explain to Hollis why he'd need to do that."

"You'd have to arrange for Nick to be on some overseas junket for six months or forget it," Ruth said. "Or find some way to attach an Indian curse to him. Aren't I the helpful one!"

"You have the wisdom of a pregnant, highly hormonal woman who has no idea what you're talking about," Sarah said. "It would be great if Nick would just go back to New York and do whatever he does there, but I don't think that's going to happen. So, let me tell you about my other idea. This one might work, if Duncan will go along with it."

But before Sarah could say another word, a male voice cut into her like Ethan's knife on Red Fire Woman's hand.

"Tell me, Sarah, what just might work to keep big, bad Nick from buying your precious ranch? I'm dying to know."

CHAPTER FORTY-FOUR

SARAH SLOWLY TURNED to see Nick leaning in the doorway between the kitchen and the living room. His twisted smile filled her with dread.

"Ruth, Nick's here. I gotta go." Sarah clicked off her phone before her sister could insist she not hang up.

"What a surprise, to find you here without your Indian escort and so full of interesting news." Nick's usual cocky tone carried an edge. He looked hungry. "Aren't you going to invite me in?"

Sarah moved away as he commandeered the armchair, never taking his eyes off of her.

"How dare you sneak in here and eavesdrop on my conversations!" With her back against the fireplace, she had no escape. Any exit required getting past her intruder.

"Eli has land for sale. Don't tell that bad boy Nick. He might buy it."

Feeling like a mouse trapped by a sadistic cat, Sarah didn't know what to say. She'd already said too much.

"Eli, let me see. Haven't heard that name before. But it won't take me long to find out who he is. Unless, of course, you'd like to save me the trouble and tell me what Eli's last name is."

"Get out of here."

Nick bristled, his eyes widened, glaring. "Now that's not very polite. I just got here. Why don't you pour us both a drink?"

"I said, get out."

Nick stepped quickly towards her. "I don't like your attitude."

Sarah stuck out her arms to stop his advance, but he knocked them aside and slammed his hands against her shoulders, pinning her against the wall. "Let's try this again." He pressed in closer. Sarah turned her head away and tried to wrestle free, but he intensified his grip. He began kissing her neck.

"Get off me!"

With a force that nearly snapped her neck, he grabbed her face and kissed her on the mouth, his tongue nearly choking her. He began rubbing up against her so hard, her pelvis hurt. One hand groped her breast, then began pulling at the buttons on her blouse.

Her whole body strained against his attack but she couldn't move. He kissed her again and she bit down on his lip. He barely flinched. "So, you like it rough." He sounded almost pleased. "So do I." Then he slapped her across the face and grabbed her hair. He made sure she looked right at him before kissing her rough and hard.

He's trying to rape me! Furious, she pushed against him. When he pulled back a bit, she jabbed her knee into his groin and he crumbled to the ground, cursing.

Sarah bolted from the room, grabbed her keys and purse from the counter and fled out the door. She gunned the truck down the drive, past the main house and onto the county road. Constantly checking the rear view mirror to see if Nick was following her, she didn't slow down until she hit the main road, and then only to yield to a truck. She was shaking so badly, she had a hard time driving straight. With one hand on the wheel, she fumbling through her purse looking for her cell phone, then realized she'd left it in the living room. She had to get to a phone. The closest place was the Ute Lodge.

Thoughts bombarded her—*How could I have been so careless? You idiot! I need to tell Ms. Jessie. She'll kill me. I want to throw up. He almost raped me! I want this to all go away. Maybe I'll just keep driving and not stop until I get to Chicago....*

When she pulled up to the Ute Lodge, her mind stilled to one thought. *That's Ms. Jessie. How am I going to tell her?*

She drove past the corral where Jessie, Patrick and Karl were standing with horses, saddled and sweated, having just finished a ride. Parking next to the office, Sarah was greeted by Mona, who was carrying a tray of lemonade and glasses out to the picnic table.

As Sarah got closer, Mona took a closer look at her and exclaimed, "What happened to you? Are you alright?"

Sarah looked down at her torn blouse and felt the dull throb of her bruised cheek. Mona put out her arms and she fell into them, sobbing. Her hope of holding it together flowed away with her tears.

Mona had her sit down as Patrick walked over. "What's wrong?" Sarah didn't want anyone to see her like this.

"I don't know," Mona said. "Pat, would you mind getting some water? Oh, and grab the box of tissues. Thanks."

Patrick headed into the office and Sarah sighed in relief. "Thank you, Mona. I'm sorry..." but she couldn't finish the sentence.

"No apologies. I'm glad you're here. What happened?"

Patrick returned and handed her a glass, a worried look on his face. After several sips, she found her voice. "I only have the energy to tell this story once and Ms. Jessie needs to hear it."

Patrick volunteered to get her and Karl. Mona stood up. "Sarah, I'll be right back." She returned with another button-down blouse that Sarah thankfully put on to cover the torn one.

When everyone had gathered on the porch, Sarah looked at their faces and prayed that they wouldn't hate her once she finished.

Jessie didn't wait to hear the end of the story. Once she learned that Nick knew about Eli, she cursed and left the table to call her lawyer. Sarah cringed. How could she have let her down, and Patrick and Duncan? She thought she had figured out what she was supposed to be doing here and then she did the one thing that would destroy it. Her mind was so filled with self-loathing, she didn't hear Patrick at first.

"Sarah, did Nick hurt you?"

She shook her head, no. As much as she wanted Nick to pay for what he'd done to her, she wasn't ready to lose her job or her relationship with Hollis, not yet. He still might be able to have some influence over the land sale. It was a crazy idea, probably, but it felt like her only hope.

Patrick didn't believe her and said so. She could tell that Mona and Karl didn't either. "He pushed me, but that's it. Really. Look, I appreciate all your concern, I do. But the real problem is what Nick is going to do when he finds out who Eli is. I'm so sorry."

"I think someone needs to teach Nick Tremaine some manners," Patrick said. Karl nodded in agreement. Sarah heard the anger in his voice and begged him not to do anything. Patrick didn't reply.

"What can we do about Nick and Eli?" Sarah said, wanting very much to fix the mess she had just unleashed.

Karl said, "I thought the plan was to get him to sign that easement."

"I've been trying," Patrick said, "but he refuses."

"Last week, I had reason to be riding near that cabin where he's staying," Karl said. "The old bird took a shot at me. Fortunately, he's a terrible shot and it didn't come anywhere near me. He's dangerous, that's for sure."

Karl put an arm around Sarah and gave her a hug. "Try not to worry yourself too much. Things have a way of working out."

"I sure hope so."

Despite Mona's repeated offers to have her spend the night, Sarah insisted on going home, much to Patrick's displeasure. Patrick had never tolerated bullies, especially those who preyed on women. Even though he didn't know Sarah very well, his protective instincts were kicking in. He knew she was lying about Nick, but he would respect her wishes to not confront him, at least for now. He informed her that he'd follow her back just to make sure she got home safely. She didn't refuse his offer.

Once at the Flat Top Ranch, Patrick saw lights on at the main house. He planned to pay Nick a short visit on his way out after making sure Sarah was settled.

Patrick walked her to the door. "I'm not being forward here, but I'd like to come in, just to make sure everything's okay."

"I can tell you won't take 'no' for an answer, so come on in. I appreciate your caring," Sarah said.

"I'll sleep better making sure there's no one inside who shouldn't be."

When he was satisfied with his inspection, he bid Sarah a good night. She gave him a quick hug. "Thanks, Patrick."

"Here's my cell number." He handed her his business card. "Call me if you need to."

She assured him she would.

Patrick found Hollis and Nick drinking brandy on the porch. Hollis greeted him with an enthusiastic handshake and slap on the back while Nick stayed seated and nodded.

"Thought I'd stop in to say 'hey' while I was passing through," Patrick said, staring at Nick. "Sarah stopped by the Ute Lodge this afternoon and was telling folks about her progress on the murals. Sounds quite exciting. She asked me to come by to give the wildlife art a once over from a biologist's point of view. Told her I'd be happy to."

Hollis was genuinely pleased.

Patrick maintained eye contact with Nick. "Sarah's made some good friends in the valley, people who care about her, who are watching out for her. Just thought you should know."

"How lucky for her," Nick replied, his stare unwavering.

"Say, Patrick. Nick and I were just talking about some ranch that may be for sale. Owned by someone named Eli. Have you heard about this?"

"No sir, can't say I have." Patrick was an uncomfortable liar.

"Have any idea who this guy Eli is?" Hollis asked. "I thought I knew everyone in the valley."

"I don't know any ranchers in the valley named Eli." That was technically true. "Well, good night, sir."

Patrick could feel Nick's glare as he walked down the steps to his truck. The bastard had been warned.

But Nick had also made his own threat perfectly clear—it would not be long before he found Eli McDermott.

CHAPTER FORTY-FIVE

THE CHILLY DAWN AIR danced as mist with each exhalation the old man made as he prayed to the rising sun, a pinch of tobacco in his left hand. He offered words of gratitude for his life, for the people he loved, for the world around him. Recalling the phone call he had received last night, Duncan said an extra prayer for Sarah, who would be arriving within the hour. She had urgent news. He sprinkled the tobacco on the ground as the sun finally rose above the mountain peaks. Patting his heart, he invited the sun to fill him with light for the dark times ahead.

Turning around, he spotted Jason by the large pine, finishing his morning prayers. He waited for his nephew and together they walked back to the house in silence.

Sarah arrived after breakfast, looking as though she hadn't slept much the night before. While she accepted Jason's embrace, she didn't meet Duncan's gaze. She wrapped her hands around the coffee mug Jason brought her as she recounted what had taken place yesterday, beginning with her phone call to Ruth. "I was so excited because I thought I'd figured out what I'm supposed to do in this lifetime to make amends for what happened before, you know, as Red Fire Woman."

Duncan looked confused.

"You don't know what I'm talking about, do you?" Sarah asked.

Duncan shook his head.

"You told me that you've come to believe that I was Red Fire Woman in a past life. From what I'm learning about this whole reincarnation thing, there must be a reason why I've come here to discover this connection and to learn about what happened to Red Fire Woman and the Utes. Duncan, you think I'm supposed to do something with her medicine bundle and learn about Indian medicine ways. I still don't know how I feel about that. But my sister thinks that one reason may be that there is something I'm supposed to do today to make up for things that happened because of Red Fire Woman. I've been thinking about that for a while. The ideas that came to me yesterday had to do with saving Eli's land from being developed.

"The only problem is, Nick overheard me telling Ruth about them. He knows about Eli and that his land is for sale. I had no idea he was in the cabin. Otherwise, I never would have said a thing."

"What the hell was he doing in your cabin?" Jason asked, with an angry edge to his voice.

Sarah couldn't look at him.

"Did that bastard hurt you?"

"He tried to, but I got away. Jason, please don't do anything to him. Not now. We've got to focus on keeping him away from Eli and—"

"Putting him the hospital would certainly accomplish that!" He slammed his fist on the table.

"I think Hollis could help us and I don't want to give him any reason to let me go."

"Have you told Jessie?" Duncan asked in a subdued tone.

"Yes. She was furious. I told her I'd come over to tell you."

Duncan, too, felt outrage, over Nick hurting Sarah and over Nick knowing about the land. But as he looked at Sarah's face, wet with tears, another feeling emerged, unexpected and intense: anger at her. The woman who was supposed to help heal the ancestors had just given Nick the information he needed to destroy ancestral lands. She had become an unintended accomplice to the harm she was trying to prevent, which, Duncan realized, was exactly what had happened with Red Fire Woman years ago on this same land. History, it seemed, was repeating itself.

Sarah interrupted his thoughts. "Ms. Jessie wanted me to tell you that she would be in touch as soon as she heard anything about Nick from the lawyer. She said it would only be a matter of time before he finds out who Eli is." Her voice quavered. "I am so sorry."

"You have nothing to apologize for," Jason said, defending her. "It's that fuckin' Nick who needs his nuts handed to him. Eli too."

Duncan cleared his throat. "Sarah, what is it that you think you can do to make things right?"

"My first thought was to talk with Hollis about buying the land and putting a conservation easement on the place. He really seems to care about preserving the land. We've talked a lot about the history of the valley and he's truly interested in that. I think if he knew about the burial grounds, he'd make doubly sure to protect the area. The tricky part was doing all of this without Nick finding out. And I blew that."

"And your second idea?"

"That one involves you, Duncan." Sarah said self-consciously.

Duncan nodded for her to continue.

"As I understand it, Eli thinks he's been cursed because he disturbed the graves. And he's afraid that the spirits will hurt him if he sells that land. Is that true?"

Duncan took his time answering. "Eli is cursed by his own hand. And from what Patrick told us, he is now so frightened, he may be losing his mind. The Spirits, when they are angry, can do that to a man." Then he fell silent.

"Can the curse be undone?"

"Why do you ask?"

"What if Eli thought the curse would be lifted if he agreed to the easement? Do you think that would get him to take Patrick's deal?"

"How does that involve me?"

"I thought there might be some kind of ceremony you could do to remove the curse from him. Is there such a thing?"

"If the Spirits want it to be so."

"I thought Eli would believe you, of all people, if you told him he could be rid of this curse."

"And what is your role in this plan, Sarah?" Duncan asked. "I believe you said there is something you need to do. And all I have heard is what others can do." He watched her hopeful gaze darken.

"Maybe it's the fact that I came up with the idea? That sounds lame, I know. Maybe there's a way that I'm supposed to help you?"

Duncan sat back and closed his eyes. An image of the seven horses from his Coyote dream flashed before him. "I will go ask the Spirits about what you have said. There may be wisdom in your words." Then he stood up, patted her on the shoulder and walked out the door.

"I want you to tell me exactly what happened with Nick." Jason and Sarah had moved into the living room and were sitting closely together on the couch.

"There isn't that much to tell," Sarah said. "Nick came over to my cabin. He was drunk. He got forward with me and tried to kiss me. I pushed him away and decided it would be best if I got out of there."

"Why didn't you call me?" Jason had wanted to ask her that all morning. "Or come over here?" *Doesn't she trust me? Doesn't she know she can count on me?*

He had tried to see her a number of times since the sweat ceremony, but she kept putting him off, saying she needed time to work. He couldn't shake the fear that her feelings for him might be changing.

"I left my cell phone back at the cabin, so I drove over to the Ute Lodge. And then once I told everybody there, all I wanted to do was crawl into a corner and hide. I felt so awful about what happened."

"What if Nick had come back? You should have come here last night," Jason said.

"I felt I could handle it. And I was afraid you'd drive over and beat him up if I did call."

"You're right, I would have. I still will."

"You have to promise me that you won't do anything to hurt him," Sarah pleaded. "It won't do any good. I don't want anything to happen to you. They could throw you in jail or worse. I couldn't live with that."

Jason reluctantly agreed, even though he knew he could hide a body where no one would ever find it.

He hugged her tightly. "I don't want you staying there any more, not until I know that Nick won't be around to bother you."

She let herself relax into his embrace, until her eye caught sight of a book on the coffee table. She pushed back to look at Jason. "Oh my god, I forgot to tell you and Duncan. I opened the medicine bundle yesterday and I found the most amazing thing. Red Fire Woman's journal!"

"Have you read it?"

"I finished it last night. She wrote about everything that happened to her since she was fourteen years old. That's when Ethan Amory first showed up in her life. He was a creep from the very beginning."

"I assume she wrote about Standing Bear and Yellow Eagle." Jason's throat tightened. Maybe her writings would tell a different story than what was revealed to him in the sweat.

"Her description matches pretty closely the vision you shared with me." Then she told him all that she had read up until Ethan's beating and Red Fire Woman losing the baby.

"What a sick fuck," Jason said. "Let me get you some water, you're starting to sound a little hoarse."

"Thanks. I'd like that." Sarah joined him in the kitchen and suggested they sit outside.

Jason scanned the yard as they sat down. No sign of Duncan.

"Can I tell you the rest of Red Fire Woman's story?" Sarah asked as she rocked gently in the weathered green rocking chair.

"Of course." Much as he hated to admit this, it gave him a small degree of comfort to know that someone had hurt Red Fire Woman even more than Yellow Eagle had. Jason had been feeling responsible for Yellow Eagle's actions, ever since the sweat, even though logically he knew it didn't make any sense. Still, he couldn't shake the guilt and shame that he imagined Yellow Eagle must have felt. There was some relief in refocusing those feelings into ones of anger for Ethan and Nick.

"After Ethan had beaten her and made her miscarry, Red Fire Woman fainted. When she regained consciousness, she could tell from the sound and movement that she was in a wagon, but couldn't see. Something heavy was covering her that smelled awful. Her hands were tied. She panicked and started screaming. When someone lifted the covering, that's when she realized it was a fresh bearskin. Ethan was on horseback staring down at her. He told her that was the skin from the grizzly in the meadow."

Jason grimaced.

"Red Fire Woman had lost so much blood, she faded in and out of consciousness for the rest of the trip. She nearly died. Ethan took her back to Fort Laramie in Wyoming. As you probably remember, he was married to her mother and she was living at the fort. When they got there, that bastard told people that the Utes had cut off her fingers and beaten her, and that he had saved her life! Can you believe that?"

Jason's jaw tightened. "That motherfucker. She didn't let him get away with that, did she?"

"She was too sick at first, it took everything she had just to get stronger. Her mother was the only one who would care for her and Red Fire Woman was afraid her mother would abandon her if she told her what had actually happened. She also knew that her mother would never believe her anyway. She only did or thought what Ethan wanted her to. So, Red Fire Woman had to make do until she could find a way to get out of there.

"The good news is, someone finally killed Ethan four years later in a fight. Her mother passed away a year after that. Red Fire Woman could finally leave Wyoming. She went to Utah and stayed with White Willow Laughing for a long while. She said that it was White Willow Laughing who encouraged her to write down her story. Seems like once she got most of her story on paper, she stopped writing for a while. The final section of the journal is more like a diary. Her handwriting became less clear. It ends with her saying that she was going to return to the mountains to be with Standing Bear, that she was going to return to what she called 'the grizzly's home'. She wrote that she was leaving her medicine bundle and bear-claw necklace with White Willow Laughing so that they could be passed on."

"And here you are," Jason said, "with her medicine bundle and her story, after all this time." A story that left him deeply moved and equally troubled. Hearing about Ethan's cruelty and Red Fire Woman's suffering made him even more determined to protect Sarah from harm, especially from Nick.

She stood up and reached out to him. "I'd really like a hug." As their bodies pressed against one another, he longed to feel her skin against his.

She spoke softly, still nestled in his embrace. "Every time I think of Ethan, it makes me think of Nick. Nick really frightens me. I think he's as dangerous as Ethan was."

Jason squeezed her tighter. "I won't let that bastard hurt you, I promise." He rubbed her back until he felt her relax, then he kissed her gently. She returned his kiss without hesitation. Maybe he wasn't losing her after all.

CHAPTER FORTY-SIX

DUNCAN BUILT A SMALL prayer fire in the fire pit used for the sweat lodge. As the kindling ignited, he offered tobacco to the flames. Then he lit a strand of sweetgrass and smudged himself with the smoke. He smudged his drum and his rattle before respectfully placing the remaining braid of grass into the fire. Picking up the rattle, he began to sing a welcoming song that called to the Spirits to join him and hear his prayers. Then he switched to the drum and sang another song to Grandpa Fire. This one asked the flames to help bring a vision that would guide him, take him further into his dream of the seven horses. Once his song finished, he continued with a steady drumbeat that matched the beating of his heart. His body felt heavy, his mind clear.

In his pocket he found a small leather bag that contained bearberry, an herb that grew in the mountains. It brought vision to those who knew how to call on the medicine of the plant. He sprinkled a small amount in the fire and sang one final song. "Oh, sacred one," he sang, "please show me the rest of my dream, show me what I need to do for the ancestors. Bearberry, hear my prayers."

With his offerings completed, Duncan sat down on a small rug in front of the fire and closed his eyes. Once again he saw the seven horses waiting in a meadow. Coyote sat on the hillside and beat a drum. Duncan watched, as one by one, a rider appeared for each horse, beginning with himself. Then Jason, Sarah, Jessie, Patrick. And then the remaining two riders appeared. They all mounted up and followed Coyote, who led them down a path to a ceremonial ground where a large fire burned. The air was filled with chanting, rattling and drumming but Duncan saw no one other than his riding companions. And Coyote.

He saw the dream continue to unfold, detailing the ceremony the Spirits wanted him to do for the ancestors. But the vision stopped abruptly before the ceremony was complete. Duncan saw himself standing in front of the Ancient One.

"Why can I not see how the ceremony ends?" Duncan asked. "How will I know what to do?"

"Once the ceremony begins, the outcome will not be up to you," the Ancient One said. "Trust what you have been shown. But know that all is not yet ready. Remember this. She must accept her medicine before there can be healing."

Duncan opened his eyes. The fire had burned down to glowing embers. He offered a prayer of thanks, even though his vision inspired as many questions as it did answers. The Ancient One said Sarah had to accept her medicine, but she had no training, no understanding of spiritual healing. How could Duncan help her? And what was his role in the healing?

As he packed up his instruments and his herbs, he noticed a shift in the air. It smelled like rain. Dark clouds blew over as the temperature dropped by a few degrees. A jagged string of lightning flashed in the western sky. *The Thunder Beings have come to bless my vision. Thank you.*

Duncan loved to sit on the porch during a thunderstorm, but he didn't like to get wet, so he hurried back to the house. On his way, he thought about the final two riders who appeared in his vision and the uncertain role they both would play. "Spirit has given me a challenging task," he said, speaking to the storm clouds. "How am I going to get Nick Tremaine and Eli McDermott to come to ceremony?"

CHAPTER FORTY-SEVEN

JESSIE ARRIVED AT THE courthouse ten minutes before the doors opened. Sally Grimm had left a message the night before that she had news and needed to meet. It had been two days since Nick's appearance in Sarah's cabin. Jessie had been an enraged wreck ever since.

The heavy wooden door to the courthouse creaked open and she marched inside, then paced in the lobby, waiting for the lawyer to arrive. When Sally walked through the door, Jessie barely said "hello" before she started to vent.

"Ms. Jessie, slow down. I know you're upset, but let's take this one step at a time. Come down to my office and let me get us some coffee."

Jessie begrudgingly followed her down the hall and pretended to be patient. When Sally returned with two mugs, Jessie sat down and said, "Okay, you've got your coffee. What's happened?"

"Well, Mr. Tremaine came by the office yesterday...."

"Nick or Hollis?"

"Nick. He sure is nothing like his daddy, is he? No sense of humor."

"What did he say?" Jessie sat on the edge of her chair and spilled some coffee on the desk.

Sally jumped up to grab a napkin, much to Jessie's irritation.

"Forget the coffee. I'll clean it up. What did Nick want?"

"To buy Eli's land, of course," she said, handing Jessie a napkin. "He had a contract all drawn up by some New York firm. He wanted to know how much he was asking for the land and where to find him."

"What!" Jessie was out of her seat. "You didn't tell him, did you?"

"I told him how much he was asking, I am obligated to do that. But I said that Eli could not be reached and that I'd be happy to pass along the contract to him myself."

"And what did he say to that?"

"At first, he tried to sweet talk me, like I'd fall for that. When he realized that wasn't working, he got very upset and demanded to know where Eli was. These rich folks can get so bossy, like they own the world. As I said, he's nothing like his daddy. Hollis is a gentleman."

Jessie glared at her friend who, in this moment, seemed to be speaking at a snail's pace.

"I didn't let him intimidate me. I just stood my ground. He stormed out with his contract. Didn't leave a copy for me. So, I think we dodged that bullet, don't you?"

"Not at all. He'll find Eli, it's only a matter of time." Jessie had to figure out how to stop him.

"If he does find his cabin, Eli might just as easily shoot him as talk to him," Sally said. "I'm worried about him, Ms. Jessie. I think he's going crazy. Last time I drove up there, I had to repeat my name several times before he recognized who I was! Frankly speaking, I'm not comfortable visiting him any more, so it's just as well that Nick didn't leave that contract. I'd be obligated to take it to him."

"I just found out Eli took a shot at Karl Maser last week. That man's a menace in more ways than one." Jessie seethed.

"Ms. Jessie, I think it best if I give you the easement agreement," Sally said, handing her a large envelope. "I'm afraid of Eli now. Maybe you can get him to sign this. I think you're the only one who has a chance of talking any sense into him. You might want to give it another try."

Jessie snatched the envelope and stuffed it into her briefcase. "I didn't do so well last time. And now, with the way I'm feeling, I'm just as likely to kill him next time I see him. Let me know the instant you hear from Nick again." Without as much as a thank you, Jessie stormed out of the office, in much the same fashion, Sally observed, as Nick Tremaine.

Jessie had no plan in mind when she drove to Eli's cabin. She did bring a pistol, which rested in her jacket pocket. She told herself it was for self-defense, but she knew better. Part of her wished he'd give her a reason to pull the trigger. She should have asked Sally who would inherit the land if he died.

"Jessibel Amanda Winde, stop that kind of thinking right now!" She cursed as she slammed the door. This damn thing with Eli was making her a bit crazy, too.

"Eli," she yelled from behind her truck. "It's Jessibel. I want to talk to you. Come on out."

To her surprise, the front door opened and a hand waved, motioning to her to enter. She walked around her truck to get a better view of the door. "Eli, get out here."

Again, the hand appeared, waving more emphatically.

"What am I walking into?" she muttered, as she slipped her hand into her pocket and wrapped it around the gun.

Approaching cautiously, she peered into the cabin to see Eli standing in the corner by the door, shotgun in hand but not pointed at her.

"Come out and let's talk."

"No!" Eli tensed, his eyes wide. "It's dangerous out there. They're watching me, always watching me. Only safe inside, back here." He turned abruptly and shuffled into another room. Jessie swallowed hard and followed him into the kitchen, unnerved by his hair-trigger paranoia. She wished now she hadn't been so persistent with the spirit warnings.

Once in the kitchen, Eli calmed a bit and even pulled out the chair for Jessie before scuttling around to the corner farthest from the door. He acted like a cornered animal, agitated and desperately dangerous.

Reluctantly, she sat down at a table strewn with empty whisky bottles and crumpled up chip bags. His demeanor shocked her into silence.

"Did he send you here?" Eli's voice was raspy from lack of use.

"Who are you talking about?"

"You know, don't play with me." Eli was trembling.

"I'm not playing with you. I don't know who you mean."

"The ghost, the Indian spirit."

"Oh, him." Jessie decided to take a risk. "I think I know him. What does he look like?"

"He comes at night, always at night," Eli whispered. "Dressed in bear hides, his face is black, huge claws hanging from his neck. And his eyes are red. I can't look at them."

"Yes, I know this spirit."

"So, he did send you." Eli fumbled for his gun and pointed it at her, but his hand shook too much to hold it up. Jessie kept hers on her pistol.

"Settle down, Eli. I didn't come here to hurt you. He doesn't want to hurt you either. But he will, if you don't do the right thing."

Is some spirit really haunting him, Jessie wondered, *or is he simply delusional? Did I drive him to this?*

She didn't have much time to contemplate that thought. She heard floorboards creaking outside. Eli heard it too and leapt to his feet, knocking his chair backwards. He started waving his shotgun toward the windows. "He's coming!"

"For god sake, calm down!"

"He's out there, I know it. He won't leave me alone. He's going to kill me!" His whole body quivered.

"Eli, look at me. No one will hurt you as long as I'm here," she said, looking out the window. "There's no one out there. Must have been an animal, a porcupine or something."

He glanced at Jessie and the shaking slowed, but his eyes kept darting nervously toward the window.

"I put it back. What more does he want from me?"

"What did you put back?"

"The bone. From the grave. I put it back, I put it back."

"A human bone?"

Eli nodded.

"How could you?" Jessie was appalled. "No wonder the spirits are upset. What were you thinking?"

Eli stepped over to the counter where an open whisky bottle sat. He took a hard sip, and then another.

"Put that down! I can't believe you kept a human bone after you promised me that you had returned everything you stole from those graves. Is there anything else you still have, anything?"

But Eli wasn't listening to her; he was only hearing his own fears racing through his whiskey-muddled mind. He began pacing and yelling like a man possessed. "He's out there somewhere. I know it. He's coming for me. I'll shoot him next time. I'll shoot him! He's not going to get me!"

Jessie kept her eyes locked on the shotgun as she backed away toward the door and pulled her pistol from her pocket, keeping it at her side. Watching him fall apart, she thought how simple it would be to shoot him and put an end to all this. She'd never seen anyone so tormented.

"I need you to sit down now," she said calmly and firmly. "Now!"

He kicked a chair and then knocked over the table.

"Eli!"

He turned to look at her. Seeing the gun, he screamed and crumbled to the floor. She heard a scrambling and a door slam. When she looked over the pile of upturned furniture, she spotted a pantry door. He must have crawled in there to hide. And he had his gun with him.

"Eli, come out of there. I'm not going to hurt you. I just need you to calm down."

No response, except heavy breathing and whimpering. What was she going to do now? If she opened the door, she risked buckshot in her face. She couldn't leave him here like this.

Picking up a chair, she sat down and stared at the pantry door, unsure of her next move. What would happen if Nick found him like this? The rush of realization hit her. "Jessie, you idiot, that's just the point. You need to make it so Nick can't find him. Why didn't I think of this before? If I can get him out of this horrid cabin, I can hide him. And I've got just the place." But in his current condition, she'd need help moving him.

She pulled out her cell phone and swore at the lack of reception. She'd have to drive to Duncan's to ask for help and call Patrick from there.

"Eli, listen to me. I can take you someplace where you'll be safe."

She could barely make out a muffled, "Go away. I'm not coming out."

"Okay. I'm leaving. But I'll be back."

Spotting two boxes of shotgun shells on the counter, she picked them up and took them with her. She hoped Eli would return to his senses by the time she got back, but feared he was dangerously close to a total breakdown. She had no time to waste.

CHAPTER FORTY-EIGHT

JESSIE FOUND DUNCAN in the corral, feeding carrots to his horse and telling Jason an old Indian joke about a medicine man, a priest and a rabbi going into a bar. Duncan turned with surprise as she piped in with the punch line.

"So, you've heard that one before," he said warmly.

"Only about a hundred times. You need new material, Duncan."

"What do you expect? I'm an old Indian. I only know old jokes." He laughed.

"Ms. Jessie, you've arrived in time for some of Old Man's famous ribs," Jason said in greeting. "They'll be done in an hour or so. Would you like to join us for dinner?"

"Thank you, Jason, maybe another time. I'm afraid this isn't a social call. I need your help with Eli. He's cracking up."

Jessie told them about her visit with the recluse, including his confession that the object he'd recently returned to the gravesite was a bone he'd kept all these years.

Duncan's eyes flashed with anger and a scowl hardened his face. Muttering in Ute, he walked out of the corral without a glance at Jessie or Jason and headed toward the house, leaving behind a heavy silence.

Jessie sighed. "I know Duncan's upset, but I need his help and yours so this situation won't get any worse. And I need that help now."

They found Duncan sitting on the porch, burning a strand of sweetgrass and singing softly. He motioned for them to sit. Jessie waited until he'd finished his song before she spoke. "We need to keep Nick

Tremaine from finding Eli. I don't know why I didn't think of this sooner, but the best way to do that is to hide Eli...at my place. I can keep him drunk enough so that he'll behave. At least, I think I can. Besides, he's so weak right now, he needs some kind of care. He may need hospitalization, the way he's going. Anyway, I need help getting him out of that cabin and over to my ranch."

"No disrespect, Ms. Jessie," Jason said, "but why do you think you can handle this maniac?"

"Jason is right," Duncan said. "He is too dangerous. Do not be offended. You are a strong woman, but this is too much for you. We should bring him here. He needs doctoring. He has a spirit sickness from his dishonoring of the ancestors."

Jessie knew better than to argue with Duncan. Eli was safer here and she certainly would be. "You're probably right. I won't fight you. But I am concerned about how we convince him to come with us without anybody getting hurt."

"Leave that to me," Jason said. "He may not come willingly, but we'll get him here. Think your biologist friend would be able to help out?"

Jessie called Patrick to fill him in on the latest developments and asked him to meet Jason at the beginning of the dirt road leading up to Eli's place. She told him to bring a gun.

Sarah was hungry and eagerly anticipated dinner with Jason and Duncan and the promised "ribs like you've never tasted before." She slowed her truck in preparation to turn into the long driveway and, to her surprise, saw Jason's truck pull out onto the road. He came along side her, stopped and leaned out the window.

"I've got to take care of something. Old Man and Ms. Jessie will fill you in. I'll be back as soon as I can." He smiled at her before driving off, but his sense of urgency worried her.

She found Duncan and Ms. Jessie working in the kitchen. They all exchanged greetings and then Ms. Jessie excused herself. "I'm going to lie down on the couch for a bit, if you don't mind." She looked weary and her normally straight shoulders seemed to slump a bit.

Duncan had Sarah cut up cabbage for coleslaw while he explained Jessie's concerns about Eli and the resulting decision to have Jason and Patrick pick him up and bring him here.

Warily, she asked, "Do you think they'll be safe going after Eli?"

Duncan nodded. "Jason knows how to protect himself. I would imagine Patrick does too. Eli is no match for them."

He handed her a bowl for the cut-up cabbage. "Put that in the refrigerator for now. Let's go out on the porch. Jason told me you have something to share with me."

Sarah's thoughts rushed back to the first time she and Duncan had sat on this porch when he'd shared the story of Standing Bear and Red Fire Woman with her. So much had happened to her the past several months.

Here they sat again, only this time she was going to be the storyteller. "I found the missing pieces to the story. I opened Red Fire Woman's medicine bundle and found her journal. Would you like to see it? I have it in the truck."

Duncan shook his head no. "Remember, Sarah. That is your medicine now. Her journal is not for me to see, only you." He leaned back in his chair and began to rock slowly. "However, if you would like to tell me a story, I would gladly listen."

Sarah was surprised at how nervous she felt. "I can't make a story come alive like you can, but I'll do my best. Although there is nothing happy in what I'm going to tell you, so perhaps it's best that I'm not a good storyteller." She sighed. "Where should I begin?"

"Tell me what happened in the mountains after Amory went after Red Fire Woman. Tell me how Standing Bear and Yellow Eagle died."

He listened intently without interruption or reaction while she described Red Fire Woman's capture, Yellow Eagle's failed attempt to persuade her to leave with him, Standing Bear's rescue and the battle with Ethan and the soldiers that claimed his life and that of the grizzly bear and Yellow Eagle. After recounting Red Fire Woman's escape and revealing that she had buried her beloved and his cousin after the soldiers had gone, Sarah paused in her narrative.

"They shared a great love, Standing Bear and Red Fire Woman," Duncan said softly. "One that could last lifetimes. Is that what you think, Sarah? In your view of past lives, does their love keep on living too?"

Sarah didn't know how to answer him. Shouldn't a love that strong reappear in other incarnations? She wasn't ready to say she was in love with Jason, still her heart was leaning that way, despite her earlier reservations. But Jason's dream made it clear that his connection was with Yellow Eagle. "Maybe," she offered, "it shows up in different ways each time, but I really don't know."

"Maybe people experience more than one lifetime so they can learn the lesson of letting go," Duncan said. "Letting go of the past, letting go of what cannot be."

An uneasy silence settled between them.

"I do know that Red Fire Woman's love came with a price," Sarah said tentatively.

"What do you mean?"

"She wrote about the terrible guilt she carried with her the rest of her life. She felt responsible for all of their deaths, Standing Bear, Yellow Eagle, the grizzly—and her unborn child. She blamed herself for the terribly cruel way that Ethan Amory treated the Ute People on that forced march to Utah. There are sections of her journal where her anguish and guilt were so overwhelming that they seemed to drive her to complete despair."

"She had much to grieve," Duncan said. "As did Yellow Eagle. I did not know of his love for Red Fire Woman or of his inner conflicts."

Duncan rose slowly from his chair. "There is much healing that needs to be done before these Spirits can rest."

Patrick arrived at the rendezvous spot a few minutes before Jason and found a place on the shoulder where he could leave his truck. No reason to give Eli any more reason to resist and the chance of him getting in a vehicle with a government logo on the side was nil.

Jason pulled up as Patrick finished parking. The two men greeted each other with a handshake and quickly got to the task at hand of figuring out how best to work together and not get hurt. From years filled with drunken bar fights, Jason had more experience with hand-to-hand encounters and Patrick, an experienced hunter, was better with a rifle.

"I think it's best if we can get him to come outside on his own," Jason said. "Let me check out the cabin and see if I can determine what state he's in. Find a place where you can have a clear shot of him coming out the front door."

"Do you have a gun?" Patrick asked. Jason pulled a large knife out of his hip holster and let the sun shine off the clean blade.

They got in Jason's truck and drove slowly down the road to Eli's place. As they turned onto the drive, Patrick said, "Drop me off here. There's a patch of trees I can hide in with a good view. Give me a few minutes to get into position before you pull in."

"Just remember not to get too excited back there," Jason replied, slapping him on the back. "I'll get pissed off if you shoot me by mistake."

Patrick made his way to the vantage point he'd used when delivering the talismans. He wasn't quite in position when he heard Jason's truck pull in. Looking back down the road, Patrick thought he caught a glint coming off a vehicle moving in their direction, but his attention was suddenly called back to the cabin with Jason's exclamation, "What the hell happened here?" He waved for Patrick to join him. He already had his knife drawn. Something wasn't right.

The front door hung from only one hinge; all around the door and on the door itself, deep claw marks had been torn into the wood.

"These were made by one big bear," Patrick said, his voice lowered. "We need to make sure it's not still around."

"I think we would have known by now," Jason said, "but no harm in checking it out."

Patrick slowly made his way around the cabin and found the back door wide open. He peered inside to find broken furniture knocked over and strewn across the room.

Jason stood in the front door, shaking his head. "Eli McDermott. Are you in here?" Cautiously, the two men stepped into the cabin and searched the interior but found no one. They decided to go outside and split up to look for Eli or parts of Eli if the bear had caught up with him.

Jason continued to call out, "Eli, show yourself. I have a message from Duncan Hawk."

After a half hour's search, Patrick heard a scuffle and screams and ran in that direction. Jason had pinned down Eli, who wasn't showing any sign of struggle except for his wailing. "Shut up, you dumb fuck," Jason said as he smacked him in the head. The screaming stopped.

"You okay?" Patrick asked.

"Yeah. Give me a hand. I've got some rope in my back pocket." Together they lifted the now limp man from the ground. Eli mumbled incoherently as Jason held him from behind and Patrick had him put his hands together. He offered no resistance as his wrists were tied.

"Eli, we're going to take you where you're going to be safe," Patrick said. "Do you understand?" Eli stood there, shaking uncontrollably.

Jason said, "He's in shock. I don't think there's any point in trying to explain anything to him right now." Patrick agreed.

They each grabbed a shoulder and guided Eli, stumbling and shuffling, out of the woods and put him in the truck.

Patrick went back to the front door of the cabin and examined the claw marks one more time. He took some quick measurements and then returned to the vehicle where he pushed in next to Eli on the seat.

"This guy needs a bath something terrible," Patrick said. Eli's head slumped forward, a string of drool hung from his chin.

Jason started the engine. "Make sure he doesn't hit his head on the dash. Let's get this drunk back to the ranch and out of my truck."

"There's something really wrong here," Patrick said. "Those claw marks in the door, those weren't made by a black bear. Only a grizzly could make scratches that wide. And we both know there aren't any grizzlies in these mountains anymore."

Jason looked a bit surprised. "Maybe a spirit really is after him, one with big claws."

"You can't be serious," Patrick said.

"Spirits are just as real as any animal you study. Besides, you don't seem to have a biological explanation for what happened here."

"There has to be," Patrick insisted.

Jason shrugged. "Whether it was a bear or a spirit, what I don't get is why Eli is still alive. Either one could easily have finished him off."

"Maybe his breath scared them away," Patrick said, rolling down the window. When they got to Patrick's truck, he slid Eli over and buckled him into the seatbelt. Jason said he could handle him on the drive back.

Patrick gave himself enough distance on the road to keep out of the dust kicked up by Jason's wheels, but his thoughts were more than cloudy. He couldn't make any sense out of those scratches. If someone had spotted a grizzly in this forest, he would have heard about it. It probably would have made the news. And it was unlikely that a bear that size would avoid detection out here. Could Jason be right?

The bear mystery occupied his mind so completely that he failed to notice the vehicle in his rearview mirror, following at a discreet distance behind him.

That pickup drove slowly down the drive to Duncan's ranch, and stopped as soon as the house became visible. Making note of all the vehicles parked in front, the driver decided to leave his so it blocked the drive, just out of view from the porch. He reached into the glove box, pulled out a pistol and stuck it in his waistband behind his back. He found a spot behind a tree where he watched Patrick, Jason and Eli go into the house. He'd wait here for a time. A large raven flew past his hiding place, cawing in distress. He raised his right hand and shaped his fingers like a gun, and with the setting sun reflecting off his sunglasses, pretended to shoot the bird as it passed over him again. The raven deposited a sticky white response on his windshield.

CHAPTER FORTY-NINE

JASON made it back to the house without Eli throwing up in his truck. He hadn't passed out but he wasn't conscious either. When he spoke, Eli made no sense and his eyes, the few times they opened, had no focus.

"You are one seriously messed up son of a bitch," Jason said as he helped Eli out of the truck. Patrick pulled in right behind him. Together they walked Eli to the house without much trouble.

Jessie opened the door before they reached the steps. "I'm so glad you're back, boys. Are you alright?"

"We're fine," Patrick said. "Eli's lucky to be alive."

They maneuvered Eli into the kitchen and sat him in a chair. "Well, first things first," Jessie said, shaking her head at the mess of a man in front of her. "He needs a bath and a change of clothes. Can you boys get him to the bathroom? I'll take care of the rest. I don't think Duncan will mind sacrificing some clothes for the cause."

"Bless you, Ms. Jessie," Jason said. "He's way past ripe. Where's Old Man?"

"He's out back, seeing to his ribs. Sarah is with him."

Patrick stayed to help Ms. Jessie get Eli cleaned up and Jason made his way to the barbecue pit where he found Duncan giving Sarah step-by-step instructions on how to make ribs the Indian way.

Sarah smiled and came over for a hug. "We were getting worried about you."

Jason dipped his finger in the bowl of barbecue sauce and savored the smoky flavor before telling them about the torn up cabin, finding an incoherent Eli, and the huge claw marks in the door that Patrick felt could only be made by a grizzly.

Duncan's eyes grew wide at the mention of the bear, but otherwise had no reaction to Jason's story.

"Hope you don't mind, but I gave Ms. Jessie some of your clothes for Eli. I think we'll have to burn his."

"Take him to my healing space and let him sleep there. I will be in soon with the ribs."

Eli was asleep as soon as he lay down in Duncan's room. The energy required to shower had exhausted him. He no longer smelled like a sewer, but he still looked like a derelict, despite the clean clothes.

"I think he'll be fine for now," Patrick said. Jessie gently shut the door.

They found Jason in the kitchen putting the final seasoning on the coleslaw. "How's the bastard doing?"

"He's asleep," Ms. Jessie said. "Maybe you can shave him tomorrow. His face and his head. I wasn't going near that mangy mess."

A loud knock on the front door turned their heads. "Who the hell could that be?" Jason asked, annoyed and suspicious. Very few people dropped in on Duncan and those folks were already here. "Patrick, check it out. I'll go around the back." The knocking grew more insistent.

Patrick opened the door to find an impatient Nick Tremaine.

"Looks like you're having a party in there," Nick said, stepping towards the door, but Patrick stood his ground and didn't let him in.

"What can I do for you, Mr. Tremaine?"

"Why so formal, Patrick? I thought we were becoming friends," Nick said sarcastically.

"Are you looking for Duncan?"

"No." Nick glanced over at the vehicles parked along the fence. "I see Sarah is here, getting another taste of the local color. I don't believe that's what my father's paying her for."

He clenched his fist. No woman had ever refused him, no one except Sarah. Her presence here surprised and angered him. Now was not the time or place to deal with her. But he would make her pay, he promised himself, very soon.

He turned his attention back to Patrick. "But that's not why I'm here. I know that Eli McDermott is here. And I need to speak to him."

"I'm afraid you're mistaken. Eli isn't here."

"Why, just the other day you told me you didn't know anyone named Eli and now you're telling me he's not here. Patrick, you're a federal employee; you're not supposed to lie." Nick's tone hardened.

"A lot can change in a couple of days." Patrick said sternly.

"I know he's here. I saw you and that Indian punk taking him for a little drive...that ended here. Let me see him."

"You're going to have leave now. I can't help you."

"You may want to reconsider," Nick said, reaching his hand behind him. In an instant, he was pulled backwards, caught in a wrestling lock.

"Don't even try it, you prick."

Jason seemed to come out nowhere. He held his grip on the unwanted visitor and forced him to drop his gun. "We might just be a bunch of redskin savages to you, cowboy, but we like our guests to have some manners, which you clearly lack. So, get your fuckin' ass off our land before my Indian instincts kick in and I decide to scalp you."

"Where the hell did you come from?" Patrick said, smiling at Jason. He picked up Nick's gun and emptied the chamber.

"Take your goddamn hands off of me!" Nick struggled, but couldn't break free of Jason's arm-twisting grip as he was forced back to his truck.

"You won't get away with this," Nick sputtered. "I'll get your Indian ass thrown in jail for assault."

Jason pushed him hard against the driver's door and motioned for Patrick to give him back the unloaded gun. "I have a mind to shoot you for trespassing, so get the hell out of here and don't come back." Before he let Nick go, Jason leaned forward and snarled one more warning in his ear. "If you ever touch Sarah again, I'll kill you."

Duncan and Sarah came into the house with trays full of ribs and found the kitchen empty. Jason, Jessie and Patrick were on the front porch, watching the dust from Nick's truck swirl in the air. Sarah cringed when she learned who had come to call.

"We got Eli just in time," Jessie said. "I'm sure that's not the last we've seen of Nick." Saying his name made her want to spit. "I'm concerned for you, Sarah. He's got a thing for you and he won't let up. A rich spoiled bastard like that is used to getting what he wants. Have you told Hollis how Nick's been treating you?"

Sarah shook her head. "Hollis left for New York yesterday. I thought Nick was going with him...."

Jason put his arm around her, pulling her close. "Then you're not going back to your place. I want you here, so I can keep you safe."

"I'm so sorry I got Nick into this," Sarah whispered.

"No apologies," Jessie said. "We've all said things we wish we could take back." She glanced briefly at Duncan. "Trust me, I know."

Jessie was too riled up to eat dinner and couldn't be convinced to stay. Patrick asked for a rain check on the ribs as well; the paperwork he was supposed to get done was still in the office waiting for him.

"I'll come by tomorrow and see how things are going with Eli," Jessie said. "Thanks again for taking charge of him."

She was part way out the door when she turned around. "I almost forgot this," she said, holding out a small leather bag. "I found this in Eli's pants pocket. I have a feeling it's from the graves. I pray this is the last thing that Eli still has from there."

Duncan had her put it on the table and wished her a good night.

"May I look at that?" Sarah asked. Duncan nodded. "I recognize this beadwork," she said, examining the pouch. "This looks like the same pattern that's on the herb bags in Red Fire Woman's medicine bundle. I've got it in my truck. I'll go get it."

Jason set out the now lukewarm dinner while Sarah went to retrieve the medicine bundle. Duncan insisted that they eat before his ribs became inedible. The beaded bags could wait.

As the shock of Nick's visit subsided, her hunger returned. Sarah ate quickly. She had to admit, they were the best ribs she'd ever tasted even at room temperature. After Duncan pushed back his plate of bones and patted his belly, Sarah cleared the table and brought out the bundle.

The beading matched perfectly. Duncan nodded. "This belongs to you now. It is a tobacco pouch. We will fill it in the morning. I will show… Jason can help you smudge it with sage tonight to clear it of Eli's energy. He will teach you how to use it."

Duncan slowly stood. "I will check on Eli, then I am going to sleep."

A few minutes later, Jason and Sarah heard a high-pitched scream from down the hall. They ran to the back room where they found Eli pressed against the wall in the far corner, cowering in fear on the floor, yelling at Duncan who stood calmly off to one side of the door.

"What the hell is going on?" Jason blocked the doorway to keep Eli from bolting.

"He thinks I am the Spirit that's been haunting him," Duncan replied.

"Let me try to calm him down, Old Man."

Duncan nodded and stepped out of the room. Sarah greeted him in the hallway. "What's wrong with Eli?"

Duncan sighed. "He needs a healing, his spirit is dying. But I cannot do anything for him while he is like this. I do not know how to help him."

The screaming continued.

Sarah moved into the doorway to get a better look and the screaming stopped. Eli stared at her with bloodshot eyes and began mumbling incoherently.

"Maybe he just needs a friendly face," Sarah said.

She took a couple of slow steps into the room, Eli's eyes locked on her, but he did not react. "Jason, why don't you let me see what I can do? It might be best to wait outside, but don't go far."

"I'm not sure that's the safest plan." Jason started to walk over to her, but stopped when Eli resumed his tantrum.

Sarah turned and motioned for him to back up. "If you leave the room, maybe I can get him to calm down."

"And then what?"

"I have no idea."

"You might find the answers in here," Duncan said, reappearing in the room with Red Fire Woman's medicine bundle. "These are your tools now." He placed the bundle on the healing table set against the wall in the corner of the room. "Sarah, the Spirits told me that you need to accept your medicine in order to bring healing. At the time, I thought they meant that I had to help you heal. But now I see that the Spirits are calling for you to be the healer. It is time. Eli needs you. I cannot help him, but maybe you can."

Putting a hand on Jason's shoulder, Duncan led him out of the room and closed the door.

CHAPTER FIFTY

"I HAVE NO IDEA HOW to heal anyone!" Sarah proclaimed to the closed door. "I'm not Red Fire Woman." The door remained shut and Eli continued muttering , but no longer had his knees pulled up by his chin.

Keeping her eyes on her would-be patient, Sarah sat down in the chair and wondered what to do next. "My name is Sarah. I have no idea how to help you. I don't even know what's wrong with you."

Her confession didn't elicit any change in his demeanor. She wasn't even sure if he understood what she was saying. Reaching into her back pocket, she pulled out the tobacco pouch and put it on the table next to the medicine bundle. Now that she was no longer sitting on the pouch, the chair felt a bit more comfortable, but her situation was anything but.

Eli watched her every move. When he caught sight of the tobacco pouch, he grew agitated again, reaching out his hand but unwilling or unable to move closer.

He must recognize it, Sarah thought as she picked up the bag. "Is this what you want?" Eli nodded his head, his eyes pleading with her.

Sarah got an idea. "Eli, why don't you come over here and have a seat on the healing table and then I'll let you see this pouch." She removed the medicine bundle from the table and put it on top of a trunk on the opposite side of the room.

Eli hesitated, but with more encouragement, he finally stood up and shuffled over to the table and sat down.

"You don't get to keep this," Sarah said, regretting the need to part with the bag. "But you can hold on to it while we're in this room."

Eli grabbed the pouch like a drowning man grasping for a life jacket. His mumbling stopped, his gaze grew vacant, no longer fixated on Sarah, and his mouth hung open slightly. She watched him gradually shut down to the point where he appeared comatose, unresponsive to waving hands in front of his face or a gentle nudge to his knee.

"Great. I've turned him into a zombie. Some healer I am." Feeling at a loss, she glanced around the room, praying that Duncan would walk through the door to relieve her, when her attention was pulled to the medicine bundle. Tentatively, she opened it up and spread out its contents. One of the pouches contained sage and she decided to burn some to smudge the room. The earthy smell calmed her but had no visible effect on Eli.

Nestled in with the herb pouches was a small turtle shell rattle with a wooden handle. She liked how it felt in her hand and gently shook it. The rattling sounded like small hailstones hitting wood. Closing her eyes, she found a rhythm that pleased her and soon she was swaying in time, absorbed in the sound and the movement.

She rattled for some time, until a low moaning broke through her trance. Opening her eyes, she saw Eli had slumped back against the wall. She put down the rattle and slowly stepped closer. Eli's eyes were shut; he appeared to be sleeping, with the leather pouch still clasped in his hand. Then he moaned again and started trembling. She swung his legs around to the side of the table to help him lie down. His forehead was hot and sweaty, signs of a high fever; his breathing was shallow and erratic.

She wondered if he was suffering from withdrawal. Jason would most likely know, and he would probably know what to do. But when she opened the door, the hallway was empty. She called out. No reply.

"Damn, where did they go? I can't believe they'd leave me here." She was about to go look for them, when Eli's chills grew more violent. She couldn't leave him alone. Dashing into the bathroom, she wet a hand towel, grabbed a couple of dry ones and hurried back to the room. He groaned as the cold towel touched his forehead. Sarah covered him with a light blanket, wiped the sweat from his cheeks and then scanned the room for a trash can, which she found just in time to catch the mess that Eli retched up. This was going to be a long night.

A blind covered the one window in the room and when Sarah lifted it to look out, she saw the glow of a fire by the sweat lodge. She could just make out the muffled sound of drumming. Perhaps Duncan and Jason were doing some kind of ceremony at the fire, offering prayers to help her with Eli. That thought made her feel less abandoned. Still she'd prefer some able hands to assist her in the room rather than spiritual support from afar. She left the blind open, finding some comfort in the view of the fire's orange and red glow.

When she checked on Eli, he felt as hot as a bonfire, so she refreshed the cold towel and tried to remember what her mother used to do for her when she had a high fever. Of course, she couldn't remember a thing because when she was that sick, she hadn't been aware of anything, just like Eli here.

His face contorted in a fearful grimace as he whimpered and thrashed around, trying to free his hands from the blanket. *He's having a nightmare,* she thought. "Eli, it's okay. Wake up. Eli, wake up." He fought against her hands on his shoulders, but was too weak to resist for long and eventually stopped flailing.

Sarah picked up the rattle and began shaking it softly, mostly to calm herself, but then noticed it had the same effect on Eli. His face softened and his breathing slowed. Eventually, he slept.

Sarah spent the rest of the night tending to him with cool towels, sips of water and the vomit bucket. She burned different herbs—sage, cedar, sweetgrass and a few she didn't recognize—from the medicine bundle; she rattled and prayed for anyone or anything to help her.

As the soft light of morning floated in through the window, Sarah was too exhausted to notice. She didn't hear the door open or remember Jason's gentle touch on her face or him carrying her down the hall to his bed where she fell into a fitful sleep full of dreams she wouldn't recall.

But she was aware of one thing as dawn filled the room. Eli had survived the night.

CHAPTER FIFTY-ONE

WHILE SARAH SLEPT, Jason and Duncan attended to Eli, although there wasn't much for either of them to do. Eli lay motionless on the table, staring at the ceiling with vacant eyes. Duncan stayed in the room, quietly saying prayers for Eli, while Jason made breakfast. By the time food was ready, Eli had closed his eyes and appeared to sleep.

Twenty minutes later, as Duncan and Jason finished eating, Jessie drove up. She opened the kitchen door without knocking, dark circles under her eyes. "I hardly slept at all. And from the look of things, neither did you two."

"And a good morning to you, my friend," Duncan said.

"Coffee, Ms. Jessie?" Jason handed her a cup before she could respond and then offered her a chair.

She nodded her thanks but remained standing. "How's Eli?"

Duncan shook his head. "You can see for yourself."

"Is it good or bad?" Anxiety pinched her voice.

Duncan said nothing.

Jessie put down her mug and walked quickly out of the room. She returned five minutes later, her face ashen.

"My god, what's wrong with him?"

"He has lost his soul," Duncan said matter-of-factly.

"What do you mean, he's lost his soul? Did I do this to him? I had no intention of...."

"No. Your tricks with the talismans did not do this to him. They had no real power, but they did serve a purpose. They made him face his own deception. The only reason they affected him so strongly was because he had something to hide. He had not honored his promise to the Spirits to return everything he had stolen. His own deceit has brought on this illness. The Spirits have taken his soul and are hiding it from him."

Jessie pulled over the chair Jason had offered her a few minutes earlier and sat down facing Duncan. "Can he get it back?"

"It is possible. We need to do ceremony for him."

"I don't understand how someone can lose his soul," Jessie said slowly, "but I trust you and I'll do whatever I can to help."

"Good." Duncan took a slow sip of coffee. "Last night, I talked a long time with Grandpa Fire. Jason and I sang and danced and burned lots of cedar. I was told what the Spirits want us to do to bring things back into balance, to make things right. It will take all of us to make this happen. I will ask you to tell Patrick what he needs to know."

"I'm sure he'll be willing to help out," Jessie said.

"You must get him to agree to do exactly what I ask," Duncan said sternly. "And you must agree to the same. Are you willing to do that?"

Jessie and Jason both nodded in agreement. As Duncan started to speak, they inched their chairs closer to learn the details of the plan to which they had just committed themselves.

Sarah woke to find Jason sitting in a chair by the door, looking tired and concerned.

"Hey, you're awake."

"Barely," she tried to smile. "What time is it?"

"Almost noon." Jason came and sat on the edge of the bed and filled her in on the morning's events.

When Jason had finished, Sarah wanted to crawl back under the covers. "Duncan is expecting me to find Eli's soul? I can't do that! I'm not sure I even want to. I came to Colorado to paint, not to pretend to be some kind of healer who lived over one hundred years ago!"

Jason gave her a hug. "I understand how you feel. Really I do. But the spirits wouldn't tell you to do something you can't do. I've learned that first hand. You just have to trust."

"Where's Duncan now?"

"He's out looking for the right place to have the ceremony. He said it would be somewhere on the bluff overlooking the valley."

"Can I call in sick?"

He kissed her neck. "You'll feel better after you've had a shower. I'd offer to help you," he said, nibbling her ear, "but Ms. Jessie is still here keeping an eye on Eli until Old Man gets back."

"I'll definitely take a rain check." Reluctantly, she pushed aside the covers, slid past Jason and got out of bed. "And I'll take a strong cup of coffee in the meantime."

Duncan returned shortly after Sarah had finished the scrambled eggs and toast that Jason had fixed for her.

"I'm glad you are awake. We have much to prepare," Duncan said. "Come with me."

Sarah looked pleadingly at Jason, but he just smiled. "Sarah, you can do this. I've got my own things to do for ceremony. You'll be fine."

"Easy for you to say. You're not the one expected to perform a miracle."

Trying to delay the inevitable, Sarah filled her cup with the last of the coffee and then made a fresh pot. By the time she followed Duncan down the hall, her heart rate had slowed to almost normal. Her anxiety returned when she stepped into the healing room. "Where's Eli?"

Duncan turned around slowly to face her. "I had Jessie take him outside for some fresh air."

"Oh, good." Sarah's knees felt weak, so she sat down.

Duncan opened a closet with shelves full of herbs, hides, pouches and ceremonial clothing. He began pulling items off the shelves and placing them on the healing table. Eventually he spoke.

"The Spirits have asked me to do a ceremony, to create a space for the spirit of Grizzly Bear to be with us. She will bring healing in her way, for the ancestors and for the land. I was shown that you will be a part of this. Eli and the others need to be there too."

Duncan motioned for Sarah to sit on the chair. "There are several parts to any ceremony. First, we must prepare the land where the ceremony will take place. We make offerings and prayers to honor all the beings there, those we can see and those we cannot. We also prepare ourselves so we are clear in our intentions and in our hearts.

"Then there is the ceremony itself. We will each have our own part in this. But once Spirit comes into us, into the ritual, we must do as Spirit tells us or shows us. This is when the healing comes. Spirit knows what needs to happen and we must follow, even if we do not understand. When we do ceremony in a good way, we trust that good will be done."

"What if you don't have a clue what you're doing?" Sarah asked.

"The important thing is your intention. Put your ego and your fear aside. Be clear in your desire for healing." Duncan put his left hand on his chest. "Act more from your heart than from your mind. When your intention is good, Spirit can work through you."

"How will I know if my intentions are good enough?" Sarah couldn't hide the frustration in her voice. She wanted something more concrete than what sounded like a philosophical pep talk.

"Always so many questions." Duncan said. "You will know soon enough. Now let me finish." He didn't give her any time to interrupt.

"The third part of any ceremony is the feast where we offer our gratitude for the healing and honor all who came to bring that gift—the spirits, the animals, the plants, the elements and the people. Back home, we would invite family and friends to the celebration so we could share the healings with others in the community. But not today. Our honoring ceremony will be for those who participate…and survive."

"You're kidding, right, about the surviving part?" Sarah stood up and looked at Duncan, who returned her gaze without any indication of whether he was joking.

"As you can see, we have much to do. I have asked Jessie to host the celebration and feast, so she will not be at the ceremony itself."

"Is she okay with that? Seems like the women are always off in the kitchen…"

Duncan cut her off sternly. "It is an honor, not a chore."

Sarah winced at his tone. "Sorry. I didn't mean to offend."

With eyes closed, Duncan mumbled in Ute. Then with a sigh, he looked over at Sarah and continued. "Patrick will have the *chore* of watching Eli and making sure he doesn't run away. Jason will have a number of things to do in the ceremony, as will you. But first, you and I will prepare the space. I will teach you."

Sarah started to speak but concern about upsetting him further made her hesitate. "Can I ask you something?"

Duncan nodded.

"This morning, Jason told me that this ceremony was going to bring back Eli's soul. Is that part of healing the ancestors?"

"The healing for Eli needs to happen before the ceremony. That will be part of the preparation. This will be your work."

"Did the spirits tell you what I am supposed to do?" Sarah wasn't sure she wanted an answer.

"No. That is for you to know."

"But I don't. Duncan, why are you always so vague? Can't you just tell me what to do?"

"I wasn't shown your path, Sarah, only mine. Trust what you feel as the ceremony unfolds. Remember your connection to the past, to Red Fire Woman and Standing Bear. They will guide you."

Sarah again caught a glimpse of sadness in Duncan's eyes. "How can I help you...I mean, to get ready for the ceremony?"

Duncan paused in his preparations and sighed. "Put these items in the bag by the door," he finally replied, pointing to the pile on the table. "Take the bag with you when we go to the ceremony site. Make sure to bring your medicine bundle, the bear claw necklace and your sweetgrass. Fill some water bottles and meet me at the barn in a half hour."

As Sarah left the room, bag in hand and a flood of questions begging for answers, she saw Duncan open a large cedar chest. She wondered what the chest contained but his posture made it clear that she was no longer welcome in the room.

CHAPTER FIFTY-TWO

DUNCAN STOPPED HIS HORSE and dismounted, signaling Sarah to do the same. They had been riding for over an hour up to the top of a bluff. While much of the trail had been forested, it ended at a large meadow.

This was the site Duncan had chosen for the ceremony. It looked out over the narrow valley where Sarah had first run into Jason by the creek. Only a few scraggly piñon pines offered any kind of protection at the cliff's edge, so Sarah grabbed a quick glance down and then backed up before her stomach got queasy.

"Don't like heights?" Duncan asked. He had unloaded the saddlebags from his horse and was walking him over to a shaded spot to tether him.

"No, not a big fan," she said, bringing her horse over to join his. "Guess that's 'cause I'm not a big fan of falling."

Sarah spent the next several hours following Duncan's instructions, burning sweetgrass and cedar to smudge the meadow, offering tobacco and prayers, gathering wood and building a fire. All of these tasks felt familiar even though she was performing them for the first time. *At least in this lifetime,* she reminded herself. Touching the large bear claw that hung underneath her shirt, she thought of Red Fire Woman and smiled with a sense of connection and purpose only her heart could fathom.

But her skeptic's mind started taunting her with doubt as soon as she heard horses coming up the trail. Jason and Patrick would have Eli with them. And she was supposed to somehow restore his soul. Her sense of dread grew stronger as the men rode into the meadow.

Patrick dismounted and came over to help get Eli off of Jason's horse.

"I don't plan on holding onto this sack of shit on the ride back," Jason said. "He'll have to walk or I'll leave him here for the mountain lions."

"He can sit by the fire," Duncan said. "We'll take care of him now."

Sarah greeted Jason and Patrick. "Nice fire," Jason said with admiration. He gave her a quick kiss.

Duncan didn't give them much time to visit before he sent Jason off on another task. "We will do ceremony here because the cave is directly below us. I would like you to go there and make offerings to the Bear Spirits in preparation for the ceremony tonight."

As Jason turned to go, Duncan added, "Take our biologist friend with you and explain about healing the ancestors. Tell him the story of Red Fire Woman and Standing Bear. That will help him understand why we are doing ceremony."

While not as gifted a storyteller as Duncan, Jason managed to pull off an abridged version of the saga that held Patrick's attention.

"Now I understand why those graves are so important to Duncan," Patrick said. "But how does Sarah fit into all of this?"

That story was too complicated and personal for Jason to share. "The easiest way to explain it is that she has a connection to Red Fire Woman that she's here to figure out. It's all part of healing the ancestors."

"Is she related to Red Fire Woman?"

Jason hesitated. "Do you, by any chance, believe in past lives?"

"You mean, like reincarnation?"

Jason nodded.

"Nope."

"Then let's go with the idea that they are related and leave it at that."

By the time they reached the mouth of the cave, Jason had tried his best to explain the Ute concept of healing ancestors, and confessed that he had little experience with the ceremony, so had no idea what to expect. "All I know is what Old Man wants me to do for my part and we'll see what happens."

Patrick listened respectfully without saying much. The two men let their horses drink from the creek, then tethered them on a patch of grass.

"Old Man had a vision back in the spring about this cave," Jason said. "He saw Standing Bear and a large grizzly near the entrance. Then they disappeared and Red Fire Woman came out of the cave and spoke to him. She was old. Half of her face was beat up. She told him that he needed to help the spirits of Standing Bear and the other ancestors."

"I have no experience with visions or their meaning," Patrick said.

"A vision is a message. Sometimes a vision will show you what took place in the past, sometimes it shows what is going to happen and sometimes what needs to happen," Jason replied. "Visions aren't always straightforward. But according to Old Man, the vision made it clear to him that this cave had been the den for the grizzly from the Standing Bear story. That's why we are here to honor her Spirit."

Jason made a tobacco offering before they entered the cave. Once inside, Patrick said, "Are you sure this is the right cave? It's much too large to have been used by grizzlies. They usually dig a den in the snow or in the ground. If they do use a cave, it would be smaller than this."

"You're the bear expert. But I do know this is the right cave."

Once his eyes adjusted, Patrick spied a smaller passageway toward the back. "If you don't mind, I'd like to look around while you do whatever it is you need to do here."

"That's fine with me," Jason said. "Just don't get lost."

Jason offered prayers as Duncan had requested and by the time he was finished, Patrick had returned with a pocket flashlight in his hand and a smile on his face.

"I found another cave at the end of that passage. Looks like a perfect size for a bear den," Patrick said. "But no fresh signs that it's been used."

"Were you expecting to find any?"

"Would have been nice," Patrick said. "The bear that tore up Eli's place has to be around here somewhere and I'd love to find him."

"Be careful what you wish for," Jason said, giving him a friendly jab in the arm. "I just got through saying a whole lot of prayers to the bear spirits in here. They're listening."

Patrick shook his head. "That would be a first. Tracking bears through the use of prayer. I'm afraid I'd have to see that one to believe it."

"Something tells me that you won't be disappointed," Jason said, offering a final pinch of tobacco before leaving the cave. "But what do I know? Come on, Mr. Biologist, we should be getting back."

As soon as Jason and Patrick left the meadow to do their work in the cave, Duncan and Sarah turned their attentions to doctoring Eli, who remained unresponsive except for breathing and blinking. Too weak to sit up, he lay on his back a safe distance from the fire.

Duncan showed her how to apply a red paint made from clay on Eli's face, hands and feet. "This will connect him back to the Earth, our mother, so he can remember where he came from. The red color also helps the soul find its way back." When they were finished, Sarah smudged Eli with sage. Duncan asked her to burn sweetgrass, cedar and tobacco in the fire while he offered prayers, spoken mostly in Ute. Then he picked up his drum and had Sarah get her rattle and together they kept time to a rhythm that seemed to emanate from the earth, moving up through their bodies and into their instruments.

Sarah had no sense of how long they played. When the music stopped, a heavy silence filled the meadow now bathed in afternoon light. Duncan put down his drum and looked at her. "There is only one thing you need to remember about spiritual doctoring. You do not do it alone. You really do not do anything at all. It is the Spirits who do the doctoring. You just have to point them in the right direction."

"How do I do that?"

"You have to be a hollow bone that Spirit can move through. You help guide the Spirits to where they are needed. But you must ask them for help. Be clear in your intention, that you want healing for this person, and let go of your expectations. You will find your own way."

"That may make sense to you," Sarah said, "but not to me."

"You will remember," Duncan said softly as he turned away. "I have done all I can to help you, Sarah. I must leave Eli in your hands now."

"You can't just walk away. I don't know what I'm doing!"

Duncan picked up his drum and his medicine bag and then walked toward the forest and disappeared into the trees, leaving Sarah alone with Eli, the fire and her own confusion.

"Ask the spirits, that's all you have to," she mumbled to herself, as she paced back and forth, kicking at stones in the dust.

Looking over at Eli's blank stare, she felt ridiculous and inadequate. And angry. "How dare Duncan leave me alone like this! And what about Eli? He's so sick. Instead of taking him to a doctor, Duncan dumps him on me and expects me to heal him. What if he dies out here?"

As her agitation grew, the trees around her began to darken with birds and the air fill with cawing chatter. Sarah looked up in to see a flock of ravens surrounding the meadow. They seemed to be waiting on her. "Tell me what I'm supposed to do!" she shouted back at the birds.

She still held the rattle in her hand; she shook it tentatively, then with more energy, moving around the fire with a halting step, trying to imitate Duncan. The cawing grew louder and so she rattled stronger until the sounds in the meadow drowned out everything else. Around and around the fire she danced, completely immersed in the vibration of sound filling her body. And then gradually, the birds and the rattling quieted and stopped. Embraced in stillness, she felt a strange peace. Without making a sound except for the soft "whoosh" of wings, the ravens circled once around the meadow and then flew off over the canyon. Sarah felt as though a part of her was flying with them. Closing her eyes, she breathed in the moment, longing for it to last.

When she did open her eyes and gaze at Eli, her elation dimmed; her rattle dance appeared to have had no effect. He lay still as a stone.

Now what do I do? She sat down on the log and covered her face with her hands. The answer she received wasn't exactly what she had in mind. A very full bladder was demanding her attention.

Stepping into the woods, she found a secluded place to relieve herself. *I don't believe this! Couldn't it have waited one more day?* Sarah rifled through her backpack for a tampon. She kept an emergency supply in a side pocket. She also found a bandana in lieu of toilet paper.

She cleaned herself up and then had to dispose of the blood-soaked bandana. Making her way back to the meadow, she prayed that no one had returned yet. The embarrassment would undo her.

Good, just Eli, she sighed, quickly tossing the bandana into the fire, grateful that it would consume the evidence. She was having a hard enough time with Eli; she didn't need her body making a mess of things like it had during the sweat lodge.

As she watched the stained fabric smolder and eventually crumble into ash, the thought came to her. Maybe she was supposed to get her period now. Would it somehow help with Eli's healing as it had for Jason in the sweat ceremony?

She put another log on the fire and then came over by Eli. She sat down on the ground and gently lifted his head onto her lap, careful not to smudge the red paint. She touched his heart. It was still beating. "Okay, spirits. I'm asking. Please heal this man. In whatever way you can. If I can help, I'll do it. Here he is. I'm pointing the way. Please. Help him."

Over and over again, she spoke these words while staring into the fire. Soon she was speaking them directly to the red-orange blaze, imagining the flames sending out her message like radio signals to the spirits. And then her call for help echoed only in her mind, as her awareness became consumed by the fire pulsating and dancing through her, lulling her into a trance.

A large raven flew into the meadow and landed at one end of the log that Sarah was leaning against. Cocking its head, it looked at her for some time, but she remained transfixed. The bird ruffled out its feathers and settled in, a sentinel.

Listening.

Watching.

Waiting.

CHAPTER FIFTY-THREE

JASON AND PATRICK RETURNED to the meadow to find Eli sitting up and drinking water from a canteen Duncan was helping him hold. Both men stood and stared, not sure whether to approach.

"Look at that," Jason said. "Eli's come back from the dead, or at least part way."

"What's with the red paint?" Patrick asked.

"I'm sure it has to do with the healing. Hope Old Man's not trying to turn him into an Indian."

After they finished taking care of their horses, Jason asked permission to come over by the fire where Eli was now sleeping. Duncan, seated on a log near Eli's feet, invited his nephew to approach.

"How's the patient?" Jason looked around. "And where's Sarah?"

"She will be back soon." Duncan paused. "Eli is conscious but not fully healed. He still needs ceremony. Now that you are back, we must prepare. It will be dark soon."

Sarah came up behind him and touched his shoulder. He turned around and hugged her tightly. "Looks like you do good work," he said softly in her ear.

"I have no idea what I did," she murmured back. As they parted, she said, "One moment I was staring into the fire, asking the spirits to help Eli, and then, it was like I was jolted out of a dream. A raven is shrieking in my ear, I see Duncan standing on the other side of the fire staring at me, and then Eli opens his eyes and sits up. Eli keeps calling me his 'angel.' But that's about all he says. He's still a mess."

She glanced over at Eli. "It's a bit freaky."

"You did real good, Sarah. I hope Old Man told you so."

"He hasn't said much at all," Sarah replied. "But what else is new."

Duncan had been talking with Patrick and walked back over to them. "Patrick will sit with Eli while we prepare for the ceremony. It is time."

Within the hour, all was ready. The early evening light colored the meadow in crisp, warm tones, with a hint of the blue-gray shadows of sunset. The air was still, as if the sky was holding its breath in anticipation. Jason and Patrick stood in the entrance to the meadow with Eli sandwiched between them, as Sarah smudged them with sweetgrass and sage. Then she invited them to stand by the sacred fire that she'd been tending all afternoon and called in the directions as Duncan had taught her, invoking the Spirits of the East, the South, the West, the North, Father Sky, and Mother Earth. When she had finished, Jason gazed at her with admiration. Patrick watched closely, having no idea what to expect, while Eli stared into the fire, then stared at the ground.

Jason walked around the fire until he stood opposite Eli. He offered tobacco to the flames and then spoke. "Eli McDermott. The Spirits of this land have called you here to make amends for your actions."

Eli started to shiver and reached out his hand toward Sarah. She stepped behind him and placed her hands on his shoulders to steady him.

A drum beat, slow and steady, filled the meadow. Eli and Patrick looked around but the drummer remained hidden.

"The Spirits know what you have done," Jason continued. "And they know that you have suffered." Eli nodded frantically.

"If you wish to make peace with them, this is what they demand of you. First, you must return all that you have taken."

Eli was still. Sarah spoke gently. "Eli, do you understand what he is saying to you?" He nodded. "Then you need to do what he says."

"But you...gave it back...to me," he stammered. "It has power against the bad spirits. It protects me."

"Eli, you need to give back the bag. It was not mine to give. And it doesn't belong to you either. It must be returned to the ancestors."

He refused at first, but then Sarah told him that the pouch had changed, that it would call bad things to him now. "You must believe me. I'm your angel, remember?"

With great reluctance, he pulled out the beaded leather pouch from his pants pocket and handed it to her. She started to pass it to Jason, but he shook his head. She should hold onto it.

"Eli, there is more the Spirits demand from you. The land that has been in your family, it has been entrusted to you. You must continue to be the keeper of this land, the Spirits call on you to honor it and protect it. Do you understand?"

Eli staggered backwards but Patrick caught him and kept him from falling. He held onto his arm in case Eli tried to run.

"I'm sorry for taking things from those damn graves. I want the spirits to know that. But that land is all I have," he pleaded. "I need money or I'm a dead man! They'll kill me!"

The drumming grew louder.

"You have a choice, Eli." Jason said, taking a stand directly in front of him. "You can pay them off and keep the land. You have a choice."

Eli tried to lunge at Jason, but Patrick kept a firm hold. "You don't understand!" Eli sputtered. "They'll kill me. I have no...."

The fire flared, shooting sparks in all directions. The booming of the drum grew louder, the vibrations palpable. Eli's face froze in mid-sentence, his eyes wide with fear.

Sarah turned, following his stare to see an apparition rising from the other side of the meadow, a shadowy hulk swaying from side to side. As it moved slowly closer, its frightening form grew visible through the dancing bonfire. The man-beast was covered in heavy fur and large bear claws dangled from its neck. With head lowered, it grunted and growled as it stepped in time to the pulsing drum that had become almost deafening. Then it rushed the fire and roared, exposing its black face, white eyes and snarling, blood-red lips.

Everyone scrambled backwards. Sarah stifled a scream. It must be Duncan, she told herself, but found no trace of him in this beastly guise.

Patrick grabbed Eli by the shoulders and forced him to face the Grizzly Spirit. "Wrong answer." Eli crumbled to ground.

As the menacing figure continued to dance just beyond the fire, a flock of ravens flew into the clearing, screaming and darting erratically only a few feet above people's heads. At first Sarah thought they were going to attack the dancer, but then a jolting sense of alarm shot through her. Raven was her protector. The birds had come to warn her, but warn her of what?

She stepped backwards toward the trees. Her left hand curled into a fist and started twitching. Then she felt an arm grab her around the chest and a cold, hard object shoved into her ribs.

"Don't move or I'll be forced to shoot you, my sweet Sarah." Paralyzed with fear, she couldn't speak.

"I think it's time to stop this primitive nonsense," Nick sneered in her ear. "You're scaring poor Eli to death." Nick shoved her forward, tightening his grip, digging the gun deeper into her back.

"Gentlemen," Nick shouted. Jason and Patrick immediately turned in their direction. Jason started towards him, but Nick warned him off. Eli continued to stare at the bear spirit, who kept dancing and growling to the drumbeat, oblivious to the intruder.

"Let her go," Jason snarled.

"I don't think so. Not until I get what I came for."

"And what would that be?" Jason took a step toward him.

"Any closer, and I'm afraid I may have to hurt your lovely white bitch," Nick said. He was pressed so closely against her, she could feel his heart pound. *Why was Duncan still dancing? Didn't he know what was going on?* She had no idea what to do. *Spirit, help me!*

"You're going to hand over Eli to me, right now."

"I'm afraid he's busy at the moment," Jason replied.

"Don't test me, you redskin punk. I get what I want. Hand him over or I'll make you regret it."

Patrick slowly slid his hand toward the pistol in his hip holster, but Nick detected the movement. "Don't try it! Or you'll have blood on your hands. Her blood." Patrick held up his hands.

"Use your left hand to get your gun and then slide it over towards me," Nick instructed, as he tightened his grip on Sarah. Patrick did as he was told. The incessant drumming picked up speed and the spirit started to spin. Sarah could barely breathe.

"Make that dancing clown stop," Nick demanded. "Or I will." Shifting his hold so he had Sarah around the neck, Nick pointed the gun at the whirling figure. She felt his stance harden as he prepared to fire. Twisting her head, she bit down hard on Nick's arm, causing him to flinch as he pulled the trigger. To her horror, the bear dancer spun backwards and fell. Nick turned and smashed his pistol into the side of her head and she fell to the ground, pain exploding across her face.

Jason hesitated for a split second, wanting desperately to protect Sarah and his uncle. But Patrick was already in motion, darting across the meadow toward Duncan. In an instant, Jason rushed forward and slammed his fist into Nick's face, sending him reeling. Another hit to the head knocked him flat on his back. Jason kicked the gun out of his hand at the same time that Eli leapt to his feet, screaming, "Stop, stop! Don't kill the spirit! I'll be cursed forever." Before Nick could get back up, Eli flung himself on top of him and started punching like a madman.

As Sarah tried to sit up, she felt Jason's arms around her, pulling her into the woods. "Are you okay?"

"I think so."

"Stay here."

She couldn't move even if she wanted to. The throbbing pain blurred her vision, but she could still make out Eli and Nick struggling on the ground. The fire flared again and the drumming suddenly stopped. The night grew deathly quiet for an instant. But only an instant. Then a fierce snarling pierced the silence, electrifying the air around them. Sarah watched in disbelief as a dark image at the edge of the clearing started to move. It was coming towards them. And then it charged. A huge bear barreled into the meadow, growling and foaming.

Eli froze, which allowed Nick to push him aside, grab the gun off the ground, and stumble to his feet. He pointed the pistol at the grizzly, trying in vain to control the shaking of his hand.

As the bear rose on its hind legs, its hulking form blocked out any light from the fire, casting Nick in heavy shadow. Jason stared at the scene he'd seen so many times before in his dreams. Rage surged through him. "No!" he screamed as he bolted across the meadow and flung himself at Nick, knocking him off balance as the gun fired. The bear snarled in pain as the bullet tore into its leg.

Both men fell to the ground. Nick tried to get up, but Jason grabbed his leg and pulled him down, hitting him square in the jaw. As he lifted his fist to hit him again, Sarah scream a warning. He turned his head to see the bear had dropped to all fours and was preparing to attack.

Suddenly, the grizzly spun around, snarling. Patrick was pelting it with rocks and yelling, trying to distract it long enough for Jason to react.

Jason scrambled to his feet and pulled Nick up with him. The bear turned back to face them, staring right at Jason. In that moment, everything around him stood still as if frozen in time and space. Looking into the animal's amber eyes was like stepping back into his dream. They were the same eyes. He knew this bear and it knew him. This animal was protecting the same people Jason would give his life for.

And with that realization, Jason loosened his hold on Nick. The bear's gaze shifted and locked onto Nick, who turned around and ran. An instant later, the grizzly charged. The ground shook as the bear rushed past Jason in pursuit, its raw, musky scent permeating the air. Jason knew they couldn't go far.

Nick raced through the brush and caught himself just before he reached the edge of the cliff. He was cornered with no place to hide. Spinning around, his whole being trembled with fear as he watched death rush towards him dressed in fur, claws and teeth. The grizzly roared and hit him with such a powerful swipe of its paw that Nick flew through the air and over the precipice. His screams echoed off the canyon walls. Then silence.

Jason watched from a short distance away. The bear slowly turned and looked at him. Its shoulder and back leg were matted with blood. A wounded bear was extremely dangerous, but Jason felt no fear.

"Blessings to you, Brother Grizzly. Thank you." The grizzly grunted and then perked its ears at the sound of footsteps running toward them. With a grace that belied its size, the bear stepped into the trees and disappeared just before Patrick arrived.

"Are you alright?"

Jason nodded. "Can't say the same for Nick. The bastard's at the bottom of the canyon. He ran right over the edge."

"And the bear?"

"Gone."

"Which way did it go?"

Jason pointed toward the west.

Patrick shook his head. "Jason, I've looked all over and I can't find Duncan. He's disappeared!"

Splayed out on the rocky canyon floor several feet from the cave entrance, Nick's broken body was no longer breathing. One eye, wide with terror, stared blankly into the night. The other half of his face had smashed against the ground. His legs and arms lay twisted at grotesque angles. From a deep gash in his head, blood ran thick and red, a rivulet that flowed around stones, over muddy ground and into the creek, where the current washed it away.

CHAPTER FIFTY-FOUR

THERE WAS JUST ENOUGH light for Patrick to pursue the bear. The blood spatters made the trail easy to follow for the seasoned tracker. He wasn't eager to catch up to a wounded bear of any kind, much less a grizzly. Even so, he urged his horse into a trot; he had Duncan's stallion on a lead behind him. After thoroughly searching the area around the meadow, Patrick hadn't found Duncan and now feared that he had run into the forest after he'd been shot and that the bear was in pursuit. Patrick hoped he could catch up to it before it found Duncan.

The bear seemed to be following a deer trail that led up onto the ridge bordering Ms. Jessie's land. Patrick was somewhat experienced with the terrain, but not enough to navigate it in the dark. Near the top of the slope, he stopped abruptly. To the right of the trail, freshly broken branches and flattened grasses smeared with blood indicated some kind of struggle. He readied his pistol and called Duncan's name. All he heard was the rustling of aspen leaves. He scoured the area but found no sign of Duncan or the bear beyond this spot. *How could a grizzly bear, one that shouldn't even be here, simply vanish?*

He decided to continue down the trail a little further. The sound of running water made him pick up his pace. Surely there would be some sign in the muddy banks of the creek. When he saw nothing directly on the trail, he checked along the stream on the uphill side. After a bit of searching, he found what he was looking for, a fresh print, but not from a bear. It was, without a doubt, a human footprint.

"Duncan!" Patrick called repeatedly. Moving quickly, he covered as much ground as possible in the waning light but couldn't find any other signs indicating where the Ute man had gone. He cursed the darkness that was forcing him to abandon his search. He'd need flashlights and Ms. Jessie's knowledge of the land to keep looking for him tonight.

Patrick called out one more time and strained in vain for any reply. He hoped that Duncan had some wilderness skills passed down from his ancestors, because he knew how hard it was to survive overnight in the mountains without any gear, especially when you're wounded.

Jason had Sarah and Eli sit by the fire while he quickly packed up everything from the ceremony in the meadow. Sarah gratefully complied. Her head throbbed from the blow from Nick's gun and moving around made her nauseated. Eli hovered around her like a lost dog. They watched as Jason offered hurried prayers to the flames before extinguishing them with water and dirt. "That's not the proper way to honor Fire," Jason said, "but we don't have time to do it in a good way."

Jason had Sarah ride with him. Eli was strong enough now to manage a horse on his own. They made their way down the trail in worried silence, until they reached the final fork in the trail. Jason wanted Sarah and Eli to return to the house while he went in search of Nick, but Sarah insisted that they go together. The dimming light left no time for argument, so Jason reluctantly led them down to the creek and along the trail that hugged its banks.

But when it came time to cross over the creek to get to the cave and the place where Nick's body most likely landed, Jason insisted that they wait with the horses while he went on alone. He wasn't gone long.

"Did you find him?" Sarah's voice cracked.

Jason swung up into the saddle and kissed her cheek.

"That bastard won't be bothering you anymore."

"He's dead? Oh, god." Sarah slumped back against Jason, overwhelmed. "What do we do now?"

"We get you back to the house so we can put some ice on your cheek. And then I'll call the sheriff. And Ms. Jessie."

"We can't leave him out here!" Sarah said. "What if the coyotes or a mountain lion find him?"

Jason urged the horses into a fast walk back up the trail. "They don't like the smell of humans. Trust me, they won't touch him tonight."

Jessie was putting the roast in the oven when the phone rang the first time. She listened as Jason hastily recounted the ceremony and its disastrous conclusion. The news of Nick's death and Duncan's disappearance shocked her into sitting.

"I called the sheriff and told him we'd all be at your place," Jason said. "He probably won't get there for over an hour. We're coming over. Keep your eye out for Old Man."

He hung up before Jessie could ask what he meant. She didn't understand why he didn't seem more concerned about his missing uncle.

Then the phone rang again. This time it was Patrick. "I think Duncan may be up on that ridge near Full Moon Rock. I'll get to your place as soon as I can and we can go look for him."

"Thanks, Pat, but I'm wasting time if I wait for you. I'm heading out."

She hung up the phone, turned off the oven, and grabbed her jacket, a blanket and a rifle. As she hurried out to the stable and whistled for her dogs, she offered an urgent prayer to the spirits of the mountain, asking them to help her find Duncan—alive.

"I want to be absolutely sure that we all agree on what happened in the meadow," Jason said to those assembled in Jessie's living room. "The sheriff will be here soon."

Sarah sat next to him on the couch, Eli had selected the chair closest to her and Patrick paced in front of the bay window. They had arrived at Jesse's place over forty-five minutes ago and she had not yet returned. Patrick felt useless waiting around, but he couldn't argue with Jason's reasoning. Ms. Jessie knew the forest better than anyone and Patrick would probably get lost in the dark. One missing person was enough.

"There's no need to tell anyone about the bear," Jason insisted. "If word gets out that a grizzly was in the area where Nick died, this place will be crawling with yahoos wanting to be heroes. No bear will be safe."

"I don't want a group of vigilante hunters going after the bear," Patrick said, "but I can't ignore the fact that there is a dangerous animal out there—a grizzly."

"I'm asking you to trust me on this one," Jason said. "This won't be an issue in the morning. But I can't prove that to you yet."

Patrick started to protest when they saw lights coming up the drive.

"The sheriff's here," Jason said. "Just forget about the bear for right now. All of you." Not waiting for a reply, Jason walked over to the front door and went out to meet the sheriff.

The investigator from the sheriff's office talked with each person in turn about what took place in the meadow. He would have a team out first thing in the morning to pick up Nick's body and investigate the scene. After that, he'd call them all in for further questioning; no one could leave the area until then. Jason assured the investigator that he'd notify him as soon as Ms. Jessie returned. He felt confident that Duncan would be with her.

Patrick didn't share Jason's optimism and couldn't stand waiting any longer. With the investigator gone, he announced that he was going to ride up the trail a ways. He had to do something. Halfway to the barn, he saw a light bobbing up and down at the far end of the pasture. "It's Ms. Jessie!" he yelled, running back to the house.

Jason met him on the porch and together they rushed out along the fencerow to meet her. "Is Old Man with her?"

"Can't tell."

After a short sprint, they had an answer.

"Anyone care to explain to me why Duncan was stumbling around in the forest without a stitch of clothing?" Jessie's stern expression gave way to a grin. "Good thing I brought a blanket."

CHAPTER FIFTY-FIVE

ONCE THEY GOT DUNCAN INSIDE, Jessie took charge of his care and gave everyone else a job to do. Patrick went back to the barn to tend to the horses. Sarah and Jason headed to the kitchen to finish preparations for the ceremonial meal. Eli, who hid in a closet when Jessie and Duncan had come in, now shadowed Sarah and sat quietly at the kitchen table.

The change that had come over Eli was remarkable. The man who returned from the mountain meadow was tentative and contrite and would speak only to Sarah, whom he now saw as his salvation. He seemed willing to do whatever she told him to, but it was clear to Sarah that he would need a lot of coaxing to face Duncan and Jessie.

With the roast and potatoes in the oven, Sarah and Jason rinsed vegetables and lettuce to begin assembling a salad.

"Do you think we should take Duncan to the hospital?" she asked. "I'm sure Ms. Jessie knows what she's doing, but still, he's been shot."

"Probably, but if he doesn't want to go, there's no way we'll get him there. Sarah, you saved his life. Nick would have killed him."

"I don't want to think about that."

"I'm not happy that Nick's dead," Jason said, "but I'm not sorry either. The bastard got what he deserved. Makes me think that maybe there is something to this karma idea."

"Why do you say that?" Sarah asked.

"When that grizzly showed up, I felt like I had stepped back into my dream. I was in the meadow where Standing Bear and Yellow Eagle had died. I didn't see Nick pointing a gun at the bear, I saw Ethan Amory. I came running toward the grizzly, just like in my dream. But this time, I saved the bear. It didn't die. I didn't die. And instead of watching life fade from its eyes, I saw them burning with life. When that bear looked at me, I felt like it knew me."

"That grizzly actually protected you from Nick," Sarah said.

"And took its own revenge." Jason kissed her lightly on the mouth.

Before they could explore a further embrace, Jessie walked into the kitchen. "Duncan's ready to see you both," she said. "I must say, he's not saying much about what happened out there, nothing about getting shot twice or why his clothes are missing."

"Twice?" Sarah exclaimed. "Nick shot him only once. I'm sure of it. The only other shot that was fired hit the bear."

"Don't know how that could be," Jessie replied. "I cleaned up two wounds. One just grazed his side but the other went clean through his calf. Didn't hit an artery, thank goodness."

"I know how it happened," Jason said. "Sarah, you do too, if you just let yourself believe it."

A loud clatter had heads turn to find Eli, wide eyed and shaking, standing in front of the chair that he'd knocked over backwards.

"Eli," Jessie said, surprised. "I didn't know you were here."

Sarah walked quickly over to him and took his hand. He calmed a bit. "Take it easy, Eli. Everything's going to be all right. Why don't you say 'hello' to Ms. Jessie?"

Eli mumbled a bit, staring down at his shoes, hands dug deep into his pockets. Then he cleared his throat. "Hello, Jessibel…Thank you for making supper for us." His voice quivered.

"Well, I'll be," Jessie said. "That must have been some healing ceremony. You look a helluva lot better, Eli. Let's hope you've come to your senses. But we'll talk about that later."

After a scan of the kitchen to assess the progress made on preparing the meal, Jessie thanked Sarah and Jason for their help and insisted that they all move into the living room so she could hear from each one of them about the momentous ceremony in the meadow.

They found Duncan sitting by the fireplace, his one leg elevated on an ottoman. Sarah hurried over and gave him a gentle hug. "We were so worried about you," she began, but Jessie interrupted.

"Before I feed any one of you a morsel of food, I demand a full recounting of the ceremony, especially the part about the bear. Everyone sit down and start talking!"

Jessie listened intently to all that was said, beginning with Sarah, followed by Jason, then Patrick.

"I tracked the bear as far as that little creek and then lost any sign of it," Patrick concluded. "But, I did find one human footprint on the bank. I'm assuming it was yours, Duncan. That's the only place I found any indication that you were on that trail. It's as though the bear disappeared and you showed up. I'm at a loss to explain it."

Jessie shifted in her chair to look directly at Duncan. "How do you explain it, my friend?" She folded her arms to wait for an answer that, based on experience, she expected would be slow in coming. But he surprised her with a quick response.

"I do not believe I can." He shook his head. "I do not remember much. I remember preparing for ceremony, dancing in front of Grandpa Fire and inviting Grizzly Spirit to come. I felt pain. I felt rage. But no explanation of why until now."

"That's it? That's all you have to say?" Jessie threw her hands in the air. "Come on, Duncan! Did you somehow become that bear?"

He managed a weary smile. "You may have to answer that one for yourself. I cannot say at this time." After a brief pause, he said, "Patrick, you are the wildlife expert. What do you think?"

"As a biologist, I truly cannot explain what I saw," Patrick said. "But as a guy who just witnessed his first Indian ceremony, I'd have to say I'm more...mystified. If you told me right now that I didn't need to worry about tracking down a wounded grizzly first thing tomorrow morning, I guess I'd sleep in. But I'm still going back out to look around for myself, just in case."

Duncan's smile broadened. "By the time we are done with Jessibel's delicious feast tonight, it will be quite late. I am going to sleep in."

"Yes, the feast," Jessie said, standing up. "Sarah, would you come help me get it on the table?"

Sarah followed her into the kitchen. "It smells wonderful in here," Sarah said. The rich aromas reminded her that she hadn't eaten for most of the day and was famished.

"First things first," Jessie said, handing Sarah a full shot glass. "You do drink tequila."

"I do tonight," she replied, taking the glass she was handed.

"This is sipping tequila, the good stuff."

They clinked glasses and took a drink.

"You've had quite the day," Jessie said. "We all have. I've known Duncan a long time and I'm here to tell you that he still finds ways to challenge and expand my belief in what is real and what is possible."

"I know what you mean," Sarah said. "Ever since I came to this valley, my sense of reality has been shifted in ways I could never have imaged. In my old life, birds didn't follow me around, I had no past lives, I didn't know what a medicine bundle was or think that I would ever have one. I didn't even know who the Utes were or what a sweat lodge was. And I've never seen anyone shapeshift, until today."

The oven timer buzzed. After another sip of tequila, the two women focused on getting the last of the food ready.

"Ms. Jessie, there's something I want to share with you...about Eli. I've had some time to talk with him," she said. "He seems to understand what he's done and he wants to make things right. He told me he'd like to do something to make sure that the spirits will forgive him."

"He can sign the damn easement," Jessie said. She emptied her glass and then poured herself another.

"He is finally open to that. But I came up with an idea that could do even more and I think he's willing to go with it."

Before she could say more, Patrick walked in the room.

"Need any help? You've got a bunch of hungry guys out there."

"Yes, of course," Jessie said. "Let's eat before everything gets cold." As she passed by Sarah, roast in hand, she said, "I want to hear about your idea, after we eat."

Once everyone took a seat at the dining room table and had something to drink, Jessie raised her glass. "I'm truly glad to see all of you here, safe and mostly sound. I'm honored to provide the meal to celebrate the ceremony you all survived today. But, Duncan, next time you decide to defy nature and man, I want to be there to see it for myself. Someone else can make the damn roast!"

"Thank you, Jessibel," Duncan said. "I am grateful to each one of you. Healing the ancestors is sacred work. And sometimes it is dangerous. But I think all will be as it should be now. It is good. I will say prayers for Nick Tremaine, that his spirit may find its way."

Everyone raised their glasses and then took a drink, each one silently reflecting on the gravity of the day and the possible repercussions.

After the meal was served and appetites sated, Jessie invited Sarah to continue with the conversation they had started in the kitchen. "You said you have a proposal worth listening to."

"I sure hope so," Sarah said. She got up from her chair and stood behind Eli, placing one hand gently on his shoulder. "Duncan, Eli wants to say something to you."

Eli fidgeted in his chair, but did manage to glance briefly at the Ute elder before he spoke. "I know what I did many years ago was wrong. I want to make things right...with the spirits." Eli started to cough and wring his hands.

"Go on, Eli. It's okay," Sarah said.

"I will sign those easement papers you want just so long as you, um, promise me that I'll have enough to pay my debts. But I need to make sure the spirits never bother me again." Eli looked pleadingly at Duncan. "I want to be free of the curse."

Duncan stared back at him, silent.

Sarah spoke up. "Eli asked me what I thought he might do. So I told him about an idea that came to me while I was tending the fire up in the meadow and he is agreeable."

Eli nodded his head. "But only because you say it's a good thing."

"I suggested that Eli look into deeding the ranch to you, Duncan, so the land could go back to the Ute People. I'm assuming you could work out an arrangement so Eli could live on the place as long as he wants to. Would that be enough to ensure that all would be forgiven, by you and the spirits?"

Duncan's face lit up. "Eli McDermott, if you do this, you would honor the ancestors and my people. I will speak to the Spirits of your gift and your desire to put things right. I believe they will bless you for walking now in a good way on the Earth." Duncan shifted in his chair and winced in pain. "I will talk with the Spirits tomorrow. Now I need to sleep. It is time to go home."

Once back at Duncan's ranch, Sarah helped Eli settle in for the night while Jason brought the horses into the barn. On her way back to the kitchen, Sarah checked in on Duncan to see if he needed anything.

"Thank you," Duncan said.

"I'm glad to help," Sarah replied.

"I do not mean for the aspirin and the water." Duncan smiled. "You did well today. You are starting to learn your medicine. I want to thank you, Red Fire Woman, for bringing the Bear medicine back to me and for finding a way to save the land."

She detected no sadness in his voice.

"You're very welcome, Standing Bear."

CHAPTER FIFTY-SIX

THE NEXT WEEK FOUND JASON driving Sarah to Grand Junction to catch a flight back to Chicago. Hollis had asked her to take a month off while he and his family came to terms with Nick's death. He offered to pay for her transportation back home or wherever she'd like to go for the time away.

Sarah had expected Hollis to cancel her contract once she told him about all that had taken place—Nick's hostile obsession with her, his unrelenting pursuit of Eli's land and his attack in the meadow which ultimately led to his death. To her surprise, Hollis didn't appear to doubt her and didn't hold her responsible in any way. Losing his son was heartbreaking for him, but so was the danger that Nick had put Sarah and Duncan in. Hollis wished he could have been more aware of his son's troubled behavior so he could have prevented the tragedy. Hollis gave Sarah the impression that Nick had given him reasons to intervene on his behalf before. He felt he had failed his son, which only added to his grief.

The sheriff was still investigating Nick's death but had given Sarah permission to leave the state. He would eventually rule the death accidental; Nick's wounds were consistent with a fall from a cliff. He was also the only one who had fired a weapon. His toxicology screen would indicate that he had been drinking before he died. The sheriff initially suspected that Jason might have pushed Nick, but Patrick's testimony supported Jason's explanation that Nick had gotten disoriented in the failing light and had gone over the cliff while running away from Jason.

"Are you sure I can't convince you to stick around a little longer?" Jason asked, as he made the final turn into the Grand Junction airport.

Sarah smiled. "I wish I could, you know that, but Ruth needs me right now." Her sister had called several days before, excited about a dream she'd had about an early arrival for her baby. She had urged Sarah to come home as soon as possible. While Jason had invited her to stay with him for the month, he understood the power of dreams and knew she needed to be with her sister.

"You are coming back, aren't you?" Jason asked, as they pulled into the departure lane at the airport.

Sarah felt tears welling up. "Of course, I am. I've got to finish Hollis' murals." Jason's frown told her that wasn't the answer he was hoping for. "And I'm leaving my medicine bundle with you, for safekeeping. Except for the diary. I want to keep that with me."

He pulled the truck into the unloading zone and put it in park. "What about us? Are you coming back for us?"

"I'm trusting you with my medicine bundle. What do you think?"

"That's not an answer."

He was right. "A lot has happened to me over the last few months. I'm still trying to make sense of it," Sarah said. "We come from such different backgrounds. I wonder sometimes if we'd be interested in each other if we'd met under more normal circumstances. We've gone through something surreal together that connects us. But I'm scared too. Is there more to our relationship than just this shared experience?"

"That's something only time will tell," Jason said, taking her hand in his. "But I do know that we can't figure it out unless you come back."

"I can tell you this." Sarah leaned forward, caressing his cheek with hers. "I love how I feel when I look in your eyes and when I'm in your arms. I am coming back for us, too. We'll figure this out together."

As the plane lifted off the tarmac, the sweet longing in their goodbye kiss still lingered on her lips.

Snuggled into overstuffed chairs in Ruth's living room and fortified with herbal tea and coffee, the sisters talked for hours. When Sarah finally completed her saga of the past week, Ruth exclaimed, "What an adventure! Do you have her diary with you? I'd love to see it."

Sarah pulled it from her bag and handed it to Ruth, who opened it and gently paged through it.

"Red Fire Woman wanted to be redeemed," Sarah said. "Do you think I've done that for her? Or is there more I have to do?"

Ruth closed the diary. "Take a look at what actually happened. Your healing ceremony for the ancestors seemed to mirror the fight in the meadow when Standing Bear was killed. But your story ended much differently. In the original story, Yellow Eagle hadn't been able to save the grizzly and they had died together. But this time, Jason got there in time and saved the bear. Nick, who certainly could stand in for Ethan, got what was coming to him. Instead of killing the grizzly, the grizzly chased him to his own death. Seems more than fitting.

"And sweet Duncan. I want to meet him," Ruth continued. "It must have been hard for him once he realized that he was Standing Bear, born too early in this lifetime to be reunited with his love. I'm so glad he received some healing when the bear medicine came back to him."

"He did seem at peace after that final ceremony," Sarah said. "Besides, I'm almost positive there's more to his friendship with Ms. Jessie than he lets on."

"I hope you're right," Ruth said, rubbing her bulging belly and adjusting herself in the chair.

"Now, getting back to your question about whether you've done what you were supposed to. First of all, you prevented Nick from killing Duncan. You saved Standing Bear, my dear. As I recall, Duncan thanked you for bringing the bear medicine back to him. And it was your vision to encourage Eli to deed the land back to the Utes."

"And the man who beat Red Fire Woman and killed her baby died this time before he could really hurt anybody," Sarah said, her voice hushed. "Red Fire Woman blamed herself for Standing Bear's death and for all the cruelty that Ethan brought on the Ute People. Do you think what I did in any way makes up for what happened in that past life? Eli's ranch is just one piece of land and the Utes lost so much more than that."

"I agree, but Red Fire Woman wasn't responsible for all of the suffering of the Indian peoples and you're not responsible for fixing the karmic burden of it all," Ruth reminded her. "You did what you could and that's enough. And I'm sure if Red Fire Woman were here, she'd tell you the same thing."

Sarah got up and hugged her sister. "I knew you'd help me make some kind of sense out of all this!"

The sisters moved into the kitchen to get more tea and coffee.

"There is one more thing that's been on my mind," Sarah said. "It's about me and Jason."

"I'm always up for boy talk." Ruth winced, then took Sarah's hand and placed it over the top of her abdomen. "Feel the baby kicking? She wants to hear about Jason too!"

"Hello, little girl," Sarah said.

Once the baby quieted down, Ruth got her sister back on track. "So, you and Jason?"

She hesitated at first and then blurted out, "Do you think we have a chance?" Her face flushed. "I mean, with the past life stuff, seems like we might not be meant for each other. I don't know. What do you think?"

Ruth laughed. "Seems to me, this lifetime is about doing things differently, not repeating old patterns. What does your heart tell you?"

"That I can't wait to see him again. That I miss him like crazy and can't stop thinking about him."

"And what about Blue? Any lingering 'what if's' there?"

"No, not any more. For the longest time, I blamed myself for our breakup; I was afraid that the mountains had somehow made me a little nuts. I thought I'd driven Blue away. But Jason helped me realize that he had had no idea what I was going through. He's not the man for me."

"And Jason?"

"Hey, no fair! I asked you that question." Sarah gave her sister a playful nudge.

"Well, I say, go for it. You'll never know until you try. Just don't go running back to Colorado before I have this baby."

"I won't. I promise."

The fire crackled and hummed, shooting sparks into the chilly Colorado darkness. Duncan threw another log on the blaze with his one good arm, his other shoulder still wrapped in bandages. He talked a while to Grandpa Fire, then came and sat down next to Jessie, who had come over every night since the shooting to change his dressings and to cook dinner. They could hear Jason playing guitar and singing on the back porch. Duncan smiled, then reached out for Jessie's hand and gave it a gentle squeeze. Jason was writing a love song.

The wind picked up and sent more sparks dancing into the sky. Looking through the fire, Duncan saw a faint image emerge from the smoke and gradually take form. It was the Ancient One, with his long white hair, bare chest and buckskin loincloth. Duncan looked at Jessie, who was staring into the flames, unaware of the visitor.

"Jessibel, look just beyond the fire. Do you see him?"

A moment later Jessie squeezed his hand. "I do."

"Greetings, Ancient One. We did the best we could to help heal the ancestors. I pray it was enough."

The Ancient One smiled broadly and placed his hand over his heart. Duncan reached into his pocket to pull out his tobacco pouch just as another wind gust made the flames flash higher. Duncan stood to offer his blessings. The Ancient One had vanished.

"Ha!" Duncan said with pleasure. "It is good." Then he moved slowly around the fire, in a sunwise direction, singing an honoring song for the ancestors. As he reached the place where the Ancient One had stood, the coyotes started singing with him.

KATHLEEN RUDE is an environmentalist, writer and shamanic practitioner trained in traditional ceremonial ways by Blackfoot, Northern Ute and Lakota elders.

Kathleen also facilitates workshops in spiritual healing, environmental and social change, and The Work That Reconnects, pioneered by Joanna Macy.

She began her career as an environmental journalist and has a Bachelor of Science degree in Wildlife Ecology and a Master of Science degree in Natural Resources.

This is her first novel.

www.GaiaWisdom.org.

Made in the USA
Lexington, KY
27 February 2014